THE TRIAD FLAME

THE TRIAD FLAME SAGA

Book One
The Triad Flame

THE TRIAD FLAME

Book One of the Triad Flame Saga

by

Michael Widger

Michael Widger
Kentucky, USA

The Triad Flame
Book One of the Triad Flame Saga

Text © [2025] Michael Widger
Cover design © [2025] Michael Widger

First edition

ISBN: 979-8-993945-80-4

Cover art by Michael Widger
Interior design by Michael Widger

Published by Michael Widger
Kentucky, USA

Printed in the United States of America

The Triad Flame

Prologue

The Day the Skies Burned

They say the sky once wore feathers of fire, and the mountains leaned close to listen when the great ones spoke. They say men and dragons shared bread and storm, oath and hearth, for a little while—a bright season like a spark blown across dry grass. But sparks either bloom to flame or stamp to dark, and this tale is of the blooming and the stamping both. Sit close to the embers and hear: how the last summer of the old world ended, how winter learned a new and terrible word, and how a single ember refused to die.

Listen.

In the elder days, when the sea still remembered the shape of the first moon, the dragons gathered in the hollow of a mountain that had been a volcano and was now a bowl for thunder. They circled in the smoke, those sky-lords and earth-kin, their wings stirring echoes from stone. At the summit stood Vaeryn Highwing, whose shadow could swallow a valley, and with him Seravelle of the Silver Vale, whose breath could peel paint from wind, and Morgrin Earth-Blood, who spoke with faults and fissures and could teach a mountain to bow. Many more there were, named and nameless, bright as kings, old as grief. They had come because the omens had soured.

A comet had split the bowl of night. Whales beached themselves along seventy shores. Eagles nested on the ground. In the north, men had dug new altars, and the smoke of those altars smelled not of meat or mead but of cold iron and spite. The dragons watched the roads of men and saw wagons with teeth, towers that moved like ships upon land, and priests whose voices made frost bloom from dry rock. Once, man's bravery had delighted them; now his cleverness had begun to itch.

"Brothers," said Vaeryn, his voice the low drum under all weather, "and sisters, bright as dawn, this is the last parley before war. If we are to avert it, it must be now."

Seravelle flared her silver wings and set the air to singing. "Their priests sing binding songs," she said. "It is an ugly tune. If we wait, we give them rhythm, and rhythm becomes a chain."

Morgrin stamped once; the volcano remembered and trembled. "Stone heeds no chain," he said, "but stone craves peace. Shall we speak to their kings once more? Once more, for the sake of the spring we shared?"

Then the storm rim cracked and three small figures came into the hollow with a courage that was almost worship and almost hunger. Men—kings among their kind: Eydis Iron-Cloak, Jarl of the Ridges; Hadran the Bold, who had made a kingdom from quarrel; and a third, a quiet priest with winter in his beard and a star's shard ringed upon his hand. They had asked for parley and been granted wingshadow and the taste of thunder.

"High ones," said Eydis, and her one good eye did not drop, "we honor old oaths. We bring gifts." She set down a coffer of rune-iron lined with gold, and it hummed like a bee-hive when the dragons drew breath. "We bring warning. South and east, your kind have taken cattle and men. Fear breeds fear. We are not many kingdoms now; we are one. We seek a treaty that holds."

"Take cattle," said Morgrin with a rumble like gravel slipping. "Return men."

"And when men take our eggs?" Seravelle's pupils thinned to needles. "Shall we return their sons wrapped in ribbon?"

Hadran the Bold did not blink. "No one will take your eggs," he said, and the star-ring on the priest's finger whispered something that made the air taste of iron rain. "By my life, no one."

The priest said nothing, but Vaeryn heard him anyway. There are words the mouth need not shape; the world knows them when they form. **Bind. Contain. Seal.** The ring sang those words under its breath as a flint sings to steel.

Vaeryn lowered his great head until his horned brow almost kissed the stone. "We kept your winters off your bones," he said softly. "We taught you where hot springs spoke to roots. We put our fire into the mouths of your forges and called it gift. We would not unlearn this friendship. But I smell a spear in the room, and it has your priest's eyes."

The priest lifted his face, and for a heartbeat the mask of the man slipped, and Vaeryn saw the shape of a starving winter behind it. "The world must be safe for the weak," the priest murmured, and every shadow leaned closer to hear. "For lambs as well as wolves. You burn too bright. You make us feel small."

"Smallness makes thieves," Seravelle said. "Not safety."

Hadran set a hand on the priest's shoulder. "We came for treaty, not taunting," he said. "For love of old summers, take your hungry from our herds and hunt in wild high places only. Leave our ships be. Promise us the safety of our towns and we will rebuild the oaths."

"Say also," Eydis added, "that your wrath will not fall upon us for sins done by the nameless and the mad among your kind. We have slain those who slew. We have tried to be clean in our vengeance."

Vaeryn looked at Morgrin; Morgrin looked at Seravelle; Seravelle looked at the shadow where the rest waited, breathing like a bellows. Some nodded, some hissed, some closed their eyes.

"Very well," said Vaeryn at last, though misgiving brushed his scales like a moth. "We will hunt the high wilds, and we will punish the mad among us, and we will leave your ships. But hear this: we will not stay caged by your fear. If you seek to bind the sky—"

The priest's ring sang louder. Runes bloomed in the dust like frost. Hadran's eyes went wide. Eydis's hand went to her sword not in treachery but in warning.

—**Too late**, said the metal, and the world heard it.

From the lip of the bowl the first arrow fell—no arrow, but a sliver of winter, blue as a bruise. It struck the stone at Vaeryn's foreclaw and grew outward in a pattern like a fern written in ice. Around the hollow, men rose from behind rune-shields, fifty, a hundred, five hundred, the air rippling with their breath. On the ridges beyond, catapults flexed. The parley had been bait; the dragons had smelled the iron and come anyway.

Seravelle moved first—silver blur, note stabbed into the staff of silence. The archers nearest melted like wax under a spilled candle. Morgrin shook his body and the lip of the crater broke like a crust of bread. Eydis drew and stood before Hadran as if her body were a wall against a storm. The priest—ah, the priest—lifted his ring and began to sing.

Hear now the song that men taught winter. Hear the old language of no.

"Bind the Sky-Lords." The vowels were long and cold, the consonants knives. Sigils crawled from his mouth and stuck to the rock. They looked like frost, but frost never bit like this.

"Contain the Flame." The wind remembered what it meant to be still.

"Seal the Fire Below." The hot heart of the mountain missed a beat.

"Break the song," Vaeryn cried, and vaulted. The priests around the rim fell like snapped arrows, but there were so many, and men had built this bowl with cunning; for every fallen voice three more rose. Seravelle skimmed the rim and the chant stuttered; Morgrin threw his strength against the slope and stone gave way in shards; the hollow emptied as dragons surged, hungry to be sky again.

They broke from the crater like sparks from a struck stone. The day above seized them.

Remember, listener, what sort of day it was.

Clouds had knotted themselves into a net. The net had teeth. Lightning stitched its own name across the stitches. The Worldspine threw up peaks like spears spiked into a dragon's back. And men had filled those spears with engines and oil and a patience that winter envies.

We skalds tell many versions of the next hours, for the war wore many faces on that day. But all versions agree on this: it was not one battle. It was nine, and then nineteen, and then innumerable, the world itself a drum struck by nine hammerers at once. So I will bring you to three fronts, and then another, and then another, as if I were walking you along a shore where nine storms were breaking.

First, the Sky Front: above Worldspine Ridge, where the air itself was a blade.

They came in flights: Vaeryn at the fore, Ilyra red as a cut, Torrik-crack-wing with the storm in his throat, a hundred more, some barely past their first molt, some so old their scales had dulled to a dignified dusk. Men met them with songs that wrote ice, arrows that carried winter in their bellies, and fires that burned with two mouths, one for air and one for hate.

"Loose!" cried Jarl Eydis, and the hel-oil bloomed blue-black, petals of flame that ate sound. Ilyra split them with a hiss, her hide crackling, the scent of singed scale like bitter spice. Torrik's roar shoved the storm aside; the priests' chorus shoved it back with word and bone.

Vaeryn stooped and rose, stooped and rose, the rhythm of the oldest dance there is—kill-because-you-must, live-because-you-can. Each pass left fewer catapults, fewer men who could still sing. But always, far beyond, another ridge of shieldwalls waited, and beyond that another: men who had set a table for winter and asked it to stay.

On the second stoop, an unnamed green took hel-oil full to the chest—the flame crawled down his throat and lit him from within, a lantern made of sorrow. He fell and the slope took his weight with a crunch. Men cheered because sometimes you must shout to keep from breaking.

On the third stoop, the sky itself shot back. The cliff-eyes opened—a row of bolt-throats hidden in whale hide —and spears went singing. One kissed Torrik's ribs and went to bone. He rolled, kept flying; kept roaring, though the roar now had a crack as if a bell had been knocked out of round.

Above it all, on the far ridge, Hadran stood with the Spear of Helgard naked in his hand. Ah, that spear—star-metal cooled in dragon's blood, rune-carved in a language that men had learned from loneliness. It did not gleam; it devoured light. The priest's song wrote a path for it. Hadran was brave enough to follow the path the song made.

"Bind," he whispered again, but this time the word came from the spear like frost breath.

Vaeryn saw it and knew—as an old stag knows when hounds have found the angle of his wind—that the day had made a knife with his name on it.

"Not yet," he told the sky, and climbed until his breath tore and the air refused his wings, then folded and fell. He fell through chant and arrow, through hel-oil and prayer, a gold hammer twice, thrice, again, until the men in the third line stacked their shields without being told. He tore a hole in the world big enough to see the old summer through it. He could not make it wide enough to climb back in.

Elsewhere, the Ashen March: a plain of basalt and steam where nothing grows and everything remembers fire.

Morgrin Earth-Blood came up from a fault with the mountain on his shoulders like a cloak. He wore stone the way men wear mail. He hated the air, but he loved the ground with a simplicity that made poets jealous.

Against him, men brought wagons with teeth and capstans with chains, oxen with foam in their mouths and priests whose hammers beat a tempo that turned sand to road. In their casks: a fog alive with winter's appetite.

The chains bit. The road melted and fused and held. Morgrin growled, and the growl traveled through the ribs of the plain. Wagons toppled. Runes crawled back up the chains and into his flesh, burning a color that is not heat. He went to one knee, then the other, and the ground panicked under him.

Seravelle fell from the white sky like a small god, her breath a shear that shaved runes from iron as if they were frost. "Up, old mountain," she hissed in the tongue of earthquakes. He heaved. The chains screamed. The fog rolled, patient as a tax collector, and set up house in his lungs.

The Gavelmasters beat time with bleeding ears. The Fog-Bearers poured what the world should never have learned to make. The old earth-dragon moved like a hill learning to run. Nothing was decided. Everything was costly.

North again: the Sea Front, where fjords bit ships and ships bit back.

Kethrax Gale-Singer rode lightning down like a thread, stitching his name into the wind. Brynja Tide-Scar took the first longship by the spine and wrung it, then dove with a harpoon blooming like a wicked flower from her shoulder. The fleet held—thirty ships, then twenty-seven, then twenty-four—oars chopping, cauldrons vomiting fire that learned to live on water. Men burned on the sea, and

the sea did not go out.

From the cliff eyes, bolt-throats spat iron into the storm. Kethrax took six and lost two feathers of cloud from his wings. Brynja found rock with her teeth and threw it at men who should not have been brave enough to hold but held anyway. A ship turned and split a breaker with a prow rune that parted the wave like cloth. Three more ships tried and failed and rolled.

The sea remembers everything. It would remember this, too. Neither side loved the memory.

West, in the Fjellwood: no glory of flight. Branch and root and sap that clings like grief.

Drakes went low, wyrmlings went high, and men did what they do best when there is no room to move: they made a wall of themselves. A shield-ring around an altar where a forest priest whispered to old stone.

Solveig the Shield-Queen, handless on one side but not diminished, set her feet and her mouth around a shout. A sable drake hit the ring like a ram; they slid and did not break. An ash wyrmling fell upon her; she took its weight with a grimace and a little grunt, then gave it back the long way with a spear up through the jaw into the thinking place. The ring sealed around the empty where someone had been.

Karok of the Old Wood came, moss-grown, eyes like wells. He did not want this. The runes swarmed him like bees anyway. "Go," Solveig said, and her voice forgot to be hard. "Sleep." The old drake obeyed. You may walk there still, generations later, and not know that the hill under your boots has teeth.

Now, listener, draw breath. The sky-front again: the

place where endings put on their crowns.

Hadran the Bold stepped forward. He had broken three swords and two ribs and fifty promises to himself this day; he had kept two promises to his people. He held the Spear of Helgard and it held him. The priest's song made a path in the air a man could walk.

Vaeryn angled for the throw. He tried to make the wind misbehave. He asked the storm to lie for him. But steel that remembers stars does not listen to weather. When Hadran cast, the spear leapt to its work like a hound that knows its master's whistle.

It struck where a plate had thinned from a thousand survivals. Cold bloomed inside the wound like a flower with too many petals. Vaeryn kept flying for one heartbeat, two. On the third, the sky let him go.

Ilyra screamed without music and dove. Torrik put himself under Vaeryn's fall and the mountain cracked its knuckles. Together they delivered him gently as kings are delivered, not to earth but to a shoulder of stone. The priests' song found its last word. The word was **No**.

Winter had always been a season. On that day it became a sentence.

Rivers went stiff with the surprise of it. Fire shattered like glass. Mountains put on crowns the color of throats. The glaciers stood up, full-grown, and said to the world: **Stop.**

Ilyra clawed and found her own pinned wing. Torrik roared and the roar turned to a nail hammered into ice. Vaeryn took one last breath and put it where it would do the most good: he set a whole range glowing within, banked coals under a blue grave. His voice went down through stone and up through teeth.

"When the ice melts," he said, and men a league away felt the syllables in their bones, "and flame breathes again, your sons shall pay the debt of their fathers."

The spell closed like a book.

Silence fell, heavy as the lid of a sarcophagus.

But the world is big, and silence cannot sit everywhere at once.

In the Ashen March, Morgrin made one last push. He rose half his height before the fog wrote its name across his lungs. He froze mid-bellow, eyes still moving, like a memory that refuses to be decent. Seravelle stretched her neck along his and sang of summers she had actually seen, until her breath frosted and her song slowed and stopped.

On the fjords, Brynja broke the new ice twice with her brow; on the third, the sea roofed itself over her like a church. Kethrax found a trench of sky the cold had forgotten to steal, beat his wings within it, and became a seam.

In the Fjellwood, Solveig's ring pivoted to face a different wind, and the snow that began to fall made no sound on leather or hair. The altar lay open like a chest whose last treasure had been spent. Karok rose into a knoll, and children would sled there someday, shrieking, and none of them would dream of moss-grown plates beneath.

And everywhere, men began to tell themselves a story that made it possible to sleep: that they had saved the world. Some of them wept when they told it. Some hammered the sadness into the song until it rang truer. Some left out the part where their hands shook.

Deep under a mountain that the spell had not quite remembered, where hot springs talk to stone in the old language, a root lifted like a kind hand. Into that cradle rolled an egg the color of sunrise seen through smoke. The cold sniffed at it, and the egg did not deny the cold entry. "Lie with me," it seemed to say, "and be tired less." The cold, which had said **no** so long it had forgotten other words, folded itself around the egg and was still.

The root drank the spring and braided itself into a nest. The egg listened to the earth and learned patience. Once a century the cave breathed. Once a century the shell dreamed of wings. Once a century the old vow rolled through the rock like thunder that had not decided where to fall.

Above, the new blue stretched to every horizon. Men stamped runes into stone and said **Never again** with voices that trembled only a little. They taught their boys the names of heroes and their girls the names of winters. Priests polished the star-ring smooth. The Spear of Helgard went to a vault and slept with one eye open.

They say the world slept then. They say dragons are only in songs and in old carvings worn smooth by the river. But I am a skald, and I know the habits of embers. Ash can look like burial and be only waiting.

Listen, then, to the last of the prologue and the first of the future:

In the far north, where glaciers calve thunder into fjords and the wind eats its own footprints, a girl will one day hear wings in a storm that shows no feathers. She will wake in the night with the taste of copper and snow on her tongue and the certainty that someone is calling her by a name she has not yet earned. When she climbs into the white and finds the cave where hot water tells stories to stone, when her hand touches sunrise through smoke and the shell answers—ah, then the debt will turn in its sleep.

And when the ice melts, and flame breathes again—

Hush. For now we end where all true beginnings hide: in a dark warm place, under a mountain that hums old songs, with a single egg dreaming the world back toward fire.

Chapter One

The Girl Who Rides a Storm

The first snow of spring came sideways, riding the wind like ash from some invisible fire. In her dream, Astrid Halvarsdottir walked through it barefoot, the sky above her a bruise of silver and flame. The storm howled, and somewhere beyond the clouds came the sound of wings— slow, powerful, endless.

Each beat rippled through the snow at her feet, bending it like grass beneath invisible wind. She lifted her face and thought she saw a shape vast as the sky itself, its eyes molten gold, its voice whispering through the storm—her name.

"Astrid."

She gasped, reaching upward, and the light shattered.

Astrid woke to darkness and the groaning of the roof timbers under the storm. The wind keened through the thatch, a long, low voice that made the shutters tremble. Her heart still pounded, echoing the rhythm of wings that existed only behind her eyes.

She lay still, listening. No wings now—only the restless sigh of the wind and the creak of wood. Still, she could not shake the feeling that something vast had passed overhead, unseen and searching.

She rose. The longhouse air bit her cheeks, and her breath smoked like a spirit as she knelt at the hearth. The coals slept under ash; she teased them with a twist of birch bark, fed them a pine sliver, then another. Flame breathed, a small stubborn thing, orange as a cat's eye. She warmed her hands over it, palms tingling, as if the heat were greeting her by name as well.

"Bad weather?" came her father's voice from the shadows. Halvar's tone always came rough from sleep, the sea salt still in it though he had not sailed all winter. His broad silhouette shifted under the furs. "Feels like the fjord itself wants to climb inland."

"Spring's first is always an old winter's last tantrum," Astrid said softly. It was something her mother would have said, and the words made her throat tight for a heartbeat. "I'll see to the goats."

Halvar pushed himself to sitting, hair a grey tangle, and frowned toward the shutter. "Take the iron staff. Ice will be thick on the path. And watch the cliff trail. Two roofs caved last night in Sandvik—Erla came by to warn."

Astrid nodded, wrapped herself in wool and fur, and took the iron-shod staff from its peg. She slid the latch and shouldered the door into the storm.

Havngard crouched at the fjord's edge like a herd of sleeping beasts huddled for warmth—low longhouses with sod roofs and smoke spires, pens and net-racks, the black ribs of longboats upturned like whales on the snow. The wind came hard from the sea, smelling of salt and iron and something metallic, like a blade licked clean. The mountains loomed where the land reared up from the water's edge, their shoulders cloud-wrapped, their crowns erased.

She crossed the yard, boots crunching, the staff tapping the hard ground as if speaking to something beneath. The goats bleated at her approach, reproachful and hopeful both. She scooped frost from the latch with her knuckles, eased the gate, and slipped inside the pen.

Warmth and smell enveloped her—hay and dung, earthy and alive. Little noses butted her palm. One of the nannies, narrow-hipped and stubborn, stamped until Astrid laughed and reached for the stale barley mash she'd tucked into her cloak.

"There," Astrid murmured. "You're not starving. You just like to pretend."

As she worked—checking hooves, smoothing a rough hide, warming one frozen teat with careful fingers—she found the rhythm that stilled the dream's pulse. This was the sort of work her hands understood without asking. By the time she closed the gate again, the snow had eased to thin blades, and the horizon held a seam of watery silver where dawn would come.

On the path back, she paused at the fence and looked out across the fjord. Ice floes drifted, a broken flock. The tide was low; black weed glistened on stones like wet hair. The wind dropped for a breath as if stooping to drink. In that moment of hush she thought she heard—no. Not wings. The groan of far ice shifting, the fjord's voice turning in sleep.

Astrid pushed the thought away and let habit take her. She hauled a pail of water up from the well where rope burned cold grooves into her palm. She split kindling. She scraped ice from the door lintel with the back of her knife. Halvar moved with her, simple choreography of long winters, their words few but not unfriendly. He always reached for the heaviest thing in the room as if the weight might spare her some other burden she hadn't named.

When the fire licked bright and the porridge thickened, Halvar sprinkled a pinch of salt into the flames with two crooked fingers. "For the drowned," he said, as he always did, voice pitched low. "And for those the sea remembers."

Astrid's gaze flicked to the carved ash pole near the hearth where a thor's hammer hung beside a wooden cross. The cross had been brought by a monk with a shaved crown and cracked smile two summers ago. He had sung in a language that bent like a river and told stories of a god nailed to a tree who loved lambs and wolves the same. The old men nodded politely, the old women sent him away with salmon and pity, and the boys mimicked his prayers for a week like crows. The cross had stayed because Halvar said a roof ought to welcome every honest story.

Astrid wasn't sure any god had listened to hers.

She ate standing, bowl warm against her palms, spoon rising and falling like oar strokes. Her father watched her over the rim of his own bowl, eyes crinkled at the edges the way they did when he wanted to speak sense gently.

"You were up in the night," he said. "Dream again?"

"Yes."

He waited.

"Wings," she said at last. She kept her tone practical so it could not turn into more than air. "Nothing strange. Only— louder."

"You always were a weather-child." He said it with a father's gruff affection, but she knew how the neighbors said it: storm-touched. Hearing-whispers. The kind of girl who burned the porridge when thunder rolled because she was listening to something the rest could not hear.

"It was only a dream," Astrid said, as if naming it could sheath it. "I promised Old Kjaer I would help mend her roof today if the wind eases. She pays in cheese and honey words, and the cheese is better."

Halvar's mouth tugged. "Take Sigrid with you."

"She's plucking eiderdown for the priest's pillow," Astrid said, not hiding the grin in her voice. The winter-sailed priest from the southern monastery had gone through two pillows since the snow came and kept offering coins no one wanted. "I'll be fine. If the drift is bad on the moor, I'll cut across the smoke field."

Halvar's brows went up. "Smoke field?"

"Thaw-steam," she corrected, though the word *smoke* fit better. "Down-valley. It rises from the ground like the earth forgot its manners."

"Hot springs," Halvar said, relieved; this, at least, had a name he knew. "Stay to the high side. Ground softens there, and you go up to your knee in muck with one wrong step. No farther than the birches."

He turned away to ladle more porridge into his bowl. It took him a breath to realize she hadn't answered. When he looked back, she was watching the door with the same fixed attention a cat gives a shadow. He followed her gaze to the latch, to the faint flurry beyond the crack.

"What is it?"

"Nothing," she said. The word sat too fast, like a skipped stone. "I'll take the staff."

He didn't press. He knew when words could not carry the weight of a thing.

By daylight Havngard softened, the hard edges of storm blunted by voices and work. Smoke climbed and shredded. Children stamped paths between house and pen and licked snowflakes off their mittens with pink tongues. Men mended net and rope, mended sled and shoe, mended whatever winter had gnawed. Old women carded wool on stoops, hair like hoarfrost, tongues sharper than knives.

"Astrid!" someone called. "Bring that halyard you promised!"

"Halvardottir, your father's seal hooks—did he find them?"

"Kjaer's roof, mind the lee beam!"

Astrid answered as she always did: with help, with small jokes, with the economy of a person used to being useful as a way to earn the right to be other things later. She ran rope through a block and tackle for Nils the netmaker, her fingers quick, her shoulders remembering strain with honest pleasure. She hammered wedges under a listing sled-pole for Thora, knuckles jolted. She carried two bundles of eel cages from the shore to a shed so swollen with salt it smelled like old tears.

But she could not keep her attention from the sky. Every time the wind dropped her gaze flicked upward. She was not looking for wings—she told herself that. She was not a child, not a fool. The old songs carved into the steading poles told of dragons in words worn thin by time: sky-lords, fire-kin, guardians, devils—choose your time and the dragons were what the time required. No one had seen one since the sagas hardened and the priests wrote winter into iron. No one would.

Still, when the wind made a hollow over the fjord that sounded like a breath drawn in, she felt the hairs on her arms lift in answer.

Kjaer's roof came last. The old woman's house leaned into the wind as if eavesdropping on the sea. Astrid climbed the ladder and dug ice from the reed-thatch with the heel of her hand until she found the lee beam and wedged it with a cut block. She tied a rope from gable to birch and cinched it tight. Below, Kjaer leaned on her stick and shouted opinions about knots until Astrid began to laugh.

"You'll stay for a bite," Kjaer said when the rope lay snug as a belt and the ladder was down. "It's a hard day, and your father will not scold an old woman if I keep you with cheese."

"I warned him first," Astrid said, conceding. She followed Kjaer into the warm stink of old wool and onion and honey. The hearth was low and bright. On the far wall a little shelf held a clay image of a woman with wheat in her hands; beside it, a wooden cross. Kjaer tossed salt into the fire, and it crackled like applause.

"You passed the field today?" Kjaer asked, tearing cheese and handing Astrid the larger piece as if it were an accident. The old woman's mouth was all angles. "Down-valley? Steam like the earth's breath?"

Astrid paused with the cheese against her lip. "No. Not yet."

"Good," Kjaer said. "Don't go alone. Not now."

"Why not now?"

Kjaer's eyes went to the hearth. The light there was small and brave. "A groan came up the ground at moonrise," she said. "Like a whale under ice. I heard it with my teeth."

Astrid swallowed, the cheese suddenly dry. "The fjord shifts in spring. Everyone knows that."

"This was not the fjord." Kjaer lifted her stick, tapped it against the packed earth floor. "Down. Under. The old ways are restless. I dreamt of a red egg wrapped in roots. I woke with the taste of copper. That is a foolish old woman's dream, and you may say so when you leave my house. But you will take someone with you if you go."

Astrid's skin prickled along her forearms. For a heartbeat her dream lurched up from its corner—storm, wings, the shape like a sky—and then she put it down again.

"I will take someone," she lied gently, because Kjaer needed the lie more than Astrid needed to be believed.

After, when Astrid stepped back into the cold, the sky had cleared in torn places. Low sun shone through like a blade through cloth. The wind fell to a mutter. She could hear the sea tick, tick against the shore, like a clock with a slow heart.

She should have gone home. There were nets to mend, a sheath to re-stitch, a stew to start. But habit tugged at her feet the way the tide pulls at a moored boat. She took the iron staff, set her boots toward the birch line, and cut across the field of snow grass where summer made smoke.

The "smoke field" had not been there when Halvar was a boy. That was how the old men talked about it—like a new wrinkle on the earth's brow. In late spring and summer, mist lifted there at dawn and stood waist-high above the ground, thick as breath, smelling faintly of stone soup. In winter the mist lay thin as promises, but today it rose in gray sheets from the hummocked field, smearing the air, beading in her hair.

Astrid stopped at the birches as her father had told her. Their white trunks stood like a row of tired women with pale arms and dark eyes. Beyond the trees the land dipped in a shallow bowl where the steam gathered.

She pressed her palm to the nearest birch. The trunk felt

cold enough to squeak. "I'll be quick," she told no one, and slipped between the trees.

The snow here had a different texture, crusted then sodden under the skin. Her boot went thigh-deep once and she swore, hauling free. The iron staff tested each step, an extra sense that could taste hollows before they took her. Steam swirled around her ankles. The field smelled not just of earth but of something older: iron, and a faint, almost sweet char—like the ghost of a burned log long hidden in a wall.

She crouched where the snow had thinned to show the ground's skin. Between lichen and stone, a trickle of water showed its teeth, unfrozen, running black and quick. She dipped two fingers and hissed. Warm. Warm as breath. She lifted drops to her nose. They smelled like rain in summer, like storms rolling in—the kind that made ships tie off their sails and men touch talismans at throat and wrist.

Wind shifted. The steam lifted and for a heartbeat she saw, across the bowl, the dark mouth of a split in the earth. Not a cave—the shape was wrong. More like a seam had opened where two stones met and forgot to touch.

Astrid straightened, the staff sinking a little as she planted it. She took three steps toward the seam and the ground answered with a sound she felt more than heard: a very old groan, long and low, like a whale singing under ice—or like a mountain remembering pain.

She froze. The iron in her hand vibrated. The hairs on her arms lifted as if lightning wore a fur coat. The steam drew in and held its breath with her.

Beneath her boots, something big exhaled.

It was not air—more a shift of pressure, a low drumbeat

that pushed snow crystals into a brief tiny dance. The seam widened the width of her thumb. A lattice of rime at its edges crackled and fell in glittering dust.

"Astrid," said the wind.

No. Not the wind; she knew the wind's voice as well as her own. This voice came from the ground, rose through her bones. It did not say her name with a mouth. It made her name ring in the hollows inside her, places that had never been named until now.

Her body decided before her mind did. She stepped back, breath coming too fast. The seam held. The steam sighed back into place like a curtain let go. The world resumed its pretending.

Astrid stood there a long while with snow melting cold trails along her calves where it had crept into her boots, with the iron staff heavy enough to anchor a ship. She could put what she had felt into any number of ordinary baskets: thaw. Spring. Ground shift. Old wives. But none of the baskets felt large enough.

"Not today," she said to the seam, because something in her wanted to name a boundary and see if the earth listened the way goats do when your voice is right. "I'll come back with a rope and another pair of hands. Not today."

The ground did not answer. The steam streamed, and a raven somewhere croaked like a hinge.

Astrid turned and made her slow way out of the bowl, testing each step. At the birches she stopped, put her forehead to the cold bark, and laughed once—short and incredulous. The laugh turned to a breath she didn't know she'd been holding. When she looked up the sky had gone a bright, mean blue between torn clouds. Sun struck the mountains and made the ice on their flanks shine like knives.

On the walk home her legs steadied. She told herself lies that felt like courage: she had imagined the voice; it had been the pressure shift of steam; she had not heard wings. She would not say anything to Halvar, not yet. There was no use worrying a man with a story that couldn't carry its own weight. She would go back tomorrow—with a rope and a wedge and maybe Sigrid if she could be pried from her eiderdown. She would prod at the seam like a loose tooth and when it did not open she would feel foolish and relieved in equal measure.

In the village she handed Nils the halyard and Thora the tightened wedge and Kjaer a promise to come again with more roof-rope. Her cheeks burned from cold and from the heat of knowing something alone. The knowing sat like a coin under her tongue: heavy, unspendable yet.

Halvar was whittling a net float on the bench by the hearth when she came in, chips gathered in the fold of his apron like pale fish. He glanced up, eyes flicking first to her boots, then to her hands, the catalog of a man who had lost and learned to count.

"You went," he said.

"To the birches," she answered. This was both true and, depending on how you measured the world, not complete.

He grunted and set the knife down. "Snow easing. Fjord's breathing. I'll check the ice by the shallows before dusk. You'll come."

"I will."

"Eat first."

They ate seal stew thick with barley. Halvar chewed with concentration. Astrid's spoon slowed halfway through the bowl. She thought of Kjaer's stick knocking the earth, of steam rising like breath, of a seam opening the width of a thumb, of her name said from below.

When Halvar rose to pull on his sealskin boots, she stood as well. On impulse she crossed the room and touched the thor's hammer with her forefinger. Then, because the cross watched her with equal patience, she touched it too. Metal and wood, old and new, both cool to the skin.

Halvar saw and said nothing. He pushed the door and the cold kissed their faces like an aunt. Together they walked down to the shore.

The fjord had laid itself out flat as a blade, ice a single skin from rock to rock. Halvar tapped at it with the butt of his spear and listened as if the sea would whisper its secrets up the wood. Astrid crouched and pressed her ear to the ice. The cold bit so hard her skull flinched. Beneath, the fjord made a sound like distant bellows, long and slow. She pulled back quickly and found Halvar watching her with that complicated expression again—pride and worry and love all folded into one.

"You hear more than is good," he said.

"I hear what is there," she answered.

"Those two things are not always the same."

They stood until the sun burned itself thin on the horizon and the cold went from bright to cruel. On the way back, Sigrid hailed them from a doorway with a twist of goose fat and a smirk. "For your lips, storm-girl," she called. "We can't have them cracking and you scowling more than usual."

Astrid took the fat, grinned, and blew a mock kiss that sent Sigrid into scandalized laughter.

They slept early, as villages do in winter when the dark is thick. Astrid lay on her pallet and listened to the wind test the thatch for weak places. When sleep came, it came like a wave; she let it take her.

No dream with wings met her. Only the field, the seam, the smell of rain that was not rain. When she woke, the dark had not yet shifted to gray. She lay with her eyes open, counting heartbeats for the comfort of the counting. Somewhere a board ticked.

She rose before dawn and took the iron staff. She did not write a note or speak to the cold hammer and the quiet cross. She stepped into the thin night with breath fogging and followed her own boot-prints from the day before until they branched and she chose the ones that led to the birches.

The sky to the east held a secret it was preparing to tell. The snow squeaked underfoot with that high bright complaint it made when the cold went far below kind. The world, for all its wide, felt close, as if the mountains had drawn in a little and the fjord listened through a hand cupped to its ear.

At the birch line, she paused and waited for fear to arrive. When it did not, she went forward into the bowl.

Steam lay thin. The warm runnel still ran black and quick, a vein under pale skin. She stepped lightly, testing each patch with the staff. At the seam she set the staff's iron tip along the hairline crack, more a kiss than a prod.

The ground answered at once.

A pulse lifted under her boots—one slow thud, like a heart waking from cold sleep. The seam cracked the width of her hand. Frost at the edges sublimed with a whisper. Warm vapor exhaled and wrapped her face; it smelled of stone and something faintly metallic, the ghost of lightning.

In the thin light she saw it: not just a seam. An edge of something not-rock under rock. A curve, faint and perfect, the surface smoother than any boulder, smooth like shell.

Her breath left in a sound that wanted to be a prayer and did not know which god to choose.

The earth shifted again, more gently, as if something inside had turned in its sleep and found a more comfortable place. The curve showed an inch more. The staff vibrated. Somewhere far above a raven barked twice, the second time as if it had seen a thing it would not say.

"Astrid," said the ground, and this time the word rang in her bones with recognition, not surprise.

She put her palm out, not quite touching the curve. Heat bled into her skin, not burning but alive, like holding a living creature against your wrist and feeling it trust you with its warmth.

"Not today," she whispered again, because fear and reverence can share a mouth. "But soon."

Behind her, on the bowl's rim, snow hissed under a boot. Astrid's head snapped around. For a heartbeat she saw no one. Then a figure stepped between birches: broad shoulders, a cloak rimed white, a spear-lug over one shoulder.

Halvar stood there, pale with cold and not fear. He took in the bowl, the steam, his daughter's stance like a worshiper at the edge of a shrine, and the crack in the earth where not-rock showed its first shy curve.

His eyes, which had seen storms wreck and spare and wreck again, narrowed in a way that meant a life could turn on what came next.

"Astrid," he said, but not as the ground had said it. A father's voice—rough, human, chosen. "Step back."

She did not move.

"Do you see it?" she asked, and her voice came out steady because the thing inside her had chosen steadiness over shaking.

Halvar did not answer with words. He nodded once, as if to someone behind his shoulder.

Astrid realized then, with the clean clarity of cold water, that the field had stopped pretending. The wind had gone to a hush the way a hall does when the skald lifts his hand. Even the steam waited.

The seam lifted—only a heartbeat, only a breath—and from far away, very far, the faintest echo: the slow, rhythmic rush of wings.

Not the sky. Not the storm.

From beneath.

Chapter 2

Road & Warning

They took the upland path while the frost still held the ruts firm. The light was the thin kind that comes before a decision, ash-pale along the ridges, gold only where it caught on ice. Halvar walked ahead with the easy patience of a man who had counted many winters by the weight he could carry home. Astrid followed in his prints, staff tapping, every third step a little off the beat because part of her was listening behind her, back toward the birches.

"Mind the heather hummocks," Halvar said without turning.

"I am," she said, though she wasn't, not really. She was minding the hollow under her ribs where yesterday's heat had gone.

They climbed until the fjord lay below like a blade left cooling on a bench. Up here the wind thinned to a whisper. The path threaded between scrub pine and old rock that showed its bones where snow had slipped. Ravens followed them for a while, counting in their harsh voices and finding them worth only three.

At the saddle where two hills leaned their shoulders together, a figure sat on a stone as if the stone had grown him: a bent man wrapped in a gray cloak the color of fog, hood up, hands folded over a staff with iron rings on it. His boots were good, though the leather had been mended often; a traveler's lamp hung cold at his belt. He might have been any pilgrim from the monastery to the south, or any old herdsman resting bones that had not learned when to be quiet.

But the air around him felt—different. The way air feels by a hot spring in winter: not warm, exactly, but attentive.

The man lifted his face as they approached. His beard was a tangle the wind had combed; his eyes were the clear gray of water over slate. He smiled like someone greeting weather he had ordered on purpose.

"Morning to you," Halvar said, neutral as a plank. "Road's thin ice along the north curve."

"So it is," the old man agreed. His voice had been sanded by many roads. "I thank you for the warning, Halvar Halvarsson."

Halvar paused half a heartbeat at the sound of his name. It was a small pause, but Astrid had learned to hear small things. She watched the lines around his mouth change shape, as if the day had put on a different coat and he didn't like the cut.

"You've the better of me," Halvar said.

"Old men hear what the wind tells them," the traveler replied, and somehow that was an answer and not one. His gaze shifted to Astrid and softened at the edges, not pity, not appraisal—recognition, like a musician hearing the first note of a tune he's been expecting. "And this is Astrid, who hears more than is good and exactly as much as is needed."

Astrid's fingers tightened on the staff. "We meet strangers on this road," she said carefully. "We don't usually meet prophecy."

The old man's smile deepened, then gentled away. "Prophecy is a large word," he said. "I am only a listener who has not yet gone deaf."

Halvar stepped between them half a pace, not enough to be rude, enough to be solid. "We're bound for the ridge. If you've business with Havngard, you can take the lower trail. It's kinder on old knees."

"I will take the trail that was laid for me," the man said, unbothered. He tapped his staff once on the stone. The iron rings chimed, not loud, but the sound seemed to go down rather than outward, as if the earth were a drum waiting to be struck again. "Tell me, fisherman—did you feel it last night? The ground turning in sleep?"

"No more than any spring," Halvar said.

"Hm." The old man's gaze wandered past them, over their shoulders, toward where the birches would be if the hill could be peeled back. "There's a pulse under your fields. The kind that writes itself into rock. I have felt it in other places too, but here it is…nearer to the skin."

Astrid hadn't wanted the words until she heard them. Now they were meat, and she was hungry in a way that made her jaw hurt. "What does it mean?"

"Astrid," Halvar said, warning in his voice.

The traveler looked at her as a father might look at a map he has not yet shown his child. "It means the buried fire remembers its name," he said. "And names remember their bearers."

Astrid swallowed. The place under her ribs went warm and afraid at once. "You speak as if fire were a person."

"Everything is a person if you have lived long enough with it," the old man said dryly. "Sea. Stone. Storm. Even winter learns to answer to a name if you are stubborn." He tilted his head. "Do you dream of wings, girl?"

Halvar moved faster than a man his age should. His hand closed around Astrid's elbow—gentle, firm. "Enough. We've work on us."

The old man did not take offense. He watched Halvar's fingers, then Halvar's face, and nodded as if a problem had shown him its shape. "Work is good," he said. "Work keeps the mind from breaking open too soon."

"Too soon for what?" Astrid asked before she could leash the question.

"For anything that can't be put back," he said simply. He rose. He was taller than she'd thought, and not as frail; the cloak had hidden a frame that had known boats and mountains both. When he leaned on his staff, it was with the economy of a man who could walk all day without making fuss of it. "Forgive an old tongue, Halvar Halvarsson. I forget that truths have weight, and some shoulders are not warmed for carrying yet."

Halvar's mouth thinned. "Some truths break the back you say you mean to spare."

"And some silences do," the old man countered, without heat. "But I am not here to teach you your house. Only to say: the seam under your birches is not a seam. It is a lid. Lids open when what is beneath them is ready." He looked at Astrid, and for a breath the gray of his eyes went to the deep kind of color you see in fjords when the sun is behind a cloud—green in the gray, light in the depth. "When the ice forgets, remember."

The words struck her the way a bell strike finds the hollow in metal. The sound went through her bones and kept going.

Halvar took a breath through his nose like a man

counting. "Your name," he said, as if offering the old man a last chance to be ordinary.

"Names are promises," the traveler said. "I will keep mine for later. For now—call me what you like. Walker. Listener. Fool." He grinned suddenly, all weather and teeth. "Wizard, if that makes the story sit straighter in your head. I've been worse."

Astrid felt laughter rise in her throat, the dry kind that comes when fear and delight bump shoulders. "Are you here for me?" she asked, and only when the words were out did she hear how much they wanted a yes.

"I am here for the road," he said, and the kind eyes did not let her look away. "If you are on it, then I am near you by accident of maps." He tipped two fingers from the brim of his hood in a gesture that was both respectful and a little mocking of respect. "Mind your steps. The earth is listening for you."

He went past them with the ease of a stream finding downhill. As he passed Halvar, he paused a heartbeat and said in a voice that did not carry, "You cannot hide a sunrise with your hand." Then he was moving again, staff tapping, iron rings giving their quiet note, and the gray of his cloak was a piece of the morning until the morning took it back.

Astrid stood with her heart in the wrong place. She felt as if the air had changed color and no one would admit it. "You know him," she said, not quite a question.

"I know the kind," Halvar said. He released her arm. His hand lingered a fraction of a breath longer than necessary, as if the letting-go cost him coin he would rather have kept. "Road-men with old songs and new mouths. They're trouble."

"He didn't feel like trouble," she said. "He felt like…
answer. Or at least a finger pointing toward one."

"That's the shape of the worst trouble," Halvar said. He
started walking again, and she matched him. The ravens
swung off the ridge and followed the traveler, as if rumor
had tugged their tails. "Keep your head where your feet are.
We'll trade for line at Stennar's and be home before dusk."

Astrid obeyed with her body and not with her mind. She
tried to put the words away like fish salted for later, but they
kept slipping free. When the ice forgets, remember. The
phrase fit under her tongue like a seed. It hurt and it
promised.

They bartered for line and hooks and a new awl, for resin
that smelled like childhood headaches, for a wedge-hammer
Halvar didn't admit he wanted until Stennar found him
holding it like a friend. People spoke of roofs and thaw and
a cow that had gone wrong in the night and righted itself by
morning. No one spoke of seams in the earth or lids. No one
spoke of dragons except in the way of jokes that keep fear
tame.

On the way back, the weather pulled one more thin cloud
over the sun, then gave it up. The light went winter-bright
and honest. From the rise between the hills, Astrid could
see the birch line like a seam sewn in white thread across a
gray coat. The hollow beyond it was only a suggestion, a
dark not-dark where the steam made the air a little drunk.

They did not speak of going there.

But when Havngard showed itself below and Halvar said,
"Home," like a man closing the door on a wind he didn't
trust, Astrid said, "I'll take the long way—drop the awl at
Nils's," and did not wait long enough for him to disbelieve

her. She trotted ahead, staff ticking, breath white, pulse loud as if the ground were echoing it back.

The birches welcomed no one. They stood like they always had: tired women keeping their own counsel. The bowl lay quiet, steam thin as the edge of a thought. Astrid went to the place where she knew the seam had been and found only snow pressed smooth by wind and the memory of her own boot prints from the day before melting into vagueness.

She knelt. Brushed snow aside. The ground looked like ground. She set her palm to it and felt—nothing but the cold tasting her bones. For a foolish, angry moment she thought of striking the earth with her staff like a child calling a sulking friend to the door. She didn't. She laid her ear down instead, cheek burning with the cold bite, and listened.

A long time. Long enough for the breath to settle out of her, long enough for the world to go wider again and less intimate. Somewhere a raven said something rude. Somewhere a stream laughed at its own joke under the snow.

No heartbeat. No voice that made her name ring in the hidden places.

She sat back on her heels. Doubt came like a tide—quiet, insistent, licking at everything. Had she dreamed the warmth? Had she wanted it so hard she'd made it out of nothing? The old man's words slid through her mind and would not stick to anything.

When the ice forgets, remember.

She pressed her palm flat to the ground one last time and —because it was foolish or holy, she could not say which— she whispered, "I remember."

Nothing answered. But when she stood, her hand burned as if she had been holding something warm and living and reluctant to be let go. She tucked it under her cloak and walked back toward the village, eyes stinging from the wind and from something else that the wind could take the blame for if it wanted.

Halvar was waiting by the fence, whittling as if the knife could cut the day into better shapes. He looked at her hand hidden under her cloak, then at her face, and did not ask. She did not tell. They stood a while in a silence that was not empty, and the fjord below them wore the light like a promise it hadn't decided how to keep.

Chapter 3

The Voice Beneath the Wind

Morning came reluctantly, as if the sun itself doubted the worth of the day.

A pale gray light seeped through the cloudbank, turning snow and sky into a single sheet of dull brightness. Astrid woke before Halvar and lay in that hush where houses remember the night. The coals in the hearth made their small brave sounds—settling, sighing—and the rafters answered with the groan of old wood. She listened to the wind at the eaves. It wasn't angry now, not like the storm two nights before. But it had picked up a strange rhythm, an unevenness, as if somewhere beyond the ridge a hand drummed its fingertips against the air.

She slid from her bedding, careful not to wake her father, and eased the door open. The cold met her like a stern aunt —bracing, not cruel. The fjord lay flat under a glaze of light, ice latticed in fine cracks that spidered from shore to shore. Breath plumed from her mouth and vanished. She waited for the usual: the creak of ice, the quiet tick of water under the skin. What came wasn't that. It was a hum—low, nearly nothing—threading through the stillness. Not sea. Not wind. A tuning note before a song.

Behind her, furs shifted. "Astrid?" Halvar's voice came rough with sleep and a winter's worth of salt.

She jumped slightly, shut the door, and turned with what she hoped was a light smile. "Checking the weather," she said. "It's calm."

"A calm sea still hides deep currents," he said, sitting up. "Best not to test them." He stood and went to the hearth; the red under-embers lifted their faces like cats to his hands. "Eat. Then the sheds."

Astrid nodded and went through motions the way a person keeps a tune going when their mind has wandered off: porridge, salt, a cup of water, the good rope coiled for later. But the hum had braided itself through her ribs. At first she told herself it was only memory. Memories, though, faded as the winter day grew. This held.

By midday they were on the fishing shed roof. The boards creaked under their weight with a conversational sort of complaint. Halvar worked with the steadiness of tide: axe up, axe down, plank righted, nail set. Astrid crouched near the ridge beam, sorting nails from a jar that had outlived three lids: true, bent, bent-but-persuadable. Gull cries came sharp and infrequent, like white chalk marks across the muted sky.

"Pass the hammer," Halvar said without looking up.

She placed it in his hand and paused, head tilted. The wind ran a finger along her hair. There it was again—thin as breath on glass. A whisper so faint the world might deny it had happened the moment it ended.

"…Astrid…"

It wasn't her name spoken with a mouth. It was her name appearing in the space just behind her eyes, as if her bones had been reminded of it.

Her skin pebbled along her forearms. She looked toward the fjord. Nothing unusual—only mist lifting from the ice in slow, uncertain curls. She swallowed.

"Dreaming again?" Halvar asked. He didn't look at her. He never looked when he was listening hardest.

"No." Her voice came steady because she made it so. "Just—listening."

"To what?"

She groped for a rope that would take the weight of the lie. "To you," she said lightly, "if you'd stop hammering long enough to tell me what comes next."

The corner of his mouth tugged. "What comes next," he said, driving the nail home with three even blows, "is learning which sounds matter and which are walking cloaks for nothing."

She pressed her lips together. On the roof's edge, a gull lifted and wheeled, circle upon slow circle, without a single flap. She thought of the old traveler from the pass—his iron-ringed staff, the way the air around him had felt attentive. She put that thought away with the bent nails.

They finished the roof before dusk. The day never quite warmed; it only changed shades of cold. Smoke rose from Havngard in mild, unambitious threads. Nets hung from racks like narrow, sleeping books. Work kept the mind honest until it didn't. All through the afternoon, the hum wove in and out of the familiar, like a fisherman's song heard three houses away.

That night the wind returned. It came down from the north with a clean blade in it, not cruel, but sharp enough to make the thatch think about its old sins. Astrid turned over and over until the blanket tangled at her ankles; then she pushed it off and sat up. Halvar was a slow hill of sleep, his breath even. The fire had settled to embers and fine ash. The walls wore their old smoke like a memory they had chosen to keep.

Do not fear.

The words arrived inside her like a hand set gently upon a shoulder. She did not hear them. She *had* them.

She held very still. "Who's there?" she whispered to the dark.

Ash answered with the smallest collapse—a faint, papery sound. The rafters breathed. Somewhere outside, a fox barked once and thought better of a second try.

You are not dreaming, the voice said. It was deep without heaviness, threaded with age and patience. *You are beginning to hear.*

"What—how—?" She touched her temples, foolishly, as if something in her skull might be hot to the touch.

Sleep, the voice said, softer now. *Morning is kinder than questions at midnight.*

A draft slid down the chimney; sparks lifted their heads and sank. The voice went with them, pulled away like a boat from a pier.

Astrid lay down because the voice had phrased it like an instruction and because there was nothing else to do in the middle of a winter night. Sleep came, but not as a tide; it came as a rope paying out, slow, as if the sea were reluctant to claim it.

She woke with her eyes gritty and her patience finer than she liked. Halvar's gaze ticked to her face once while they mended net and again while she salted a cod by habit. He said nothing until the ropework between his hands made sense of itself without him and he could afford to look at her directly.

"You're not yourself," he said. His voice made the observation gentle.

"I'm myself." She kept hers matter-of-fact. "I'm also

short on sleep."

"Dreams again?"

"Something like that."

"Best to let them pass."

She nearly laughed. *If only I could hand them a cloak and point at the door,* she thought. "I'll try."

She did not try. She waited.

She waited through the afternoon as snow lightened, then stopped pretending, and then started again as if remembering a promise. She waited through the long chores of winter village life, which are half action, half talking-through-your-body so your mind can wander unnoticed: wedge this; stitch that; thicken the stew; rub the goat's ear where frostbit turned the tip sweet-numb. She waited while Sigrid bargained like a cheerful brigand over three eggs and a comb, and while old Kjaer stood at her door and told the wind to keep its nose out of people's houses.

When evening pulled the sun down into the edge of the world and left a rim of bruised light, Astrid slipped her cloak over her shoulders and told Halvar too many truths.

"I'll take the long way," she said. "Nils's awl needs a new handle. And Stennar's boy says the smoke hole leaks." All these things were real. None of them were where she was going.

Halvar looked up from the bench. Knife in hand, he had been turning a block of wood into something that might later confess what it wanted to be. He studied her fastened cloak, the set of her mouth, the way her boots pointed already at the door. "Be back before full dark," he said.

"I will."

The promise ran out of her mouth on its own legs and sprinted into the night.

Havngard's narrow lanes crunched underfoot. Children were being pulled in by their names; lamplight spilled from doorways and lost courage three paces from the threshold. Astrid passed the last house, the last net-drying rack, the last sensible reason to turn back, and took the path that led to the birches.

The grove had the hush of a place that listens to itself. Their white trunks stood like a row of tired women with patient backs and hard hands. Beyond them, the bowl lay quiet. Steam lifted in a soft, stubborn veil from the hummocked field. The air smelled faintly of iron and rain.

At the edge she stopped and let the cold find all her unbuttoned places. The world arranged itself in the old way: birches; bowl; the snow like a garment laid carelessly over a sleeping thing; the seam she *knew* all the shapes of by now even if the eye could not find it.

"You came back," the voice said.

She didn't gasp this time. She had expected it in every moment she told herself she did not. "Who are you?"

Names are promises, the voice answered, amused without unkindness. *And promises bind. If you need one to hold, call me what men did when their hearing was better—the Listener.*

"Why are you speaking to me?"

Because you can hear. Because you are the one who answered when the ground said your name. Because it is time, and also not yet time.

"I don't understand."

You will. If you walk instead of run, the Listener said. *And if you do not tell the man who guards you with his fear.*

"My father." The words came out before she set them

loose. She winced. "He has a right to—"

To fear. Yes. He remembers waters that took what he loved. He will sign his name under "Never again" and try to make the weather obey it. Love writes stubborn stories. A pause, a feeling like the world considering. *But your story is older than fear. The buried fire wakes. Do not stand too close when it first remembers its name.*

"Buried fire," Astrid repeated. Down in her bones a small thing leaned forward to listen with both hands.

You felt it.

"I—" She stopped. Lies did not like the air here. "I did."

You will feel it again. A breeze came up the bowl, kinder than the cold. The mist curled around her boots, a cat welcoming a person who cannot resist not-pretending they like cats. *Now be very still. We are not alone.*

Astrid turned her head in the tiniest degree. Even tiny was too much—whoever watches in winter learns smallness by heart. The birches whispered in their sliver-leaf language. Between two trunks, where blue-gray deepened, a darker shape stood, moored to its shadow. A man-sized fact. A staff. A hood. The very idea of eyes.

She could not see the face, and yet she knew—knew in the way a hand placed on a door knows when someone stands on the other side—that he was the traveler from the ridge. Knew it as surely as she knew the smell of her father's work-gloves and the weight of the iron staff on her palm.

She did not move. She did not call. The fog wrote strange, fragile letters around her ankles and then forgot them.

He does not come because he knows what arrival costs, the Listener said, gentler now. *He will teach you at a distance until you are strong enough to bear nearness.*

Astrid swallowed. "Teach me what?"

To listen without drowning. A note, lower: *And to stand when the world chooses you for something bigger than your fear.*

It should have sounded like boasting or prophecy. It sounded like someone offering her bread in winter and expecting her to eat because people must.

Wind leaned, then let go. The shadow near the birches unmoored and was gone, like a thought before a word can catch it. Astrid let the breath leave her slowly. "If I tell my father—"

He will tell himself a story that makes the world safe, the Listener said. *He will tell it in the most loving voice he has. It will feel like a roof and be a box.*

"He's only trying to—"

—keep you alive. Yes. The voice did not argue. It had no need. *You must keep yourself true. Between those two kinds of keeping, a person grows.*

They stood like that—girl and voice and absent watcher and bowl and patient birches—until the cold reminded flesh of its limits. Astrid's toes numbed in waves; the second wave was always the worst. "I have to go," she said.

Go, the Listener said. *But hear me: do not try to open what is not ready. A lid is a lid for reason's sake. The first lesson is waiting. Tomorrow, at the shore—*

"The shore?"

Where the fjord breathes. Dawn. Bring only your staff and your stubbornness. Leave your fear at home if it insists on being in charge of the journey.

The voice folded in on itself like a sail taken in neat hands. The bowl was only a bowl again, and the steam only steam.

Astrid ran because running warmed feet faster than dignity did. By the time she reached the lane, the moon had climbed above the ridge and put a cold thumbprint on the roofs. She stopped at the door and made her breath behave.

Halvar was waiting. He had whittled the block into a fish and then into something that might have been a bird if birds had had the good sense to be square. He looked at her hand hiding under her cloak and then at her face.

"You were gone too long," he said.

"I was at Nils's," she said. "And Stennar's. And Sigrid cornered me to scold my lips into goose fat."

Halvar raised one brow in skeptical, weary benediction. "And the field?"

She didn't lie this time. "I looked at it," she said. "From the birches."

He closed his eyes for a heartbeat—the kind of closing that looks like relief and hurts like surrender. "Astrid," he said quietly, "there are cliffs you don't test by stamping near the edge. Promise me you'll stay away from that place."

She owed him the truth. She gave him peace instead. "I promise."

It wasn't true. The lie took up lodging behind her tongue and tapped its foot like an impatient guest.

They ate in quiet, the kind that isn't empty. Halvar salted the fire for the drowned and those the sea remembers. Astrid touched the hammer amulet and the small wooden cross in turn, as she had before. The gods said nothing. Perhaps they had learned from winter when to keep their mouths shut.

That night, the wind played its old song along the rafters —notes as familiar as scars. Astrid kept her eyes open until the roof beams drifted and the shadows forgot their lines. Sleep was a shore she reached one foot at a time.

The promise you made was for his peace, not yours, the Listener said, voice no louder than the thought that names the thought before it.

Astrid didn't start. She hadn't been fully asleep. She answered without moving her mouth. *Will you always walk into a room like that? Quiet as a cat and sure you're welcome?*

Only until you learn to lock your doors, the Listener said, with a glint of humor. *Dawn. The shore. Come.*

If I do, she thought, *you'll stop telling me my father is wrong?*

A father is not wrong to love his child, the Listener said. *But love can build walls as easily as houses. Come learn which is which.*

He left the way the tide leaves—so slowly you don't see it go until the wet line has crept into absence.

Astrid slept in a choppy way that made morning feel farther than it had a right to be. She woke before it. The air had the thinness that comes just before the world changes color. She dressed in wool and leather and wrapped her cloak so the wind would have to work for the privilege. She wrote nothing because there was nothing worth writing that Halvar would read with anything less than his whole heart.

She pushed the door and the predawn met her—clean, indifferent, expectant. The village held its breath; the sea held its stories. She followed her own sense of the shore, a path her feet had learned before memory had bothered to name it.

Havngard crouched at the fjord's edge like a herd of tired beasts waiting for day to pat them and say "Up." The black-ribbed longboats wore the snow like fur. Ice had scabbed itself back together in the night, thin and slightly ashamed of its crack-lines. Astrid walked the line where land and water have never quite made their minds up and stood on a rock that made her look a little braver than she felt.

The light was the idea of light, not the fact. East, the clouds had begun to thin into the first agony of color. The sea ticked, slow and patient.

Stand as if you meant it, the Listener said. He was nowhere. He was entirely present.

Astrid planted the iron-shod staff. It made a small, honest sound on the rock. *Now what?* she thought.

Now you listen to what is not your fear, the Listener answered. *Close your eyes if your eyes are greedy. Open them if your hands are. The fjord breathes under the ice. The mountains hum to the roots of themselves. The old pulse is not a sound; it is an agreement. Find it.*

She snorted, forgetting to be reverent. *"Find the agreement." That's like telling a goat to compose a hymn.*

Goats are better composers than men admit, the voice said dryly. *Quiet. Down.*

She tried. The first try sounded exactly like a person making a noise called Trying in her head. She tried again and discovered that trying is a busy verb and listening does not like company. She let her shoulders drop. Let the jaw unclench. Let the staff carry some part of her weight that had no business being carried by ankles. Let the breath go in without being counted like coins.

The fjord's ice made its slow, continental sounds. The wind rehearsed a phrase and let it go. Far up-valley a raven mentioned the morning to another raven. Beneath all that—something like a hand under a blanket, shifting to a more comfortable place. Not a sound. A *near-sound.*

Her heart raced because hearts have poor timing. She

breathed out until the heart remembered it was a guest in a house with other guests to consider.

Good, the Listener said. His approval felt like a weight taken from the back of the neck where worry sits and whispers. *Now lower.*

She lowered, not in her knees but in the place inside where alertness lives. She thought of the seam under the birches. She did not *think* of the seam. She let the field and the birches and the vein of warm water come sit quietly in the room with her. She waited until that room was big enough to hold the fjord and the mountain and the row of tired clouds trying to decide whether to snow or behave.

There. The agreement. A long, slow Yes moving through rock. The faint turn of some old wheel under the world. It brushed her bones like a name remembered.

Her eyes opened. The seam of dawn broke like a promise kept past its due. The mountains put on a little gold grudgingly and were surprised to find it suited them.

She laughed—once, very small and very from-the-middle. The sound made her feel foolish and holy at once. She wasn't sure she liked either feeling; she liked them both enough to say nothing against them.

You hear it, the Listener said, with a satisfaction that had nothing of pride in it.

I hear… something.

Something is more honest than nothing named loudly, he replied. *Remember this feeling. When the ground speaks in winter's language, it will use this grammar. When your own fear tries to mimic it, this will help you tell the difference.*

She didn't ask how fear spoke. She already knew. Fear-drum is quick and personal. This was old and disinterested, like a tide that happens to love you but would be itself if it didn't.

Sound moved behind her. Not his voice—*sound.* A deliberate scuff of boot leather. She turned slowly.

Halvar stood three paces back, a silhouette above the ice's pallor, cloak rimed with frost at the hem. He had come like fog comes, present before acknowledged. The look in his eyes was not anger. It was the complicated anger of love that has been told it is the villain in a story it wrote to save you.

"Dawn," he said. Not a question.

"I couldn't sleep," she said, which was true and not at all the truth he wanted.

He studied her face—the particular stillness of it, the way the shoulders sat, the way the staff had become an extension of her intent. Something in him recognized something in her and did not like that recognition one bit.

"There are things you don't understand," he said softly.

She swallowed. "There are things you do and won't tell."

"The not-telling is the only way I know to keep you whole."

She looked down because looking up would make her say uncareful things. The fjord's skin had taken on a faint color, the way faces do when a secret has been spoken nearby. "I promised," she said. It tasted like ash and kindness.

Halvar blew out a breath. "Come, then," he said, after a long beat, as if bargaining with himself in a language he thought she did not speak. "Help me check the east shore nets before the sun lies to us about the thickness."

She went with him because love deserves accompaniment even when it is not given permission to be in charge. They walked the line of low water and kicked at the ice with the heels of their boots where it had pulled away from rock. He told her stories about winters when men had been brave at the wrong times and right at the wrong places. She listened to the stories and to the small, constant hum the fjord made to itself.

By noon the village had woken into the ordinary. That ordinary had bright spots—Sigrid's blue scarf; little Arnul cracking a smileful of ice with his heel; Kjaer's broom chasing geese who did not respect old women's doorways; someone's laugh throwing a stone at the day and making it ripple. The ravens followed rumor as always.

Astrid worked with her body as if her body had asked for the work. She bartered for a bundle of dry moss with a stubborn old man who believed moss had opinions; she carried eel cages and tried not to breathe the salt that had become a fog inside the shed; she mended a tear in a sleeve with neat stitches, each stitch a gratitude for hands that had learned to make order where cloth forgot itself.

Twice, three times, she felt the Listener's attention like a hand near a shoulder. He did not speak. The non-speaking spoke enough: *Practice the grammar of the ground. It will teach you how to hear me without breaking yourself on the learning.*

By late afternoon, thin snow had resumed in air so still each flake felt like an idea the sky was trying out. Astrid found herself at the fence above the birch path with no memory of choosing it. She leaned into the post and let the day swing below her like a door. In the distance, the grove kept its counsel. Beyond it, the bowl wore its veil.

Halvar came to stand beside her. He did not speak. The two of them could build a fire from a silence like this if given kindling and time.

"Do you believe in prophecy?" Astrid asked at last,

surprising herself.

He didn't flinch. "I believe in old stories that have sharpened themselves on many tongues," he said. "I believe in men who use those stories like spears. I believe the sea takes the same kinds of people every year while we tell ourselves different reasons."

"That isn't the same as no."

"No," he allowed. "It isn't."

"Did Mother—" She hadn't meant to say it. The word came and stood there between them, refusing polite company.

Halvar's face changed shape as if a wind had moved under it. "Your mother believed that the world knew her name," he said, each word placed with care. "She believed it knew mine. She believed it would know her child's name too, in a way that was not ownership but welcome." He swallowed. "She was often right."

"And when she was wrong?"

"She had courage anyway."

Astrid breathed. The breath had edges. "There is a man —" she began, and then stopped, because love may not deserve to be in charge, but it deserves not to be made to feel foolish in its own house.

Halvar saved her the trouble of choosing. "A road-man with a staff and eyes like storms that have learned manners," he said. "He was at the pass. He will be everywhere a person like you goes until he has to stop pretending the road is the thing that brought him."

She turned her head, startled and not. "You knew he—"

"I know his kind," Halvar said, and his voice, for a moment, let the salt out. "He will call himself Listener or Walker or Friend and he will be all those things. He will bring the world closer and make you think it has less appetite for you than it does." He drew a breath. "He will teach you something I cannot. If he harms you, I will take his staff and teach him the language of breaking."

Astrid's laugh skated close to tears and turned at the last moment, breathless and grateful. "You'd have to catch him."

"I would," Halvar said simply. "And then I would."

They stood a while longer, the way two trees will stand— roots touching rock, crowns taking what the light gives. When the cold proved it had the better patience, they went inside and shared stew with the kind of hunger that makes conversation optional. Halvar salted the fire for the drowned and for the ones the sea remembers tenderly. Astrid laid her hand over the old hammer pendant and then over the small, carved cross. She did not ask for anything. She said thank you to a roomful of gods and left it unclear which one she meant.

Night gathered itself in the corners and on the roof. Sleep came to Havngard house by house like a sensible visitor with a list. Astrid lay awake, counting the beat in the rafters and the small settling of the hearth and the way winter makes a silence you can stand on.

When the voice came, it did not startle her.

You did well, the Listener said. *You heard the agreement and did not mistake it for your own pulse.*

You were there, she thought, without accusation. *Watching.*

Teaching, he corrected. *From where I can do least harm.*

Are you a wizard? She didn't mean to sound like a child asking if a story had come outside to play. She failed to not sound like that, and decided to forgive herself.

I am old at listening, he said. *Men have called that wizardry when they were in a generous mood and witchcraft when they were in a fearful one. Call me what you like when the naming helps you do the work.*

And the work is…?

To become the person your name expects when the ground says it, he said. *To learn not to drown when the buried fire lifts its head. To stand where the world is thinnest without breaking it or yourself.*

It should have sounded like arrogance. It sounded like chores.

Tomorrow, he added, *we go to the birches. Not to open. To learn the language of lids.*

And if I cannot—

Then we wait. Waiting is not failure. It is the first spell any sensible wizard learns.

For a wonder, Astrid smiled in the dark, and the smile did not cut her mouth. *You're not as grim as you pretend.*

I am as grim as weather and as kind as patience, he said, amused. *Sleep, Astrid.*

The fjord groaned once, far off, the sound a great thing makes when it rolls in sleep and remembers an old ache in a new place. Astrid's eyes slid shut. She dreamt of birches that bent over a seam and whispered not of secrets but of timing, of a lid that would open when asked by the right hand, in the right season, with the right word.

She woke before dawn with the word still in her mouth and no memory of its shape—only the certainty that it would not be borrowed from any language men spoke to each other when the harvest was good.

Outside, the world considered a new color. Inside,

Halvar's breathing marked the measure of a life made of more love than skill and more skill than pride. Astrid lay very still and let herself feel both kept and called, and did not apologize to either feeling for the other.

Chapter 4

The Whispering Wizard

Dawn unstitched the night seam by seam. Astrid rose before the last star left its post and followed frost prints she'd made the day before, the iron-shod staff tapping a quiet cadence ahead of her. The fjord lay hushed, the ice a pale page thinly scraped. She stood on the same rock as yesterday, planted the staff, and waited for the Listener to arrive in the way only he did—by reminding her she'd already known he was there.

You came back, he said.

You asked, she answered, and felt foolish for answering in thought and relieved not to have to choose a voice.

Today we learn to listen with bone, he said. *Ears tire. Bones keep better records.*

She shut her eyes because the eye was a greedy guest and listening preferred an emptier room. Wind rehearsed and forgot. Ravens traded rumors. Beneath the ice, the fjord made the slow adjustments of a sleeping thing turning on its side. She let those layers stack without climbing any. When her breath stopped trying to lead, the quieter things rose.

There—a faint, regular ticking under the ice in the cove to her left. Not crack, not current. A pulse with purpose, like teeth testing wood.

What is it? she thought.

Name it, the Listener said. *Don't ask me. Teaching is a kind of theft if I always hand you the words.*

Astrid shifted her weight, let the staff carry her questions. She widened her attention as if opening a door and waiting to see which smells entered with the cold. Tick, tick, pause; tick, tick. She pictured eel cages, the way ropes iced after spray, the way trapped air complains inside thin ice.

"Otters," she whispered, surprised by her own mouth. "Two of them. Testing for a weak spot where the stream from the marsh meets the fjord."

Good, the Listener said, approval like warmth between shoulder blades. *Stay in the bones. Now listen farther.*

She did. Beyond the otters, farther out where the ice turned from skin to glass, something massed—a heaviness she could not hear so much as *recognize.* Not a thing. A place deciding to be a thing. The fjord there held itself differently, as if bracing.

Don't fix it with a name yet, he warned. *Only acknowledge. We seek the agreement—not a trophy.*

She nodded. The iron staff tapped once, lightly, in the rhythm of a thought.

Boot scuff behind her. She kept her body still and let only her attention turn. Halvar stood at the path's edge, cloak rimed with the glitter that comes when air has not yet decided to be day. He watched her a long breath without interrupting either of their silences.

"You'll freeze," he said at last.

"I'm listening," she said.

"To what?"

"Not to danger," she answered, and it was true—the way you can be truthful standing under a sky full of weather that has not yet chosen your village.

He came down the slope and stood beside her, not on the rock but close enough to borrow its lie about courage. He said nothing more. His presence arranged the cold into something bearable.

The otters found their channel. The ticks moved downstream. The farther heaviness shifted and stopped, like someone settling a weight on a shelf. Astrid opened her eyes.

"You've stood like that since you were little," Halvar said lightly. "Listening to silence until it agreed to speak first."

She smiled with half her mouth. "It's rude to interrupt."

"Hmm." He looked out across the ice. "Where shall I throw the spear if it cracks?"

"Not there." She pointed to the glass-blue stretch. "The fjord is listening that way. It might answer with teeth."

He studied the place she indicated, then her face, then the place again. He didn't argue. He didn't promise to obey. He only nodded once—the smallest treaty.

They walked the shore line back; he checked the ice with the butt of his spear, she the inside of the air with the ribs she'd been born with. Work waited and tried to remind her it was the entire world. She made room for both.

Word travels oddly in winter villages. By noon, old Kjaer had told three people that the fjord sighed "like a married man seeing spring," and Nils had decided this meant the nets should be shifted two posts to the east. Children argued about whether ice could be jealous. A gull stole a fish head and nobody called that an omen because gulls steal and calling it fate would only encourage them.

Astrid kept to chores with a mind like a door left just unlatched. Underneath the ordinary, something kept humming—steady as a loom, faint as a held breath. Not danger; intention. It made her hands careful.

Midafternoon found her mending ribs on a small boat near the slip. She worked with a curved awl and waxed thread, fingers moving as if they had been practicing this very mend all while she was learning the grammar of the ground. Snow came down in an indecisive drift. Halvar's voice carried from two sheds over, steady as ever, bargaining rope against blades with a man who believed every knot was an opinion.

"Astrid!" Sigrid's voice from the lane—half shout, half laugh. "Come tell Joren his geese aren't cursed; they're stupid."

Astrid wiped her hands and stood, grinning despite herself. That was when her bones said *No*.

It wasn't a sound. It wasn't even a word. It was a pressure that came from the direction of the slipway: a weight lifting where no weight should lift. Her heart lurched—hearts always late or early. She turned and listened the way a deer listens when the woods change their mind.

The ice at the slip groaned—common enough. Then it clicked twice like a jaw finding an old break. Children were playing near the lip, pushing a sledge. One step more and the thin new ice would be sledge and boy and bad story.

Astrid didn't shout. Shouting arrives after, and after breaks things. She ran, hand up, not to wave but to pull the attention of whoever's eyes would obey. The youngest—Arnul—saw her face and stopped because fear is contagious, and so is trust. Astrid reached him, scooped him back with an arm, slid the sledge by its rope two paces right, and said in the calmest voice she could borrow, "Here. If you must race death, at least insult it properly."

They laughed because children cannot help themselves. The ice where the sledge had been pressed—just left of where she moved it—popped a line and sugared over into slush. It would have held another week if no one had touched it. It would have swallowed a boy if she had come one breath later.

Halvar was there in five strides and a lifespan. He looked at the ice, then at Astrid's face, then at Arnul, who was busy pretending he hadn't almost learned a legend's ending. Halvar's hand found Astrid's shoulder—heavy, grateful, foreign to explanation. "Good," he said simply. To Arnul he added, "Tell your mother you owe Astrid cheese."

"I'd rather honey," Astrid said, which made them laugh again and reset the day.

Sigrid reached Astrid at the same moment Kjaer did, and between them they made enough noise to convince the weather to behave. "Storm-girl," Sigrid scolded fondly, then softened when she saw Astrid's hands shaking now that the room had been righted. "You heard it, didn't you? You hear everything before it decides to be loud."

Astrid shrugged. "Sometimes the world whispers because it's tired," she said. "We should be polite and answer before it has to shout."

Kjaer's old eyes sparked. "You sound like a story," she said. "Careful. Stories tire people out too."

"Only if they're badly told," Sigrid said, then kissed Astrid's cheek with a smack and went away joyful, which was Sigrid's best revenge on winter.

The hum in Astrid's bones eased, the way a drum does after a dancer bows. She returned to the rib mend and found her fingers steady again.

Well done, the Listener said, so near she could have mistaken his voice for her own thought if she'd wanted an easier day. *You *answered the agreement with action. No thunder. No display. Yes is a quiet word when it works.*

It wasn't magic, she told him, stubborn.

No, he agreed. *It was listening that remembered to move its feet. Men call that magic when they need to forgive themselves for not hearing it first.*

She snorted, then hid the sound in a cough when Halvar glanced over.

Now, the Listener added, *we make it harder. Come at dusk to the birches.*

Why harder?

Because soon it will cost you to hear, he said, and his voice wore sadness without bitterness. *The world grows louder around awakenings. You will need to choose which sounds to put down even when they carry names you love.*

Astrid's mouth went dry. She did not ask him to explain. Explanations were tools; sometimes they were nets.

Dusk poured like ink into the folds of the valley. Astrid took the birch path with a measured pace, each footfall a vote for the kind of courage that fits in boots. The grove held its listening. Beyond it, the bowl wore a thinner veil; the steam was more insistent, as if the ground had found an old breath and decided to keep it.

The Listener stood on the far lip of the bowl, a tall shape against snow, as real as anything can be when you've spent days wanting it not to be a dream. He had the road's coat and the staff from the pass, and the patience of someone who had learned to arrive early so the world could catch up.

She did not cross to him. He did not beckon. That felt like a lesson too.

"Show me what you mean by bones," she said aloud,

because the birches deserved to hear words shaped properly.

He lifted his staff, set it on the rim, and the sound it made was small but specific—a click that found her ankles and climbed to the small of her back. He spoke then, the voice she knew now bent by air and distance, and it still reached a place in her that had no furniture but a chair and the right light.

"People listen with ears because ears have drama," he said softly. "They prefer the obvious. But bone hears pressure and direction; skin hears temperature and intention. To listen with bone, you must let your fear sit down and stop correcting you."

"That sounds like telling the sea to mind its temper," she said.

"It is," he said, and smiled—the kind that does not split the face so much as admit warmth to the corners of it. "We begin with pressure. Set your staff in the ground and tell me where the seam lies without looking."

She did. The staff stood like a name written too clearly to be mistaken. She closed her eyes and sank attention into her shins like a person wading, slow, in a black stream. Pressure gathered—left, then forward—then eased, then gathered again somewhere farther. The seam was not a line; it was a possibility stretched thin, a choice the ground could still unmake.

"There," she said, and pointed to a place a hand's breadth right of the mark she'd chosen yesterday.

"Open your eyes," he said.

The dark line in the snow was exactly where she'd pointed. It hadn't been there a breath ago. Or perhaps it had been and the eye had refused to assist until bone had done the courtesy.

"Again," he said. "But now with wind. It comes," he added, tilting his head. "With purpose."

She listened. The breeze at first seemed ordinary, the kind that carries the day's gossip to the wrong ears. Then she felt —not sound, but texture—like a hand moving through fur the wrong way. The wind was sliding down-valley with the weight of the fjord behind it, then pooling, then lifting as if testing the bowl for purchase.

"It wants to pull the steam away," she murmured. "It won't. The steam won't let it. The warmth keeps its own counsel."

"Good. Now tell me: if you were a careless boy with a torch looking for a story to set on fire, where would you stand to make the wind your accomplice?"

She traced the movement, mapped it against the bowl's lip and the grove's protection, and pointed to a notch where birch trunks leaned aside as if by habit.

"There," she said.

"Then tell old Kjaer to set her broom there tomorrow," he said. "And tell Halvar you have a reason you will not waste on words."

"I can't keep him out forever," she said quietly.

"Nor should you," the Listener answered. "But there is a difference between a shield and a wall. You are learning the former. He will try to build the latter out of love."

She stood with that a long moment, because standing is what you do with truths that aren't going to move for you. Wind skimmed the bowl; steam refused to be taught its manners; the seam held, like a mouth that knows when to keep shut and save the line for later.

"You said it would cost me," she said at last.

"It already does," he said. "You saved a boy today. Now every mother will look at you with gratitude edged by worry. Some will call you lucky. One will call you touched. Soon someone will say cursed because winter always needs a word to fear."

Astrid's jaw tightened. "I didn't do anything but listen."

"That will not matter to ears that prefer thunder," he said. "Your task is to go on listening anyway."

He turned a fraction, head cocked—not to her, but to the bowl—as if the ground had put up a hand. Astrid felt it too: a slow turn underfoot, the seam settling deeper. Not opening. Not yet. But remembering a path to the word.

"When?" she asked, though she didn't mean the seam.

"When you can hear your father's fear without borrowing it," he said. "When you can hear your own name from the ground without trying to be worthy of it. When the world stops whispering and starts asking." He nodded toward the village. "And when hunger and cold and rope and net and neighbor are not made smaller by your listening, but bigger. I will not teach you to escape your life. Only to belong to more of it."

He lifted his staff. The sound it made when he moved was the smallest of agreements.

"Tomorrow," he said, "we learn to listen to lies. Not other people's. Your own."

"Wonderful," she said dryly.

"It is," he said, and the smile reached his eyes this time.

He stepped back, and the birches accepted his absence the way they had accepted his presence—without fuss.

Astrid stood until the cold reminded her that bodies are not suggestions. She went home with the staff tapping a measure that had nothing to do with music and everything to do with keeping time with a world that had begun, at last, to speak to her in a language she could learn without burning.

At the door, Halvar met her with a basin and a towel and no questions. He waited while she washed her hands as if she'd come from a birth or a burial and he did not yet know which it had been. When she finished, he set the towel aside and said only, "Eat." It was a prayer disguised as a command.

They ate. He salted the fire for the drowned and for those the sea remembers. She touched hammer and cross and added a third thing in her mind—a small, round shape that had not yet asked to be named.

In the rafters, the wind rehearsed. Under the floor, the old pulse kept time. Somewhere in the winter-dark, the Listener sat down and listened to the same world, and the knowledge that someone else held the other end of the thread was—if not comfort—something very much like it.

And deep beyond the birches, where stone keeps its own counsel and steam writes its thin letters into cold air, the seam cooled and waited, as lids do, for the proper hand.

Chapter 5

The Song Beneath the Ice

The thaw came early, or else the world had lost patience.

By morning the air above Havngard shimmered faintly, not with heat but with the memory of it. The sea fog that had always stayed politely offshore crept closer, curling around the headland like a listener leaning in. Astrid woke to it pressing against the shutters, damp and persistent.

Halvar was already gone. She found his note carved into a birch shaving on the table:
North nets. Mending line. Back by dusk.
Beneath, a small cross — his way of saying *don't follow.*

She smiled and packed food anyway.

Outside, the fog muffled the world until even her own boots sounded far away. Somewhere a gull laughed in a tone that belonged to cliffs, not shore. Astrid stopped at the edge of the yard and listened the way the Listener had taught: with skin first, bone second, ears last. Beneath the sea's pulse came another rhythm, slower, not quite regular. A tremor, or a breath.

You feel it, the Listener said, sudden as thought.

The ground moves.

It remembers moving.
His tone held no fear — only recognition. *Something old turns in its sleep.*

Astrid knelt, pressing her palm to the frozen mud. The vibration was so slight she could have mistaken it for the echo of her own pulse, except the beat came from *below* the beat. The fjord's buried heart.

Will it wake? she asked.

All hearts do, in time. The question is how loudly.

A dog barked then — one of Nils's — a sharp, startled sound that broke into a whine. The hum vanished like a fish darting to deep water. Astrid stood and brushed her palms clean, though nothing clung to them.

The Seer's Return

By mid-day, Havngard's usual chatter had taken on an edge. Nets tangled twice as often, children argued about nothing. And then the old traveler appeared again — the one from the ridge, the one Halvar had hurried away from weeks ago. He came on foot through fog that clung to him like loyalty, staff ringing small truths against the stones.

People paused their work without admitting they had. He nodded to each in turn, a courteous ghost.

"A mild day for such noise beneath the ground," he said to no one in particular.

Kjaer spat over her shoulder. "Old bones hear what they expect."

"Perhaps." He smiled faintly. "Or perhaps old bones are the first to notice when the world starts tuning its strings again."

Astrid met his eyes. The world tilted almost imperceptibly — a recognition without introduction. He inclined his head as if greeting an equal. She felt the Listener's presence flicker, then withdraw, leaving a quiet that rang.

Halvar returned as the traveler was leaving. Their gazes struck like flint.

"I told you to keep south," Halvar said.

"And yet north kept calling," the traveler replied, gentle as weather.

Halvar's hand tightened on the net rope. "You bring talk that stirs children."

"I bring warning."
His staff touched the earth once. *thrum*
Even those too far to hear felt it in their ankles. "The pulse grows. The buried fire breathes."

Halvar's jaw set. "Then we smother it."

"Try," the traveler said softly, and went on toward the cliffs.

The Pattern

That night the wind reversed. It came from inland, from stone instead of sea. Roofs sighed. The goats stamped uneasily in their pen. Astrid sat by the hearth pretending to mend a glove and listening to the wrongness of it.

Halvar sharpened his knife slow and deliberate. "You'll keep inside tomorrow," he said.

"Because the wind changed?"

"Because men like that seer bring storms they don't have to row through afterward."

Astrid looked into the fire. The coals shifted, small echoes of the same slow rhythm she had felt under the ground. *thrum — pause — thrum — pause.* She matched it with her breath until the space between beats widened into meaning. The pattern was not random. It was *counting.*

One for waking.
Two for waiting.
Three for… listening?

She wasn't sure, but the knowledge arrived whole, as if it

had been waiting for her to quiet enough to receive it.

At the Fjord's Edge

Before dawn she was walking again, the staff steady in her hand. Frost cracked under her boots; mist drifted in threads that clung to her calves. When she reached the birches, she stopped. The seam still slept, but the air above it quivered. She knelt, palm flat.

The beat was stronger now—three notes, a rest, three again. The same pattern she had counted by the fire. Her heart tried to match it and failed.

You hear the measure, the Listener said.

It's calling something.

No. It is remembering what calling feels like.
He hesitated. *Do you see how the world listens back when you listen first? That is your craft, Astrid. Not to command—only to remind.*

"I can remind it to stay asleep?" she murmured aloud.

Perhaps. Or perhaps you can remind men not to break what they don't understand.

A shout carried faint through fog—Halvar's voice, closer than she expected. "Astrid!"

She rose, brushing snow from her knees, pulse steadying with reluctance. "Here."

He came through the birches, breath white. "You shouldn't be alone."

"I'm not," she said, before she could stop herself. Then, softer, "I mean, I'm listening."

He followed her gaze toward the bowl, to the faint mist curling upward in slow spirals. "You hear it still."

"Yes."

He was silent for a long moment. "Your mother said the same before the glacier broke. Said the mountain was restless. We laughed. Two nights later the pass took half our herd." His voice roughened. "I will not laugh again."

Astrid touched his arm. "Then help me listen."

The request surprised them both. Halvar looked at her, the refusal forming and faltering. Then, grudgingly, he set his palm beside hers on the frozen ground.

Nothing happened for a breath, then another.

Then they both felt it — the third beat, faint but deliberate. The buried heart acknowledging two listeners instead of one.

Halvar drew back sharply. "It knows we're here."

"It's *alive*," she said.

"It's *old*," he answered, voice low. "And old things wake hungry."

He stood and turned toward the path. "We'll tell no one yet. Panic is worse than truth."

Astrid followed, eyes lingering on the bowl until the fog closed over it like a secret folded back into its envelope.

That night, the fjord sang. Not loudly—just enough that those who slept lightly dreamt of thunder without storms, of warmth under their feet. Astrid lay awake and traced the rhythm in her ribs, three and rest, three and rest, until she realized she was no longer sure whether she was hearing or remembering.

The Listener spoke once before sleep found her.

The buried fire is not evil, Astrid. It is a promise forgotten. When men built walls of fear, they sealed it away with their own breath.

Can it stay sealed? she asked.

For a while. But nothing that once taught the sky to listen stays silent forever.

Chapter 6

Echoes in the Frost

The frost that morning had a sound.

Not the crisp crackle of boots through ice, but something deeper — a faint hum beneath the cold, as though the world itself were shivering awake. Astrid noticed it first when she opened the shutters. The air seemed to hold its breath; the silence was too perfect to be silence at all. It rang, thin and hollow, like a single note drawn out so long that it began to tremble under its own weight.

The fjord below was still. No gulls cried, no boats creaked at their moorings. Even the smoke from the hearths rose straight upward, frozen mid-gesture in the cold.

Astrid leaned on the windowsill, listening. The hum was faint but constant, vibrating through her fingers where they touched the wood. It was not imagination. It was alive.

"Too quiet," she murmured.

The words fell flat against the air. No echo came back.

Morning Unease

The path down to the village was lined with frost-furred birches. Every branch glittered, but the shine was wrong— blue-white instead of silver, as if the ice held light from some other world. Her breath plumed ahead of her, joining the mist that clung to the ground in thin, restless bands.

Halfway down the hill she met Sigrid, who was leading her goats back toward their pen. The animals bleated low and uneasy, tugging against the rope.

"They've been like this since dawn," Sigrid said. "Won't

eat. Won't go near the lower field."

"Why not?"

Sigrid gestured toward the fjord. "You don't hear it?"

Astrid hesitated. "Hear what?"

"That sound," the woman said. "Like someone singing under the ice."

Astrid's heart skipped. She wanted to deny it, to tell Sigrid that the air was playing tricks, but she could hear it too — faint, wordless, a vibration more than a voice. It wasn't the same tone she'd felt before. It was stronger now, and sadder somehow, like a song caught between waking and remembering.

Sigrid crossed herself. "It's not natural. My grandmother said the sea can call people when it's lonely."

Astrid forced a smile. "Then best not to answer."

But she was already listening harder.

You hear it because you're meant to, came the Listener's voice, soft and close.

What does it want?

Not what. Who.

The Frozen Well

The sun never rose properly that day. It only climbed far enough to pale the sky, then hovered there like a tired coin. The air tasted sharp, heavy with the smell of iron and brine.

By midday, word spread through the village: Joren's well had frozen from the bottom up.

When Astrid arrived, half the townsfolk were already there, clustered around the rim of the old stone well. Joren, red-faced and sweating despite the cold, was shouting into the darkness.

"It's cursed!" he cried. "The water turned to glass overnight. It's glowing!"

Astrid leaned over the edge. The light was faint but real — a ghostly blue radiance far below, flickering like breath against the ice. It reminded her of the wells she'd dreamed of as a child, the ones that looked back when you stared into them too long.

Halvar was already there, his expression grim. "Bring the iron," he said. "We'll break through."

Two men came with bars and hammers. The first strike rang like a bell, clear and bright. The second cracked the air so sharply that even the children clapped their hands over their ears.

The ice didn't break.

Instead, a low vibration shuddered through the ground, rolling outward in invisible ripples. Astrid stumbled back, heart pounding. The humming in the air deepened, settling into her bones like a heartbeat not her own.

"What was that?" someone whispered.

Halvar's jaw tightened. "The earth settling."

"No," Astrid said before she could stop herself. "That was *breathing*."

All eyes turned toward her. The silence that followed was heavy, suspicious.

Halvar's hand closed gently around her arm. "Enough," he murmured, low enough that only she heard. "People are frightened. Don't feed it."

She bit her lip and nodded, but the truth pulsed in her chest like fire: whatever slept below them was *not still.*

Stories in the Smoke

That evening, the villagers gathered in the longhouse. Firelight painted the walls in shifting gold and shadow. The talk was nervous — tales of strange lights under the ice, of frost that crept upward instead of down. Old stories resurfaced like ghosts.

"They say when the last dragon fell," muttered one fisherman, "its heart burned so hot that the ground had to swallow it. Maybe it's waking."

Another spat into the fire. "Superstitions. The gods turned their faces from such beasts long ago."

"Maybe they shouldn't have," said an old woman by the door. "The dragons kept balance. When they slept, the land slept with them. Now the land turns in its sleep and wonders where they've gone."

A shiver passed through the crowd.

Astrid sat quietly near the back, her hands clasped around a cup of broth gone cold. Every story sounded too close to truth. The hum was still there, faint but insistent, threading beneath the crackle of the fire.

She caught Halvar watching her, worry hidden behind his stern calm. He hadn't said a word since the well. His eyes told her enough: *you know something, and I wish you didn't.*

The Stranger Returns

At dawn, the fog rolled in from the sea like a curtain being drawn. When it cleared, the traveler was standing at the edge of the village.

He was older than she remembered — or maybe the light

made him look that way. Frost clung to his beard, and his cloak gleamed with a faint film of ice. In his hand he carried the same staff, carved with runes that seemed to shift when you looked at them too long.

"The fire beneath the world stirs," he said to the first person who met his eyes. "The time of silence ends."

Halvar came striding from the smithy, his voice sharp. "You again."

"Still," the man corrected. "And still the same warning."

Halvar's knuckles whitened around the haft of his hammer. "You bring fear where we already have enough."

"I bring truth." The traveler's gaze turned to Astrid. "You hear it, don't you? The song beneath the frost."

Astrid hesitated. "It's not a song. It's—"

"A memory," he finished for her. "The world remembering what warmth felt like."

The villagers murmured uneasily. Someone muttered about omens. Another spat.

Halvar stepped forward. "You speak riddles, old man."

"Then let me speak plain." The traveler pointed his staff toward the mountains. "Beneath that ice lies the buried heart of the first fire. Men called them dragons, but they were older than that name — the pulse that kept the balance between warmth and cold, life and silence. When they slept, they left one ear open to the world — one who would hear them if silence grew too deep."

He turned back to Astrid. "And she hears."

The crowd shifted, eyes flicking between them. Fear smelled like smoke in the air.

Halvar's voice hardened. "Leave."

The traveler inclined his head. "I will. But remember this: the ground hums louder each day. When it breaks, you'll wish you had listened."

He turned and walked into the fog. The sound of his staff striking the frozen ground lingered long after he was gone.

Night of the Frost Song

That night, Astrid woke to a sound that wasn't quite wind.

It was music — thin, crystalline, rising and falling in the rhythm of breathing. She threw on her cloak and stepped outside.

The village was drowned in moonlight. Every rooftop shimmered, every fencepost glittered. Frost had grown into patterns along the walls — spirals, circles, lines that looked almost like runes. When she brushed one with her fingertips, it sang. Not loudly, but enough that her heart answered.

She looked toward the fjord. Mist rose in silver veils, and far out on the ice, faint lights flickered — blue, then gold, then gone. The hum in her bones grew stronger, matching her pulse beat for beat.

It's close now, the Listener whispered. *The silence is breaking.*

"Is that good or bad?"

It depends who wakes first — the world or those who would burn it again.

Astrid turned her face to the wind. It smelled of salt and something older — ash buried deep. She felt small, and yet, in a strange way, chosen.

"Why me?" she asked softly. "Why can I hear it when no one else can?"

The Listener's voice gentled, almost mournful. *Because you were born with the world still inside your ears. You hear not just sound, but intent. And the earth remembers kindness — it listens back.*

The Echo Beneath

She walked to the edge of the frozen shore. The mist parted as she approached, revealing the ice like a mirror stretching to the horizon. Beneath it, shadows moved — slow, massive, ancient. Not shapes exactly, but the *idea* of shapes, like something dreaming just under the surface.

Astrid knelt, pressing her palm flat against the ice.

Warmth pulsed through it — faint but steady.

The hum rose, no longer one note but many, a harmony just beyond understanding. It spoke without words, and though she couldn't translate it, she felt its meaning all the same.

It was calling for balance.
It was calling for light.

And buried within that harmony, she heard something else: a heartbeat that wasn't the world's or her own. Familiar. Human.

Father.

Halvar's voice came from behind her. "Astrid!"

She turned, startled. He was running toward her across the frost, face pale, eyes wide.

"What are you doing?" he demanded. "You shouldn't be here!"

"I was listening—"

"I told you to stay away from this place!" His voice cracked with fear. "You don't understand what's waking!"

He reached for her arm, but the ice beneath them groaned

— a low, resonant note that silenced them both. A thin crack shot outward, spidering toward the fjord's center.

Astrid's breath caught. "It's answering."

Halvar stared down, trembling. "Then pray it doesn't finish the song."

The Final Note

They made it back to the village without speaking. Behind them, the mist closed in, hiding the ice, but not the sound. The hum followed them all the way to their door, faint but relentless.

Inside, Halvar slumped into a chair, rubbing his temples. "I should never have brought you back here."

Astrid hesitated by the hearth. "You mean after mother died?"

He didn't answer.

"You knew this might happen," she said quietly. "Didn't you?"

Halvar looked up, eyes hollow. "Your mother heard it too. Just before the glacier broke."

A silence fell between them, heavy and full of things unsaid. Outside, the frost sang again, its thin melody winding through the night.

Astrid stared into the fire, her hands clasped tight.

The world is waking, the Listener murmured. *And you are the first to hear its name.*

Chapter 7

The Sound That Sleeps

Morning came thin and blue, as if the sky had been washed too often and the color had leached away. Frost webbed the eaves and stitched the fence rails with fine white thread. When Astrid pushed open the door, the air struck her cheeks clean and sharp. Somewhere a raven talked to itself on a roof beam. Somewhere a net creaked as if remembering wind. Between those small sounds there lay a space that was not quiet so much as *held*—a pause in which the world waited to see what it would be next.

She stood with her palm on the lintel and listened the way she had learned to listen: not with her ears first, but with her bones. The fjord below the village answered with a steadier rhythm than yesterday—three slow pulses and a longer rest, then three again— the measure of something testing its strength after a long stillness. It wasn't menacing. It wasn't kind. It simply *was*, like tide.

You are early to the day, the Listener said, his voice light as breath on cold skin.

I didn't sleep much, she answered, not moving her mouth. *Everything hums.*

It is not humming, he said gently. *It is tuning.*

She let out a breath she hadn't known she was holding. "And to what?" she murmured, so softly the frost on the step did not dare crack.

To itself. To what it remembers. To what you will ask of it.

"That last part is the most frightening," she said, and stepped out into the thin blue morning.

Nets and Rumor

They began the day with broken line and quiet tempers. Halvar had taken the nets down early to patch the long winter's work out of them. Astrid knelt to her task beside him, binding frayed cords with new hemp, the small muscles in her hands finding their old rhythm. The smell of tar and salt rode from the sheds, familiar as her father's voice. It should have been a comforting morning, all repetition and work. It should have been ordinary. The not-ordinary lived under everything, like warmth under ash.

"Pass the shuttle," Halvar said. His tone was flat, not unfriendly; the voice of a man saving his words for when they would buy him something.

She handed it over and tested a knot till it bit her thumb. "Sigrid's goats were restless again," she offered. "Kjaer says the frost sings because the gods are sharpening knives."

"Old women say sharp things," Halvar said. He cut a fray with his knife and smoothed the splice with the pad of his thumb. "Knives or no, we fish when the thaw lets us. The sea has its own mind. It never asked ours."

Across the yard, Nils the netmaker and two lads argued soft but pointed. Astrid didn't look toward them; she simply let her attention slip sideways until the sound of their talk thinned and the intention underneath it showed. The words were of rope and knots; the thought under the words was of fear. *If the well has light, what else has light?* one mind asked itself. *What if the ice breaks wrong? What if it breaks when my boy is out there?* thought another.

She pulled her attention back like a hand from a flame. She wasn't stealing anything; it felt like standing near a door and hearing a phrase, a cadence. And yet the knowledge of it made her skin feel thin. To hear was to carry. The more she heard, the more she carried.

Halvar's knife paused. "Stay out of the low fields today," he said without looking up. "You'll find work enough on the ridge."

"I wasn't—" she began, and stopped, because she had been. "All right."

"Good," he said, in the tone of a man who knows bargains never stay kept for long.

A child ran by with a stick for a sword. He whooped once, then looked embarrassed by the sound and turned it into a cough. Across the lane, Kjaer clattered a pot lid with unnecessary firmness until someone offered to help. The village went about being a village—because what else should it do?—and all the while the fjord below gave its steady measure, the sound of a giant heart deepening its beat.

A gray shape shouldered the fog at the lane's end. The traveler emerged from the cold as if he had been standing in it a long while and the day had finally remembered to draw him. Rime furred his hood. Frost had drawn transparent leaves along the length of his staff.

Halvar's hand tightened on the net. The old man didn't turn toward them at first. He paused by Nils, said something that made the netmaker's mouth twist, then came on through the thin light until he stood at the yard's edge.

"I have no time for teaching today," Halvar said before the traveler could open his mouth. "And no appetite for prophecy."

The man's pale eyes warmed. "Prophecy is for those who cannot hear. I bring report."

"You've brought enough of those as well."

The traveler inclined his head—as if conceding a fair hit—and let his gaze settle on Astrid without pressing. "The tones under the fjord doubled in the night," he said. "The pattern is not only stronger; it is *clearer*."

Astrid found that she did not resent his announcement. It matched her bones. "Three beats, a rest, three beats," she said. "Each beat deeper than yesterday."

The traveler's mouth tilted; it wasn't quite a smile. "And between the beats?"

Astrid hesitated. She had not known there was a *between*. She closed her eyes a moment and laid down her mind as if it were a tool she meant to sharpen. Beneath the three beats, beneath the space, something cool as meltwater ran. Not a fourth beat. A current. A path.

"There's a…way," she said, groping for words. "Not a word. Something that leads."

"A channel," the traveler said softly. "The first of the old roads opening."

Halvar's patience frayed. "You speak like a priest in a bad mood. If you know something, say it clear."

The traveler met Halvar's stare squarely. "Clear then: when the ice remembers how to move, it will not move along the lines men have cut into it. It will move along its own old lines. If your boats sit wrong when that happens, the ice will teach them its lesson."

Halvar stood, tall in a way he forgot to be until something asked it of him. "We've ridden winter longer than your staff has wood left in it," he said. "We'll make our own judgments." His voice made the air irritably solid.

"And I will not wrestle them from you," the traveler said with a dip of the head. He set the staff and the frost-leaves chimed. "Only—listen. The ground is not against you. It is simply done pretending to be something else."

He turned and went away as if the fog were his door and he had business on the other side of it. When Astrid glanced at her father, the muscle in his jaw stood out a fraction, as if it too had something it wished to say and had been told to wait its turn.

"We'll pull the traps above the rock shelf," he said briskly. "The lower ones can rot if they want. Tie that splice tighter—you've left it with a lie in it."

She tightened it without argument. The knot corrected itself obediently under her fingers.

The Stalled Sky

By midday the color had changed in the light. It wasn't a thing you could point at. If a stranger had come and asked what hue the sky was, Astrid would have said *pale*, as she had said yesterday and the day before. But between moments the day picked up a shade of tin, as if the world's brightness had been packed away and the earth was using what was left by careful handfuls.

She took the higher path to the ridge to gather brush, as she had promised, and kept her steps on frozen ground. At the birch line she paused and touched the nearest trunk with her knuckles. The tree's sap slept hard, but the wood gave back the faintest shiver. Not wind. Not weight. A communication, the way good wood speaks to a carver when the knife is honest.

Half down the ridge, she stopped again and looked toward the fjord. The surface lay like hammered metal, dull where the light failed it, burnished where a thin sun scraped its edge. Nothing moved. Not a seal's head, not a gull's drift. The stillness felt less like peace and more like a soldier standing parade-rest—motionless, but full of readiness.

Careful, said the Listener, not warning so much as reminder. *Listening is what opens doors.*

And you want me to open this one?

I want you to know which one you are opening.

She would have asked him which that was, but at that moment the ground made a sound like a low note on a deep drum, or the first plank of a bridge finding the weight put on it after a long season. Once. Twice. The hairs on her forearms lifted under her sleeves. A ripple passed through the thin brush, not wind-rustle but a soft jolt, the way grass trembles when a horse far off puts its hoof down. She set her feet wider without thinking. As though something under the ridge had changed its position, testing where the world allowed it to belong.

The sound eased. The hum remained. The birches stood and pretended nothing had happened.

She let her breath out slow, then gathered the brush she had come for and carried the armload home, because the body's work is a counterspell to panic.

Halvar's Ledger

They ate in a silence that heard itself. Halvar chewed like a man who had bitten more than hunger. When he had finished, he reached beneath the bench and brought out a narrow wooden box Astrid rarely saw him open. He set it on the table and worked the small brass hasp loose with the careful hands of a man who has learned that what is most valuable is also most easily broken.

Inside lay a ledger so old the leather had taken on the color of smoke. The pages had the soft stiffness of hide. He turned to the middle where a strip of blue cloth kept a place. The writing there was her mother's—a steady, tidal hand, as confident on the first line as on the last.

Astrid felt the ache of it before she recognized the letters. Halvar's thumb pressed the edge of the page as if to keep the words from dissolving.

"Your mother kept weather like a priest keeps names," he said, not looking at her. "She wrote down every shift. She thought the world could be convinced to repeat itself if only we paid it enough attention."

"Was she wrong?" Astrid asked.

Halvar smiled without humor. "Repeat is not the same as obey. She wrote here—" He found a passage by memory and tapped it. "—'The day the pass fell, the frost sang three tones before dawn. The sound was low as buried bells. The goats would not drink.' She thought that mattered."

"It *does* matter," Astrid said, and the words surprised her with how quickly they came. "It matters because the world told her. It matters because she listened."

Halvar's gaze flicked up and softened despite itself. He lifted his hand from the page. "She wrote the same the winter before you were born. Not about the pass; about the lake breaking its skin. Three tones. Then quiet. Then the ice… moved."

"As if it remembered how," Astrid said.

He shut the ledger, gently, the way you fold a child's blanket in a room where the child no longer is. "As if something under it changed its weight."

They looked at each other across the table as if across a narrow river. It wasn't an argument. It wasn't peace. It was a recognition: they had both been taught by the same woman to hear the world, and they had learned opposite lessons from the teaching.

"Keep away from the fjord tonight," he said at last. "If it breaks, it will not ask you where your feet are."

"And if it calls?" Astrid asked. She kept her voice level. "If it asks me where *its* feet should be?"

"Then you come and ask me," Halvar said. "Because I will always tell you to live first."

She nodded. It was not consent so much as gratitude.

When he went to split wood in the yard, she opened the ledger again and read her mother's old, clean words. Between lines of salt weights and net tallies lay small notices: *Ravens nested low this year. Fog came inland and stayed. A cousin dreamt of thunder under ice. A girl born and did not cry until she heard the wind.* The last one had a fingerprint beside it where the ink had blurred. Her mother's print. Astrid put her own fingertip there and felt the ghost of oil. For a foolish heartbeat she imagined the oils would match.

The Tremor and the Door

Night built itself one careful board at a time. The sky hung iron-gray and then lost even that. Lamps came on early across Havngard, each small circle of yellow like a vow to endure. Astrid moved through the longhouse setting small things right—straightening a bench, setting a drying rack level, checking the salt on the sill—rituals that told the dark that people lived here. Halvar hummed as he carved a float, low and tuneless, the way men hum when they want to pretend no one else can hear them thinking.

The tremor came on soft feet.

It began as a long exhale under the hearth and became a tone that the ear could not catch but the body could not ignore. The rafters answered with a whisper, boards giving back a tuned sigh. Astrid's spoon rattled in a bowl and then stood still as if ashamed of itself. Halvar's knife paused half a heartbeat and resumed as if he could make the world believe it had imagined him.

Astrid moved to the door and put the back of her hand

against it. The wood was warm from the inside fire, cool from the night, and thrummed like a string touched lightly.

"Astrid," Halvar said, sharpened by worry. He didn't raise his voice, but the tone made doors act like walls. "Leave it."

"I just want to"—she almost said *listen*, then swallowed the word—"look."

He set the float down with care. "If you go out now, you won't choose how far your feet carry you."

She could have argued that her feet had always been hers. In another life, perhaps she would have. She looked at his hands instead—scarred, capable, the nails clean because he was clean even in the work that made men easiest to despise. "I won't stray," she said. "By the shed and back. I swear it."

He weighed something invisible in his palm, then nodded once. "By the shed and back, then."

Outside, the night was bright with frost and low cloud, the kind of brightness that isn't light. She walked to the shed and stopped, as promised, and let the world arrive. Sound carries farther over cold ground. The fjord's voice came to her under the air's hush—not speech, not song, but the conversation water has with the edge that holds it. Except the tone had changed again. The three beats were there, but in the space after them a new note lifted: an answering hum, faint as breath through hollow bone.

As though something beneath had shifted its weight and found its edge.

She closed her eyes and put two fingers to the pulse at her throat. *I am here*, she thought without words. The hum steadied. *I hear you.* A warmth rolled through her boot soles up into her calves, the way hot water sends news up a pipe. She did not mistake it for comfort.

It was notice: *you have been recognized.*

Do not step farther, the Listener said, and his voice no longer came from somewhere in the air. It stood beside her, within arm's reach, though when she turned her head the yard was empty. *Sometimes listening is stepping. Sometimes it is the thing that keeps you from the step.*

She let her breath out and opened her palms. "Then speak," she whispered. "If I cannot walk, let the words move."

For a moment there was only the frost-breath of the shed and the soft tick of wood shrinking back from its knots. Then the Listener said, in a tone she had not heard from him, almost formal, as if he were quoting a text learned long ago and not dared aloud since:

When the sea forgets its voice and the mountain hums with a buried chord; when winter eats its own footprints and the nets come up with light; when a child of the storm hears the deep lay a path—then follow the sound that sleeps.

She tasted the lines more than heard them. They had the old cadence—the kind that makes men argue and women set bread on the sill and call it piety. She did not want to ask the next question. She asked it anyway. "And where does it go?"

Down, he said simply. *And forward. The old roads are only ever those two ways.*

"Is there a third?"

A long time ago there was. It was called together. Men forgot the word. The earth did not.

A laugh tried to be born and failed. "You speak like a priest too."

I was one once, he said, not rueful, not proud. *Before I learned to keep my voice low enough to hear the ground answer.*

She wanted to turn and make the empty yard give him back to her with skin and breath. She didn't. To demand proof was another kind of not-listening.

"What do I do tomorrow?" she asked instead.

Be where you can see the fjord before the sun decides what to do with itself.

"That's a riddle."

It's a courtesy. If you asked the sea when it would change, it would say: when I am ready. It is nearly ready. Do not be where the ice will teach you.

"And where is that?"

He was quiet long enough for her to hear three complete measures from the fjord. *Any place that has forgotten the old lines.*

She nodded, though the dark did not need her to.

"Back," Halvar called softly from inside, the shape of his voice gentled by the door. "You promised."

"I did," she answered, and went.

When she lay down under her blanket, the world's rhythm threaded itself through her sleep like a low river under the mind's bridge. She dreamt of no wings. She dreamt of a path drawn in faint blue, winding like a vein beneath ice.

Spiral

Fog from the sea met fog from the land at dawn and the two recognized each other like family. The village wore their union as a shawl. Astrid woke to a sky with no edge and a window furred with sugar. Halvar was already pulling on his boots.

"The shore," he said. It was not a command. It was the name of the place where truth would sit down today and look them in the face.

They took the high path where the slope is honest about how steep it is and reached the headland where the cliff looks down on the fjord like a careful father. The ice below lay unblemished at first glance: a great clean sheet hammered flat by weather and blessed by cold. Astrid narrowed her eyes until the light lost its glare and the surface showed its thoughts. A hairline crack ran from a cove half a mile south like a scratch made by something that had tested its claw and then reconsidered.

"Do you see it?" Halvar murmured.

"Yes."

They watched.

The first sound was so soft even Astrid only felt it in her teeth. The second was a little louder, a low *thukk* that might have been a distant oar finding a rowlock. Then the line moved. It did not rush. It did not snake like a frightened thing. It widened with the patience of a seamstress setting a hem. A second line bled from it at an angle and curved toward the center of the fjord. Another answered from the north side, found the curve, and took its hand.

"Not straight," Halvar said under his breath. "Never seen that."

The lines did not craze the whole surface as winter breaks sometimes do, wild and wasteful. They turned each other, found each other, made a pattern the eye wanted to call a flower and the mind wanted to call an intention. Round the center of the fjord they curled and grew, not tight to begin but closer with each pass, until Astrid realized she was looking at a spiral. Not perfect, because nothing wise is. A spiral nonetheless. A path inward.

As though something beneath had shifted its weight and the ice was learning its shape.

Down on the flats, two boys had come to show each other how brave they were and now stood staring, mouths open, sticks in their hands dangling. Halvar cupped his hands and shouted a word that had sent men off boats and children out of gull-nests since before Astrid was born. *"Back!"* The boys ran with that joyful terror only children and hunted deer have.

The spiral widened by a hair's breadth more and stopped, not by exhaustion but by decision. The fjord held itself still as a held breath. Air flowed over it and seemed to hesitate.

Astrid did not feel triumph, or fear. She felt recognition, as if a door she had gone through blind many times had been opened for her in full light at last and she could see the hinges.

"It isn't breaking for us," she said. "It's making room for itself."

Halvar scrubbed his face with one gloved hand. "Room for *what?*"

She almost said a word she hadn't been taught—*heart*—and bit it back. "For whatever knows that pattern."

He looked sideways at her, calculation and worry and love all sitting down at the same small table behind his eyes. "We pull every trap above that line," he said. "We tell Nils to do the same. We mark it with poles. And if anyone puts a foot on that ice today, I'll—"

"You won't need to," she said, because the villagers were already doing what good villagers do: telling each other what to fear and then obeying themselves. Men on the beach had gathered, pointing with their chins, the way men point when they don't want to give a thing the courtesy of their finger. Kjaer stood with her stick planted, lips white with the pressure of not saying I told you. Sigrid held a child so tight the child squirmed and then leaned into it because sometimes fear feels like safety from the inside.

You kept your feet to the high place, the Listener said, approval without ownership. *Good.*

It would have been foolish to do otherwise.

Brave and foolish look alike from a distance.

She made a small sound that might have been a laugh if the day had been less ready to teach humility. "What now?"

Now, he said, *you listen to silence.*

She thought he was teasing her. He was not.

In the space after the spiral had stopped and before the day remembered to be a day again, a quiet lay over the fjord so pure that sound would have embarrassed itself trying to exist there. Astrid felt it settle on her shoulders like a cloak that had been made for her. Under that quiet, beneath even the three-count rhythm, something else stirred—not motion, exactly. Presence. The particularity a room has when the person it belongs to steps into it.

As though something beneath had opened an unseen eye.

A pressure kissed her ears and was gone. She put two fingers to the pulse at her neck and found it sure.

Halvar let his breath out in a long line. "Come," he said. "We do the work men can do. The rest will do itself."

She wanted to stay and watch the pattern until it moved again. She went with him because you do not nourish the strange by starving the ordinary.

Work and Watch

They spent the daylight telling people where not to stand. This is more complicated than it sounds. Men hear *do not* and make a list of exceptions in their minds; children hear it and conceive of a hundred ways to turn the rule into a game. Astrid found herself speaking in short, clear phrases and discovered that people obey better when you give them reasons shaped like things they can see. "Not there," she would say, and touch a pole of driftwood to the ice, listening for the low note the spiral had taught her; "here instead," and the wood would give back a different sound, safer. She became, without asking, the person you checked with if the next step felt like an argument.

By midafternoon the village had a strange look—alert and cautious, like a house where a sleeping child lies in the center room and everyone speaks in lets and careful hands. Nets lay in neat coils. Sleds were pulled back above the drift line. Even the sea seemed to hold itself with deliberate care, its small chop never quite daring the new edges. In the smithy, the man who rode the bellows slowed his rhythm and matched it to something that did not come from his foot. He would have denied it if accused.

Astrid drank thick broth standing, her bowl almost too warm for her gloves. She ate without tasting and listened without looking like she was listening. When the Listener spoke again, he did so as if addressing the space just over her left shoulder.

You felt the path.

I felt a…shape, she said. *Not a way wide enough for men. More like the thought of a way.*

That is where roads begin, he said. *In thought. Before men lay stone across a river they choose the line it will be glad to carry.*

And what river is this?

An old one. It has other names in other tongues. Here, men used to call it the fire-vein. The elders in this fjord forgot the word. Their elders did not.

She tipped the last mouthful of broth into her mouth and swallowed with difficulty. *If I follow it—*

You cannot yet, he said, as gentle as you can be when you contradict someone you respect. *The ice will allow passage when passage is the right word for what is needed. Not today. Perhaps not for many days. This is not a riddle. It is a mercy.*

You speak as if the thing below could hurt us.

Everything worth waking can.

She lowered the bowl and watched cloud shadow make a slow movement across the white. "Are you afraid?" she asked aloud before she could decide to keep the question inside.

The answer came at once and surprised her with its honesty. *Yes. But not of what you think. I am afraid we will forget to be one thing while we try to be another.*

"You sound like my father."

Then your father is wise when he is tired of being brave.

She smiled into the cold where he could not see it and felt the world smile back with a small tightening of the air.

Evening's Lesson

Toward dusk, the spiral breathed again. It did not widen this time. It *deepened.* The ice did not sink; it found a new note, lower and truer. Astrid felt it in the meat of her shoulders. Halvar felt it, too— she could tell because he stopped speaking in the middle of a sentence and put his palm against the wall of the shed as if to steady himself. No one cried out. No one laughed. A dozen people straightened, then went on with what their hands were doing. That is courage, of a kind that does not show its teeth.

Astrid walked to the headland when the work had become merely repetition and stood until the cold reminded her that bodies have rules even when souls are listening to old music. The spiral held, darkening toward its center as twilight gathered there first. She imagined laying a finger at that center and finding it warm, the way the first ember under ash hides. She did not indulge the image. What you imagine too clearly can call you to it like a landmark.

The egg remembers, the Listener said. The words arrived so quietly that the wind did not notice them and therefore did not take them away.

She closed her eyes. Heat, sudden and particular, woke in her palm as if her hand had been named. It wasn't physical warmth. It was the memory of warmth. She spread her fingers and let it go.

"What if we leave it sleeping?" she asked. "What if the old things are old because they learned to be quiet?"

Old is often only another word for patient, he answered. *You will not decide whether it wakes by wanting or not wanting. You will decide how you greet it. With fear that teaches knives. Or with fear that teaches care.*

"Those are both fear."

Yes. The world is made of brave kinds of fear.

She stood long enough that her boots bit deeper into the crust and frost painted a ring along the edge of her cloak where her breath had met the cold. When she turned back toward home, Halvar waited for her halfway, as if he had measured the distance of her stubbornness and chosen the exact place where meeting would look like coincidence.

"How far?" he asked, without framing the question, because the day had given them both the same lesson and there was no point putting school around it.

"Not to the center," she said. "Not today."

He grunted, which in Halvar meant agreement. "Kjaer says she dreamed of summer wheat growing in the snow," he said as they walked. "Sigrid says her child spoke a word in his sleep she's never taught him. Nils says his bellows sings in a different key."

"And you?"

"I say we eat. And tie down what can blow loose."

She nodded. It was a theology she could respect.

Last Light

Night found them again, this time with a sky clear enough to show stars pricking holes in the dark. The cold turned from honest to harsh. In the great silence after the lamps were pinched out, Astrid lay with her hands folded on her stomach and counted the beats that were not her own.

Three. Rest. Three. A curl through the middle, like a path drawn with a warm finger.

She did not try to sleep. Sleep would have taken that as a challenge and stayed away just to win. Instead she let her mind drift along small things—the feel of twine smoothing when it wants to catch; the exact sound of her father's knife on wood when he is half a moment from speaking; the way the frost at the window learns the pattern of the grain and imitates it without mockery. She let the world be particular. Particularity is how you love something without breaking it.

When the Listener spoke once more before morning, he did so from very far away or very deep down; it is hard to tell the difference when you are underground and the world is large.

Tomorrow, the breath will quicken. Stand where the headland meets the old path. Bring no fire. Bring no iron you do not trust.

"What do I bring?" she asked, and found herself embarrassed by the eagerness in her whisper.

Your listening, he said simply. *And a rope.*

"A rope?"

For whatever you love enough to try to keep.

The room did not move. The rafters did not wake. Her heart gave one strong, unsteady thud.

"And if the village asks me what I'm doing?" she asked the dark.

Tell them you are making ready for the thaw, he said, with a smile in his voice that she felt against her skin more than heard. *It will be true.*

She slept then, not because the world allowed it but because she chose it the way you choose a word and then honor it.

In the gray before dawn, when lamps are a cruelty and roosters are liars, Astrid woke to a sound like a great thing drawing breath where breath has not been drawn in a very long time. It did not sound like triumph. It did not sound like doom. It sounded like a body remembering itself.

She rose, put on the clothes that know the path to the door without being told, took a coil of rope from the peg, and stood for a moment with her palm on the ledger box the way a pilgrim touches a shrine in passing. Then she stepped into the cold.

On the headland, the spiral darkened toward its center as if tender meant *close to heat.* Along its curve, frost had grown taller in the night, as if listening makes things grow. Down on the flats, shapes moved—men keeping distance, women making sure men kept distance, children promising to obey with their mouths while their eyes wrote maps.

"Astrid," Halvar said behind her. She turned. He had dressed for work that makes hands bleed. He had brought no iron he could not trust.

"What are we doing?" he asked, and there was no

mockery in it, only a man asking to be included in a thing he can't lift alone.

"Making ready for the thaw," she said, and felt the Listener's wry approval warm the place between her ribs.

"Good," Halvar said, and took one end of the rope without asking.

Together, they walked toward the old path, where rock shows itself the way a scar shows a history. The fjord held its breath and the day leaned down to hear.

Chapter Eight

The Song Beneath the Ice

The thaw came early that year, though no one trusted it. Rivers cracked like breaking glass, and the mountains loosed sighs that rolled down to the fjord in soft avalanches. In Havngard, men muttered that the sea was waking wrong. The priests said it was only the breath of spring finding its lungs again. But Astrid knew the difference between breath and heartbeat.

For three nights she had dreamed of light moving under the ice. Not fire—something deeper. A pulse she could almost hear, slow and steady, like a drum wrapped in snow. It called to her between heartbeats, in the hush between waves, in the groan of the roof timbers.

On the fourth morning she woke before dawn, skin prickling as if her name had been whispered just behind her ear. Halvar still slept. The coals in the hearth glowed faintly, orange under ash. Outside, the wind was still, and that stillness frightened her more than any storm. She dressed quietly, took her iron staff, and stepped into the half-light.

The world was colorless—gray sky, gray snow, gray sea —yet it hummed. A sound below hearing, more felt than heard. It came from the direction of the smoke field. The same place she'd promised herself not to go alone.

She went anyway.

The path through the birches had changed. Where frost had once glittered on every branch, now beads of water clung like glass tears. A raven followed her for a while, croaking once, twice, then veering toward the cliffs. When the trees thinned, mist rose in ribbons across the field. Beneath it, the ground steamed as though the world were dreaming through its mouth.

Astrid paused at the edge of the bowl. The air smelled of iron and rain, sharp enough to taste. She pressed the iron tip of her staff into the snow. It came away wet, not frozen. The earth was breathing again.

She stepped down slowly. Steam curled around her ankles, stroking her calves. Beneath the thin crust of snow, the ground was warm—alive. The fissure where she had first seen the curve of something not-rock lay ahead, crusted now with translucent frost. She half-expected to find it sealed entirely, another trick of the world's forgetting.

Instead, it glowed.

A faint light pulsed within the crack—golden, rhythmic, alive. With each beat, warmth kissed her skin. Astrid knelt, her breath catching in her throat. The light grew brighter, then dimmed, then brightened again, like a creature sleeping and waking by turns.

"Hello," she whispered before she could think. Her voice sounded too loud. "Are you… still there?"

The answer came as vibration through her knees, through the soles of her boots. A pulse she knew as well as her own heartbeat. The rhythm matched her breath. When she exhaled, the light flared. When she inhaled, it softened.

"I'm here," she murmured. "You remember."

From the ridge above, a figure watched—hooded, half-hidden by birch trunks.
The wizard.
He leaned on his crooked staff and whispered words that tasted like weather. *The fire quickens,* he thought. *And she is the spark.*

But he did not call out. The rhythm was delicate. One wrong sound might break it.

Astrid brushed snow away from the fissure with her gloved hand. Beneath it, the surface she'd once thought to be stone shone faintly pearlescent. Her fingers tingled. Heat throbbed up through the earth, steady and insistent.

Then the ground gave a soft, sharp crack.

The fissure widened, and steam hissed from it in a spiral. The heat became intense, not burning but fierce, like the breath of a forge. Astrid fell back onto one hand, blinking against the light. The earth's hum deepened until it matched the pounding of her heart.

Another crack, louder this time. Then another.

The ice split fully, revealing a hollow beneath the snow—a nest of tangled roots and stone, and at its center, a sphere the color of sunrise through mist.

The **egg**.

It was larger than she remembered, half-buried in melting soil, veins of gold running beneath its translucent surface. The warmth radiating from it made the steam shimmer. Within the shell, something moved—slow, graceful, undeniable.

Astrid's mouth went dry. "You're real," she breathed.

The movement inside quickened. The egg quivered once, twice, as if recognizing her voice. A sharp line appeared across its surface—a crack thin as a hair—and from that crack seeped a thin thread of light.

Far behind her, Halvar called her name. His voice carried faint and uncertain, the sound of a man afraid to believe what he feared. The wizard turned toward him and lifted a hand in warning. "Too soon," he murmured. "She must stand alone."

Astrid barely heard. She was kneeling again, hands hovering above the egg. The light from within shifted through colors—amber, red, gold—then steadied to a hue that matched the flame of her hearth at dawn. The shell split wider. A sound rose from it—neither cry nor roar but a trembling tone that made her eyes fill without reason. It wasn't in her ears; it was *inside her chest*, resonating through bone.

She knew, without knowing how, that it was asking a question.

She touched the shell.

Heat surged through her palm, not pain but power, the feeling of something immense recognizing her. The hum rose into a chord that filled the bowl and the birch valley beyond. Birds took flight. Snow slid from branches. Far out on the fjord, the ice cracked like a whip.

The egg broke open.

Light spilled upward, a column that turned the mist to fire. Astrid stumbled back, shielding her eyes. When the brightness softened, a shape uncurled from within—a creature no larger than a yearling foal, slick with steam and trembling. Scales shimmered pale gold and silver, still soft with newness. Two wings folded awkwardly against its sides. Its eyes blinked open—molten amber with pupils like pinpoints of night.

The hatchling saw her.

FoThe dragon's breath thrummed against her skin—warm, damp, startlingly sweet, like air that had been sleeping in a cedar chest. Close now, Astrid could see the soft fringes at the base of each scale—new growth that caught the light in halos. Its throat fluttered as it swallowed, confused by a world that arrived all at once.

"Slow," she whispered. "We have time."

Time? The sense returned to her like a bell struck far off—curious, muddled, young.

"Yes," she said aloud. "Time enough."

The hatchling tried to plant its feet. The talons—milk-white and soft as candle wax at the tips—slid in the thaw, sending it splay-legged. Instinct made Astrid brace under the small chest and shoulder the weight as if it were a yearling calf finding legs for the first time. Heat bled through her cloak; her arms prickled with it, and yet she did not let go.

"Up," she encouraged, as if her voice could lend bones.

The dragon obeyed with awkward dignity, hindquarters rising before the forelegs quite remembered what to do. A wing half-unfolded, shook, and cast droplets in a glittering arc. The membranes were pearly where the light touched—smoky-blue in shadow, veined with gold so fine it looked like frost traced backward.

The dragon sneezed.

It was a ridiculous sound, delicate and explosive together, and a thimble of blue fire flicked from the nostrils and died—more light than heat. The patch of snow in front of it sighed and subsided, leaving a glassy skin.

Astrid laughed before she knew she would. The laugh was breathless and wet, tangled up with tears she hadn't asked for. "We'll keep that pointed away from hayricks, I think."

Hayricks? The echo came puzzled, the way a child rolls a new word in its mouth to learn its shape.

"Later," she promised. "You'll meet them later."

The hatchling leaned. Its forehead—cooling now—bumped her collarbone again as it learned the geometry of closeness. In the back of its mind—where she could just hear when she held still—threads of meaning tangled and untangled: *Warm. Near. Yours.*

"Not mine," Astrid corrected softly, though her heart leapt at the word. "Together."

The dragon paused, tasting the shape of that. *To…gether,* it tried, and the near-miss of the sound inside her made her smile.

They practiced walking.

It lasted only minutes—small steps in a circle within the bowl, Astrid's hand always at the shoulder, the hatchling's tail scribbling uncertain notes into the snow. Twice it planted a forefoot, tested the ground with an intent little bob of the head, then shifted weight as if listening. **There**, Astrid realized—the same way she listened for the seam's pulse, it listened for the earth's. When it settled, its stance aligned with a rhythm she could feel, faint as a thought.

"Do you hear it?" she asked.

Hear, the dragon affirmed without words, a simple yes braided with the taste of hot stones and rain.

Another sneeze. Another spark, this one longer, a silken thread of pale flame that stitched and went out. The dragon startled at its own light and then made a sound so doubtful —half-apology, half-pride—that Astrid had to put her forehead briefly against its brow to stifle a second laugh.

"It's all right," she said. "The world is allowed to surprise you."

Up on the ridge a raven—perhaps the same that had followed her through the birches—settled and watched with a philosopher's slant to its head. It croaked once, then bowed as if conceding that for once the story below required silence.

The hatchling's breathing steadied. Astrid felt her own breath fall into that pace, then her heartbeat, then the soft, old sound the ground made when it remembered how to be warm. For a few breaths the bowl held only that—three rhythms learning each other, the simplest music in the world.

Name, the dragon nudged into her mind—tentative, a finger brushed against a bell.

"You have one already," she said. "I don't know it yet."

The hatchling considered. *Yours?* it offered, yielding the choice back.

"Not yet," Astrid said, and meant it. Names were promises. Promises were doors.

r a moment, nothing moved. The world seemed to wait for the choice between flight and fear.

Astrid went still as stone. Slowly, she extended her hand, palm up, the way she might greet a frightened animal.

The dragon tilted its head, steam curling from its nostrils. Then it leaned forward—tentative, curious—and pressed its forehead to her palm.

Sound filled her mind. Not words, but meaning. *You were the first voice.*

Her knees gave out. She laughed and wept all at once. "Then you heard me."

Always.

The dragon's breath warmed her wrist. It made a soft rumbling noise, somewhere between a purr and thunder. When it spread its wings, droplets flew like rainbows.

The light that had flared upward did not fade—it *traveled.* It streaked along the roots, through the thawing earth, down to the fjord where the ice cracked in long ribbons. On the far shore, fishermen dropped their nets as the water shimmered red and gold for one impossible heartbeat. Deep under the mountain, something ancient shifted its weight, sensing a change in the pattern of silence.

And far to the south, in a temple of black stone, a priest stopped mid-chant. His breath frosted in the air. "The seal weakens," he whispered, eyes wide. "Fire walks again."

Astrid did not know any of this. She only knew that her hand rested on warm scales, that the air shimmered around them, and that her heart no longer felt like it belonged to her alone.

The dragon tried to stand. Its legs wobbled. It fell forward with a small, startled hiss. Astrid caught it without thinking, her arms circling its chest. The heat nearly burned through her cloak, but she didn't let go.

"There," she said softly. "Slowly. The world is big. You'll learn it."

It blinked at her, confused and curious, and she felt laughter—not hers—bloom in her mind like sunlight through fog. *Big,* it echoed. *Cold. Bright. Yours.*

"Mine?" she whispered.

The dragon pressed its snout to her collarbone. *Yours.*

From the ridge, the wizard lowered his hood. The wind tangled his white hair.

"So it begins," he whispered.

Halvar came to stand beside him, awe and fear at war in his eyes. "Is that... what I think it is?"

Halvar's fingers tightened on the haft of his axe until the knuckles went sallow. He had carried that axe to funerals and to fish runs, through lean years and good; it had lived long enough to learn the weight of his hand. Now his grip said what his mouth did not: if the world changed in the next breath, he would meet it standing.

"Tell me it is a trick," he said, very quietly.

The wizard's eyes were still on the bowl, on the two figures at its heart—girl and not-quite-lizard, old as story and new as breath. "It is not," he said. His voice held no triumph. "Halvar Halvardsson, do you remember the winter the cod fled the fjord and the priests sang over the ice until even your pots cracked?"

Halvar's mouth flattened. "I remember too much of priests and not enough of cod."

"They did not invent that song," the wizard said. "They copied it from a worse one. The first binding was not made by men—it was learned from a hunger that wanted the world tidy and cold."

Halvar looked at him for the first time instead of the bowl. "Speak plain."

The wizard's staff planted into thawed earth with a small, convincing sound. "Your wife knew," he said, softer now. "The old blood chooses—every few generations, the hearing is born where it is needed. She used to stand on the cliff after storms and listen for ships. That is not a habit learned from grief; it's a habit grief recognizes."

Something moved under Halvar's stony face—pain, yes, but also a quick, almost guilty relief at hearing the truth put where he could reach it. "She told you this?"

"She told the goats," the wizard said. "I happened to be there."

Halvar snorted once despite himself. The sound thawed

the place where fear had packed itself tight under his ribs. Then he sobered. "If the old songs wake, the old enemies will wake with them."

"They already stir," the wizard said, and glanced south where clouds stacked as if to bar a road. "Men who love order more than life will hear this day as clearly as the birds do. Some will come with cages made of kindness. Some with cages made of iron. Both harm."

"And our people?"

The wizard's mouth turned. "Fishermen tell the truth better than priests. But fear is clever. If the hatchling sneezes in the wrong yard, a good man can be taught to light a bad fire."

Halvar studied his daughter a long moment, the line of her back as she leaned into the new creature, the exact angle of her head when she listened. He had seen that angle when she was five and pressed her ear to the fish barrel to count the living. He had seen it when she was ten and put a palm on the doorpost to learn the song the wind made there. He had worried it was strangeness. Now he understood it was inheritance.

"What would you have me do?" he asked.

The wizard's answer came with no drama. "Hide them, teach them, and be brave in front of your neighbors without mocking their fear. Brave men who feel mocked become cruel." He tipped his chin toward the bowl. "And… when she chooses a name, say it aloud as if it were always meant to live in your house. Names need room."

Halvar breathed once through his nose and nodded. "I can do three of those."

"Which three?"

"We will find out," Halvar said dryly, and started down the slope.

The wizard followed, letting the birches take his sleeve one by one like old friends reluctant to see him go. Beneath their feet the thawed earth gave a low, contented sound—as if, in some quiet layer the priests had forgotten to freeze, the land approved of the mess that was about to begin.

The wizard's gaze did not leave the girl and the hatchling. "No," he said quietly. "It is what the world remembers it can be."

Halvar gripped his axe handle as though it were the only solid thing left. "If others see—"

"They will see soon enough," said the wizard. "And not all will call it miracle."

Astrid looked down at the dragon. Its chest rose and fell against her knee. The light from its scales played across her face, soft and flickering. She felt its heartbeat through the ground, echoing her own. The bond was already sealed—simple, ancient, unbreakable.

Above them, the sky shuddered. Clouds pulled apart in slow, spiraling trails. The wind carried a low, distant sound—like thunder, or perhaps like other wings answering across the mountains.

Astrid lifted her eyes. "You're not the only one, are you?"

The dragon's gaze met hers. *No.*

She drew in a breath that burned with cold and wonder. "Then we'd better learn to fly."

The hatchling rumbled, as if amused, and leaned closer into her hand.

By dusk, the bowl lay still again. Steam curled from the earth, and the light faded to ordinary gold. The wizard and Halvar approached at last, moving slowly, reverently. Neither spoke. Astrid sat in the snow with the young dragon beside her, both watching the last rays vanish beyond the fjord. The ice there was breaking in long, straight lines, as though the world were drawing its first breath in centuries.

When the final crack of sunlight slipped behind the peaks, the dragon turned its head and made a sound—a soft note, rising. Astrid heard it not in her ears but in her blood. The sound meant *promise*.

She smiled through tears. "Then we'll keep it."

They did not move for a time after that—three figures in a bowl of steaming earth, watched over by a sky trying to remember how to be blue without being brittle. The hatchling's head sank by degrees until it rested on Astrid's knee, eyes narrowing to glowing almonds as drowsiness learned its own weight. When its breath evened, a faint wisp of vapor puffed with each exhale, as if sleep itself were visible in this place.

Halvar crouched, boots squeaking in the wet, and very carefully—so carefully the care itself felt like a prayer— extended the back of his knuckles toward the hatchling the way he'd greeted skittish farm dogs all his life.

The dragon's pupils widened, caught scent, and did not flinch. It made a small sound that lived somewhere between greeting and warning.

"No harm," Halvar said, voice low. He held the hand there long enough for the meaning to travel. The hatchling blinked, then dismissed him the way small, newly fed things dismiss everything not immediately edible.

Astrid's mouth tugged. "He thinks you are less important than sleep."

"He is right," Halvar said. "He has a better claim."

The wizard stood with his palms spread, collecting the lay of the bowl in his skin, the way some men taste a stew by scent alone and can tell you which hillside the thyme grew on. When he spoke again, the words came not as orders but as furniture: solid, needed, inevitable. "There is a lava tube under the south rim—collapsed long ago, but the back of it holds dry. If we lay bracken and old sail, it will bed soft. The steam vents near it will keep the chill from the bones."

"Will it hide the light?" Astrid asked automatically, already protective in ways she did not pause to name.

"It will persuade the light to mind its manners," the wizard said. "Light listens when it can."

Halvar rose. "We'll fetch bracken by moonrise," he said. "And salt meat. And water." His practical mind tabbed the list with relief—a boatman is never happier than when an impossible problem breaks into a stack of small loads. "What does a dragon eat?"

"Everything it shouldn't," the wizard said, not unkindly. "We'll begin with fish."

Astrid's eyes went wide. "Fish?"

"You wish to keep neighbors," the wizard said. "You do not begin with goats."

She pictured Thora's face if the kids went missing, then the hatchling's face learning guilt too early, and made a face of her own. "Fish," she agreed with sober gravity, as if it had been her idea all along.

They made a sling from the old cloak Astrid kept rolled in her pack, and when the hatchling woke—startled by the unfamiliar rustle around its middle—they soothed it with voice and touch and that simple word it loved now: *Together.*

The carry to the lava tube was a lurching promenade of compromise. The hatchling wanted to walk. The ground wanted to help. Astrid wanted to carry. Halvar wanted to test every foot of path with the staff first because fathers look for broken edges even in meadows. In the end they moved as a small herd does, unhurried but determined, and the night watched with interest as if it had not seen this exact shape of procession in a very long time.

The tube-mouth yawned where the bowl's south lip crumbled—dark, dry, ribbed with old flowstone like frozen waves. Inside, the air was warmer, the sound closer. The wizard struck tinder with quiet competence and set a lamp that burned without smoke; its little gold light stitched the rough walls and made a second, cozier dawn in the hollow space.

Astrid laid the cloak in a nest of bracken. The hatchling tested the bed with its chin the way it had tested the earth, then folded down with a sigh so deep she felt it in the bones at the back of her mouth. Its wings arranged themselves by instinct into an untidy tent. One talon gripped the cloak's edge because new creatures are offended by edges that do not answer.

"We can't stay the night here," Halvar said eventually, as if arguing with his own reluctance to move. "If we do not show our faces at the hearth, we'll wake a rumor that will grow legs by morning."

"I will stay," the wizard said. "The mountain owes me a favor here."

Astrid looked from the dragon to her father. The pull to

remain—fierce, physical—tugged at the muscles in her chest. The pull to be the kind of daughter who returned when the stew needed tending tugged the same place. She swallowed. "I'll go with you, fetch fish, come back before first light."

Halvar nodded, accepting both pulls as honest. "Bring the blue net. It does not tangle as quick."

Astrid brushed the hatchling's brow with two fingers—quickly, as if the moment might make her too soft to walk away. *Together,* she promised, not aloud.

The thought came back drowsy and content: *Together… later.*

They left the wizard in the warm dim of the tube, his lamp a second star. Outside, the valley had taken on that particular blue that happens between day and night when the world forgets which story it is telling. The steam had thinned. The birches had put away their glitter and stood sober as pillars.

Down in Havngard, lamps pricked awake one by one. A child shouted laughter; a dog answered with ownership. Two women argued cheerfully about a man's uselessness and then, without pausing, about the uselessness of arguing. Normal life made its round, and over all of it lay a thin ash of new rumor—the kind that starts as weather and becomes a tale if you give it bread.

Astrid and Halvar crossed the smoke field the long way, skirting the warm runnels where ice had the decency to admit defeat. When they reached the birches, Halvar paused and set his palm to one trunk. He did not pray, not in words, but the gesture admitted: I am out past soundings.

"You'll tell me when to be afraid?" he said, not looking at her.

"I'll tell you when to be brave," Astrid answered. "The rest you know."

That won a small grunt that meant respect. They walked on.

By the time they reached the huts their breath came white again in the new cold. A wind had risen, gentle at first, then pushing—wind with news. It twined the smoke into ropes and laid them flat along the snow where they drew gray lines like writing.

At their own door Halvar paused a second time. He lifted the latch and let the hinge speak its familiar syllable. "We'll eat," he said. "Then nets."

Astrid hesitated. "I need a word for him," she blurted, surprising herself with the urgency of it. "Not now, not spoken—but ready. It feels wrong to leave him unnamed."

Halvar studied her face the way he studied weather—a quick catalog of details, a slower consideration of what those details meant for boats. "In the morning, when we bring fish, we'll bring the word too," he said. "Names ought to be carried with both hands."

She nodded, relieved by the simple promise. The stew smelled of fennel and seal fat and the last of a dried apple Halvar had been hoarding since late autumn for a day when sweetness would help more than thrift. They ate without speaking much, words worn thin by the weight they'd already carried.

When the bowls were clean and the lamp trimmed, Halvar fetched the blue net—the one with knotted wisdom older than his father's father—and the two of them stepped back into the cold.

As they crossed the hard ground between house and

shore, a shadow passed over them—fast, silent, the shape of a bird too large for the night. Astrid looked up, heart hammering at a silhouette that might have been a trick of cloud.

Only cloud.

Still, she felt more watched than alone.

On the far side of the world, in a city that had put its lamps behind stone, a priest closed a book and frowned into a wind that should not have carried warmth so far. He licked a finger, turned a page back, and found a line his predecessors had ironed flat until it behaved. That line rose like bread. He rang a bell. Other men woke. Winter itself listened from a high shelf and considered whether it had been insulted.

Back in Havngard, where winter was a matter of boots and stew and ordinary stubbornness, Astrid and Halvar took a skiff to the ice's edge. The blue net went out the way a good story goes out—cleanly, with a shape that invites return. Fish came because fish are nosy and because something in the water had started telling a rumor they found exciting. They took enough, then no more, and set the rest free with thanks said in Halvar's bent-headed way.

They were back at the birches by first light, breath burning, arms made heavy by kindness. The wizard's lamp still glowed in the lava tube like a remembered star. Inside, the hatchling lifted its head at the scuff of their boots and made a sound that flipped Astrid's heart over like a fish.

She knelt with the first fish cradled in both hands. "We brought breakfast," she said solemnly.

The dragon sniffed, decided this was a marvelous idea invented moments ago for its exact benefit, and took the fish too fast. It coughed—astonished at the simultaneous existence of bones and haste—then managed. A small puff of resigned smoke escaped its nose like a sigh that had been practicing to be a warning.

"Slow," Astrid advised, choking on a laugh. "The world will not run away if you chew."

They fed it a second, and then a third, and stopped before greed taught a lesson hunger should teach later. After, the hatchling made the small, satisfied rumble of a forge banked properly and put its head on Astrid's thigh as if that were the proper place for heads in a well-run cave.

Halvar leaned against the wall, watched them, and made a decision that did not fit in his mouth yet. He turned it in his hands a moment, then held it out.

"Say it," he told Astrid.

She blinked. "What?"

"The name," he said. "It's time you teach my house the right word."

Astrid's first answer rose too quick and she set it down again. She let the silence work—the same way she let nets sink the right amount before drawing. A dozen words hovered. A half-dozen tried to please. She ignored those. At last one came with the quiet confidence of a knife that knows its sheath.

"**Embla,**" she said.

The wizard looked up sharply, eyes bright with the inward surprise of a man who had not expected to be surprised today. Halvar's brows went up, then down, then softened as the rightness of it found the joints in his thinking.

The hatchling—Embla now—lifted her head, tasted the word in Astrid's mind, and answered with a sound that felt like the opening of a warm hand. *Emb…la.* The echo landed and stayed.

"It will do," Halvar said, but the roughness in his tone gave way to pride as he added, "It will more than do."

The wizard smiled into his beard. "The first woman of the old stories," he said, approving the courage of the choice. "Made from tree and breath. A begin-again name."

Astrid stroked the soft young scales between Embla's eyes. "Begin-again," she whispered, and the cave, the lamp, the thawed earth—all of it—seemed to nod.

Outside, day gathered its shoulders. The valley looked ordinary from a distance—smoke, snow, people who deserved simple weather. Inside, a promise breathed, fed, and put its head down to sleep.

When they left the tube, Astrid paused at the mouth and looked back the way a person looks at a cradle before closing the door. She did not say the prayer that rose, because prayers are timid in the face of work. She only touched the stone and committed every line of the place to memory—smell, sound, the exact way the light pooled, the nick on the floor where Halvar's boot had kicked a pebble— so that no matter what came she would be able to find her way home to this beginning.

On the slope the wizard waited with his staff, face lifted to taste the new wind. "The world will come looking," he said without drama. "Let it find your courage first."

"It can have all of mine," Halvar said.

"And mine," Astrid added.

"Good," the wizard said. "It will bring friends."

They went down out of the birches with their empty basket and their full morning. In Havngard, a bell rang the hour. Nets came up. Someone shouted that the first gulls of spring had arrived. Someone else declared that gulls never left, they only criticized more loudly in warm weather.

The day pretended hard to be only a day.

Under the south rim, in the warmth of old fire and new breath, Embla dreamed. Her sleep flickered with small flame and pictures that were not yet pictures—sound-images of river stone and cloud-edges and the exact pitch of the girl's voice when it said together. Far below even that, the land dreamed too. In that layered drowse where mountains remember the shape of their first names, something turned —not a threat, not a promise, simply the great slow shift that happens when a story decides it will go on.

That night, when the others slept, Astrid woke again. The dragon dreamed beside her, small puffs of smoke curling from its nostrils. In its sleep it made faint sounds—half-formed thoughts. *Light. Voice. Sky.*

She reached out, her fingers hovering above its neck. "Someday," she whispered. "Someday you'll have all three."

The hatchling's tail flicked once. In the distance, the fjord moaned softly, ice shifting under the stars. The sound was almost a lullaby.

Astrid closed her eyes and let the rhythm of its breathing carry her into sleep.

Outside, the wind rose for the first time in weeks. It swept the valley clean of mist and carried the faint, new scent of smoke— *dragon-fire, reborn.*

Chapter Nine

The Whispering World

Morning came slow and bruised. Cloud rolled down from the peaks like wool brushed in ash, and Havngard's chimneys trailed thin, uncertain threads of smoke. The thaw had reached the village at last. Water ran in restless veins beneath the ice, unseen but insistent — like a voice rehearsing its own name.

Astrid woke to that sound and thought, for a heartbeat, she was still dreaming. The air in the longhouse smelled of brine and burnt pine. Her breath smoked above the blanket, and when she rubbed her hands together, she could still feel warmth from another fire — not from the hearth, but from within.

Embla.

The dragon's name came to her like a remembered song. It filled her with light and a strange ache she couldn't name. She saw again the small body curled against her knee, wings folded like silk, breathing in tiny sparks. The sound of it — the low, rhythmic purr that seemed to come from the earth — had followed her even into sleep.

Across the room, Halvar sat at the table mending a net. He didn't look up when she stirred. His shoulders were drawn tight, his jaw unshaven. Each knot he tied was small, precise, and angry.

"You're awake," he said finally, without turning.

"Yes."

"There's porridge on the hearth."

The porridge had the clean, thin taste of the last oat-scrapings from the bin. Astrid ate standing, one hand around the wooden bowl, and let her eyes learn the morning the way her ears already had. The shutter leaked a line of pewter light. When the wind pressed, the rawhide hinge made a soft, wet creak like new boots. Beneath the floor, somewhere in the seam between packed earth and the piles that lifted the longhouse, water threaded itself through old stone. It moved with a purpose that wasn't hurrying and wasn't idle either—like a messenger repeating its message to itself so it didn't lose a word.

She finished and set the spoon across the bowl. "I'll fetch wood."

Halvar made a small sound that meant gratitude and disapproval at once. "Take the back way. The front drift will take you to the knee."

The back way shouldered between two sheds. Hoarfrost furred the eaves, shaggy as a tired dog. The world out there had forgotten to be white; it had turned the color of weak tea where snow slumped to slush and soaked the dun earth beneath. Smoke kept low, unwilling to climb.

Havngard awake was a list you learned with your body: the cadence of Nils's mallet on net-floats (three quick taps, a pause, a fourth), the way Thora cleared her throat before she swore (loud courtesy, then judgment), the shore dogs' chain-rattle (they were not savage, just bored and full of opinions). Astrid's hearing had always been a hand extended toward those sounds; today it felt like her hand had grown three more fingers.

At Old Kjaer's stoop she paused. The woman's door stood open like a missing tooth. Inside, a kettle argued with itself. Kjaer herself leaned on her stick and glared at the sky.

"Storm-girl," she said without turning, which made Astrid

smile. "The thaw is a liar. He says go, and your feet go, and then he eats a boot."

"I brought wood for the liar," Astrid said, stacking split birch by the hearth until Kjaer's mouth, which had been a blade, softened into something like a tired ribbon.

"You hear it?" Kjaer asked, not specifying what "it" meant because in Havngard words did not waste themselves on things that didn't matter.

Astrid, who had meant not to say yes to anyone today, said yes.

Kjaer nodded once. "I dreamt the fjord put on a mask. Not to hide. To breathe differently." She tapped her stick. "Priests change the way air moves."

"Priests?" Astrid said carefully.

Kjaer spat into the corner where she kept unlucky thoughts. "What else marches without wondering why its feet hurt?"

Down the lane, men argued in low, brisk tones. The words rolled like round stones—no edge to nick you unless you stood in their way. Astrid could have told you who spoke without looking: Rurik, whose s's came out like rope slipping through a hand; Leif, who made every statement a question when he was nervous. She didn't look. It was becoming too easy to know things she had no right to know.

At the well, Thora had gathered a parliament of shawls. "Black sails," someone said. "Iron ribs," someone else answered. "Supply barge," said a third voice in the way people say a thing they don't believe and hope will persuade the world into becoming true.

"A barge doesn't take a priest," Thora said. "A priest

takes a barge."

"Maybe he comes to bless the thaw," Leif said, hopeful because his youngest had coughed all night and hope is the only coin a parent can afford to spend freely.

"Blessings that smell of oil tend to stick where they shouldn't," Thora snapped, and the shawls clucked agreement.

Astrid kept her face ordinary and her step slow. Havngard had been her whole map once, a dozen longhouses stitched to a strip of shore, a net of work that caught each day and held it still long enough to live it. Today she felt the net lift and strain. Something big was swimming under it.

Back at the house she stacked wood under the eave and wiped slush from her boots on the threshold. Halvar tied off his last knot, bit the end to tighten it, and tugged with a small, satisfied grunt.

"Thora says black sails," Astrid offered, pretending to be casual.

"Thora always says black something." But the line at Halvar's jaw sharpened.

"She said a priest might be aboard."

He didn't answer for a breath, and in that breath Astrid heard the creak of a door in his mind she hadn't known was there. It opened on memory: a winter not this one and not long ago, a prayer in a language too clean, a man in white telling a village how grateful it should feel to sleep without fear and waking with the taste of iron anyway.

"We'll gather bracken," Halvar said at last, and his voice had the shape of a decision that didn't want questions hung on it.

She rose and moved toward the pot, the floor cold beneath her feet. "Did you sleep?"

"Enough."

She doubted it. His eyes were red at the corners, and he flinched once when the wind groaned against the shutter. Neither of them mentioned the cave, or the hatchling, or the way the air itself had seemed to change when Embla breathed her first breath.

When she finished eating, Halvar stood. "Roof needs patching. We'll gather bracken before noon."

Astrid nodded. They both knew what "bracken" meant.

The world outside looked half-born. Snow sagged from rooftops, turning to slush where it met the ground. Water dripped from the eaves like clockwork. The fjord cracked and sighed, sending faint echoes between the cliffs. Steam rose from the smoke field, thicker than the day before, coiling upward in pale threads.

As they walked, Astrid felt each patch of warm ground before her boots touched it. Her palms tingled. Somewhere beneath the crust of thawed earth, the deep pulse she had first heard at the wellspring throbbed again, faint but familiar — a heartbeat that matched her own.

Together, came a sleepy voice at the edge of her thoughts.

Astrid smiled despite herself. "I'm coming."

Halvar looked sideways. "What?"

"Nothing," she said quickly. "Only talking to myself."

"Best not do it out loud in front of the neighbors," he muttered. "They already think we're odd."

She grinned. "Then let's give them something to talk

about.”

But Halvar didn't smile. He shifted the basket on his shoulder and quickened his pace.

At the mouth of the cave, warmth breathed out to meet them — damp, heavy, alive. The wizard sat cross-legged near the old lamp, his eyes closed, hands spread on the stone as if listening with his skin. Embla slept nearby, her sides rising and falling in a rhythm that seemed to echo the mountain itself.

When the wizard opened his eyes, the gold flecks in them caught the light like sparks. "You came."

"You said she'd need fish," Astrid said, lifting the small net bag from her shoulder.

He smiled faintly. "She will always need something."

Halvar set down his basket. "And you? What do you need?"

The wizard considered. "Patience. And perhaps less company."

"You'll have neither," Halvar said.

Embla stirred, one eye slitting open. When she saw Astrid, a pulse of warmth fluttered through the air, a low hum that touched Astrid's ribs.

"Good morning," Astrid whispered, crouching. "We brought breakfast."

The hatchling sniffed the air, caught the scent of fish, and half-climbed, half-stumbled toward her. Her scales shimmered where the light touched — silver at the tips, deep blue near the belly, colors that shifted like oil on water.

"She grows quickly," the wizard said softly. "Dragons

remember how to live before they learn how to walk."

Astrid fed her one fish, then another, careful to keep her fingers clear of the teeth. "She doesn't remember manners."

"They remember much worse things," he said.

She looked up. "You've seen dragons before, haven't you?"

"Long ago," he said. "When I was young and foolish. I am less young now."

Halvar folded his arms. "But not less foolish."

"Correct," said the wizard. "Wisdom is a burden; foolishness keeps a man light enough to walk the paths that matter."

Astrid hid a smile behind her hand.

Later, when the hatchling slept again, the wizard motioned for them to sit. He drew a circle in the dirt with his staff, marking it with small runes that flickered faintly like the eyes of fireflies.

"This place is old," he said. "Older than Havngard, older than the fjord. The dragons used to come here when the world was young — when fire was still wild and free. It's a wellspring of living heat. That's why you heard the earth speak before the egg hatched. It was calling for someone who could listen."

Astrid frowned. "Why me?"

"Because your blood remembers," he said. "Your mother was of the Hearing Line. The old families that could sense the pulse of the world. Most forgot. A few were silenced. You were born when the silence began to crack."

Halvar looked away, jaw tight. "You talk too much of

things that should stay buried."

"And yet," the wizard said gently, "your daughter found the unburied thing, didn't she?"

Halvar didn't answer. His hand went to his axe as if to reassure himself that some truths could still be cut in half.

Astrid felt the tension thicken like smoke. "I can't do magic," she said quietly. "I only hear things. Like… like the earth breathing, or water thinking, or people before they speak."

"That is magic," the wizard said. "Not the loud kind that shatters mountains, but the quiet kind that keeps them from falling apart."

Astrid met his gaze. "And the priests in the south? What do they want?"

He drew another rune, this one shaped like a cage. "To keep the world still. To keep winter eternal. They believe safety is worth any silence."

Halvar spat into the dirt. "They call that peace."

"They call it peace because they've never met fire that was kind," the wizard said. "They will smell her soon. Fire cannot hide for long."

"Once," the wizard said, "fire didn't need to."

They were seated in the wider mouth of the tube, where the steam's breath thinned and the slope let you look down into the bowl without being seen from below. He kept his voice low, but the story carried anyway; some tales arrive wearing their own quiet.

"When I was a boy," he said, "summer lasted longer. I don't mean by the calendar the priests keep under lock, I mean in the body. Old knees hurt less. Bread stayed soft longer. The fjord gave back more than it kept. The elders said winter had manners then."

"What changed?" Astrid asked, though she knew the shape of the answer and only wanted to see the words he used to carve it.

"Men learned to make a season out of a sentence," he said. "To say No and make it last. The first time, it was fear. The second, it was pride. The third, it was habit. They forgot that No is a tool, not a house."

Halvar shifted. "And dragons?"

"They were the part of the world that reminded it how to say Yes," the wizard said. "Not to everything. To breath. To heat. To the way water wants to move. That's what the priests hated. Not the fire. The permission."

Astrid thought of Embla's sneeze-thread of blue, thin as a hair and bright as a promise, and felt a twist under her breastbone—fear and home knotted together. "If the priests come, what do they do first?"

"Nothing," the wizard said. "That's their trick. They say they have come to observe, to ensure safety, to bless a harbor. They measure. They write. They ask if anyone has seen anything unusual and are very kind to those who say no. Then they build something that looks useful and hums wrong. Then they ask for cooperation. Then they put the word *containment* in a sentence with *temporary* and forget where they set the end."

Halvar rubbed a thumb over a nick in the haft of his axe as if he could rub it out of history. "I won't let them put a cage around my house."

"You won't," the wizard agreed. "But cages are clever. They arrive as gifts."

Astrid's hearing, which had been busy with the small work of the world—rocks shifting wetly under melt, a beetle somewhere in the bracken making a sound like a single hair plucked from a fiddle— opened wider without her telling it to. For a heartbeat she heard beyond the bowl and the birches, beyond Havngard's rude chorus, into the pass where snow leaned close over the road. The pass returned a single word in a stranger's mouth: *Soon.*

She flinched.

"What?" Halvar said.

"Nothing," she lied, then corrected herself because she had just promised herself she would not lie to him unless it kept him safe. "Something moving in the pass. Not close. Close enough to think it has a right to come."

The wizard sighed. "They're ahead of my best guess."

Halvar turned his face toward the south and set his jaw. He had a face made for weather; it could be storm or it could be stone. "Then I'll fetch line and two men I trust and set a fish story at the headland—the sort that eats a day to untangle."

"You'll be seen," the wizard said.

"I can be seen," Halvar answered. "It keeps eyes busy while my daughter is not seen."

Astrid wanted to put a hand on his arm and tell him not to be brave where she could see it. Instead, because she had learned from her mother that a woman's hand on a man's sleeve can say both *go* and *come back*, she put her hand there and let him read what he needed.

Astrid looked toward the hatchling, her heart pulling in two directions — fear and fierce love. "Then we'll have to teach her to be quiet."

The wizard's smile was thin. "You cannot quiet a storm.

But you can teach it which houses to spare."

"Then we begin with sparing," Astrid said.

The wizard mislaid a smile in his beard. "With sparing—and with not setting fire to your own hair while sneezing."

Embla had woken again with the restlessness of creatures who have discovered their body and find it both miracle and insult. She planted her feet like a foal—hock first, then a funny, earnest stab of the forefoot—tail trying to learn when it was part of her and when it was a tool. Astrid circled two steps ahead, one hand lifted wide in a steadying gesture, the other ready at the shoulder.

"Here," she coaxed, and made her voice a rope someone would trust to hold. "Turn. No, the other… yes."

Embla turned the wrong way and wound up facing her own tail, which startled and flicked her nose. She sneezed, and a thread of pale blue licked out and died on the damp stone.

"Good," Astrid said on instinct, and felt the word land inside Embla like a small heat-stone. The hatchling wobbled with pride. Pride made her overconfident. Overconfidence made her try to leap a patch of wet that her legs couldn't measure yet. Astrid caught the chest again and took the weight, laughing breathlessly.

Halvar rebuilt the nest with his hands the way he made a boat-stern hold together—finding the lay of each bracken frond, overlapping the brittle with the springy, testing give before he let a thing go. He didn't look up while he spoke. "No village for two days. We use the back gully to the north when we come and go. We clean our boots before we set foot on the lane, wash our hems when we can so the smell of steam stays here."

"Smoke or steam?" the wizard asked, which was the sort of question people mistake for unhelpful until they name the difference and live longer because they did.

"Steam," Halvar said. "Smoke tells on you. Steam pretends to be weather."

They set a rhythm that felt like a kind of liturgy. Astrid would coax Embla through half-circles—left, right, then left again—pausing to let the dragon plant a foot and listen to the ground each time. Halvar carried fish from the cool mouth of the tube to a shallow stone bowl. The wizard marked his small blue chalk runes higher up the wall, one hand always on the stone as if asking permission. Between tasks they spoke little, because speech wasted breath that balance and caution needed.

"Again," Astrid murmured, and Embla repeated the steps without blunder, the way a child repeats a nonsense rhyme for the joy of getting it right. She leaned her head into Astrid's palm—soft pressure, a test of boundaries—and Astrid let the weight rest there, not pushing back, simply existing with it.

Warm-near, the little mind said, content.

"Warm-near," Astrid echoed, and thought how many things in her life she had called by longer names: duty, kin, home. The two-syllable was simpler and not less true.

When Embla tired, she folded with that boneless grace new creatures are gifted, all at once, as if sleep had been standing behind her and finally decided to sit. Astrid tucked a frond under the jaw and the wizard dimmed his lamp to a whisper.

"She'll learn faster than you can," he said softly.

"I'm not racing," Astrid said, but pride and fear both

tugged; she had never wanted to be enough for something so badly and never doubted herself more.

"You'll need to," he answered, not unkindly. "People always think danger comes loud. Priests don't. They arrive telling you stories about how much safer you are already."

Halvar's mouth made a line. "We'll not be home when they knock."

"You can't hide forever," the wizard said mildly.

"I will for two days," Halvar said, which was both true and a lie and therefore accurate for a father.

Astrid's head had begun to ache the way a bone aches before weather—deep and humming. She pressed two fingers to her temple. The wizard's eyes flicked to the gesture and away, not prying, which made her like him better and trust him only a little.

"What will she eat when she is not a baby?" she asked.

"Less than a god, more than a goat," the wizard said. "Fish now. Mountain hare when the snows ease. In time, words."

"Words?"

He tilted his head. "Words are food. They shape what you allow yourself to be. Men who eat only 'duty' starve differently than men who eat only 'freedom'. Mind her diet."

Astrid thought of Thora's shawl-parliament and Kjaer's stick and Leif's worried questions, the way words had begun to slant in Havngard since the thaw. She nodded, and the wizard looked pleased the way teachers do when a student understands something they didn't know was being taught.

When they left the tube at last, the day had thinned. Even the light looked tired, a poor man counting coins twice to see if they'd learned to multiply. Astrid paused at the lip and turned to look back. The lamp's faint gold ringed the sleeping dragon and made the bracken shine as if each frond remembered a summer it had known by heart.

"Two days," Halvar murmured, reading her wish without needing her to spend a word on it. "Then we do not come this way. We circle through the thorn gully and the sheep cut. People look where paths teach them to."

By afternoon the snow had stopped. They left the cave together, the three of them climbing back toward the birch ridge. The wizard's staff tapped softly, keeping time with the rhythm of the thaw.

"Does she sleep much?" Astrid asked.

"For now," he said. "Dreams are lessons. The world speaks to her there. One day she will answer back."

Astrid thought of the small warmth that bloomed whenever Embla breathed. "When she speaks… will others hear her?"

"Only those who listen as you do."

Halvar glanced over his shoulder. "Then we best hope no one else in Havngard was born with her mother's gift."

The wizard's smile did not reach his eyes. "There are always listeners, Halvar. Some simply pretend otherwise."

They reached the village by dusk. Smoke curled from every chimney, but fewer lights burned behind the shutters. People walked in clusters, whispering. The air felt colder, not from weather but from worry.

"What's wrong?" Astrid murmured.

Halvar's neighbor, old Thora, was standing by the well with her shawl drawn tight. When she saw them, she lowered her voice. "A ship's been sighted on the southern fjord. Big as a hall, with black sails and iron ribs. The priest says it's a supply barge. The fishermen say it's a curse."

"A barge?" Halvar said, too quickly.

"That's what they're calling it." Thora's eyes flicked to Astrid, then away. "Strange weather, strange ships. Maybe the gods are counting heads again."

Halvar forced a laugh. "Let them count mine last."

Thora didn't smile. "They never do."

As they passed, Astrid felt a chill that had nothing to do with the cold. The hum of the earth below her feet trembled once, sharp and uneven. She caught her breath — it was as though something vast had stirred in its sleep and rolled onto its side.

"Father," she whispered. "Do you feel that?"

He frowned. "Feel what?"

"The ground. It—" She stopped. He wouldn't hear it. He never did.

That night, Havngard was restless. The wind shifted, bringing with it the smell of oil and smoke. Dogs barked until their voices cracked. Men muttered prayers to gods they hadn't named in years.

Astrid sat by the hearth, staring into the coals. Halvar had gone to bed, though she doubted he slept. Every sound felt louder tonight — the drip of thaw water outside, the whisper of wind through the thatch, even the small, nervous tick of the rafters cooling above.

Then, beneath it all, came another sound.

It was deep — not heard with ears but with the bones. A steady rhythm, like drums wrapped in frost. She closed her eyes and reached for it. The world blurred. Her heartbeat slowed until it matched the pulse she felt under her feet.

The darkness behind her eyelids opened like a curtain.

She saw snow whipped sideways by hooves. Men in iron, their breath steaming through runed masks. A column moving through the pass — riders with black banners, their symbols carved in frost. At their head rode a priest, his eyes closed, his lips moving soundlessly. The air around him shimmered with a cold that looked alive.

Astrid gasped, trying to pull away — but the priest's eyes snapped open. They were white, colorless, and they turned as though he could see her across the miles between them.

For an instant, she felt him in her mind — a voice that didn't speak in words, only intent: *The fire breathes again.*

Astrid jerked backward, breaking the connection. Her breath came ragged. The coals hissed in the hearth, throwing sparks like frightened birds.

She turned toward her father's sleeping shape by the wall. "They're coming," she whispered, her voice shaking. "And they already know."

The whisper made frost bloom along her teeth. She closed her mouth against it, the way you close a door softly when a child is sleeping, and sat very still so the sound wouldn't find new cracks to creep through.

On the other side of the room, Halvar's breath caught and fell back into its old rhythm. A log in the hearth settled with a tired hiss. Somewhere under the floor a mouse reconsidered its route and chose a quiet death tomorrow instead of an excited one tonight.

Astrid stood. The room tilted—the way a boat tilts when a wave forgets its manners—and then steadied as if embarrassed by its own enthusiasm. She crossed to the door on careful feet and lifted the latch with an up-breath, the way Halvar had taught her when she was small. Outside, the night had that stretched blue-black that happens when the clouds remember they have somewhere else to be and go there all at once.

The village slept with one eye open. Lamps guttered. Ropes creaked and then remembered they were meant to behave. The skin of ice that had reformed in the trough by the door had already learned to crack itself into a map of small islands. She stepped over it and went to the fence.

From there she could see the fjord. It lay like a blade and like a wound, honest about both. She let her hearing off its leash. It ran. It brought back more than she wanted.

The riders did not sound like hooves. They sounded like decisions. Each footfall nailed something to the world. The metal at their belts sang to itself in a key cold enough to be mistaken for reason. Banners make a sound, too, if you know how to listen. These banners sounded like pages turned harder than pages should be.

Astrid followed the sound back the way a hand follows a scar. The pass opened in her mind, bare rock wearing a crown of wind. The column wound through it—orderly, competent, patient. No shouting, no laughter, because noise is a tax undisciplined men pay and these men were too rich in purpose to waste coin.

At the center, a white figure rode with eyes closed. The priest had a face that would be easy to forget if you didn't look directly at it. When you did, your eye didn't know where to rest. His mouth had that small, perpetual gentleness that means a person enjoys the sound of their own mercy.

She did not try to touch his mind. She merely looked at him too clearly across too much night.

He looked back.

It wasn't sight—sight can be blocked by cloth and distance. It wasn't hearing—words need air to carry and there was not enough air in the world for this. It was recognition, clean and ugly.

Ah, said the place in her that receives voices. Not fear. Identification.

Not the egg, said the place in him that throws voices. *The listener.*

Astrid flinched so hard her shoulder thumped the fence post. The post told the blow to the ground and the ground told the bowl and the bowl told Embla. A sleep-sound rose from the south rim of the valley under her feet—a curious hum that meant, in dragon, *Near?* and, in girl, *I'm here.*

She pressed both palms to the fence and hunched around the sound, the way a mother stands between a stranger and a child without making a show of it. "Sleep," she breathed. "Please sleep."

The priest's lids did not lift, but the corner of his mouth did, the way a man smiles when a plan he made for purely practical reasons also pleases him quite a lot.

A smaller sound intruded—the trivial sort that saves people's lives because it breaks a line of attention. From the lane to her right came a muffled curse and the slop of a boot coming out of suction. Rurik, impatient even at midnight, had decided to check the moorings himself. The spell of looking snapped. The priest's head turned, noticing the world again. The column went on.

Astrid pulled her hands from the fence. The wood had printed its grain into her skin.

She stood a long time, counting breaths until numbers stopped helping. When she finally moved, it was to do something small and cheaply useful: she dragged the wood-basket to the door, set two sticks ready for Halvar to grab without looking, filled the water bowl for the dog that dragged its blanket to their threshold every thaw and called itself theirs without consultation.

At the lintel she paused. The thor's hammer hung beside the little wooden cross; both had settled into truce in their corner. She touched them with the same finger and then, because tonight had taught her that touch doesn't have to choose a church, she pressed that finger to the beam between, where the house itself might listen.

"Hold," she asked it. "Just hold."

The house, which had been built from trees that had practiced holding for a hundred winters before they were persuaded to become walls, agreed.

Back under her blanket, she lay on her side and watched her father's back become a hill and a coastline and finally only her father's back again. When sleep came, it came like a net tossed by a tired man—wide enough to catch a little, sloppy enough to miss much.

The last thing she heard before the net took her was the fjord. It had begun to crack in a tempo that matched the riders' pace. The sound made a rhythm in her bones. She despised it for a heartbeat and then forgave it because even water must do as it must.

In the thin hour before dawn, the crack-rhythm changed. It softened and learned to count like a lullaby. Astrid surfaced with that music in her mouth and realized two things at once:

The priest had left the pass and entered the low roads.

And Embla—under the south rim, in the warm dark—had started to dream deliberately. The dream's edges felt like choices.

Together, the dragon said, not sleepy this time. Not asking either. A statement, not a plea.

Astrid rolled up, hair wild, heart steadying. "Together," she said into the almost-morning, and meant the word in both directions at once: toward the cave, toward the road.

Chapter Ten

The Riders of the Frost

Dawn peeled itself thin over Havngard, the light the color of a blade rinsed in cold water. The thaw had crusted overnight and then set again; the lane wore ruts that glittered like old scars. Ropes creaked. Nets hung from pins in limp, salt-stiff curtains. A gull cried and, hearing something in its own voice it did not like, went silent.

Astrid woke already listening.

The sound of the riders was not loud; it was exact. Iron met packed snow with a polite knock, a rhythm careful men keep when they have no need to hurry. Under it came a second music—paper stiff with cold, the burr of rune-stones knocking each other in a leather pouch, the small hiss of breath through cloth meant to warm and to hide.

Halvar had slept in his boots. He rose, tied his hair back with a strip of sailcloth, and said without preface, "If they ask you questions, answer as if your mouth is a door and you are choosing what the room behind it looks like."

"What does that mean?" Astrid asked.

"It means don't lie," he said. "But don't let them inside either."

He crossed to the peg where the iron staff hung and pressed it into her hands. "Carry this. Old wood snaps when stared at. Iron pretends it's a tool."

She took the weight. The staff hummed against her palm, faint as a cat purr. It had been Halvar's father's before him; the grip remembered other hands.

They stepped out together.

Havngard stood facing itself in the way villages do when guests arrive who are not guests. Men drifted toward the shore on errands made suddenly urgent; women lingered at doorways, shawls high, cheeks wind-bitter; children were gathered briskly into tasks that kept them inside and busy counting. On the slope above the lane, Old Kjaer planted her stick and leaned on it with the fierce entitlement of age.

The column entered at the north path where the birches bowed to the wind. The riders wore grey like sky, black like wet rock, white like breath. Their horses steamed and did not toss their heads; good stock, trained to think obedience first and later. Banners hung on crossbars, rune-stitched and heavy. At their center rode the priest on a white mare. His hood was back now, face open to the cold, as calm as if he'd planned the weather.

"People of Havngard," he said, and the air liked his voice the way snow likes to fall—too easily. "Peace on your houses and good thaw to your nets."

No one answered. Thora folded her arms. The shawls behind her made the careful rustle of women who have been polite farther than it has profited them to be.

The priest smiled, modest, practiced. "I am Brother Calven of the Southern Cloister. This is a standard inspection. The winter has been long; the thaw is unpredictable. Runes have been… unsettled." His eyes passed over the roofs, not lingering. "We are here to ensure safety. We will inconvenience you as little as possible."

Astrid felt the word *safety* set itself like a coin on her tongue—shiny, weighty, counterfeit.

A man in a leather officer's coat nudged his horse forward. "We will require a ledger of births and deaths this season, a list of travelers through your port, and a look at your store salt. The Cloister will replace anything it uses."

Halvar muttered, "They measure your salt to see how much life you can afford to lose."

The priest's gaze found him as if the mutter had been called aloud. Not hostile; noting a piece on the board. "The headman?" he asked.

"We don't have a headman," Thora said, before Halvar could decide whether to become one. "We have work. Tell your list the work will be late if you take the men from it."

The priest inclined his head. "Then we will be quick." He made a small signal. Soldiers dismounted, soft-footed. They moved in pairs, as into a house they already knew the shape of.

Astrid's hearing widened on instinct. The world swam back—cloth scuff on wood, the low murmur of a rune prayer repeated by habit not belief, the skitter of a mouse departing a beam just in time to escape a pole's thump. Beyond those small noises came the ground-tone she had learned to trust: steady, patient, warm as a hand under a blanket. Embla slept under the south rim, deep and deliberate. The wizard had layered chalk light across the rock and whispered through the stone until even Astrid, who could hear thunder in ice, could barely sense the cave.

Together, the little mind said, very faint, as if speaking from inside a pocket.

Still, Astrid breathed back. *Still and small.*

Brother Calven let his mare stand. The horse took the opportunity to consider a knot in its rein. He turned slightly in his saddle to admire the shore. "Your harbor is honest," he said conversationally. "The fjord's breath is very clean."

"Today," Halvar said.

The priest smiled with an appreciation that might have been sincere. "Today counts. Yesterday is not a place you can live in."

Leif, who owed the priest nothing and knew it, blurted, "What do you smell that we don't?"

The priest's lashes lowered—the look a man gives when he is about to be generous with information he could hoard. "Snow that is not committed to being snow," he said. "A tide of warm under a roof. Small things. I pay attention to small things."

Astrid had to force herself not to look south.

The soldiers began their work. Two stood at the well, sorting parchment and a small intriguing machine made of brass sliders and knotted cord. Two moved to the store shed and measured salt in long, even strokes, as careful as surgeons. Two knelt by the net racks and wrote numbers no fisherman had asked to know. The officer in leather—Luth, someone said under their breath—checked latches with two fingers, as a guest might.

Brother Calven dismounted at last. He moved like a man who walks much and mostly indoors. "We will begin with questions and end with thanks." He lifted his hands to shoulder height, palms open, a gesture that looked like surrender and was not. "Has anyone seen any unusual lights over the water?"

No.

"Flocks behaving strangely? Seals out of season?"

A murmured chorus of normal.

"Steam where it ought not to be? Warmth in the ground?

Places where snow lies differently?"

Astrid felt the village hold its breath. In a place like Havngard, every person knows the shape of everyone else's silence.

Thora said briskly, "We have a smoke field. In thaw it breathes."

"And this has always been so?"

"As long as I've been old enough to complain about it," Thora said. A few people laughed—relief that had to go somewhere or it would sour.

Brother Calven smiled into the laughter. "Excellent. Then you will allow us a look. Two men only. To observe." He turned that open-palms gaze around the circle. "If there is nothing to see, we will see nothing. If there is something to see, we will advise you how to be safe."

There was the coin again. Astrid tasted the metal, thought of Kjaer's stick tapping the earth, thought of the wizard's chalk hissing softly on stone.

Luth, the officer, approached Astrid and Halvar with the nod people use when they mean to be civil and purposeful. "We will need those ledgers," he said to Halvar. "And your last inspection mark. The Cloister seal."

Halvar's mouth tightened. "Burned in a house-fire three winters ago."

"Of course," Luth said, as if that were one of the options he preferred to hear. "We'll make a note and issue a temporary grace." He looked to Astrid's staff. "You work the cliff road?"

"When it needs working," Halvar answered for her.

"Good." Luth's attention slid on. "We'll be no trouble."

They were trouble the way cold is trouble: not an event, a condition.

By midmorning, the village had been measured six different ways. The priest tasted the well water and declared it pure. The salt was weighed, blessed, and weighed again with the blessing on it. A list of births and deaths was written with a script that left neat wounds on the page. The smoke field was marked on a map with a tidy dot.

Brother Calven kept near the lane. People drifted close to him against their better judgment. He had the kind of face you wanted to impress even if you resented wanting it.

When Astrid passed within two strides, he said mildly, "You carry iron like a woman who knows the ground."

"It keeps my feet honest," she said.

"A good habit." His gaze slipped—no more than that—toward her hands. "Do you ever hear the ice?"

Astrid felt Halvar go still beside her. She made her mouth a door and chose a room with a hearth and not much furniture. "Everyone hears the ice," she said. "In thaw it refuses to be polite."

He nodded, unfazed. "Does it now." His eyes went to the fjord, pale under the noon. "Some places speak through the soles. We're all listeners if we let ourselves."

Halvar said, "We can't always afford to let ourselves."

"Ah." The priest's lips softened with professional sympathy. "Work is a jealous god."

Old Kjaer planted herself between them without preamble. "If you're going to bless anything, bless my knees."

"I have a balm," Brother Calven said, and produced from his sleeve a small corked bottle that smelled of mint and discipline. "A gift. No charge."

Kjaer eyed it like a fish eyeballs bait. "I'll take it and I'll see if it tells stories."

"Do," he said, amused. "Tell the stories back to me if they're kind."

He let Kjaer shuffle him down the lane with questions about dosage and side effects a woman who could barely read numbers should not have the vocabulary for. It was a pleasant theater. It demonstrated his gentleness to an audience he could feel arranging itself.

Under that scene, a quieter one unfolded. Two cloister-men in plain wool drifted toward the south gully with a cart that looked like a surveyor's toy. They laughed softly together; one told a joke with his hands. The cart had a brass belly, small glass windows, a funnel that would not have looked out of place on a kitchen kettle if you didn't know what metal can be made to remember.

Astrid kept her feet still. Inside her, everything sprinted.

Wizard, she thought, not sending the word, simply letting her fear shape it.

The word did not need sending. It arrived where it needed to be. A long way under stone, a man in threadbare robes lifted his head. Chalk dust made a pale crescent along his jaw where he'd rubbed a thought off with the back of his hand. He did not look toward the south rim; he looked at a small shallow dish he had set in a crease of rock. The water in it was quiet. He breathed once and it dimpled.

"Still," he said to the stone. "That's my clever girl."

Embla did not move. Dragons learn stillness from eggs and practice it well when asked by a voice that is not afraid.

The cloister-men parked their toy at the lip of the smoke field. They opened a little door in its side, removed a sheaf of copper leaves etched with tight sigils, and slid one leaf into a gap in the machine as if feeding it gossip. The brass took on a color that was not a color—what blue would be if it were colder than it could get.

Halvar turned to Astrid without turning his head. "Go to Thora's. Bring me a net-repair awl and three coils of tarred twine."

"We have both at home," she said, puzzled.

"Thora's," he repeated, and she understood. He needed her out of the line of sight that would soon be drawn across the gully.

She went. She did not hurry. Hurrying is a language men like these are fluent in.

Thora had seen the cart too. Her mouth was a thin seam. "They measure heat with that," she said, without hello. "Not the kind from hearth or hand. The kind that chooses its own work."

"How do you know?"

"I was married to a fool who wanted a winter without wood," Thora said shortly. "He studied with them a season. Came back saying words like *containment* and *just for now* and *think of the children.* He froze faster after that. The cold likes the sound of itself."

Astrid's fingers closed around the awl until the wood grip bit her palm. "If they point that at the cliff—"

"Then your father will distract them," Thora said, as if

remarking on the weather. "And Old Kjaer will ask loud questions about the proper way to bless a birthing stool. And Rurik will 'accidentally' snap a pin on the cart. And Leif will cry because he is a kind man and his baby wheezes, and the priest will make a gentleness for a coin. People cannot pull a rope the same way if you give each a different end."

Astrid looked at her, startled and grateful. "You planned this."

"No," Thora said. "We have been alive a long time and we do not enjoy being told that was a mistake."

Outside, the cart made a small purr. One of the cloister-men peered into the glass. The other shaded the pane with his hand. "There," he said softly. "Warm seam. Southward."

Astrid felt the word *seam* travel through the ground like a rumor and almost ran. She did not run. She walked back into the lane with the awl and the coils and found that Halvar had already moved.

He stood at the cart as if at a neighbor's boat, hands tucked into his belt so the fists they wanted to be could pretend to be polite. "Beautiful," he said, which is the kind of compliment men in uniforms expect of themselves.

"It is," said the technician, pleased by the appreciation. He had kind eyes you could imagine liking if they met in any other life. "Measures flux. Helps us detect leaks."

"Leaks," Halvar repeated, as if learning a new tool word. "From what?"

"From places the ground keeps too much for itself." The man scratched his nose. "You've a steam pocket there." He pointed in a way that would have been careless if Halvar were not already standing in the pointing. The finger indicated the cliff. Halvar's shoulder intercepted the line before it could extend.

"Pocket," Halvar said. "Always had it."

The other cloister-man, less kind-eyed, more in love with brass, frowned at the glass. "The seam shifts. That's not old steam."

Astrid's hearing tightened to a point. She felt the wizard's breath hold a long way under her. Felt Embla's heartbeat settle into the slow patience of a lizard on a warm stone. Felt the fjord pick up its crack-tempo and set it down again, indecisive.

Brother Calven appeared at Halvar's shoulder like fog resolves into a man. "A look," he said. "No more than that. The Cloister doesn't bind what it can bless."

Thora coughed a laugh into her shawl. Calven did not look at her.

Halvar lifted his chin. "You can look at stone from where you stand. It's very stoic. You'll like each other."

"Kindness," the priest said softly, to the air. "It's a better word than *permission*, less… legal." He turned the smile on Halvar. "Kind to let us look. For the children."

There it was again—the coin. Astrid wanted to spit it into the snow.

Rurik chose that moment to step forward with a coil of fresh tar line, grin wide as a split log. "You boys know how to splice?" he boomed. Before anyone could decline, he had thrust the line into the kinder-eyed man's hands and was demonstrating—with theatrical incompetence—the art of a long splice. "Right over left, left over right. No, your other left. Ha!"

The brass-man looked trapped between duty and curiosity. The glass-man huffed and stooped again. Thora stepped up to Brother Calven with Kjaer's bottle. "If I put this on my knees and my knees get worse, do I bring them to you for repair?" she demanded. Behind her, Leif's child —coached within an inch of decency by his mother— managed two damp coughs that sounded like failure.

Brother Calven's attention braided itself: a strand for Rurik, a strand for Thora, a strand for the baby. That left fewer for the cliff.

"Gently, then," he said to the glass-man without looking. "Only a glance. I won't sour a village over a dot on a map."

The technician turned the cart's mouth a degree south.

In the cave, the wizard pulled a thread. Not from fabric— from water. He had strung three shallow bowls along a seam; he had taught the bowls to listen. He touched the farthest with one finger. A ripple moved to the second, then to the first, so small that only a mind that loved small things would have named it a wave. The ripple climbed the rock like a shy thought and lay down over the chalk-runed wall.

On the cliff, the glass fogged as if someone had breathed on it from the inside.

"Condensation," said the kinder-eyed man, grateful for the obvious.

"Hmm," said the other, dissatisfied by mercy.

Brother Calven's head tilted. "Another time," he told the air in a voice that pretended to be a promise and was, in truth, a note to himself. "We won't be tedious guests."

He clapped his hands softly. "Enough measuring. I'd like to meet your stories." He turned to the shawl-parliament. "Who tells here?"

Kjaer bristled. "We do."

"Then tell me over a pot," he said, and for the next hour he drank thin beer and asked grandmothers about the way summer used to taste. He laughed in the right places. He remembered names he had heard once. He left each conversation with a blessing that had the correct number of syllables and a faint aftertaste of ash.

By late afternoon, the column packed its brass and cord and courtesy. Brother Calven mounted with a tidy swing and looked down the lane as if at a long table he had been invited to sit at again. "We will return tomorrow to finish our notes," he said. "To be thorough is to be kind."

No one waved. That did not trouble him. He had the face of a man who can applaud himself.

They left the way they had come: accurate, quiet, inevitable. The banners did not flap—they hung, confident of the wind's manners.

Only when the last horse's heel had stepped past the birches did Havngard exhale. Voices rose on their own and crashed into one another like thaw water trying all the rivulets at once. Rurik whooped too loudly. Leif hugged his coughing child and cried for real. Thora leaned on Astrid for a moment as if the girl's shoulder were a post she had set in this lane when she was sixteen.

"Tomorrow," Thora said.

"Tomorrow," Astrid agreed.

Dusk came blue and wary. The wizard arrived under its edge, walking with the careful speed of men who would rather not be seen and will be if they look like they regret it. He did not go to Astrid first; he went to Halvar. Some courtesies live deeper than speech.

"They have a flux cart," he said. "Clever. Cruel by

neglect, not intent."

Halvar grunted. "If they come at dawn, we move before dawn."

"Where?" Astrid asked.

"Not far," the wizard said. "Far is suspicious. Different is protective." He touched the iron staff where her hand had polished it shiny. "Can you hear the gully west of the sheep cut?"

Astrid put her palm to the staff and closed her eyes. The world pivoted. She turned her hearing like a lantern. West: the sheep cut, a narrow throat where wind learned to sing poorly; a gully beyond, shallow and littered with winter's broken fingers; a seam there too, but sleeping, and the sleep was honest. "Yes," she said. "It is quiet. It doesn't want to be important."

"Good," said the wizard. "Important gets visited. Quiet gets walked past."

"We can move her?" Halvar asked, skeptical of any sentence that began in certainty and ended in hope.

"Wrapped," the wizard said. "She'll hate it and she'll forgive us. A bracken cradle. Nets outside, so the shape is what men expect to be burdened with."

"And if they come while we carry—" Halvar began.

"Then I talk," the wizard said. "I am very boring when necessary."

Astrid almost laughed, then didn't. The night had a taste to it, metal, not from the priest—he had taken his smell with him—but from the village, panic turning its pockets out for things that felt like tools. "We'll need a noise," she said. "Something that asks for eyes."

"Rurik," Halvar said at once, and they smiled together, father and daughter, not because they took delight in using a neighbor's habits but because they knew how to place people in the pattern so it held.

They made their plan on the packed earth by the hearth, drawing lines with the awl's tip, erasing them with a finger. Not a long plan. Long plans make winter laugh.

Before first light, Astrid stood in the cave with her hands in the bracken and Embla's breath in her bones. The hatchling woke badly —dragons are not elegant when roused before they've decided to be —snapped once at the air to show her opinion, and then, hearing Astrid's voice wrap around the word *Together*, consented to be a bundle.

They bound her not like a prisoner but like a child— layers that could be loosened in a heartbeat, weight balanced so one person could take it and not stumble. Halvar shouldered the nets. The wizard took the head of the cradle. Astrid took the tail.

"Still," she murmured.

Still, Embla agreed—resentful, loving, awake.

They went out under a sky that had not chosen a color yet. Rurik, punctual and loud, began a row at the net racks about whether a bridle knot should be square or imaginary. Men drifted toward the argument because men like to, and the lane filled with enough theater to distract a god.

The trio moved along the sheep cut where the ground pretended not to notice them. At the lip of the west gully, the wizard stopped and laid his palm to the dirt. He breathed. The gully accepted what he asked of it the way a stubborn animal sometimes does: with the insult of a delay, then with a reluctant grace. They lowered Embla into a pocket the world had not admitted it had, turned her cradle, and tucked the bracken to look like nothing at all.

The hatchling's mind touched Astrid's—flint against flint, spark and ache.

Dark, she complained.

Safe, Astrid answered.

Silence, then the soft consent of a creature who trusts the rope because she trusts the hand.

They climbed out in time to see the birches take on their first vein of color. From the north path came the column again: accurate, quiet, inevitable.

Brother Calven rode in smiling. He liked being a man who kept his word.

"Good morning," he said to the world. "Let us be thorough and kind."

He lifted a hand. The flux cart turned south; the glass-men leaned in. Astrid felt the ground under the cliff make a choice: it would sleep harder than sleep; it would imitate old stone; it would pretend to be boring.

The cart hummed. The glass fogged. Runes walked a thin circle and sat down.

Brother Calven's smile did not change. In his eyes a note moved and tried to find a place to rest. It did not. He turned his mare in a small, neat circle and let her stand.

He looked from the cliff to the village and found Astrid's face as though he were checking a column of numbers and she was the one figure that didn't quite add up. Not suspicion—just an alertness wrapped in politeness, the kind a man might use when he's turning over a stone to see what lives underneath.

"Would you walk with me a moment?" Brother Calven asked, tone mild, as if all he wanted was a better view of the fjord.

Halvar's hand tightened on the iron staff until the leather wrap creaked. Astrid felt the shift in him—the way a fisherman tightens the rope when he senses something deep tug once, then wait.

But she stepped forward before he could answer for her. "A moment," she agreed.

They walked only a little way, to where the village lane bent toward the water. The wind carried the smell of salt and cold moss. Brother Calven folded his hands behind his back, the picture of easy conversation—yet something in his posture suggested he already knew what he wanted from her, and was only choosing how gently to ask.

"You keep your eyes low," he said lightly. "Most young people look up. Toward the world they want. Toward the trouble they hope will find them."

Astrid didn't take the bait. "Some of us have chores," she said.

He smiled—not mocking, but… assessing. "True. Though people with chores sometimes notice more than people with ambition."

They paused near a break in the birches. From here one could see the thawing gully beyond the fields and, if they stepped two paces farther, the faint line of steam that still rose from the earth.

Brother Calven didn't look at it directly. But he didn't need to.

He angled his head slightly, as if listening for a distant

bell.

"Tell me something, Astrid Halvarsdottir," he said quietly. "When the world shifts—when something old stirs underfoot—do you hear it before others do?"

Astrid's breath snagged. She kept her face calm, but her heart gave itself away in a single, guilty thump.

"I don't know what you mean," she said.

"Don't you?" he murmured.

He didn't press. He didn't even look at her. Instead, he watched the steam drifting in thin threads far across the field, like the earth exhaling thoughts it hadn't decided to share.

Calven's voice softened. "There are people who listen differently. People who catch the shape of things in the space before they happen. It's a rare gift. Rare… and often misunderstood."

Astrid felt heat climb her neck. "And you came here to tell me that?"

"No," he said. "I came here to see the land. To learn its wounds."
His eyes flicked to hers. "And to see who else could hear them."

A pulse touched the ground beneath her feet—not movement, not sound, just a faint recognition, like a memory brushing past her.

Astrid stiffened.
His gaze sharpened, too quickly for politeness.

So he *had* felt it.

Halvar called from behind them, voice terse. "Astrid.

Come back."

Brother Calven stepped aside gently, as if releasing her from an invisible thread. "Your father worries," he said. "Listen to him. Worry is its own kind of wisdom."

Astrid hesitated. "You're being strange."

He laughed—bright, warm, almost disarming. "I'm a monk who studies old things in a cold country. Strange is an occupational hazard."

But as she turned to go, his tone changed—becoming almost reflective.
"Astrid," he said softly. "If the ground speaks to you… don't ignore it. And don't think you're alone in hearing it."

She didn't answer. She walked back toward her father's waiting shadow, the iron staff, the safety of the ordinary. But the whole way she felt Calven's quiet certainty following her like a second set of footsteps.

When she reached Halvar's side, he searched her face.

"What did he want?" he asked.

"To talk," she said.

"That man never 'just talks.'"

Astrid gripped the staff. The birches ahead were still. The fjord was still. Even the wind seemed to have perched on a distant rock, watching.

"Father," she asked quietly, "do you think the land can… wake up?"

Halvar's jaw worked. For a long moment he didn't speak.

Then—too quickly—"No."

Which meant, of course, *yes*.

He took her elbow and guided her homeward. "Stay away from that monk," he muttered. "He listens to the wrong things."

Astrid barely heard him. The pulse beneath her feet echoed again, faint and certain, as if answering her earlier question in a voice only she could hear.

Not today, it seemed to say.
Soon.

Behind them, Brother Calven remained at the bend in the lane, hands folded, face lifted toward the birches and the steaming land beyond—listening with the stillness of someone who had been waiting a very long time for exactly this.

CHAPTER 11

The Weight of Dawn

The first true thaw of the year came quietly. Not with triumphant warmth or generous sunlight, but with a whisper in the earth — a loosening, a long-held breath released beneath frozen soil.

Astrid woke before the dim light had settled into the rafters. She knew, without thinking, that Embla was already awake.

Not magic.
Not prophecy.
Just… a pull.
A listening that lived under her ribs like a second heartbeat.

She dressed quietly so as not to wake Halvar and stepped into the cold from the longhouse, breath blooming white. The wind carried the smell of birch sap and thawing moss — the earliest hints of spring.

And beneath it, faint but unmistakable, a sound like a stone shifting against another stone.

Embla was moving.

Astrid followed the familiar path behind the houses, crossed the brittle crust of morning snow, and slipped through the birches to the lefthand descent where five days ago the earth had opened its secret mouth. The entrance to the hidden cleft looked ordinary again, disguised under the wizard's careful runes and Halvar's clever bracken-work. Only Astrid's eyes and bones knew what was truly beneath.

She knelt and placed her hand on the rock.

A warm thrum answered her.

"I'm here," she murmured. "I know. I'm coming."

The bracken parted with a soft sigh as she descended into the dim pocket that held the hatchling.

Embla was no longer small.

Five days had changed her dramatically. Though perhaps "changed" wasn't the right word — more like revealed. The tiny creature that had melted snow as she breathed now reached Astrid's knee when crouched. Embla's scales, once soft and underlit like wet opal, had begun to harden along the edges into a faint prism of golds and faint copper. Her wings — gods, her wings — had grown like buttercups after rain, unfurling and stretching with each passing hour, thin membranes shot through with veins that glowed faintly when the hatchling grew excited.

This morning, Embla's eyes caught Astrid first. Wide, amber, and ancient in a way newborn creatures should not be. When she saw Astrid, her whole body quivered with a squeaking chirp.

Astrid smiled despite herself. "There you are."

Embla trotted forward on awkward legs, nearly tripping on her own wings. Astrid dropped to her knees just in time to catch the little creature's snout as it bumped her shoulder, then slid down to her lap as though she belonged there.

Her warmth soaked through Astrid's cloak. The dragon's breath smelled faintly of flint and warm riverstone.

"You've grown again," Astrid whispered.

Embla rumbled softly, her version of agreement.

Astrid stroked the ridge beneath her jaw, feeling scales

that were firmer than yesterday. "This is going to get harder. To hide you, I mean."

A small huff.

Harder, came the wordless sentiment. But not impossible.

Astrid swallowed.

"You must stay quiet. And still. The village isn't ready."
I'm not ready, she didn't say.

Embla's tail wound loosely around her hip, a gentle warmth pressing through wool.

The hatchling pushed a small thought into her:
Warm. Light. Above.

"I know." Astrid pressed her forehead to Embla's, letting the dragon's warmth spread into her skin. "But not yet. The sky will still be there when it's safe."

Embla blinked, understanding the shape of the words if not the weight. Then she curled closer, her wings folding like pages of a book.

Astrid sat with her for some minutes, listening to the slow drip of thawwater and the faint hum of Embla's breath, until a footstep sounded faintly above.

Halvar.

He wasn't trying to sneak — but the ground carried his approach like a drumbeat.

"Astrid?" His voice came low, cautious.

She pulled herself free and climbed out of the pocket. Halvar stood at the top of the cleft, the iron staff in one hand, his face cut by both worry and tenderness.

"She's louder every morning," he said quietly.

"I know."

"You can hear her when you sleep?"

Astrid hesitated, then nodded. "It's like listening to weather from the inside."

Halvar's eyes softened with concern, not fear. "Your mother called it 'bone-hearing.' She said some people are born with a piece of the world still ringing in them. And the world rings back."

Astrid swallowed the strange ache that came then — of wanting to ask a thousand questions about her mother, and knowing Halvar gave only what he could bear.

"She's growing fast," he said. "Faster than the stories say."

"There were stories?" Astrid looked up sharply.

Halvar exhaled through his nose. "Old ones. Rare ones. A hatchling's first week is meant to be a sleepy thing. But Embla…" He glanced at the bracken that shifted faintly with the dragon's movement. "She's hungry for the world."

Astrid drew in a breath. "We can keep her hidden. For now."

Halvar didn't argue, but neither did he agree.

Instead, he motioned toward the village. "Come eat something. You'll think clearer."

The longhouse smelled of seal fat and old smoke. Halvar ladled broth from the pot over the hearth, and Astrid sat with her bowl while steam curled over her face and thawed the last of the morning chill from her fingers.

Halvar ate in silence for several minutes before he spoke.

"I know you think you can protect her alone," he said at last, stirring his spoon slowly to avoid meeting her eyes.

Astrid stiffened. "I know I can."

"You're one girl," he said simply.

"She's one hatchling."

Halvar set his bowl down, leveling her with a steady look. "A hatchling who could draw danger from a hundred leagues away without meaning to."

Astrid's heart thudded. "She's getting better at staying quiet. I'm teaching her."

"You shouldn't have to teach her alone."

Astrid frowned. "Then who—"

Halvar motioned toward the cliffs. "There are people who know more of dragons than we do."

Astrid stiffened. "You mean the wizard."

Halvar did not deny it.

"He said he'd help," Astrid admitted.

"And he has. But Astrid…" Halvar rubbed a thumb along the rim of his bowl. "He may not always be enough."

Before she could answer, a faint hum pressed into the air like a finger dragged along glass.

Astrid's head lifted sharply.

Embla.

Not fear.
Not pain.

Restless.

Like a child pacing in darkness.

Astrid pushed her bowl aside. "I need to—"

Halvar raised a hand gently. "Go."

Astrid hesitated only long enough to see gratitude flicker through his eyes — not gratitude to be rid of her, but gratitude that she wasn't angry with him.

Then she ran.

Embla met her halfway between the bracken and the shadow of the birches — not physically, but in sensation. A low resonant ache of impatience thrummed through the ground. Astrid hurried down and found the hatchling shifting her weight from claw to claw, wings trembling with wants too big for her small body.

"Easy," Astrid murmured, dropping into the hollow.

Embla's wings fanned briefly, catching the low light in a ripple of copper-gold.

Then the dragon leaned forward and pressed her forehead to Astrid's chest.

Out, came the sensation.

Astrid pulled in a breath. "You can't. Not yet."

Embla huffed, pushing harder.

Astrid steadied her gently by the jaw, noticing not for the first time how warm Embla had become. Nearly hot to the touch, as if a tiny furnace lived under her scales.

"We'll go above for a moment," Astrid said softly. "Just to feel the air."

The hatchling brightened instantly.

Astrid led her out — carefully, quietly, casting frequent

glances toward the village below. Embla's claws clicked softly on the stone, her breath fogging gently in the cool morning.

They stepped behind the farthest birch, where the ridge curved like a cupped hand away from the village.

"Here," Astrid whispered. "Just for a little while."

Embla lifted her head and inhaled deeply. The breeze rippled her wings; her tail swayed with delight.

Then she attempted her first true stretch of wings outside the cave.

The movement was clumsy, unbalanced — but beautiful. A soft glow pulsed along the wing's inner veinwork like light traveling through amber.

Astrid watched, breath held.

And with a tiny hop—

Embla lifted from the ground.

Only for the space of two heartbeats.

But when she landed, her eyes were bright with pride.

"You'll fly," Astrid whispered, her voice breaking. "You truly will."

Embla chirped, tail winding around Astrid's calf.

But suddenly she stiffened.

Her wings drew tight.
Her head lifted, nostrils flaring.
Her body went still.

Astrid froze too.

Embla stared toward the ridge beyond the birches.

A presence moved there.

Quiet.
Measured.
Observing.

A figure watching them from far enough to be shadow, yet close enough to know this was not a goat or gull.

Astrid's breath caught.

"Back," she whispered, guiding Embla toward the hollow with calm she did not feel.

Embla obeyed — reluctant, confused — but she obeyed.

Astrid hid her quickly and covered the entrance just as the figure stepped into clearer view.

Halvar.

She exhaled hard in relief—until she saw his face.

His eyes were not angry.
Not frightened.
But they held a weight she had not yet seen.

"What did you see?" he asked quietly.

Astrid swallowed.

"Nothing," she said.

He waited.

Astrid's throat tightened. "She wanted to feel the wind."

Halvar closed his eyes, pressing fingers to the bridge of his nose.

"Astrid…"

"She didn't go far," Astrid rushed. "Just a stretch. A taste of the air. No one saw."

"No one?" Halvar asked gently.

Astrid hesitated.

The wizard.
He had been somewhere. Watching. Feeling.

Halvar studied her silence and breathed a weary sigh.

"You have to be more careful," he said. "The snow is thinning. Tracks will hold shape. Smoke rises straighter in warm air. Sound travels differently in thaw."

Astrid's eyes burned.

"I know."

"Do you?" Halvar asked—not accusing, only tired. "You love her. I see that. But loving her means protecting her from more than cold and hunger. It means protecting her from the world. And protecting the world from her."

Astrid turned away, blinking fast.

"I won't let anything happen to her."

Halvar stepped closer and rested a hand on her shoulder.

"And I won't let anything happen to you."

Astrid's breath trembled.

Under the earth, Embla shifted again — just a tiny movement, as though adjusting her weight.

Astrid felt it like a heartbeat in her bones.

She wasn't sure if she or Embla took the next breath first.

Chapter 12

Games the Sky Remembers

The thaw didn't ask permission. It simply arrived—softening the edges of ruts, loosening ice's grip on the shore stones, turning the hard-packed paths of Havngard into long glistening stripes. The village smelled of wet rope and sap and seal fat and something else Astrid could never name, a scent that came only when the land gave back what winter had borrowed.

Astrid woke with a certainty already humming through her hands.

Today we play.

Not a voice. Not magic. Just the knowing that lived between her ribs now, the one that answered whenever Embla's small body shifted or wanted or brightened. She dressed quickly, knotted her hair, and slid the latch with the quiet she'd learned from nights like this.

Halvar's breath moved evenly under the furs. He would not stop her; he rarely did. The iron staff stood upright by the door as always, the way a guardian stands when it cannot change a mind but will walk beside it anyway.

Outside, dawn had not yet chosen a color. The fjord lay between blue and iron; the mountains wore a paler shadow of themselves. Astrid cut across the yard, boots finding the shallow places, and followed the narrow trail to the birches. Steam lifted in thin skeins from the low field, beading on her lashes as she ducked branches.

The entrance to Embla's hollow looked like a fox den badly forgotten. The bracken Halvar had woven was nothing special to look at, which was precisely the point. Astrid peeled it back and slid down the narrow stone throat.

Warmth met her. Not spring-warm; *Embla*-warm.

The hatchling chirruped in delight and came at her in a tumble of knees and wing-edges, mouth open as if laughter had a shape. She'd grown again—Astrid felt it in the heft against her shins, saw it in the way the wing membranes carried themselves with a touch less clumsiness. Scales along Embla's jawline had firmed into tiny plates, each catching the soft cave-light with a whisper of copper.

"You're very proud of yourself," Astrid said, trying to sound stern and failing, because Embla had already discovered a game she loved: nudging Astrid backward until she was sitting, then attempting to curl onto her lap like a cat who had misjudged her own size.

"You won't fit much longer," Astrid laughed, bracing the warm weight. "That's not a complaint."

Embla's eyes—clear amber with a darker ring near the pupil—blinked slowly as if to say: *It is not my fault if laps were made too small.*

They began with the old game. Astrid would trace slow circles in the air; Embla would follow the shape with her nose, then her eyes, then—with intense concentration—by moving her whole head without moving her feet. Patience was difficult for a creature built for the future tense, but Embla wanted to please, and so she tried. When Astrid's finger drew a loop-the-loop, Embla echoed it with a small whirl of her neck and shivered with pride afterward as if she had flown.

"Very good," Astrid whispered, and felt the approval land in Embla like an apple dropped into a bucket—*thump, ripple, glow.*

They played a new game next, one the wizard had taught them

only yesterday evening from the shadow he preferred. He had not given Astrid his name and did not seem in a hurry to wear one. He was simply *there* when needed, like a warm stone to sit on when your knees went weak, like the last steadying note of a chant that keeps a pattern from fraying. He spoke little aloud. Astrid heard him more easily the way she heard the river under ice: a low thought in the bones.

Quiet your song. Not gone—quiet. Dragons sing without meaning to. The land listens. Today, we practice silence in motion.

Silence in motion proved to be hard for both of them. Embla quivered when she was happy and hummed when she was calm and let off a dozen tiny sparks of thought whenever Astrid laughed. But the wizard had shown Astrid how to cradle those sparks, how to fold feeling back toward its source.

"Like banking a hearth," he had said, and Astrid had watched his weathered hands mime the motion: push coals inward, tuck ash around them, let heat stay heat without letting it leap.

Now she tried.

"Ready," she told Embla softly. "We can play like the river—no splashing."

Embla didn't understand the words but felt their shape. The hatchling laid herself low, chin to forefeet, wings tucked so neatly it hurt Astrid with love. The little body vibrated with trying-not-to.

"Inhale," Astrid whispered, breathing with her. "Exhale."

They moved. Astrid crept to the hollow mouth and Embla padded behind, each step a careful placing of weight and will. The world narrowed to the sound of thawwater counting itself along stone, the wet thread of air through

Astrid's nose, the tiny whisper of membrane against membrane whenever Embla's wing-edge brushed her own side. Together they eased into the birch shade and paused.

No splash in the mind. No bright flare.

Only the warm presence of a creature who trusted the rope because she trusted the hand.

The lesson held for three heartbeats. On the fourth, a raven croaked from the ridge and Embla's joy leapt like a fish.

Astrid laughed helplessly and caught the spill with both hands the way the wizard had taught her—*shhh, shhh, no harm, back you go*—and the moment steadied.

"Good," came the wizard's thought from someplace that felt like the left side of air. "She is learning. So are you."

Astrid did not turn. She had learned not to. If she respected the wizard's distances, he stayed.

Can we try the fjord? she asked without sound.

Silence on the surface. Beneath it, consent.

They made for the water.

The fjord's skin had loosened night after night, and now the edge lay bright and messy—cats-ice breaking to slush, clear sheets shoving up against rock like discarded glass. Astrid led Embla to a narrow inlet where the cliffs cupped the water and threw back the sound of even small things. A boulder sat like a seal a few strides from shore; beyond that, the world went immediately deep.

"Here," Astrid said. "Careful."

Embla sniffed the line where ice met water and sneezed in dignified offense. The sneeze produced a pearl of heat the size of a rosehip—light without flame—that rolled off her lip, touched the water, and sighed out with a faint hiss. Embla looked both startled and pleased. Astrid clapped once, softly.

"We shall *not* do that near nets," she said, and Embla's tail flicked sheepishly.

They invented a game on the spot. Astrid found a strip of driftwood as long as her forearm and set it on the water where the current came in lazy and small. Embla watched with the total belief of a child waiting for a miracle. Astrid gave the plank the gentlest push and the current took it, slipping it along the little arc of the inlet before nudging it back ashore. Embla pounced the last handspan like a fox taking a mouse under snow—carefully, proudly—then looked up as if expecting applause.

Astrid bowed extravagantly. "The bravest hunter of wood in all the north."

They played until Embla figured out how to nose the plank herself without tipping it, which made her sit even taller and hum even more loudly. When Astrid laughed, Embla hummed louder, and when Embla hummed louder, Astrid looked over her shoulder with a sharpness that spoiled her smile.

"Quiet," she murmured, and smoothed Embla's head until the hum softened back to a purr.

They rested on the boulder afterward, Astrid's boots braced and Embla's foreclaws kneading the rough top with the same contented absentmindedness goats used on salt licks. Astrid could feel the fjord's voice through the stone— long breaths alternating with small ones, old water making new paths under skin. She let it speak, and she listened.

A thought brushed her cheek.

Today, be wary of the high trail, the wizard sent. *Three men went to check the lines beyond the narrows. They will not come this far if the weather turns. But if the weather holds, they might.*

We'll keep to the hollow, Astrid answered. *She needed air.*

And you needed joy, he said without censure, and withdrew again until he was only a weight at the edge of what could be heard.

Astrid touched Embla's shoulder. "Time."

The hatchling made a small sound of polite complaint, exactly the tone of a child told to leave the last honey cake on the table. Still, she followed readily—down from the stone, back over the salt-slick rock, up past the field where steam came like thin flags. Her claws left neat crescents in the softening dirt; Astrid brushed them with a fir branch on the return without thinking, the way she had brushed them on every path this week. Little habits. The work love makes.

Back in the hollow, Embla curled herself into a perfect coil, tail to nose. Astrid tucked bracken around the outside curve, more for ritual than secrecy, and leaned there a moment, palm on the warmest part.

Sleep, she sent, not as a command but as a blessing.

A tiny, wordless assent.

She would have stayed, but life had a list and it did not shorten itself. Thaw took roofs and gave them to gravity; nets wanted mending; wood wanted splitting before it softened to rot. Astrid returned to the longhouse and found Halvar already at the bench with his awl, re-lacing a boot whose sole had decided it belonged to someone else.

He looked up, his mouth shaping the ghost of a smile. "You were gone longer."

"She wanted the water."

He nodded, as if he had always known that answer would come. "Keep to the southern side if you can. Nets on the north are set wider—more eyes."

"I know."

They worked side by side for the better part of an hour. Halvar's silences were never empty; they carried weather, memory, the weight of things that didn't need repeating. From time to time he winced and flexed his fingers. Astrid reached for the awl.

"Let me finish."

He hesitated, pride and relief striking hands like men who meant to wrestle and wound up embracing. He gave her the boot. She set the stitch straight. It was good work, satisfying the way a rope feels when it is just tight enough and no more.

When the stew had warmed and the light had climbed a thumb-width up the wall, Sigrid popped her head through the door with the wind still braiding her hair. "Astrid! If you have two hands you don't love, the kelp rack ate another peg."

"I have exactly two," Astrid called, setting the awl aside. To Halvar: "I'll be back before kitchen shadows reach the post."

He grunted his blessing.

The day held steady until it didn't.

Astrid was halfway home from Sigrid's rack when the fjord made a new noise. Not the slow breath of meltwater or the long yawn of ice letting go, but a short, clean *tock* from the high trail—the sound of a boot heel finding stone. Not village—no one walked with that careful weight here unless they didn't know where the loose rock waited.

Astrid's heart learned a new step on the spot.

She didn't run. She didn't look toward the birches. She did exactly what a girl with nothing to hide would do: bent, lifted a skeltered length of rope from the mud, and shook it as if her whole day were no more complicated than getting rot out of the twist.

The figure came into view where the path narrowed above the gully. A man a little too tidy for Havngard, with travel on him but not the right kind. His cloak had been well-mended by someone who had never mended at sea; his boots had not learned to cringe at fish scales. His hair lay flat under a cap that had seen many chapels and very few storms. He walked like a person who trusted roads.

Astrid recognized him before he spoke.

Brother Calven.
Back again.
Too soon.

He smiled when he saw her, and the smile asked to be liked—but beneath it lingered the faint crease of a man who had come looking for something and disliked not finding it.

"Good day, Astrid," he said, as if they were familiar, as if they had shared warm bread and old stories. His voice carried the same soft authority she remembered—gentle, almost apologetic, and wholly out of place on a muddy path above a northern fjord.

"Brother Calven," she answered, shifting the rope to her other hand. "You've returned early."

"The headland roads were kinder than I expected," he

replied. "Or perhaps the wind favored me." His eyes drifted —calmly but deliberately—to the line of birches behind her.

Astrid's stomach tightened.

Calven's gaze returned to her face, mild as milk, unhurried. "Your village is lively this season," he said conversationally. "People moving about. The thaw stirring everything awake." Then, with a tone too light to be casual: "Have you heard… unusual sounds in the hills these past nights?"

Astrid kept her expression flat, practical, uninterested— Halvar's expression, borrowed like a shield. "Ice cracks. Water moves. Storms complain. Sounds carry farther this time of year."

"Of course." His smile warmed, but the warmth didn't touch the eyes. It rarely did. "Last time I passed through, I thought I heard—" He paused, as if taste-testing the right word. "—a resonance. Something below the frost. But perhaps I let the wind fool me."

Astrid said nothing.

Calven nodded, thoughtful. "Your father is well?"

"As always."

"That is good." His hands folded behind him—a scholar's posture, not a traveler's. "I may ask him about the springs near the smoke field. I was told there are… shifts there. Curious ones."

The rope in Astrid's hand seemed to shrink, as if trying to disappear.

Calven watched her a moment longer, his expression pleasant, unburdened, wrapped in harmlessness like a winter wolf wrapped in sheepskin.

"If you ever feel uneasy," he said gently, "or hear things the others don't… you may come to me. Listening is part of my calling."

Astrid forced her shoulders to settle. "Thank you for the reminder. Good day, Brother."

His smile deepened—kind, friendly, and so wrong it left a cold behind it.

"Good day," he echoed, and moved on with that same steady tread of someone who knew exactly where he was going, and why.

Astrid stood very still until the rock swallowed him.

Her mouth had gone dry.

He did not see, she told herself. He did not ask the wrong thing. He did not smell smoke.

But she felt the ground's attention change in some small way—as if a new weight had been added, not enough to tip the balance, just enough to make a scale know it was being used.

She went home, set the rope down, and told Halvar everything she could remember without using the word fear.

He listened, carving nothing from the wood in his hands while he did. When she finished he set the knife down.

"If he is what he says," Halvar said—softly, as if speaking too loudly would give the sentence to the walls —"he will ask the old questions in the old way. If he is not, he will already know the answers he wants."

"What do we do?"

"We be villagers," Halvar said. "We fix pegs. We stir stews. We complain about prices. We do not go to the high trail unless we have a bucket in our hands to make it worth his notice."

"And Embla?"

"The hollow for two days," Halvar said, and the words cost him. "No air. No inlet. If she must be warm, we warm her with hands. If she must be happy, we make her glad with our foolishness. But she does not sing to the sky."

Astrid nodded because her throat had turned stubborn.

Night took its time arriving, as it does when someone wants it quickly. Astrid carried stew to Sigrid's mother and patched a sleeve and pretended not to hear the same raven make the same croak twice from the same birch. At the last good light, she slipped away to the hollow with a blanket under her arm.

Embla greeted her with furious dignity: a small dragon convinced the world had forgotten its manners.

"I know," Astrid said, and the apology came from someplace low. "Two days. I'm sorry."

Embla pushed her nose hard into Astrid's chest and did not move, as if she could hold her own patience in place by bracing against something that loved her. Astrid sat and wrapped the blanket around both of them, not because either needed it, but because the act itself made the cave feel smaller and kinder.

They did not play the quiet game. They invented a different one that did not ask Embla to be less than she was. Astrid put her palm on the hatchling's heart—just there, where the beat could be felt without searching—and began to breathe with it. In on two. Out on three. In on two. Out on three. Embla matched her within a handful of breaths. After that, the warmth changed from a thing pressing outward into a thing filling the exact shape of their two bodies together.

"Tell her a story," came the wizard's thought from the mouth of the world.

Astrid didn't ask if he meant Embla or the land. She began, quietly, with the only stories that felt clean: the ones about boats and rope and how certain knots could be learned by hands before minds, the ones about Halvar as a boy who fell through a roof and laughed about it while someone stitched his knee. Embla fell asleep halfway through the part where the old netmender swatted Halvar with a birch switch for stealing a float and then fed him dumplings while calling him a thief.

When the little body went slack and her breath found the middle of the world, Astrid let herself lean back and close her eyes.

Something small ticked at the edge of hearing. Not danger. Not yet. More like the land counting. A pebble shifting because it had learned a new comfortable. The fjord organizing its own thoughts about spring. Or perhaps the wizard keeping watch while pretending not to.

Astrid woke once to Embla dreaming. The dragon's feet made soft running motions in her sleep; a pale thread of glow moved along the membrane of her right wing and winked out. Astrid cupped the wing with both hands the way you might cup a moth you planned to set free.

"Hush," she whispered. "I'm here."

Morning came without ceremony. The air in the hollow smelled faintly of copper and stone and a sweetness Astrid had begun to think of as Embla's breath on linen. She stretched, joints clicking, and felt the weight of the world arranging itself for another day.

She climbed to the birches for a look she promised herself she would not take, and saw him—Brother Calven—on the far path beyond the smoke field, speaking with two men from the village near the line where sled tracks ended. He stood as if he belonged in conversation anywhere. His hands moved with the clean economy of a person trained to lift chalice and book. He pointed once toward the narrows, as if the direction mattered.

When he turned, he looked where the birches grew thickest.

Astrid stood as still as a fence post.

He smiled—friendly, harmless—and lifted a hand in greeting, a wave any traveler might give to any girl in any village.

Astrid did not wave back.

The ravens were silent. The fjord inhaled and held.

She withdrew without breaking a twig and returned to the hollow.

Two days, Halvar had said.

Astrid tucked the bracken closer and set her back against the rock.

"New game," she told Embla when the hatchling stirred. "It's called stay."

Embla cheeped in polite despair and pressed her nose once more into Astrid's sternum like a key finding the right lock.

Astrid's hand rose of its own accord and found the rhythm that calmed them both.

Outside, meltwater stitched a path through old snow,

needle going and coming, needle going and coming, the seam growing flatter where it needed to hold.

They would hold.

For now.

CHAPTER 13

The Crack in the Quiet

The thaw deepened, not in great sweeping gestures but in small rebellions: the drip from the eaves that refused to stop, the way snow pulled apart like bread soaked too long, the thin gray lace of fog that rose from places where, last week, even breath had frozen. Astrid moved through the village with the careful efficiency of someone performing ordinary tasks while listening for a sound no one else could hear.
Not the fjord shifting.
Not the ravens gossiping.
Not the wind curling around the cliff.
Embla.
Always Embla.

The hatchling had grown. Not wildly — but enough that Astrid's arms noticed when she carried her, enough that the bracken hollow no longer felt like an extra pocket the world forgot, but like a place shrinking in its own skin. Embla had begun stretching her wings in her sleep, little spasms of membrane and bone that flickered with threads of red-gold light. She sneezed sparks when startled. When she dreamed deeply, her breath skimmed the surface of the stone and left it warm.

"Too bright," Halvar had muttered two nights ago when he checked the hollow with her. "Spring light gets into everything. Even secrets."

Astrid kept checking the birches every time she passed. Every time, she expected to see Brother Calven where the path bent — his cloak too neat, his boots too clean, his mild blue eyes pretending not to measure.

And though she did not always see him, she always felt

the change in the air when he was near. A shift like a hand brushing the side of a tent, curious and patient.

Astrid swung a basket of fish scraps toward the midden heap behind the sheds. Dogs barked in the distance, chasing each other through the first soft patches of ground. Children shouted where they played "ice-fox" across the thinning crust on the lower slope.

And then—
A pause.
Not in the world. In her.
The moment before a ripple reaches the shore.

Astrid turned.

Calven stood at the well, speaking with Nils the netmaker and old Ragna. He smiled, gestured lightly toward the fjord as if asking about tides. Nothing alarming. Nothing unusual.

Except he wasn't asking about tides.

Astrid kept moving. She did not linger. She turned the corner toward the goat pen, but her hearing clung to the fringes of their conversation like a hand refusing to let go.

"…unusual warmth, even for this early thaw…"
"…just the earth remembering its springs…"
"…a hum, perhaps? No? I may have mistaken it…"
"…tracks? Something small?"

Astrid gripped the fence rail.

Brother Calven was widening his circle.
Yesterday, he asked her.
Today, he asked the elders.
Tomorrow… he would choose someone who gossiped too easily.

"Astrid."

She flinched.

Ragna had come up beside her, leaning on her stick. "You dropped the last fish scrap. There." She pointed to the ground with her toe.

Astrid blinked and forced her hands to unclench. "Thank you, Ragna."

"You've been looking over your shoulder like a goat who hears wolves," the old woman said, her voice thin but sharp. "Storm coming?"

"Maybe," Astrid answered.

Ragna nodded once, as if storms were honest neighbors. "Then take care."

Astrid did.
She hurried toward the birches.

The Hollow Grows Too Small

Embla greeted her the way she always did lately: with a chirrup that was half hunger, half delight, and entirely too loud.

Astrid ducked into the hollow and knelt quickly, hand pressed gently to the dragon's snout. "Shh—"

But Embla nudged her chest hard and made a sound like a kettle beginning to boil.

"You're getting bigger," Astrid murmured. "Bigger and louder."

Embla huffed, as if proud.

"No, that's not praise."

Astrid checked the hollow. The bracken was dry. The stone warm—too warm. Embla had begun to heat the place without meaning to. Her scales shimmered faintly even in shadow, copper brightening into gold.

Astrid fed her a scrap of dried herring. Embla swallowed it whole and butted her forehead into Astrid's shoulder, tracing the shape of her collarbone with the tip of her nose as if counting bones.

Then came the thought.
Not words. Not pictures.
A feeling sent upward like steam from a spring.
Want sky.

Astrid's heart stung.

"Not now," she whispered. "Not for a while. You must stay hidden a little longer."

Embla pressed harder.
A small glow rippled across her wings.
The air warmed.

Astrid put her forehead against Embla's. "Please."

The warmth dimmed.

Embla curled into her chest with a small, wounded sound, as though she understood the truth behind the plea:
If Brother Calven sees you, if he even suspects you are real… it will not be a hunt. It will be a purge.

The wizard's voice stirred up from the depths like a breath through stone.
She is outgrowing safety. You will need a new hollow soon. One with rock that remembers heat. One the priest's eyes do not know.

Astrid clenched her jaw. "I know."

The Wizard Speaks

"Tonight," his voice murmured, "move her. After third bell. Take only what warms. Leave nothing a man could read.”

“Where?” Astrid asked aloud without meaning to.

A drop of meltwater slid down the stone and answered nothing.

Then—
North. Toward the ridge. The old storm-well. It slept even before winter had a name.

Astrid swallowed.

The storm-well was deeper. Colder. Closer to the cliffside paths Calven walked.

She would have to move Embla along the birch-shadow and cliff tracks — **above** the lanes where lanterns wandered. Past Calven if he chose the wrong moment to look up.

Her pulse quickened.

I will guide you, whispered the wizard. *Fear shapes you, but it does not own you.*

Astrid touched Embla's neck, tracing the warm scales. “Tonight,” she murmured. “We'll find someplace better.”

The Day Tightens

Halvar returned early from checking nets.

He set down his sack of cord and narrowed his eyes the same way he did when watching a storm build from three directions at once.

“You're stiff as a mast in crosswind,” he said.

Astrid hesitated. “Calven's been asking questions.”

“Who?”

“Nils. Ragna. Two men from the headland.”

Halvar swore softly in old Norse, the kind only used for dangerous weather and dangerous men.

"He'll widen his net," Halvar said. "Priests always do. They call it listening."

"He looked toward the birches again."

Halvar's hand tightened on the sack. "Then we move her."

"I know."

He studied her face. "Can you carry her still?"

Astrid nodded. "Barely."

"Then tonight," Halvar said. "After supper. I'll walk the long loop below with the lantern where he can see me. **You keep to the birch line and the cliff path.**"

Astrid's stomach knotted. "If he sees me—"

"He won't," Halvar said simply. "He'll see me. I'll make sure of it."

That was the thing about Halvar:
He didn't talk loudly about love.
He didn't need to.

Embla's Hunger

By dusk, Embla was restless.
Her tail flicked.
Her breath steamed in little amber puffs.
When Astrid touched her wing, the membrane shivered.

"You must be quiet," Astrid said, tightening the cloak she'd prepared to wrap Embla in.

Embla made a small grumbling chirp.

Astrid hugged her. "I know. I wish we could run through

the fjord right now. I wish I could let you climb the birches and glide. But not yet."

Embla pressed her head under Astrid's chin.
She always did that when she sensed Astrid lying.

"I'm not lying," Astrid whispered. "Just… promising something I don't know how to give you yet."

The wizard whispered through the stone:
She grieves the sky. But she chooses you over it. That is rare. Do not waste it.

Astrid closed her eyes.

The Move Begins

The third bell drifted across the fjord in three thin strokes.

Down in the lanes, Halvar stepped out with his lantern, making a show of checking shutter hinges and talking to a neighbor about wind. Anyone watching would see a man worrying about storms, as he always did.

Up at the birch line, Astrid wrapped Embla in the thick gray cloak. Not a perfect disguise. But enough. Embla tucked her snout against Astrid's chest without argument, the way she did when frightened.

Astrid lifted her carefully.
Heavier, yes.
But still hers.

She waited for Halvar's small signal — the lantern raised and lowered once at the lane's end — and then **moved from shadow to shadow along the birches,** keeping above the houses rather than between them, feet choosing the narrow deer-track that paralleled the cliff.

Embla stirred once.
Astrid hushed her with a soft hum.

Then—
A sound.

Bootsteps.
Measured.
Deliberate.
On the ridge path below.

Calven.

Astrid flattened behind an ice-scabbed boulder, breath caught in her throat. Embla went still in her arms, recognizing the shift of Astrid's pulse.

Calven paused where the upper track split, lantern faint. Too faint to pick her from the rock…
…but bright enough to catch a silhouette if she crossed open ground.

Astrid pulled the cloak tighter around Embla's head. She pressed her shoulder to the cold stone.

Calven stood a long moment, looking out across the slope toward the birches.
Toward the hollow.
Toward what was no longer there.

His expression was mild.
Almost bored.
But she saw something else under it: **calculation.**

He stepped forward.

Astrid held her breath until her ribs begged.

He walked on along the lower shelf of trail, the lantern dipping, his path **below** her hiding place by no more than ten strides.

Embla trembled.
Astrid tightened her hold.

Then Calven stopped.
Turned his head.
Listened.

Astrid could feel Embla's heartbeat beating through her palms like small fists.

Finally—
Calven moved on.

Astrid's knees nearly buckled in relief.
She waited a full minute before moving again.

The Storm-Well

The path narrowed as she climbed toward the ridge. Snow crunched beneath her boots in small, traitorous sounds. Twice she stopped, certain she heard Calven behind her.

But it was only the fjord settling.
Only the night breathing.

At last, she reached the storm-well.

It was not truly a well — more a round, scooped-out hollow of basalt and old snow, sheltered by two leaning boulders shaped like jaws.

Embla raised her head inside the cloak and chirped softly.

"I know," Astrid whispered. "It feels better here."

She knelt and unwrapped the cloak.

Embla crawled out, sniffing the stone. A faint glimmer of heat pooled at her feet, warming the frost. She made a small delighted rumble.

"This will be home for a little while," Astrid said. "Just until he stops looking."

Embla pressed her head into Astrid's chest again. Not fear this time.
Trust.

A warmth spread through Astrid's ribs.

"You really do choose me," she whispered.

The wizard's voice rose gently:
She chose you the day your name shook the steam. Remember that when winter sharpens its teeth.

Astrid stroked Embla's back. "Rest. I'll bring food soon."

Embla huddled into the curve of the stone, wings tucked tight, tail curled like a question mark against her side.

Astrid stayed until Embla slept.
Then she rose.
Started back along the birch track.

Stopped halfway.

The shelf below was not empty.
A lantern moved — Calven — searching the dark seam where her route had crossed.

Astrid pressed herself against the rock.

Calven paused at a patch of disturbed snow and bent to inspect it. His breath fogged faintly. His hand brushed the surface.

Astrid's heart seized.

But then—
The wizard's voice tremored through the stone:
Step back. Slowly. The earth will cover you.

The snow settled into her prints, softening the edges, easing them until they looked like nothing more than melt.

Calven straightened.
Looked up the slope.
Directly where she stood.

Astrid did not breathe.

Calven's lantern flickered.

Then he turned away.

He walked back toward the village, posture unhurried, expression unreadable.

Astrid didn't move for a long time.
Finally, she exhaled.
And the night exhaled with her.

CHAPTER 14

The Three Doors

Morning found Astrid with a fisherman's tasks and a smuggler's nerves.

She worked as she always had—coiling line, scraping scales from a board, turning herring with numb fingers—but every sound had a second meaning now. A lad shouting for a lost mitt might be a warning. A raven's double croak might be the wizard asking her to listen. Even Halvar's cough had a code in it today: *careful, careful, careful.*

Embla slept through the first light in the storm-well, heat gathered under her like a hand conserving a coal. The new hollow held warmth the way old stone does when it remembers fire. Astrid had chosen the place for that, and for the way wind knotted and lost its breath in the cleft—no smoke to carry, no steam to rise and draw an eye.

But safety was a practice, not a place.

By mid-morning, Calven stood in the lane with three men —a friendly cough of conversation that made the day look ordinary. He had a knack for that: asking questions as if he were lending a cup of flour.

"Has anyone heard the ground hum above the birch line?" he asked Nils, as if asking about the weather.

Nils shrugged, rope in his fist. "Ground hums every thaw. Your monastery must be quiet if you think the earth is supposed to stay still."

Calven laughed, easy. "We pray for stillness," he said. "The world seldom agrees."

His eyes slid—not sharply, not hunting, just… taking stock. They passed over Astrid the way a breeze passes over a field and still every blade of grass feels counted.

She took her basket and left the lane before the breeze could become a draft.

The wizard's lesson

Make a den with three doors, the wizard said that night, voice rising from the stone like warmth.

Astrid crouched in the storm-well, Embla drowsing with her chin on Astrid's knee. "Three?"

One to use. One to make a man think you used. One to bury.

She thought of Halvar's tricks with nets—how a clever fisherman gave a smart fish two wrong ways out and kept the right one for himself. "Show me."

The earth showed her the way hands show rope: by giving her things to do. With her knife she pried loose a slate of rock along the well's rim and leaned it to shape a false break in the basalt. She scattered old, frozen lichen she'd scraped from the cliff over trampled snow to make it look untrampled. She picked a path for feet that left the faintest story and made sure that story ended in drift the wind would mend.

The third door was no door at all. A heap of windblown needles, a seam of shadow, a shelf just wide enough for a girl and a hatchling if you believed in smallness hard enough. Astrid lay in it with Embla, counted her heartbeats to the rhythm of the young dragon's breath, and told herself she could be a needle too.

Embla exhaled, a pleased whuff—warm sugar and copper. Astrid felt it through the wool at her throat.

"You like this," she whispered. "Secret air."

Embla's mind brushed hers with that now-familiar texture: not

words, not pictures—*preference.*
You and warm and hush.

"Me, warm, hush," Astrid agreed, and felt how the answer settled the hatchling. Some days, love was grammar you learned one conjugation at a time.

Practice in the fog

On the third morning after the move, the fjord gave back a fog like milk spilled from a tall cup. Havngard blurred to smudges: boat ribs, a woodpile, a man who might be Halvar or a tree. The air tasted of wet wool and iron. A perfect curtain.

Astrid brought Embla down the birch-shadow only as far as the first boulder above the ice. There, in a pocket where wind forgot to look, she let the cloak fall and set both hands against the hatchling's chest.

"Breath game," she said softly. "Two in. Three out. Slow."

Embla blinked, head cocking. Her nostrils flared. *Imitate.* She followed.

"In… two," Astrid murmured. "Out… three."

They matched. After a dozen breaths the little quiver that always lived along Embla's ribs quieted. The glow that sometimes chased itself across her wing webbing softened to a pulse the fog could drink.

"Good," Astrid said. "Now wings."

Embla unfolded them with the solemnity of a queen putting on her shawl. The membrane was silk and lamp-light, smoke's cousin stretched thin. Astrid half-spread them with her hands and then gathered them again, small push, smaller pull, teaching muscles their own version of whispering.

"Again."

They did it until Embla's breaths came quick and her eyes drooped, and Astrid learned where "enough" lived in a creature who did not know the word yet.

A lump rose in her throat that had nothing to do with fear. It tasted like pride salted with worry.

"I will get this right," she told the fog, because the fog would not repeat it to anyone.

Somewhere beyond, a gull called. Closer by, a lantern clinked against a man's thigh. Astrid drew the cloak up and tucked Embla close.

They melted back into birch-shadow.

Halvar's gift

That afternoon Halvar brought home a scrap of old sailcloth patched with beeswax and ash.

"It was good canvas once," he said, spreading it on the bench. "Watertight enough to wrap a child. Or a secret."

Astrid ran her fingers over the rough weave, felt the wax under her nails. "Smells like old voyages."

"Good," Halvar said. "Memories confuse dogs. And priests who think like dogs."

She looked up at him. "You think he's that close?"

"I think he knows enough to pretend he knows less," Halvar said. "And I think he's collecting things that look like proof."

He did not say the rest. He did not need to. Proof for whom.

Halvar cut the canvas into a long sling and showed her how to knot it low across her back so the weight would carry high. He laid a hand once on her shoulder and once on the place above her heart where fear and courage kept their books.

"You'll walk the cliff line at dawn tomorrow," he said. "Empty. No Embla. Leave the tracks he wants."

"And you?"

"I'll fetch the net mender's stone," he said, as if that were news the whole village had been waiting for, and smiled with half his mouth. "Heavy thing. Needs a good back."

Astrid laughed in spite of herself. The laugh broke carefully and healed stronger.

Calven's palm

Calven made himself smaller the next day.

He traded the neat cloak for one with a salt stain on the hem. He fetched water for old Ragna and listened to her talk about nettles as if nettles were scripture. He stood with Halvar when Halvar fussed about the price of iron hooks and commiserated without offering solutions. He learned how to look as if he had nowhere else to be.

Astrid watched him from the corner of her sight and practiced not flinching when his gaze drifted near. He did not look up the birch line that day. Not once. That, more than anything, put cold in her.

At dusk she carried a coil of line past the well. Calven stood there alone, palms pressed together as if warming them. When she came within speaking distance he opened his hands and the gesture was so simple, so kind, that her heart almost punished her for hating him.

"You were right about the narrows," he said. "It thinned from beneath before noon. A man would have gone swimming if not for the wind telling him no."

"Wind's smarter than most men," Astrid said.

His smile creased—a little pain at the edges. "I suspect that's true."

He did not ask a question. He did not need to. His open hands were the question: *Trust me.*

Astrid let the silence answer. She lifted the rope and kept walking. After she had gone six strides, his voice came again, gentle, not trying to catch—only to follow.

"You care for things," he said. "I can tell."

She did not turn. "Everything breaks if you don't."

A breath—perhaps a chuckle. "Yes," he said. "Yes. That's so."

Later, when she told Halvar the exchange as exactly as memory allowed, he said, "A man who uses your goodness as a door will not knock next time."

Astrid slept lightly and dreamed of doors.

A scale no bigger than a thumbnail

The storm-well held secrets well; Astrid kept making it better.

She carried in dry bracken by the armful and then carried half of it back out again, because too much signal was as loud as too little. She rubbed the rim with pine pitch to give the air a smell that meant "forest" if anyone's nose asked. She learned where her boots squeaked and taught them not to.

Embla grew.

Not much. Enough to matter.

A copper scale loosened along her shoulder when she wriggled against basalt. Astrid caught it before it fell, pinched between finger and thumb, heart suddenly frantic. The thing was nothing—a crescent no bigger than a thumbnail, light as a flake of onion skin, but it shone like a secret that wanted to talk.

"What do we do with this?" she whispered.

Eat proof, the wizard advised.

Astrid carried it to the kettle she'd set over a small, smokeless heat of stones and meltwater and watched the scale curl and darken and unmake its own story. She stirred until it vanished. She drank the metal-taste down and did not gag.

"Gone," she told Embla, who watched with solemn eyes. "Gone means safe."

Embla nosed the cup as if confirming.

Astrid held her then until the trembling left her hands.

The ring remembers

On the fifth evening, the priest's ring sang.

Astrid did not hear it with her ears. She felt it along her teeth, a thin bright itch like ice tracing the edge of a bucket. She was halfway down the birch path with her empty canvas sling when the sensation shivered through her jaw and into her toes.

She stopped. The world held its breath for one… two… three… and then the itch withdrew, courteous as a bow.

He's using it to find heat, the wizard said, voice quiet and hard. *Not light. Not sound. The after-warmth of places a fire has loved.*

Astrid glanced back toward the storm-well. "Will he know?"

He will know a place is kind to warmth. He will not know why, if you keep the surface true and the air still.

Halvar, down in the lane, raised his lantern once, twice—the pretense signal they'd chosen for *he's abroad.*

Astrid went on. She walked where she would have walked if she had never learned to doubt her steps. She crossed a patch of old snow where her track would print and then print again in the same exact stitch, as if her feet remembered a dance. She descended among the nets with the air of a girl thinking of supper, because she was, and because soup would not stir itself.

Behind her, not close, not far, bells talked to metal in a language human mouths could not shape. For a long time afterward, when Astrid bit thread to make a clean end she would taste that note again.

Embla learns "still" and "fly"

That night the fog returned, a little less generous, a little more curious. Astrid brought a strip of salt fish to the storm-well and watched Embla eat with her whole body—tail set, wings balancing the tearing of her jaw, the small satisfied shake when the last sinew parted.

"Lesson," Astrid said when the hunger eased. "Two words."

She touched Embla's brow ridge, the way you touch a thought you want to keep. "Still."

Embla's pupils widened to the size of doorways and then narrowed to polite slits. She went statue-quiet, only her nostrils working. A perfect still.

"Good," Astrid whispered, and a little laugh escaped her—half joy, half terror.

She set her palm under the warm ridge where neck met breastbone. "Fly," she said, and dipped her knees, a body-cue for lift.

Embla did not leave the ground. She did not need to. She lifted her chest and shoulders and gave two powerful, silent draws with her wings, exactly as Astrid had taught—no more glow than a coal under ash, no more sound than the fog would allow. Dust rose. A pebble ticked. The hatchling's eyes shone with effort and delight.

"Enough," Astrid said quickly, hands up, and Embla settled, immediately, as if the word itself were a perch.

They did it three times. The fourth time, a tiny chirp slipped out—uncontainable pride.

Astrid scooped her close and hid the sound against wool. "Shh. I know. I know. You're perfect. Later we'll shout."

Embla stilled, pleased by a future in which shouting was permitted.

The line tightens

By now Calven knew the names of everyone who would sell him a crust and those who would give one for free. He had mended a broken hinge for Sigrid's mother and carried water for the woman whose oldest boy limped when the weather turned. He led evening prayers for six souls in a kitchen that smelled of cabbage, speaking a God as if he had met Him personally and liked Him.

Astrid watched him from the shadow near Halvar's woodpile and tried to make her mind into stone. It did not work. She could feel him thinking even when he merely smiled. Not with magic. With patience.

That patience walked him, slowly, almost idly, up the track that ended near the birches.

He did not go in. He looked the way a man looks at a knot before he pulls it.

He turned away.

He would be back.

The imprint of a hand

On the seventh day after the move, Astrid returned to the storm-well just after dawn and found a handprint on the rim.

Not Calven's. Smaller. Callused in the pattern of rope and oar. One of the village boys, probably, daring himself to climb where he knew he was not supposed to. The ice had been thin there yesterday; a boot could have slipped, a wrist could have caught.

Embla hissed—soft, curious, not afraid.

Astrid laid her own hand over the print. Her palm could have swallowed it. She pictured a boy finding the warmth the stone sometimes held and telling himself it came from sun.

She brushed the print away with her sleeve, then opened her fist and let the boy keep his hand. If she started hating children for being curious, she would have no one left to forgive herself when she erred.

"New rule," she told Embla. "We go higher after breakfast."

Embla's mind sent back a vivid certainty like a rung on a ladder: **You choose; I follow.**

Astrid smiled without showing teeth. "Then up we go."

Calven and the seam of heat

That afternoon, the priest went alone to the ridge when most men were mending or dozing or putting a last stitch to a net. He did not carry a lantern. He did not look up.

He walked like a man considering a sermon and paused where the birch shade thickened. He knelt, gloved, and pressed his palm flat to the snow. He held it there, counting.

When he lifted his hand there was nothing to see but the memory of pressure.

He moved on. He did the same at three other places— places Astrid had chosen for the false door, the made track, the seam the wind would mend. At the last, he took off his glove and touched the stone itself.

He closed his eyes.

The ring on his finger cooled the air above his knuckles. The metal was quiet. The rock was quieter. He waited long enough for waiting to be a question.

Then he stood, brushed his palm on his cloak, and smiled a very small smile that meant nothing a village could read.

On his way down he passed Halvar, who had chosen that moment to be a man with a heavy stone on a sledge. They exchanged names for the second time as if it were the first. Halvar let the sledge pull a little as if it cost him more than it did. Calven put his shoulder to the rope and helped, the way a good man would.

At the bottom, they parted like two rivers that only met because the ground wanted a story to happen there.

The cliff edge

That night Astrid took Embla not down but sideways,

along a deer path that stitched the cliff's face. The stars were small and mean with cold. The fjord lay black and sure. The village breathed behind them like a sleeper deciding whether to wake.

At a shelf that felt like a pause in the mountain's thinking, Astrid stopped and set Embla down. The hatchling stood with her forepaws on the lip and looked out—a child on a windowsill meeting the idea of distance.

"Still," Astrid breathed.

Embla stilled.

"Fly," Astrid whispered, cupping the warm breastbone.

Two silent draws. A third. Dust rose and fell like a held secret.

"Enough."

Embla settled, leaning her weight into Astrid's shins as if to promise not to run without being asked.

Somewhere below, in the tangle of rock and birch, a small sound answered the night—boot on stone, only once, and then the kind of quiet that thinks it has a right to be there.

Astrid swallowed and did not lean forward or back. She put her palm over the place where Embla's heartbeat wrote its steady line. She did not look down.

The wizard's voice slipped into her ear as if it had been there all along.
He is counting our breaths. Let him count. We will take his numbers from him when the fog returns.

Embla's breath eased. Astrid's did too. The mountain kept being a mountain.

The sound below did not come again.

When they went back, Astrid brushed her fingertips over the cliff's grit as if signing her name and took care to leave no letter anyone could read.

The count to three

In the dark of her bed that night, Astrid counted:

One: a priest with open hands.
Two: a ring that sings to winter.
Three: a hatchling who trusts the rope because she trusts the hand.

She fell asleep with the number three in her mouth like a coin she would not spend unless she had to.

By morning, the fog would lift. By evening, the village would have news it did not know how to value. Between the two, Astrid would teach Embla a new word—*hide*—and Calven would find something he did not expect to find at the edge of the storm-well.

Not the dragon.

Not proof.

Only the exact place where a small warmth had been… and a single thread of copper-gold hair snagged on a bracken stem, bright as a thought.

He would roll it between forefinger and thumb and smile the smile a patient man smiles when the world agrees to give him something almost like an answer.

And far above him on the cliff, a girl would feel the world shift its weight, just slightly. Not a quake. A choice arranging itself.

Tomorrow, the mountain seemed to say. *Come back tomorrow and see what you think you know.*

CHAPTER 15

The Day the Sky Almost Opened

The morning broke thin and bright, the kind of light that made every shadow sharpen into a blade. Havngard woke slowly, yawns turning into chores, footsteps turning into the rhythm of a village that believed the world held no secrets larger than nets and weather.

Astrid wished she could believe it too.

She left Embla nestled in the storm-well, hidden under a blanket of bracken and basalt warmth. The hatchling slept curled tight, wings tucked, tail over her snout like a cat trying to become smaller than she was.

Astrid brushed her fingers along the hot scales.
"I won't be long," she whispered.
Embla's dream-mind nudged hers with a sleepy sensation that meant **safe because you said so**.

Astrid swallowed guilt and climbed back toward the village.

A village pretending nothing is wrong

Halvar was splitting driftwood on the path by their house, each strike measured. The rhythm was wrong—too quick, too sharp—and Astrid knew he was listening for Calven as much as she was.

"He's in the lower lane," Halvar said without looking up. "Asking about the goats now."

Astrid winced. "The goats don't know anything."

"Priests aren't talking to goats," Halvar said. "They're talking to shepherds."

She nodded and took up a bundle of rope for appearance's sake. Villagers greeted her with normal words—good morning, cold day, storm coming, help with the sled?—but their eyes flicked toward Calven all the same.

He had become part of the landscape, like a stone too round to have rolled there naturally.

Astrid kept to the edges of the lanes, working where she could listen without being seen. Calven moved among people like smoke—light at first, then inescapable.

He did not look at the birch-line today.

That was worse.

The air shifts

By midday the frost melted off the roof beams and steamed faintly, the sign of a warmer front drifting in. Astrid knew what that meant: Embla would be awake soon. The storm-well held heat too well. Dragons did not sleep long in warmth.

Astrid reached for a ladle of stew when the first warning came—not sound, but feeling, a tug along the back of her skull like a breath drawn beside her ear.

Awake, Embla's mind whispered.

Then:

Where? Where you? Where sky?

Astrid nearly dropped the bowl.

Not now. Not with Calven so close.

She wiped her hands and stepped outside. The air crackled with thaw and nerves. She made for the birches, quick but not quick enough to be suspicious.

A voice stopped her.

"Halvarsdottir."

Her heart leapt painfully.

Halvar?
No.

Brother Calven stood in the narrow path between two houses, hands folded neatly before him, expression mild as milk.

"A word?" he asked.

Astrid forced a breath. "I was—going to check—"

"The cliff paths," he finished gently. "Yes. I've noticed you walk them often."

She froze. Her blood felt suddenly cold.

He smiled politely. "You look toward them with such… intent. Forgive me if I'm curious. A girl your age should have less weight in her gaze."

She almost said something—anything—but then Embla's thought brushed her mind again:

Come? Come now. Hot. Crow-noises. Scare.
(Astrid had learned "crow-noises" meant men's voices.)

Panic bloomed behind her ribs.

Not now.
Not him.

Calven took a single step closer.

"Is someone hurt?" he asked softly, as if offering comfort. "You look as though you're listening to something very far away."

Astrid muttered, "I have to go," and slipped past him before he could block her.

He didn't chase.
That was the worst sign of all.

Calven simply watched her, eyes calm, curious, calculating what kind of truth she had just revealed by running.

The birch-line breaks

Astrid reached the birches at a half-run.

"Embla?" she breathed.

A soft, frightened chirrup answered from deeper in the brush.

Astrid dove between the trunks.

Embla wasn't in the storm-well.
She was in the open—three strides below it, standing in a patch of melted frost, wings half-raised, trembling.

"Embla—no—no, no, no, you can't be out—"

Embla darted to her, pushing her warm head beneath Astrid's arm, desperate, scared.

Astrid wrapped her cloak around the hatchling. "Something frightened you?"

Embla nuzzled hard under her jaw—**Yes. Yes.**

Bad-noise.
Then came a pulse of feeling that made Astrid's gut twist:

Heard him.
A mental picture followed—blurred but clear enough:
The priest's voice.
Too close to the hollow.

Astrid's breath left her in a cold gasp.

She gathered Embla fully under the cloak. "We have to

go. Now."

But as she turned—

The air behind her shifted.

Bootsteps.

Measured.
Deliberate.
Close.

Astrid spun.

Brother Calven stood ten paces away among the birches.

Quiet.
Expression unreadable.
Lantern unlit in his hand.

"Astrid," he said softly.

Her heart slammed against her ribs.

Embla trembled under the cloak.

Calven stepped forward one pace—no threat, no shout, no drawn weapon. That was what made him terrifying. He behaved as a man who had already solved the problem in his head.

"You shouldn't be out here alone," he said gently. "Dangerous footing. Treacherous ground."

Astrid said nothing.

The wizard's voice flickered through her bones:
Do not run. Not yet. He expects it. Wait for the break. It will come.

Calven glanced toward the storm-well.
Once.
Too long.

His eyes narrowed slightly.

Not suspicion.

Recognition.

"Astrid," he said again, softer. "What are you hiding?"

She couldn't answer. Her tongue was stone.

Calven took another step.

Embla let out a tiny, frightened peep.

Calven froze.

Astrid felt it—the moment his world changed shape. His posture shifted, like a man listening to a sound inside his own skull.

"A child?" he asked. But his voice was wrong. Off-note, off-balance.
He knew it wasn't a child.

Astrid backed up, hands tightening around Embla.

Calven lifted one palm in a gentle placating gesture. "I'm not here to harm anyone. Let me help—"

Embla pushed her snout into the air, cloak slipping, a tiny red glow beginning beneath the fabric—

Astrid made a decision with her whole body. "Wings," she whispered. "Break the air for us."

Embla understood enough. She sprang to Astrid's shoulder, wings flaring wide—not to carry, but to **fight the fall**.

Astrid ran for the snow gully just below the cliff lip and **threw herself onto the chute**, boots braced, one hand catching a root. The world tipped; snow hissed. Embla skated the air beside her, **beating ragged downstrokes** that slowed their slide and shoved them toward the safer, lower ledge.

They **zipped ledge to ledge**, half-scramble, half-sledge, Embla's wings thudding the air like a bellows. A final shove of wind from the hatchling's frantic flapping **bled off speed**, and they **tumbled into a drift** on the shelf below.

Astrid coughed, laughed once, breathless. Embla shook herself and **pressed her hot head under Astrid's chin**—not triumph so much as *we didn't die.*

Above, a lantern's glow combed the cliff edge. Brother Calven stared down to where they'd vanished. He turned and ran for the village.

Astrid's blood turned to ice.

"He's going to warn them," she whispered.

Embla nudged her with a soft, urgent sound.

The wizard spoke through the stone beneath her knees:

The peaceful days are over. Choose now, Astrid Halvarsdottir—
Hide her deeper...
or learn to fly again before dawn.

Astrid stood.

Embla pressed against her leg.

Astrid set her jaw.

"Flying," she said. "We're learning to fly."

Embla chirped once—bright, fierce, loyal.

Together, they climbed into the dark.

CHAPTER 16

The Longest Night Begins

Astrid didn't wait for her breath to steady.

The moment Calven vanished toward the village, she grabbed Embla — hot, trembling, wings still quivering from the fall-break — and half-dragged, half-carried her along the narrow trail carved into the mountainside.

"Come on," she whispered. "We need to be invisible before he reaches anyone."

Embla pressed close, tiny claws hooking the front of Astrid's cloak.
Her breath came in bright puffs — little bursts of molten heat fading to steam.

Astrid felt every pulse of the hatchling's fear.

And for the first time, she didn't have the village to run back to.

Leaving Havngard Behind

They climbed until the lights of Havngard were no more than a small cluster of orange beads far below.
Astrid stopped at the high ridge — the last place she could still see the smoke lines of home.

Her home.

Her father was down there. Her friends. Her life.

But also Calven.

And Calven had seen enough to turn suspicion into certainty.

Astrid swallowed the ache in her throat and turned away from Havngard.

"We can't go back," she whispered.

Embla answered with a soft, forlorn chirp.

Astrid brushed the smooth ridge of the dragon's head. "I know. But we need a place he doesn't know, somewhere outside his prayers, outside his guessing."

She faced the northern range — jagged, snowbound, mostly untraveled except by hunters, wolves, and storms.

A place where a priest's boots would not easily go.

"We head north," she decided.

Embla flicked her tail and nudged Astrid's chin as if agreeing.

The First Lesson

Wind tore across the ridge, cold enough to bite exposed skin raw. Astrid hunched low and glanced at the drop on either side — sheer enough to end anyone careless.

"We need to practice," she told Embla quietly. "If we're going to fly tonight… even a little… you need to learn to feel the air."

Embla blinked, head tilting, wings shivering open a few inches.

"Not high," Astrid promised. "Just enough to glide with me without slipping."

She crouched, placed Embla on a flat piece of rock, and held out her hands.

"Wings," she whispered.

Embla stretched them — small, luminous, still too soft at the edges but strong enough to rustle the snow.

"Good," Astrid murmured. "Now—"

A downdraft hit them, sudden and sharp.

Embla squawked and flapped, lifting a few inches off the stone — startled — then drifting clumsily into Astrid's waiting arms.

"You felt it," Astrid said breathlessly. "You *felt* the wind."

Embla chittered proudly, her scales warm enough to thaw the small flakes landing on her back.

The wizard's voice rose faintly from the stone beneath their boots:

She answers the sky faster than she answers words. Teach her wind, not commands.

Astrid nodded. "Then wind it is."

Into the Frozen Juniper Wood

They descended from the ridge into a lesser-known forest — one Halvar had spoken of only in warnings. The Frozen Juniper Wood.

Twisted trees hunched under thick snow. Shadows leaned strangely. Even the ravens avoided the place.

But the wood was vast, thick, and silent — the perfect place for hiding from a man who relied on questions and listening.

"We'll find a hollow here," Astrid murmured.

Embla's claws pricked her arm as she pointed — not quite a gesture, more a feeling pushing through their bond.

Toward the deeper trees.
Toward the sound of trickling water.

Astrid followed.

The River That Shouldn't Be There

They reached a break in the trees where snow thinned unusually.

A warm fog curled up in faint tendrils.

Astrid knelt. The ground beneath her palm was warmer than it should be — like earth shifting under its own breath.

A stream cut through the clearing, small and narrow, but unfrozen.

Embla dipped her snout into it and drank, tail curling with contentment.

"This shouldn't exist," Astrid whispered.

It remembers fire, the wizard murmured.
Long ago, dragons nested in these woods. Heat lingers beneath old places.

Astrid stood straighter.

"Then this is where we stay," she decided. "For tonight. For however long we can."

Embla hopped into her arms — warm, soft, trusting.

They found a small cavern at the base of a juniper root — not large, but sheltered and invisible from every angle. The perfect temporary den.

Astrid set Embla inside and spread her cloak across the entrance like a curtain.

"There," she whispered. "Hidden."

Embla curled up, blinking sleepily.

The Priest in the Dark

Astrid had just started gathering fallen branches to conceal the entrance further when a sound froze her spine:

Crunch.

Snow.

A single footstep.

Not close — but not distant.

Astrid stiffened, ducking behind a twisted trunk. Embla stirred inside the hollow.

A lantern glowed faintly between the trees.

Calven.

He was alone. He was cold. His cloak was dusted with frost.

He was… *following the heat.*

Astrid held her breath until her chest cramped.

Calven paused, touched the trunk of a juniper, sighed into his hands to warm them.

Then he prayed — softly.

But not a gentle prayer.

A searching prayer.

A binding prayer.

Astrid pressed herself deeper into her hiding place, barely daring to breathe.

The lantern swung once.

Then Calven turned and walked back the way he came — not satisfied, but exhausted.

Astrid released a shaking breath only after his light disappeared fully into the trees.

She crawled back to Embla and wrapped her arms around the little dragon, burying her face in warm scales.

"We stay hidden," she whispered. "No matter what."

Embla purred faintly.

In the darkness, the wizard's voice came softer than ever:

He will search again at dawn. Move her deeper tomorrow. The north hides more than he knows.

Astrid stroked Embla's back, feeling the heat pulse through her.

"No," she whispered back. "Tonight we rest. Tomorrow we fly."

A promise.
A challenge.

A new beginning.

CHAPTER 17

The Sky Remembers Her Name

Two months is not a long time for mountains.
But for a girl and a growing dragon, it is enough for the
world to change shape.

The forest below the ridge had become their refuge—an
untidy sprawl of pines, old storm-fallen trunks, and pockets
of mist that clung to the earth like secrets. Astrid learned its
paths the way she once learned the tide calendar: by heart,
by sound, by necessity. Embla learned it by instinct,
bounding through undergrowth with a grace that wasn't
grace yet, only promise.

In the early days of their escape, Astrid had spent every
waking breath listening for pursuit—Calven's voice,
Calven's lantern, Calven's winter-prayers rolling across the
snow like iron filings in dust. But the priest had never
followed past the cliff. Not then. Not at first.

For a time, the world was narrowed to survival.

And then survival grew room for joy.

Embla grew, too.

Her wings, once flimsy as wet parchment, grew taut
under Astrid's fingers, the membranes streaked with veins of
gold that shimmered brightest at dawn. Her scales thickened
from down-soft to plate-light, cool on the edges, warm
down the center. Her legs lengthened, her stride steadied,
and her tail—always expressive—now held its own balance
against wind. Astrid could feel the change every time she
lifted the dragon. Embla was no longer something to cradle;
she was something to stand beside.

They found a high den tucked beneath an overhang of granite veined with quartz. A waterfall peeled over the edge above, thin and silver, spraying the air with diamonds whenever the sun rose behind the peaks. Embla adored the place. Astrid suspected the stone below remembered the old fire-drakes—it hummed sometimes when Embla slept, a low, contented purr that had nothing to do with wind.

They were safe here.

Safe enough, at least, to let hope grow again.

Fire

The first flame arrived by accident.

Astrid had been gathering sticks at the treeline, breaking the thin, crispy branches that clung to fallen trunks. Embla, as usual, mimicked her, tugging at twigs and proudly presenting them as if she had hunted them herself.

"Good," Astrid praised, tucking her own bundle beneath one arm. "We'll make a small fire tonight. No higher than my knee."

Embla puffed up with importance—and sneezed.

A tiny bead of fire shot across the clearing, hit a dry tuft of grass, and blossomed into a flame the size of Astrid's thumb.

Astrid yelped, dropped her sticks, and dove to smother it with her sleeve.

Embla froze, eyes wide, tail straight, like a child who had broken a sacred bowl.

Astrid lifted her head. "Did you just—"

Embla hiccuped.

Another bead. Astrid slapped it out with her palm before it could take.

"Oh no," she whispered. "No-no-no-no—fire already? You're still little!"

Embla slunk to the ground, pressing her snout against the dirt in dramatized sorrow.

"It's not your fault," Astrid said quickly, rubbing her hands together to get the soot off. "Just… maybe aim it away from the trees next time?"

Embla made a pitiful whine.

Astrid laughed despite herself and hugged the dragon's neck. "You're impossible."

The wizard's voice drifted from somewhere deep, like a tide running beneath the stone:

A spark is a promise. All fire begins small.

"Well, it's going to stay small," Astrid said aloud, though she wasn't sure who she said it for—herself, the wizard, or Embla.

Embla chirped, unconvinced.

Flight

Training began with gliding.

Astrid learned quickly that dragons did not flap to lift themselves; they fell to lift. Embla would scramble up a rock, crouch, wiggle her haunches, and leap. Her wings would snap out, catch a pocket of wind, and slow her fall to a gentle slide across the moss.

Sometimes.

Other times, she face-planted into pine needles and came

up with twigs stuck between her scales.

Astrid always laughed, even when Embla sulked, which only made Embla sulk harder.

"Try again," Astrid encouraged. "From the flatter part this time."

Embla chirped her argument.

"No, you didn't glide *perfectly*. You glided into a bush."

Argument intensifies.

"Yes," Astrid sighed, "a very forgiving bush."

Embla launched herself again—this time catching the wind properly, sailing a full twenty paces before landing gracefully. She puffed her chest as if she had invented gliding.

Astrid clapped. "See? You're getting it."

Empowered, Embla tried three more times, each better than the last. It wasn't flight. Not yet. But it was something close—a whisper of what wings meant.

And Astrid began to imagine the sky differently.

Not as a ceiling, but as a road.

The Wizard's Warning

The wizard rarely spoke now, and when he did, it was always during the quiet—those moments when the wind paused as if listening.

One morning, as Astrid washed Embla's scales at the river, the voice slid into her thoughts like a tide rising:

The priest has left the village.

Astrid stiffened. "Left?"

Returned to his monastery.

Astrid's breath shook. "He's… gone?"

For now.

The water rippled gently around Embla's claws. Astrid rested both hands on the dragon's neck.

The wizard's next words were softer.

Your father waits for a sign of you. His hope is thin. But it breathes.

Astrid's throat tightened. Embla sensed it and pressed her head gently into Astrid's shoulder.

"I want to see him," Astrid whispered. The words felt dangerous and warm. "Just once."

You must not, the world might have said once.

You cannot, Calven would say now.

But the wizard said only:

When the sky is clear and the wind is kind, she can carry you.

Astrid's heart lurched. "She can't fly that far."

Not alone. But with you? Yes.

Embla chirped sharply, as if agreeing.

Astrid stared at her. "You want to?"

Embla nudged her cheek.

A yes, then.

A fierce, burning yes.

Preparation

Learning to ride a dragon is not like learning to ride a horse.

It is more like learning to trust a storm.

Embla crouched low, flattening her shoulders so Astrid could lie along her neck. Her scales warmed to Astrid's legs; her wings flexed, stretching wider than Astrid had ever seen.

Astrid's stomach fluttered. "You're sure?"

Embla huffed, stamping one foot.

"All right. All right." Astrid took Embla's crest like a handle. "On three. One… two—"

Embla leapt on two.

The ground vanished.

Wind punched Astrid's face, cold and wild. Embla's wings snapped open, wobbling, then catching. They slid sideways, dipped, and for a terrifying moment Astrid thought they were going to tumble straight into the river.

But Embla corrected—wings beating once, twice, with the determination of a creature who refused to fall while Astrid clung to her.

They rose.

Twenty feet.
Thirty.
Fifty, the treetops shrinking beneath them.

Astrid gasped. Laughed. Sobbed all at once.

Embla roared—a small, bright roar, more joy than power.

"You're flying!" Astrid cried. "Embla, you're truly—"

Wind stole the rest of her sentence.

They circled the mountains once. Twice. Embla's wings wobbled with each banking turn. Astrid leaned where the dragon leaned, learning balance together. By the time they landed—awkwardly, skidding into an ice patch and rolling into a shallow drift—Astrid's cheeks hurt from smiling.

Embla headbutted her proudly.

Astrid hugged her. "We can go home."

The Return

They chose dawn.

The sky streaked gray-blue, the fjord a sleeping mirror. Embla crouched low, wings trembling with anticipation.

Astrid wrapped her arms around Embla's neck. "Let's go home."

Embla leapt.

This time, the lift was clean—wings slicing upward, wind catching them like a promise fulfilled. They soared over the ridge, over the pines, over the river's winding path. The fjord appeared, bright as polished silver, and something inside Astrid cracked open.

She hadn't realized how deeply she'd missed the sight until now.

The village—her village—came into view. Smoke from a few hearths. Nets hung to dry. Sheep moving like stones with legs. And standing on the cliff path, looking smaller than she remembered but no less strong—

Halvar.

Astrid's breath left her.

Embla spiraled downward gently. Halvar did not run. He stood still, hands at his sides, eyes wide with awe and recognition that battled each other for space.

Astrid slid off Embla's back the moment they touched the ground. Her knees almost buckled with emotion.

"Father—"

Halvar crossed the distance in three strides and pulled her into a fierce embrace, one hand on the back of her head, the other gripping her shoulder as if anchoring himself to the moment.

"My girl," he murmured into her hair. "I thought winter took you."

Astrid clung to him, shaking. "I'm here. I'm here."

Embla stepped forward cautiously. Halvar looked at her —the dragon who had become Astrid's shadow—and after a long, steady moment, he bowed his head.

Embla, catching the gesture, lowered hers softly.

"You kept her alive," Halvar said. Not praise. Not fear. A statement of truth.

Embla exhaled warm breath against his palm.

Astrid smiled through tears. "She's family."

Halvar's eyes softened. "Then you chose well."

For a moment, the world felt whole.

And then the world shattered

Hoofbeats thundered.

Shouts echoed from the lower path.

Astrid stiffened. Embla growled softly, positioning herself between Astrid and the sound.

Halvar's head snapped toward the road. "No…"

Astrid knew before she saw.

Calven.

He came riding hard at the front of a small detachment of soldiers—four, no, six—each carrying spears, some with crossbows slung over their backs. Their cloaks bore the monastery's winter-mark: a silver ring crossed with iron.

"Inside," Halvar hissed. "Go—GO!"

But it was too late.

Calven reined in his horse at the sight of Embla and Astrid standing together on the cliff.

He stared up at them, lantern-light catching the sharp angles of his face.

Shock.
Vindication.
And something colder—like victory sharpened on a whetstone.

"The fire-blood lives," he whispered.

Then louder:

"Archers—READY!"

Astrid screamed, "Embla—FLY!"

Embla lunged forward, wings snapping open. Halvar shoved Astrid upward, boosting her onto the dragon's back.

"Go," he rasped. "Go now."

Astrid grabbed Embla's crest. "Father—"

"LIVE," Halvar commanded, voice cracking like a ship's mast in storm.

Embla leapt.

Bolts whistled past.

Calven shouted, "AFTER THEM! Do not let them reach the mountains!"

Embla caught the wind, beating hard, rising past the cliff, past the last safe ledge, past the reach of crossbows. Astrid looked back once—just once—and saw Halvar standing alone before Calven's men, spear in hand, defiant as the sea.

Embla roared.

And together, they vanished into the clouds.

The chase had begun.

Chapter 18

Toward the Spine of the World

The wind tore at them as Embla banked hard over the fjord, her wings cleaving the icy air. Astrid clung to the ridge of warm scales along the dragon's neck, fingers gripping instinctively each time the young dragon dipped through a thermic shudder. Beneath them, Havngard shrank into a scatter of rooftops and smoke-twisted chimneys. And behind them—

Shouts.
Boots striking rock.
A horn blast, sharp enough to crack the quiet of dawn.

Calven and his soldiers had seen. There was no undoing that now.

Astrid looked back only once. She saw Calven standing on the ridge above the village, his cloak snapping like a raven's wing in the wind. His soldiers surrounded him — a half-dozen already pointing upward, not arrows yet, but fingers, disbelief mixed with fear.

We've been marked, Astrid thought.
She didn't say it aloud. She didn't need to. Embla felt the thought ripple through her chest and answered with a low, trembling growl that vibrated beneath Astrid's legs.

Fly, Astrid urged through the bond. *Higher. North. To the mountains.*

Embla beat her wings once — twice — and the world dropped away beneath them.

The Northern Wilds

The land transformed as they fled. The familiar green of Havngard gave way to ragged stone ridges, then to endless stretches of snow and ice that gleamed under the sun like polished bone.

Astrid squinted as the air thinned. Frost clung to her lashes. Embla's breath came out in smoky bursts.

Below, the world was empty — no tracks, no homes, no safe harbor. Only the spine of the world rising like a jagged scar against the horizon.

Embla shivered. **Cold…** Her thought brushed against Astrid's mind like a small animal seeking warmth.

Astrid pressed her hand to the warm scales. *We'll find shelter. Just a little farther.*

The bond carried more than words. It carried Astrid's stubborn hope, a spark of determination she didn't know she possessed until the world demanded it.

A Warning on the Wind

They flew for hours. When the sun dipped toward the west, a strange heaviness settled over the air. Embla faltered, wings wobbling.

"What is it?" Astrid whispered, throat raw from the cold.

Embla didn't answer at first. Then the dragon's mind flickered with sensations — not quite images, not quite sounds. A deep rumble. A sense of something ancient beneath the surface. A call pulling at her bones.

Old place… Embla whispered finally. **Old fire.**

Astrid frowned, tightening her cloak. *Is it danger?*

Embla's wings stiffened. **Not danger. Memory.**

That frightened Astrid more.

The Cave of the Falling Sky

Dusk washed the mountains in violet when Embla spiraled downward. She landed clumsily on a narrow ledge overlooking a chasm, her talons scraping stone. Astrid slid off, legs shaky, boots sinking into powdery snow.

A dark opening yawned in the rock face ahead — tall, jagged, rimmed with ice that glittered faintly blue.

Embla lowered her neck, sniffing. A faint heat pulsed from within the cave, almost too subtle to notice.

Astrid touched the stone. Warm.

"This shouldn't be warm," she murmured.

Embla's pupils constricted. **Old fire. Old home.**

The wizard's voice flickered faintly in Astrid's mind, distant as a memory carried on the wind:

If you flee north… the land will remember what you do not. The mountains keep their stories. Some are welcoming. Some are hungry.

His presence faded again, leaving Astrid with a shiver not caused by the cold.

She swallowed hard. "We don't have a choice."

They stepped inside.

The Remnants of Dragonkind

The cave tunnel sloped downward, carved by something other than water or wind. Astrid ran her hand along the wall — grooves spiraled through the stone in intricate patterns, too smooth, too purposeful to be natural.

Embla's wings folded tight. She padded forward in cautious steps.

The tunnel widened suddenly into a vast chamber. Astrid gasped.

Fallen pillars of obsidian ringed the chamber like the ribs of a collapsed giant. Strange runes spiraled across them — some glowing faintly as Embla drew near, responding to the presence of dragonblood.

At the center of the chamber sat a massive stone basin filled with crystallized ash. Embedded in the ash were shards of something iridescent, shimmering like scales.

Astrid's heart beat faster. "Embla… what is this place?"

The dragon stared, eyes widening. For a moment, Astrid felt the echo of something through their bond — a vision blurred with emotion:

A larger dragon, wings like thunderclouds, lowering its head over the basin. Flames curling and dancing within it. A ritual of memory. Of birth. Of farewell.

Embla whimpered softly, a sound Astrid had never heard from her before.

Home… once. Long ago.
A sorrow threaded the thought. **Gone. All gone.**

Astrid touched Embla's cheek, feeling the heat beneath her scales. "You're not alone anymore," she whispered.

The dragon leaned into her, trembling. The chamber lights pulsed brighter — responding to their bond.

A Message in the Runes

Astrid stepped closer to one of the fallen pillars. The runes shimmered as she reached out.

A sudden sharp voice cut into her mind — not the wizard, not Embla, but something older, more fragmented.

A keeper must rise…
The bond must be reborn…

Fire chooses the heart that can carry it…

Astrid stumbled back, breath hitching.

Embla growled softly, protective.

"It's okay," Astrid whispered. "I think… it was speaking to me."

To them.

She traced another rune. Warmth flared beneath her fingers, and words formed in her mind again — clearer this time:

When the hunters return, the mountain will shield the chosen. But only for a time.

Her stomach twisted. *Calven.*
Even here, the warning followed them.

Nightfall in the Ruined Sanctuary

They made camp behind a fallen pillar. Embla curled around Astrid, creating a cocoon of warmth. The chamber hummed quietly, like the heartbeat of an old creature slumbering beneath the mountain.

Astrid lay with her back against Embla's side, staring up at the high cavern ceiling.

For the first time since fleeing the fjord, she allowed herself to breathe.

But peace did not last.

A faint echo drifted down the tunnel — a sound carried by the shifting wind outside.

A long, low horn.
Distant… but not distant enough.

Astrid sat up sharply.

"Embla." Her voice came out thin, trembling.

The dragon lifted her head, pupils narrowing.

They follow.
The thought was cold, certain.

Astrid's chest tightened. Calven's soldiers were pushing into the mountains.

He wasn't giving up.

"We can't stay here," Astrid whispered. "Not if they've tracked us."

Embla unfolded her wings, stretching them wide in the glowing chamber. She nudged Astrid toward her back.

We fly.
But there was fear beneath it.

Astrid touched her forehead gently to Embla's. "We fly."

The Storm Begins to Gather

Outside the cave, the night sky churned with thick clouds rolling in from the west. Lightning flickered deep within them — strange lightning, twisting unnaturally through the dark.

Embla tensed. **Storm... wrong storm.**

A prickle ran down Astrid's spine. The air smelled metallic, sharp. As if something in the sky itself recognized Embla's return.

Another horn blared, closer now.

Astrid climbed onto Embla's back. "Let's go."

The dragon leapt from the ledge, wings slicing through the rising stormwinds.

Behind them, torchlights flickered in the lower ravines.

Calven was coming.

And the mountains were waking.

Chapter 19

The Mountain That Remembers

The storm chased them north like a living thing.

Embla's wings strained against the spiraling winds as she climbed, higher and higher, trying to outrun the darkness boiling over the sky. Astrid felt every tremor in the dragon's muscles, every shudder of cold slicing through the air. Snow whipped past them in frantic sheets, driven by gusts that tasted of iron and old magic.

Below, torch-lights flickered like a trail of angry embers as Calven's soldiers wound their way along the ravine. Their horns carried through the mountains, distant but relentless — a reminder that no matter how high Embla flew, the world below was still hunting them.

Astrid tightened her hold on Embla's neck ridge, her heart aching with each breath. *We can't keep running forever,* she thought.

Embla felt the thought instantly, and a low rumble vibrated through her chest in response.

Not forever… just tonight.

The dragon's thought came back small and determined, like a spark refusing to die.

Astrid buried her face briefly against Embla's warm scales, the heat comforting against the icy wind. "Alright," she whispered. "Just tonight."

The Sky Breaks

As they reached the mountain's highest ridge, the storm struck.

Lightning split the sky overhead, branching like veins across the clouds. Thunder rolled through the peaks, a deep-bellied growl that felt too close, too aware — as though the storm itself had turned an eye toward them.

Embla faltered mid-flight as the wind slammed her sideways. Astrid clung tighter, legs straining, the world tilting in a dizzying blur. Embla recovered — barely — but her wings beat unevenly now, fighting against the pulling currents.

Another blast of wind tore through the air.

Hold! Astrid urged, though her voice was lost to the roar.

Embla's answer was not through words but a desperate heave of her wings. She surged upward, driving herself toward a jagged outcrop of stone where the cliff face formed a narrow ledge sheltered by an overhang.

They reached it seconds before the storm unleashed a sheet of ice needles across the sky.

Embla landed hard, her talons scraping sparks from the stone. Astrid slid off, collapsing briefly to her knees as the wind howled past them.

Embla folded her wings tight, panting.

Astrid rested her forehead against the dragon's shoulder. "You saved us."

We saved each other. Embla's thought came tired, but warm.

Lightning in the Blood

The storm raged with unnatural fury. Astrid peered past the edge of the ledge, watching lightning dance across the clouds like luminous serpents. She'd seen storms her whole life — this was not one of them.

The sky pulsed.

Once.
Twice.
A thrice-fold heartbeat.

Then a crack split the heavens, and lightning struck the far slope with a force that shook the cliff beneath them.

Embla recoiled, eyes wide. She pressed closer to Astrid, trembling in a way Astrid had never felt from her before.

"What is it?" Astrid whispered, stroking the warm ridge between Embla's eyes.

After a long moment, an answer formed in the dragon's thoughts:

The sky remembers dragons.
A pause.
It… looks for us.

Astrid swallowed. "You mean it knows you're here?"

Embla didn't respond with words this time. Instead, she stretched her neck toward the churning clouds, nostrils flaring. A strange, electric hum shivered along her scales, making the cave runes engraved in her hide glitter faintly.

Astrid pulled her cloak tighter. "This storm isn't natural. It's magic. Old magic."

The wizard's distant voice drifted across her mind, faint as fog:

The mountains remember their keepers. Storms answer to blood once forgotten.

Astrid steadied herself on Embla. "We'll get through this. And then we find deeper shelter."

Not here, Embla agreed. **Not safe.**

The Watching Peak

When dawn broke — or tried to — the world was washed in gray. The storm lessened but did not leave; it lingered like a living presence, crawling between peaks, curling around cliffs. Embla stretched her wings.

I can fly.
She sounded stronger, but Astrid could feel exhaustion woven through her thoughts.

"We'll fly," Astrid said softly, "but only as far as we must."

They took off from the ledge, Embla gliding more than flapping this time, letting shifting pockets of wind carry them. The land continued to rise beneath them — higher ridges, deeper scars in the stone, larger shadows hiding within cavern mouths.

Then Astrid saw it.

A peak unlike the others — sheer, blackened, crowned by a ring of swirling clouds. It loomed like a sentinel watching the world.

It *felt* alive.

And as they drew closer, Astrid heard something. Not through her ears — through her gift.

A pulse.
A call.
A rhythm older than time.

Embla felt it too.

Fire-heart… calling…
The dragon's scales brightened, as if responding instinctively.

Astrid shivered. The mountain called to dragons.
To *this* dragon.

But they weren't alone.

Shouts echoed faintly behind them, carried across the vast emptiness.

Astrid looked back.

Tiny figures, but unmistakable — Calven's soldiers scaling a ridge two valleys south. They were relentless. Even the storm hadn't turned them back.

Embla hissed.

They come.

"We have to move."

The Ancient Stair

The path toward the black peak was steep and narrow, barely a shelf cut into the stone. Embla landed at the base, wings folding tightly to avoid scraping the cliff.

Astrid slid down and touched the stone beneath her boots. It was warm. Not just compared to the cold around them — *truly* warm, like the belly of a hearth.

Carved into the rock was a winding staircase, old but precise.

"Somebody made this," Astrid whispered.

Dragons, Embla answered, her mind quiet with awe. **Long ago.**

The staircase spiraled upward into the clouds. Embla nudged Astrid's shoulder.

Climb. I follow.

"You can't fit through that path."

The dragon examined the narrow ledge, then spread her wings slightly.

I can climb. Dragon-climb.
She gripped the stone with the hooks of her wings and talons,
demonstrating.

Astrid blinked. "Alright then. But stay close."

They climbed together — Astrid on the steps, Embla
scaling the cliff beside her with unsettling agility, claws
scraping stone, wings gripping like extra limbs.

The higher they climbed, the louder the pulse became.
Astrid pressed a hand to her chest.

It wasn't her heart.

It was the mountain's.

The Heartforge

They reached a ledge where the clouds broke, revealing a
vast crater carved into the mountain's summit. The center of
it glowed — a wide circle of smoothed stone engraved with
runes that spiraled outward like sunbursts.

Embla's breath hitched.
Astrid felt the shock ripple through her.

She stepped forward cautiously.

Heat rose from the stone without flame — a gentle
warmth, steady and rhythmic.

Embla walked toward the center and placed one talon on
the runes.

The entire circle brightened.

Astrid staggered back as a deep hum filled the air, rattling
her teeth. The runes pulsed beneath Embla's foot. Then her
chest.

Then her eyes.

The dragon froze, suddenly rigid.

"Embla?" Astrid reached for her.

The dragon didn't move — but she wasn't frightened. She was listening.

A voice, deep and ancient, unfurled inside Astrid's mind:

Welcome, fire-child.
Welcome back to the Heartforge — where dragons were born in flame and memory.
Where bonds were forged… and broken.
Where the old world ended.
Where the new one must begin.

Astrid's knees weakened.

Embla exhaled slowly, flame shimmering behind her teeth.

I remember…
Her thought was soft, reverent, full of newborn wonder.
Not my memories. Old ones. All dragons.

Astrid touched her wrist. "What do you see?"

Embla closed her eyes.

Fire. War. Shadows taking wing. Humans and dragons side by side — then apart. Betrayal. A song ending too soon.

Astrid swallowed.

"What does it mean?"

Embla opened her eyes.

That Calven cannot take me.
A pause.
That I must grow. Fast. Before he comes.

Astrid's breath caught.

"Embla… do you mean the Heartforge—?"

Yes.
Embla's voice warmed.
It can help me become what I must be.

"But is it safe?"

Embla nuzzled her cheek.

Not safe. Necessary.

The Horns of the Hunter

A sound split the air.

Astrid spun.

On the horizon — movement.
Lines of figures climbing the slope.
Horses struggling against the ascent.
Torches glowing like fiery beads along the mountainside.

Calven's forces.
Dozens now — maybe more.

Astrid's stomach crushed inward. "How did they track us so fast?"

The answer came from the storm — a single bolt of lightning striking a nearby ridge, illuminating the sky in ghastly silver.

The clouds churned in response.

The sky remembers dragons.
And through remembering… it betrayed them.

The Choice

Embla rose to her full height, scales flaring with faint golden light, the Heartforge responding under her claws.

I must learn. Here. Now.

Astrid's heart pounded. "If they reach the summit while you're in the Heartforge—"

You protect me. Like I protect you.

"That's not—"

We are one.
Her thought was fierce, steady.
If I leave the Heartforge early, I stay small. Weak. I cannot save you. I cannot save anyone.

Astrid's throat tightened. "Embla, I don't have magic or strength—"

You have me. And they fear that more than fire.

Astrid blinked through burning eyes.

"Alright. I'll hold them off as long as I can."

Embla pressed her warm forehead against Astrid's.
The rune-light surged around them.

Thank you, Astrid.
My heart. My storm-rider.

Astrid whispered back:

"My dragon."

Embla stepped into the center of the Heartforge.

The runes ignited.

The ground shook.

Golden fire spiraled upward around her, cocooning her in a wreath of shimmering flame.

Astrid turned toward the mountain path, gripping her father's old hunting knife with trembling fingers.

Torches climbed closer.

Horns sounded.
Footsteps thundered up the slope.

"Astrid Halvarsdottir!" Calven's voice echoed through the storm.
Cold. Pure. Triumphant.

She stood alone on the peak, facing the approaching army.

"No," she whispered.
"I'm not alone."

Behind her, Embla's cocoon of fire blazed brighter — and the mountain began to wake.

The Hunter on the Mountain

Calven's voice rolled up the slope, carried by the wind.

"Astrid Halvarsdottir! By the authority of the Holy Monastery of Solvengarde, I command you to stand down and surrender the beast."

Astrid stepped to the edge of the Heartforge plateau, boots scraping grit. She could see them clearly now — Calven at the front, cloak snapping, his shaved head bare to the storm. Behind him, two dozen soldiers climbed, shields strapped to their arms, spears strapped across their backs. More figures trudged behind, leading packhorses.

They looked small against the immense face of the mountain. But small things could still be deadly.

Astrid felt Embla's presence behind her, burning like a small sun. The dragon's body was no longer visible — only a towering column of golden fire, runes whirling within it like a storm of symbols. The cocoon roared without sound, its fury felt more in the chest than in the ears.

Calven stopped halfway up the final slope, perhaps fifty paces below. His eyes climbed to the blazing Heartforge, and for the first time Astrid saw him hesitate.

He made the sign of his faith across his chest, fingers slow.

"Saints preserve us," one of the soldiers muttered.

Astrid lifted her chin. "You're not welcome here."

Her voice sounded small, but it did not tremble.

Calven focused on her. His eyes were pale — the color of worn bone — and took her in like a puzzle piece that suddenly completed an old picture.

"You," he said softly. "You were always at the edge of things. Quiet. Watching." His gaze flicked briefly upward. "Hearing."

Astrid stiffened.

"You have no authority here," she said. "This mountain belongs to no monastery."

Calven's lips tightened. "Everything under the sun belongs to the Light, girl. Including abominations."

He lifted his arm. Spears shifted, shields tightened. The soldiers' boots bit into the snow.

Astrid felt the mountain's pulse beneath her feet. She took a slow breath.

Listen, she told herself. *Hear everything. Find the points that bend.*

She let her awareness sink.

The storm's roar dulled. The sound of her own heartbeat thinned into distance. Beneath it all, she heard the crunch of boots in snow. The scrape of metal. The grind of weight on a narrow path of rock.

And deeper still — the slow, steady rhythm of the mountain itself. Not a heartbeat. More like a drum that had been beating since the world was young.

She listened to the path they climbed — the fragile edge where stone had cracked and settled. A hairline fracture no one could see.

Except her.

Earth and Fear

"Astrid," Calven called. His voice had softened now, almost gentle. "You're alone up here. You cannot possibly hold this ground."

"Then go back," she said. "Take your men. Leave."

"You know I can't." His eyes held something like regret, buried deep. "The world has seen what rises again. The stories my order carries are not lies. Dragons bring fire and ruin."

Astrid's hands balled at her sides. "Who swung the blades in those stories, Calven? Who lit the torches?"

His jaw worked.

He gestured up at the blazing cocoon behind her. "That is not a hearth-fire, child. That is a weapon waiting to be forged."

Astrid looked back at the Heartforge. Embla's fire spun faster, brighter, streaks of white-blue now threading through the gold. The runes around the circle thrummed so hard she could feel them in her teeth.

Embla?

No words came — only a dull, focused heat. The dragon was far away, deeper than any dream.

"A weapon," Astrid said, turning back. "Or a shield. Or something you cannot control, and that terrifies you."

Calven's face tightened. For a moment, something almost like admiration flickered over it.

"You're braver than I thought," he said quietly. "But bravery without obedience is just defiance."

He raised his hand.

"Advance. Take her alive if you can. Kill the beast if it breaks that circle."

The front rank of soldiers began to climb.

The First Fall

As they climbed, the edges of their fear pressed against Astrid like cold hands. She could feel it radiating from them in trembling pulses: dread of the storm, dread of the fire, dread of the girl standing alone at the mountaintop.

She could use that.

Astrid stepped closer to the edge, boots inches from the drop.

"You should turn back," she called. "The mountain doesn't want you here."

A few soldiers glanced at one another.

Calven's voice snapped like a whip. "Eyes ahead!"

Astrid forced herself to breathe slowly. She sank her awareness again — not into the men this time, into the stone beneath their feet.

The fracture in the path ran along the edge of a narrow

shelf, where centuries of ice had eaten away at the rock.

She reached for it with her strange hearing — and for a terrifying moment, nothing happened.

Then the mountain's rhythm shifted.

Not much. Just a slight relaxing of pressure here, a tightening there. As if the stone acknowledged her presence. As if it were listening.

"Please," she whispered under her breath. "Just a little crumble. Just enough to scare them. Not to kill."

The path shuddered.

One boot slipped. A soldier cursed.

A slab of rock cracked beneath him, tilting. Snow sloughed off like flour from a cutting board. The soldier threw himself backward, grabbing his companion.

The slab broke off entirely.

It dropped in a rush of rock and ice, taking two more stones with it. The men clung to the mountain, panting, feet scrabbling for purchase. One lost his grip and slid — caught at the last second by a comrade who slammed his spear into a crevice for leverage.

Shouts erupted.

"Avalanche!"
"Hold the line!"
"Saints— that was no avalanche—"

Calven lifted his hand, and the soldiers went still.

He looked up at Astrid, eyes narrowed. "That was you."

She swallowed. "That was the mountain. I just… asked."

His face hardened. "You consort with dragons and bend the earth. Do you have any idea what you are, child?"

Astrid thought of Embla as a hatchling, curled in her arms. Of the warmth in her father's eyes when he first agreed to help hide the egg. Of the wizard's voice calling her *earth-listener.*

"I'm someone who won't let you hurt her," she said simply.

Calven stared at her for a long moment.

Then his gaze slid past her, to the blazing Heartforge.

"So be it," he murmured. "If you stand between the world and fire, then you stand as an enemy of the Light."

He turned to his men. "Archers!"

Storm-turned

Astrid's blood ran cold as three archers stepped forward, bows in hand. They planted their feet firmly, drawing arrow to cheek.

She saw exactly what Calven saw: not a girl, not a bond, but a single silhouette between his men and their target. Remove the silhouette, and the path to the cocoon opened.

She inhaled sharply.

"Loose!"

The arrows flew.

Time slowed.

Astrid heard their flight through the air — each feathered shaft cutting a line of sound. She felt the wind curl around them, the thinness of the air, the closeness of the storm.

She reached without thinking, not with hands, but with the part of her that listened.

Turn.

The storm answered.

A gust slammed across the mountaintop, furious and sudden. Two of the arrows were yanked violently off course, spinning away into the abyss. The third veered at the last instant, scraping past Astrid's arm and burying itself in the stone at her feet.

Pain lanced her upper arm. Warmth oozed through the fabric of her sleeve.

She staggered, hand flying to the wound. The arrow had grazed her, leaving a deep, burning cut.

Calven's eyes widened. Just a fraction.

"The storm," one of the soldiers breathed. "Did you see —? It bent the wind."

"The storm is just the storm," Calven snapped, but doubt had crept into his voice. "She's standing in its heart, that's all."

Astrid hissed softly through her teeth, clutching her arm. Blood soaked the sleeve, dark against the snow.

Behind her, Embla's cocoon flared orange-red, as if tasting Astrid's pain.

The ground vibrated.

Hurt?

The thought erupted in Astrid's mind, raw and instinctive. Embla's consciousness brushed hers — not fully awake, but aware enough to feel her.

I'm all right, Astrid thought quickly. *Finish what you're doing. I've got this.*

The fire of the Heartforge roared higher.

Calven flinched.

A Shadow in the Light

"Astrid!" another voice called, faint behind the thunder of the storm.

For a heartbeat, she thought it was the wizard.

It wasn't.

Down a separate path, narrower and less used, a single rider struggled up the slope on a shaggy mountain pony, cloak whipped by snow. No banner, no shining armor — just a weathered leather coat and a wool hood dusted white.

Halvar.

Astrid's heart lurched into her throat.

He'd followed them. All the way into the mountains.

"Papa?" The word tore from her before she could stop it.

Calven spun toward the sound, eyes narrowing.

Two soldiers turned with him, already moving to intercept.

Halvar swung down from the pony, nearly slipping in the snow. He was breathing hard — his face ruddy from cold and exertion. But his eyes were fierce, and once they found Astrid, they did not leave her.

"You couldn't just run without your old man, could you?" he called, breath fogging.

Astrid laughed, half-sob, half-hysterical. "You were supposed to stay safe!"

"Terrible at that," he wheezed. "Always have been."

Calven lifted his hand.

"Hold!" he called sharply to the soldiers moving toward Halvar. "Let him come."

Halvar stopped midway, glancing warily at the armed men around him. Then he squared his shoulders and climbed the rest of the way to Astrid's side.

Up close, she could see the exhaustion in him — the hollow under his cheekbones, the stiffness in his movements. He had traveled hard and fast to reach them.

He looked past her at the blazing Heartforge and whistled softly. "Well," he said. "That's… bigger than the one we hid under the bracken."

Astrid nodded numbly.

Halvar's jaw tightened as he took in her bloody sleeve. "You're hurt."

"It's nothing," she lied.

He reached out, squeezed her uninjured shoulder.

Then he turned to face Calven.

"Brother Calven," Halvar called. "Turn your men back."

Calven's expression cooled. "Halvar. I wondered how long you would keep your secrets hidden."

"Long as I could," Halvar said simply. "Not long enough."

Halvar's Sin

"You of all people know what dragons bring," Calven said, his voice carrying easily now. "You fought beside us when we purged the last of them. You saw the fires they called down from the sky."

"I saw people light those fires," Halvar snapped. Snow clung to his beard. "I saw fear turned into slaughter. It wasn't justice. It was vengeance."

Calven's eyes flashed. "Saints give us the right to protect humanity from destruction."

"Saints don't swing swords," Halvar shot back. "Men do."

The soldiers shifted uneasily.

Halvar took a breath, steadier now.

"You want my sin, Calven?" he called. "Here it is. I did as you asked, once. I hunted. I burned. I believed. And every night since, I have heard their screams in my sleep. The dragons'. The people's. The children's."

Astrid stared at him, stunned. He had never spoken of it like this. Not with such rawness.

Halvar pointed up at the blazing cocoon. "And when the earth whispered that one egg remained, I didn't turn my back. I hid it. I hid *her.*"

Calven's jaw clenched so hard Astrid thought his teeth might crack.

"You committed treason against God and crown," Calven said, his tone dangerously quiet. "For what?"

Halvar looked at Astrid.

"For a chance to do it right this time," he said. "For my daughter to see that not everything needs a sword taken to it."

Something twisted in Astrid's chest.

Calven nodded slowly, as if something had clicked into place.

"I see," he murmured. "You're further gone than I thought, Halvar. That's a shame. You were once a good man."

"I still am," Halvar said. "Which is why I'm telling you, as one who marched beside you — if you try to take that dragon, this mountain will be your grave."

The Wizard's Whisper

The storm thickened, clouds swirling tighter over the peak like a closing hand.

Calven lifted his hand. "Enough. I've heard your confession. I am not moved."

He gestured to his men. "Form up."

Shields locked with a dull clatter. Spears tilted.

At Astrid's back, the Heartforge shook, sending vibrations through her bones. Embla's presence flared, hot and worried.

They hurt you.
The thought was clearer now, closer.
Hurt him. Hurt us.

Not yet, Astrid thought quickly. *You're not ready, remember?*

The fire roared in answer, but didn't break.

Then, for the first time since they'd reached the mountains, the wizard's voice poured through Astrid's mind like warm tea over frozen fingers.

Astrid.

She almost cried in relief.

I can't come to you, he said, his thought thin and flickering. *Calven's net of zealots is spread too wide. Every path is watched.*

Then why—?

I can do one thing. His presence wavered, then steadied. *I can lend my strength to yours. Once. No more.*

Astrid tightened her grip on her knife. *What do I do?*

What you were born to do, earth-listener. There was pride in his tone. *Ask the mountain to speak loudly.*

She looked down at the soldiers arrayed on the path.

At Calven, standing unbent beneath the storm.

At Halvar, beside her, fists clenched, shoulders squared.

She stepped forward, just enough that the wind tugged at the hem of her cloak.

Then she closed her eyes.

The Mountain Speaks

Astrid inhaled deeply. She let the air fill her chest, then sink deeper. She listened.

To the crunch of snow.
To the rattle of armor.
To the restless whisper of men's fear.

Then she went deeper still.

Into the stone beneath their boots — not just the crack in the path now, but the bones of the mountain itself. Layers upon layers of rock, pressed by time into patience. Caverns beneath. Fault lines curled like sleeping serpents.

She laid her consciousness gently against them.

Please, she thought. *We don't want to kill. We just want them to stop.*

From somewhere far below, a slow answer rose — not words, but intention. The mountain was not kind. It was not cruel. It was simply… vast. Old. Aware in the way trees or oceans were aware.

The wizard's presence twined with hers, thin but steady.

Now, he whispered.

Astrid exhaled.

The mountain shuddered.

At first it was subtle — a tremor running through the path like a muscle tensing. Snow rolled off ledges in soft cascades.

Calven frowned. "Hold steady," he barked. "It's only—"

The ground bucked.

A section of the slope collapsed ten paces below the vanguard, taking snow, rock, and three men with it. They vanished in a spray of white and gray, their shouts cut off as they plummeted out of sight.

A wave of stone crashed down the ravine, roaring like a river.

Soldiers screamed. Horses reared and slipped, eyes rolling wide.

Half the formation broke rank automatically, scrambling backward.

"Saints save us!" someone yelled.

Calven staggered, catching himself on one knee.

Astrid gasped, horror slicing through her triumph. *Not so much—! I didn't mean—*

The mountain's motion slowed, then eased, settling into a low rumble. The path above the collapse was now narrow and cracked. Passable if they moved single-file and carefully. No place for a charging line of soldiers.

Halvar stared at Astrid, eyes wide.

"You did that?" he whispered.

She shook, bile rising in her throat. "I asked for… less," she said hoarsely. "I didn't want to—"

He gripped her shoulders.

"You *warned* them," he said. "They pressed on. That's not on you."

She swallowed hard.

Below, Calven dragged himself to his feet, face pale with fury and shock.

He stared up at Astrid, eyes burning.

"You dare." His voice rang out, steady again. "You dare use earth and storm as weapons."

Astrid didn't feel like she'd used a weapon. She felt like she'd tried to nudge a sleeping giant and accidentally roused it.

"Go back," she said, her voice cracking. "Please. That was a *warning*."

Calven's face smoothed suddenly, becoming almost calm.

"No," he said. "That was an act of war."

Retreat and Resolve

He turned to his men.

"Fall back."

They hesitated, stunned.

"Fall back!" he roared.

Slowly, reluctantly, the soldiers began to descend, some casting fearful glances at the churned stone and the blazing

Heartforge above. A few looked at Astrid — not with hatred, but with something like awe.

Calven remained where he was until the last of them had pulled back to safer ground.

Only then did he step carefully down the damaged path, his boots sure despite the fractures.

He stopped at the ragged edge where the slope had broken away. Snow swirled around him; lightning illuminated his profile for a heartbeat, carving him in stark white.

"Astrid Halvarsdottir!" he called.

She stepped closer again, but only just. Her wounded arm throbbed.

"There will come a reckoning," Calven said. "You've sealed your path now. There is no forgiveness for what you've done."

She swallowed. "For… defending myself?"

"For choosing the dragon," he said. "For choosing *it* over God, over your people, over the safety of the world."

His gaze flicked to the blazing cocoon behind her.

"Enjoy your mountain," he said softly. "We will return. With more men. With fire that does not listen to you. With blessings that make storms kneel."

He made the sign of his faith again, but this time, the gesture held something darker — less like prayer, more like promise.

Then he turned and began the descent, cloak snapping, boots steady. The soldiers parted for him below like water.

Astrid watched until he vanished into the whirling snow.

Only then did she realize her knees were shaking.

Aftershocks

The wizard's presence flickered again.

You did well, he murmured. *Too well, perhaps. That will give him stories to tell.*

"I killed men," Astrid whispered, throat tight. "Three of them. Maybe more."

You warned them. You gave them chance after chance. The mountain chose its price, not you, the wizard said gently. *But I know that does not make it easier.*

Halvar's hand settled on her shoulder.

"You saved us," he said roughly. "You saved Embla. You saved me. You might have saved the whole valley. If he'd come with that many men to Havngard…"

She thought of cottages burning, of children screaming, of the storm's lightning called down on roofs.

She squeezed her eyes shut.

The wizard sighed through her mind, the sound like wind through bare branches.

I must go, he said. *Calven will spread his net wider. If I stay near, I will draw it to you.*

"Will we see you again?" Astrid whispered.

A pause.

When the time is right, he said. *And if not in this life, then in the stories told about you.*

She almost smiled. "You're terrible at comfort."

I'm a wizard, not a nursemaid, he sniffed faintly. Then softer: *But I believe in you, Astrid. And in her. Don't let the weight of today break you.*

His presence faded, like smoke on cold air.

She was alone again — except she wasn't.

The Dragon Emerges

The Heartforge reached a peak of brightness so intense Astrid had to shield her eyes. The column of fire that had wrapped Embla now twisted inward, condensing, folding like wings closing.

The runes pulsed one last time and then detonated in a ring of golden light that washed across the plateau.

Astrid staggered back; Halvar threw an arm up to shield his face.

When the light cleared, Embla stood at the center of the circle.

She was still smaller than the dragons in old stories — no mountain-sized titan — but she had grown. Her neck was longer, more graceful. Her wings had broadened, the membranes veined with faint lines of silver-white that flickered faintly with leftover lightning.

Her scales, once a soft dusk-gold, now gleamed with hints of stormlight, like sunlight reflected off a distant sea. The ridges along her spine had sharpened, and the horns at the back of her head swept backward in elegant arcs.

Most striking were her eyes.

They burned with molten amber — and deep within, in their very center, small sparks flickered like trapped stars.

Embla took a breath.

When she exhaled, a plume of flame burst from her mouth — not the small, startled gout she'd produced at the hollow, but a controlled stream laced with crackling blue threads.

It scorched the air, leaving the scent of lightning behind.

Halvar whistled low. "Well," he murmured. "That's…
new."

Embla turned to Astrid.

You're hurt.
The thought carried more nuance now, layered with worry, anger,
guilt.

Astrid lifted her injured arm. The bleeding had slowed,
but the cut was ugly.

"I'll live," she said. "Are you…?"

I am more. Embla's voice was deeper now, but still undeniably
hers. **And I remember things that were not mine to remember.
Old flights. Old fires. Old endings.**

She stepped closer, lowering her head until her snout was
inches from Astrid's arm.

Warmth flowed from her — gentle, nothing like the roar
of the Heartforge. Astrid felt her skin tingle, then cool. She
risked a glance.

The wound had not vanished, but it had closed, edges
knotted together, the worst of the damage soothed.

Astrid stared. "You can heal?"

No. Embla shook her head, scales shivering. **Not fully. I can…
encourage. Remind the flesh what it wants to be.**

Halvar let out a shaky laugh. "I could use a bit of that in
my knees."

Embla's pupils narrowed in amusement. **Later.**

Astrid managed a breathless smile.

Then it faded.

"Calven's gone," she said quietly. "For now. But he'll return. With more men. Better prepared."

Embla's gaze turned south, toward where the soldiers had disappeared into the veiled valleys.

Let him come, she growled.

Her fire flared at the edges of her teeth.

Astrid reached up, placing a hand on her snout.

"Not yet," she said. "We still don't know what he'll do to find us. Or… what he'll do to everyone else if he can't."

Halvar's expression sobered. He looked south as well.

Smoke, thin and distant, was beginning to smudge the horizon. Too dark, too thick to be from cookfires alone.

Astrid's stomach turned.

"He won't like being turned back," Halvar murmured. "He'll find somewhere else to vent his anger."

Embla snarled softly. **He hurts others because he cannot hurt us.**

Astrid's hand tightened on her scales.

"Then we have to decide," she whispered. "Do we stay up here and let them burn the world looking for us? Or do we go down there and make them stop?"

The question hung in the cold air, heavy as stone, hot as dragonfire.

Neither Halvar nor Embla answered immediately.

The mountain, newly awakened, listened in silence.

Astrid looked from her father to her dragon, feeling the

storm's electricity still humming faintly in her veins, the echo of the Heartforge still buzzing under her skin.

She had wanted to hide.

Now, for the first time, she wasn't sure hiding was enough anymore.

The wind shifted.

From the south came the smell of smoke — and of something else beneath it.

Ash.
Char.
A village, or something like it, burning.

Embla lifted her head, nostrils flaring, eyes narrowing.

They've started, she whispered. **The world burns while we stand on a rock.**

Astrid's throat closed.

Calven had begun his hunt in earnest.

The choice that would define them no longer lay somewhere far in the future.

It was already here.

And the mountain that remembered watched as the girl and the dragon turned their gaze toward the fires below, knowing that sooner than either of them wanted, they would have to carry storm and flame back down into the world.

Chapter 20

The Smoke in the Valley

The fires spread long before the smoke reached the mountain.

Astrid saw them at dawn — streaks of orange smoldering along the southern horizon. Faint at first, like distant lanterns, then growing as the wind shifted, revealing the shape of devastation below.

Embla stood with wings half-open, her body held taut as a bowstring. Halvar paced a short distance away, cursing under his breath and squinting through the smoky haze.

"Astrid," Embla murmured, her voice trembling through their bond. **They burn homes. They burn people.**

Astrid swallowed hard. Her heart felt like it was being squeezed by a fist. "He's started early."

Halvar rested a heavy hand on her shoulder. "He's angry. You humiliated him in front of his men. A man like Calven will scorch half the world just to remind it who holds the torch."

Astrid looked down the mountain, toward the jagged path Calven had traveled the day before. She could still see broken sections of rock, blackened from lightning and the Heartforge's glow. But now new scars marred the valley — curling smoke, tiny figures fleeing through snow, horses bolting in panic.

Her breath trembled.

"We should've gone after him," she whispered. "Stopped him before he got down there."

Halvar shook his head. "He had twice as many men as we do arms between us. And Embla wasn't ready. You did the right thing."

But doing the right thing did not make the world less on fire.

Astrid clenched her jaw, blinking back the sting of tears.

"We can't hide here any longer," she said quietly. "No matter how strong the Heartforge makes Embla, it doesn't protect anyone else."

Embla's scales shivered with rising heat. **We go. Now.**

Halvar frowned. "And hit where, girl? He could be anywhere down there."

"He'll be where the screams are," Astrid said bitterly.

The wind carried those screams faintly now — muffled but unmistakable. The sound cut like thin knives.

Embla lowered herself, wings spreading.

Climb on. The air remembers his trail. I can follow it.

Astrid nodded, climbing quickly onto Embla's back. Her heart hammered. Fear and fury and determination churned inside her like three storms colliding.

Halvar hesitated. "Astrid… if you go down there—"

"You're not staying behind," she said, grabbing his wrist. "You followed me once already. Follow me again."

A small, pained smile crossed his face.

"You're too much like your mother," he muttered. "Stubborn as frost on a blade."

Astrid returned it with a thin, trembling smile. "You say that like it's a bad thing."

He climbed up behind her, seating himself between

Embla's back spines, holding tight.

Embla crouched.

Hold.

Then she leapt from the mountain.

The Long Descent

The wind seized them immediately, cold and biting, but Embla dove with confidence that hadn't been there before the Heartforge. Her wings cut clean arcs through the storm's remnants. Lightning flickered far above, but it no longer reached for them. It simply glowed silently, like an eye watching.

Astrid pressed herself close to Embla's neck as they plunged downward through layers of cloud. The valley stretched out beneath them in a wide sweep of frost and pines.

Smoke rose in dark pillars.

Lots of them.

Astrid's breath hitched.

"Saints," Halvar murmured. "He's not searching. He's punishing."

Embla's wings beat faster, angling toward the nearest burn.

The smell hit them first — acrid, heavy, choking. Ash drifted upward like black snowflakes. The closer they flew, the more the world shifted from white to gray.

Embla slowed, gliding lower.

They passed above a small settlement — or what remained of it. Houses lay in smoking ruins, timbers collapsed inward, roofs charred. A barn still smoldered at the edges. Chickens scattered wildly through snow, feathers blackened. Two horses lay on their sides, unmoving.

Astrid gagged.

Halvar clenched his jaw so hard his teeth creaked. "This was Torndal," he said hoarsely. "They had no quarrel with anyone. They trade fish and wool. That's it."

Astrid's stomach twisted. "Where are the people?"

Embla angled downward slightly, following faint traces of footprints in the snow — a stampede of them. Some small. Too small.

"They ran," Halvar whispered. "By the gods, they ran for their lives."

Astrid closed her eyes. For one terrible second, she wished she hadn't opened them again.

When she did, she saw what Embla had been following.

Bodies.

Not many. But enough.

A few lay in the snow near the village's edge. A woman curled protectively around a child. A man sprawled nearby, his back burned so badly his tunic had fused to him.

Astrid's throat shredded itself trying not to scream.

Halvar bowed his head, jaw trembling.

Embla growled so deeply the ground itself vibrated.

Calven did this. Not dragons. Not storms. Him.

Astrid wiped her eyes roughly. "We find him. And we stop this. Whatever it takes."

Halvar nodded grimly.

Embla launched upward again.

The Survivors' Hollow

They followed the trail of smoke and screaming.

Three more settlements burned behind them, each worse than the last. Embla's fury grew like fire itself — but Astrid could feel something else beneath it.

Fear.

Not for herself.

For Astrid.

He wants you, Embla whispered. **He won't stop until he takes you away. Or kills me. Or both.**

Astrid reached forward, pressing her palm against Embla's warm scales. "He won't take us apart. Not while I breathe."

The dragon trembled under her touch.

They flew onward until Embla slowed suddenly.

Beneath them lay a narrow hollow nestled between two ridges — a small pocket of trees, smoke rising faintly from the center.

Not fire-smoke.

Campfire.

People, Embla murmured.

They descended.

As Embla landed, villagers emerged from between the trees — women clutching children, men holding makeshift spears or axes, teenagers with soot on their faces.

Their eyes widened at the sight of a dragon, and they recoiled in fear.

"Wait!" Astrid jumped from Embla's back, landing lightly on the snow. She raised her uninjured arm. "We're not here to hurt you!"

One man stepped forward, axe raised. "Ke—keep that thing back!"

Embla hissed, offended rather than threatened.

"Please!" Astrid cried. "We saw the burned villages. We just want to help."

A murmur rippled through the group.

A gray-haired woman stepped forward. "Help?" she said bitterly. "With what? Our homes are gone. Our kin are dead. The monastery's men said they were looking for a girl with a beast." Her eyes traveled to Embla. "And I suppose that'd be you."

Halvar stepped forward. "Listen to her. Please. My name is Halvar Vennson. This is my daughter. And we're trying to stop the slaughter. But we need to know — where did Calven go?"

The villagers exchanged dark looks.

Finally, the axe-wielding man jerked his chin to the east.

"They headed toward Skarlund," he said grimly. "Bigger place. More people to terrorize."

Astrid's stomach clenched. Skarlund wasn't just bigger — it was fortified, crowded. Hundreds of people lived there.

Halvar swore under his breath. "He's escalating. Trying to draw you out."

Astrid nodded. "Then we go to Skarlund. Right now."

The villagers drew back as Embla crouched again.

A child — a boy of maybe eight — tugged at Astrid's sleeve before she mounted.

"Mistress?" he whispered. "Are you… going to stop the bad men?"

Astrid's heart cracked.

"Yes," she whispered, kneeling. "I'm going to try."

He nodded solemnly and slipped something into her hand — a wooden token carved with the shape of a fish. "For luck. Mama said heroes always need luck."

Astrid blinked rapidly and closed her fingers around it.

"Thank you."

She climbed onto Embla's back.

Halvar swung up behind.

Astrid looked down at the villagers one last time.

"We'll come back," she said softly. "And we'll help you rebuild."

The gray-haired woman nodded, tears streaking her ash-covered cheeks.

Embla opened her wings wide, casting a long shadow across the hollow.

Hold tight, she whispered.

Then they were airborne.

The Road to Skarlund

The land eastward sloped gradually upward — rocky

outcroppings, patches of frost-hardened grass, tall pines bent by the wind. Smoke curled in the distance — but this time, it wasn't a dozen small plumes.

It was one enormous column.

"Astrid," Halvar said quietly, "Skarlund is burning."

Astrid's stomach dropped so fast it nearly took her breath.

"Embla," she whispered, voice tight, "faster."

I'm already trying.

The dragon pushed herself harder, wings beating with fierce precision. Snow blasted outward beneath them as they surged forward.

Skarlund's wooden outer wall rose into view — or what remained of it. One section had been torn apart by fire. Flames licked the edges of rooftops. People ran through the streets like ants scattered from a kicked nest.

And through it all moved a dark line of shapes — armored soldiers marching in coordinated rows, pushing families aside, dragging people into the center square.

Calven stood at the heart of it all, robes whipping, hands raised like a conductor in the midst of an orchestra of screams.

Astrid's vision tunneled.

Embla's fury exploded across their bond like molten iron.

We stop him now.

And then — before Astrid or Halvar could prepare — Embla folded her wings and dove.

The wind screamed around them.

Astrid held on with both arms as the ground rushed up to

meet them.

"Embla—!"

He burns the world, Embla snarled. **I burn back.**

She opened her jaws — and the sky answered.

A torrent of blue-gold flame erupted downward.

It struck the street in front of Calven with a roar that shook the earth, sending soldiers flying, shields melting, torch-bearers stumbling backward in terror.

Calven staggered, his cloak catching fire — he ripped it off, eyes blazing with both fear and triumph.

He had wanted her to come.

Now she had.

Embla landed hard, claws skidding, wings cutting down soldiers like scythes. She threw her head back and roared — a sound that split the snow-choked air like shattering glass.

Astrid leapt from her back, knife drawn, heart pounding so violently it felt like it might burst.

Calven stepped through smoke and flame, face illuminated by the dragonfire still burning behind him.

"Finally," he breathed, smiling. "The dragon comes to the slaughter, and brings her rider with her."

Astrid's pulse turned to ice.

This was no hunt anymore.

This was war.

Calven's men recovered first.

"Form up!" he shouted, voice cutting through the chaos. "Shields! Bows!"

The training drilled into them took over. Soldiers scrambled into position even as Embla's flame still crackled along the cobblestones, leaving glowing veins of heat in the stone. A few lay groaning or silent where the first blast had thrown them, armor blackened, shields warped.

The people of Skarlund scattered in every direction — dragging children, clutching bundles, stumbling over fallen barrels and broken market stalls. Some dove for doorways. Others huddled behind toppled carts, eyes wild.

"Get them clear!" Astrid shouted over her shoulder.

Halvar was already moving, sprinting toward a cluster of villagers trapped behind a burning cart. "This way!" he bellowed. "Move!"

Embla lashed her tail, sending two soldiers flying into a wall. Spears thudded against her scales and skittered off, leaving only shallow scratches.

Little needles, she snarled. **They sting but do not bite.**

"Don't get cocky," Astrid muttered, backing toward her. "There are a lot of needles."

"Archers!" Calven snapped.

A dozen men lifted bows almost in unison.

"Aim for the eyes!" he roared.

Astrid's heart lurched. "Embla!"

The dragon threw her head up, wings snapping open. Arrows flew — and the wind hit them like a wall.

The storm hadn't left the mountains; it had followed her.

Gusts spiraled around Embla's head, knocking most of the arrows off course. A few found gaps — one sliced along her jaw, another lodged between two scales on her shoulder. Embla flinched with a roar of pain.

Bugs, she spat. **Persistent bugs.**

Astrid's knife felt very small.

She darted forward anyway, slashing at a soldier who got too close. He raised his shield; the blade scraped along the rim. He shoved her back with its weight, and she stumbled.

Another soldier lunged in, spearpoint aimed at her ribs.

Embla's foreleg came down between them, claws gouging the cobbles. The spear splintered against her scales. The soldier gaped up — then Embla flicked him aside like a twig.

Stay close, she growled. **You are not for their spears.**

"I can't just hide behind you!" Astrid protested, breathless.

Why not? Embla demanded, scandalized. **That is exactly what you should do.**

Astrid didn't have time to argue. Calven raised one hand, palm outward, murmuring something under his breath.

The air around him shimmered, heat warring with the cold of the snow.

"Back!" Astrid shouted, recognizing the feel of magic. "Embla—!"

Too late.

Calven thrust his hand forward.

A blast of white-gold fire erupted from his palm — nothing like the sprawling roar of dragonflame, but focused, narrow, vicious. It struck Embla full in the chest.

She screamed, stumbling backward, wings flaring. The fire licked over her scales, clinging like oil.

Astrid's heart stopped. "Embla!"

HOT! Embla's thought was pure, shocked agony. **Wrong fire!**

She rolled, crashing into a row of empty stalls, flattening them. Wood exploded into splinters around her.

Calven panted, shoulders heaving. The skin of his outstretched hand was red and blistered, but his eyes glittered with fanatical satisfaction.

"See?" he shouted, voice cracking with exertion. "Dragons burn — but the Light burns them back!"

Soldiers roared in ragged approval.

Astrid ran to Embla's side, dropping to her knees.

"Embla, Embla, look at me—"

The dragon's chest heaved, soot streaking her scales where Calven's fire had struck. The light on her hide dimmed, then steadied.

She turned her head toward Astrid, pupils thin with pain.

I hate him, she said simply.

Astrid swallowed. "Good. That makes two of us."

"Archers! Nock!" Calven cried.

Astrid's eyes darted around wildly. Too many soldiers. Too many bows. Too many lines of fire — and civilians still trapped everywhere.

They couldn't win this in a straight fight.

They needed fear.

Not theirs.

His.

The Dragon Who Stepped Close

"Embla," Astrid whispered, heart pounding. "We have to break them. Not just their bodies. Their *certainty*."

Embla's nostrils flared. **How?**

Astrid's gaze snapped back to Calven.

He stood in the street's center, surrounded by men but still somehow alone — a dark pillar against the blaze of burning roofs. Confidence clung to him like a second cloak.

"He thinks he's above you," Astrid snarled. "Above all of us. He thinks he can stand there and call dragonfire down like it's just weather."

She leaned close, her hand flat against Embla's cheek.

"Show him what it means when a dragon chooses to *aim*."

Embla's pupils dilated.

Slowly, her lips curled back from her teeth in something that was not quite a smile.

Very well, she said. **Stay with me. And be ready to move.**

She surged to her feet, shaking off splintered wood. Calven's eyes snapped to her, jaw tightening when he saw she was still standing.

"Loose!" he shouted.

Arrows flew — but Embla didn't leap skyward this time. She charged.

Her claws tore furrows in the street as she barreled forward. Soldiers scrambled to brace, shields coming up too late, too scattered. Embla plowed through them like a living avalanche, batting men aside with her shoulders, knocking shields from hands.

"Hold formation!" Calven bellowed. "Hold—"

Embla stopped three strides from him.

Close enough that Astrid could see his pupils constrict, skin gleaming with sweat despite the cold.

Close enough that if he reached out, he could have touched her snout.

He had to tip his head back to see her fully.

Embla lowered her head slowly, deliberately, until her eyes were level with his.

For the first time, Astrid saw it.

A tremor.

Not in his hand. In his faith.

Embla inhaled.

Not a great heaving breath for a wide, sweeping jet of flame.

A controlled, narrow draw, the way a glassblower might gather fire.

Calven realized what she was doing a second too late.

He tried to step back.

Embla exhaled through her nose.

Two streams of fire burst from her nostrils — thin, whip-quick, impossibly precise. They shot past Calven's shoulders, crossing behind him in a circle of blue-gold that traced the air around his body like a ring drawn by a giant hand.

The flames hit the cobbles and caught, racing around him

in a perfect loop.

For one breath, Calven stood untouched.

Then the circle of fire rose.

It climbed like a wall, weaving itself into a cylindrical cage of flame that licked upward higher than his head. Heat washed over him in a suffocating wave. His cloak edges smoldered where they brushed too close.

Soldiers stumbled backward, eyes wide.

Calven spun, trapped inside the ring, his expression finally stripped of smugness.

For the first time, he looked exactly what he was:

Terrified.

Fire Without Touch

He flung his burned hand outward, calling upon his own magic again. White-gold light crackled against the blue-gold flames of Embla's breath — but they did not part. They hissed where they met, sparking like oil and water at war.

Astrid stood just beyond the circle, chest heaving, knife forgotten in her hand.

Embla's flared nostrils still glowed faintly, thin tendrils of smoke curling from them like breath on a winter morning.

I will not burn him yet, she said, voice low and dangerous. **But he will feel what he has made others feel. Surrounded. Trapped. Small.**

Calven's composure cracked.

"This— this is nothing!" he shouted, though his voice shook. "Fire is fire! All fire answers to the Light!"

He thrust his hand outward again, hurling a bolt of his

pale flame at the circle.

It splashed against Embla's fire and fizzled, leaving only steam. The ring didn't budge.

"Calven." Astrid's voice rang clear over the roar.

He turned, face slick with sweat, eyes wild.

"You wanted to see a dragon up close," she said. "You wanted to judge us. To purge us. To burn us away." Her hands were shaking, but her voice did not. "You stand in judgment now."

"You're a child," he spat, but there was a thread of panic in it now. "You don't understand what you're toying with."

"I understand villages turned to ashes," she said. "I understand mothers dying to shield their children. I understand people running with nothing but the clothes on their backs because one man decided they were acceptable kindling."

She stepped closer to the ring, the heat making sweat bead on her skin.

"I understand *you*," she finished.

The crowd had stilled.

People peered from behind barrels, half-collapsed doorways, shattered wagons. Soldiers who'd kept their footing were frozen where they stood, weapons clutched uselessly.

Halvar moved quietly among the civilians, urging them farther back from the ring of flame, putting distance between them and whatever would come next.

Calven's lip curled.

"You think this changes anything?" he snarled. "You think scaring me in front of frightened peasants will undo the truth written in blood and scripture? Dragons corrupt. Dragons destroy. They cannot coexist with men."

Embla's eyes narrowed.

You burn villages and say *we* cannot coexist.

Her thought crashed into Calven's mind like a wave.

He flinched, eyes widening as if a voice had shouted inside his skull.

"You—" he gasped. "You speak—"

"Of course she speaks," Astrid snapped. "She listens better than you do."

A Fracture in Faith

For a heartbeat, silence hung heavy.

Then a voice piped up from the edge of the crowd — shaky but clear.

"If dragons are so evil," a woman called, "how come she hasn't roasted you where you stand?"

Heads turned.

Calven snapped his gaze toward the speaker — a young mother clutching a soot-smeared toddler to her chest, a burn on her arm hastily wrapped with cloth.

"Blasphemy," he hissed. "You have no idea what—"

"She hasn't killed any of us either," an older man added, voice rough. "Just your men. The ones who torched our homes."

Murmurs rippled through the crowd.

Embla's gaze slid over them, then back to Calven.

They see.

Astrid's chest ached with something like hope.

"This is how it begins," she said quietly. "With people seeing the difference between who lights fires—and who puts them out."

Calven's face twisted.

"You think they'll follow you?" he snarled. "You, a girl who talks to stone? A beast who breathes storms?"

His eyes glittered with something dark.

"They'll follow whoever keeps their children alive," Halvar said from the side, stepping forward. "And so far, that isn't you."

Calven's patience snapped.

With a roar, he hurled himself bodily toward the ring, thrusting both hands outward, magic flaring bright enough to hurt to look at.

His white-gold fire slammed into Embla's blue-gold circle.

For a moment, the two mingled, merging into a blinding wall of molten light.

Embla flinched, stumbling.

He pushes—

The circle wavered.

Astrid felt the strain like a pressure in her skull. Embla wasn't just holding the fire with her lungs now — she was shaping it with will, with everything the Heartforge had woken inside her. And Calven was pouring his own fury into it.

"We can't let him break through," Astrid gasped. "If he gets loose—"

I know.

Embla's mental voice was tight with effort.

Astrid did the only thing she could think of. She reached for the bond between them and shoved everything she had into it.

Not power.

Resolve.

She poured in memories — of holding the egg in the hollow, of Embla's first clumsy steps, of the joy the first time Embla's wings had carried them both.

Of Torndal's dead in the snow.

Of the boy's token in her hand.

She fed Embla the simple, burning certainty that *they could not let this man win.*

The dragon roared.

The blue-gold flames surged, swallowing Calven's white-gold in a flood. The circle brightened, then snapped inward, tightening like a noose.

For a terrifying heartbeat, Astrid thought it would close on him completely.

"Embla, no!" she cried.

The dragon's flame halted — stopping inches from Calven's skin, the heat so intense his hair singed, eyebrows curling, lips cracking. He screamed, staggering to his knees.

His faith didn't look like armor anymore.

It looked like a mask melting.

Choices in Firelight

Astrid staggered closer to the ring, ignoring the burn on her own skin.

"Calven," she said through gritted teeth. "Look at me."

He did, panting, eyes wild with pain and hatred and something like dawning horror.

"You feel that?" she asked. "That's what it's like. To be hemmed in. To be given no choice but burn or die."

She took another step, feeling the tips of her hair curl in the heat.

"You did this to Torndal," she said. "To all of them. You stand here in your robes and talk about Light, but all I see is a man who would rather set the world on fire than admit he might be wrong."

He bared his teeth. "There is no wrong in purging evil."

"You're standing in a cage made of the thing you claim to control," she snapped. "And the only reason you're still breathing is because the 'evil' you fear doesn't want to become you."

Silence followed.

Some of the soldiers lowered their weapons.

Calven saw it.

"Listen to her and you'll damn your souls," he rasped, desperate. "She's ensorcelled the dragon. They're demons, both of them. They show mercy now only so you'll trust them before they turn on you."

Embla's nostrils flared.

If I meant to kill you, I would have, she growled. **I do not need your trust to end you. Only your location.**

A few of the soldiers flinched at the voice in their heads.

Halvar stepped closer to Astrid, close enough that she could feel his presence at her back.

"We can kill him," he said quietly. "Right now. Make it quick. End this, before he gathers more men, before he burns more towns."

The words hit harder than any spear.

Astrid stared at Calven.

At the burns on his hands. At the way his breath came fast and shallow. At the sweat and soot streaking his once-immaculate robes.

She thought of the villagers' bodies in the snow.

Of the mother wrapped around her child.

Of the smoke on the horizon still rising.

Her fingers tightened on the knife's hilt.

It would be so easy.

One thrust. One choice.

The ring of fire flickered, waiting.

Embla waited too, eyes locked on Astrid.

If you say it, she whispered, **I will close the circle.**

Astrid's heart slammed against her ribs.

She could feel the weight of the decision like a stone in her chest — not just for her, not just for Embla, but for the shape of the world that would come after.

Kill him, and they might stop this wave of burning.

But they would also set a precedent.

A girl and a dragon taking lives in judgment.

Becoming executioners.

The sort of monsters Calven already *saw* when he looked at them.

Astrid swallowed, throat dry.

She lowered the knife.

"No," she whispered.

Halvar sucked in a sharp breath. "Astrid—"

"No," she repeated, louder this time. "If we kill him now, we prove him right. That dragons are just fire with teeth. That people like me are just another kind of weapon."

She looked at Calven, voice shaking but steady.

"I won't be what you say I am," she said. "And I won't let her be what your order made her kin into."

Calven stared at her as if she'd grown a second head.

"You think mercy makes you strong?" he hissed. "It makes you weak. It makes you easy to cut down."

"Maybe," she said. "But at least I'll know what I am when I look in a mirror."

She turned to Embla.

"Let him go."

Embla recoiled as if she'd been struck.

Astrid—

"Let him go," she said again, voice breaking. "If he comes after us again, then… then we'll be ready. But this time, *we* won't be the ones who started the killing."

Embla's gaze searched her face.

Long seconds passed.

Finally, with a sound like a sigh made of flame, she lifted her head.

The ring of fire uncoiled, stretching up and outward, dissolving into the smoky air. Heat washed over them as it went, leaving scorched cobbles and a circle of glassy, melted stone where it had been.

Calven collapsed to his hands and knees, coughing, steam rising from his robes.

Soldiers rushed toward him.

Embla bared her teeth, and they froze.

Astrid stepped back, toward Embla's side.

"We're leaving," she said to the gathered crowd — villagers and soldiers alike. "We didn't come here to rule you. Or to burn you. We came to stop this."

She gestured toward the charred ruins of Skarlund.

"And we'll keep trying to stop it. You can choose who you believe after we're gone. Him." She jerked her chin at Calven. "Or the dragon who spared the man who murdered your homes."

The crowd murmured.

Some faces were still tight with fear.

But others…

Others watched Embla with something else in their eyes.

Not worship.

Not hatred.

Possibility.

Leaving Skarlund

Halvar gripped Astrid's shoulder. "You sure about this, girl? Once we leave, he'll twist this tale to whatever suits him best."

"I know," she said tiredly. "But we'll still be out there. And so will they." She nodded toward the villagers. "They saw what happened. Even if he twists the story, something won't sit right when he tells it."

Halvar's mouth flattened, but he nodded.

"You're braver than I ever was," he muttered.

Embla knelt, lowering her shoulders. Astrid climbed up, every muscle aching. Halvar joined her, settling in behind.

Calven dragged himself upright, leaning hard on two soldiers. His eyebrows were gone, his hair singed, his skin reddened and raw.

He looked, for the first time, *mortal.*

"Astrid!" he croaked.

She hesitated, looking down at him.

"This isn't over," he rasped, voice shredded. "I will hunt you to the edge of the world. I will purge this land. You may win their hearts for a day, but the Light—"

"The Light doesn't need you to speak for it," Astrid said quietly. "And if it does, maybe it isn't what you think it is."

His face twisted with fury.

Embla spread her wings.

The people of Skarlund scattered back as wind blasted through the square, snuffing small fires, sending ash swirling.

For a moment, Astrid and Embla and Halvar hung over the burning town, silhouetted against the smoke-stained sky.

Many eyes watched them.

Some full of fear.

Some full of wonder.

A few, quietly, full of hope.

Then Embla leapt upward, beating her wings, carrying them back into the ever-watchful sky.

Smoke Behind, Storm Ahead

They flew until Skarlund was a gray smear behind them.

Astrid's muscles throbbed with exhaustion. Her mind hummed with the echo of too many choices. The smell of smoke clung to her clothes, her hair, her very skin.

She leaned forward, resting her forehead against Embla's neck.

"Did I do the right thing?" she whispered.

Embla's thought brushed hers, weary but warm.

Right and wrong are human words, she said. **I know only this: you chose not to kill when you could have. And you hurt because of it. That feels... right, to me.**

Halvar snorted softly behind them. "You made a choice you can live with," he said. "That's all any of us can do. I... did not, once." His voice thickened. "I envy you."

Astrid closed her eyes, letting the wind sting her face clean.

Far ahead, beyond the next range of hills, stormclouds gathered again — not the wild, ancient storm of the mountain this time, but the slow, heavy brewing of something else.

Consequence.

Resistance.

Change.

Embla angled toward a line of untouched forest, where no smoke rose and no horns sounded.

We need to rest, she said. **You are small and soft. You fold if we push too far.**

Astrid almost laughed.

"Put that on my grave," she muttered.

Halvar chuckled. "Not yet, girl. Not for a long time, if I have anything to say about it."

They descended toward a quiet clearing, the world below them, for this one small moment, not yet on fire.

Behind them, in Skarlund, stories were already beginning.

Of a dragon who burned soldiers, but spared a killer.

Of a girl who spoke with storm and stone.

Of a man of the Light who had screamed inside a ring of dragonfire and lived to swear vengeance.

And ahead of them, in chapters yet unwritten, the war between all those stories was only just beginning.

Chapter 21

The Gathering Storm

The forest swallowed them like a great green veil.

Embla glided low between the towering pines, her wings angled carefully to avoid the branches. Snow fell in soft, lazy spirals through the needles above, settling on her scales in delicate crystals that melted instantly from her warmth.

Astrid clung to her neck, exhaustion tugging heavily at her limbs. Halvar leaned behind her, holding on more tightly than he let on. Their clothes were singed, their faces smudged with soot, and every breath carried the faint sting of smoke.

But for the first time since dawn…

There was quiet.

Embla touched down in a small clearing beside a frozen stream, her claws sinking into soft snow. She folded her wings with a tired grunt.

Down, she murmured. **We rest now. My fire is… hollow.**

Astrid slid off instantly, stumbling as her knees buckled. Halvar caught her arm, steadying her.

"You're running on will alone," he muttered. "Sit, girl. That's an order."

Astrid gave him a weak smile. "Since when do I follow orders?"

"Since you nearly fell off a dragon," he said. "Now sit."

She did. Her whole body trembled with aftershocks — adrenaline draining, fear settling, guilt simmering beneath it all like a restless ember.

Embla sank beside her with surprising delicacy for a creature her size. She curled her tail around them protectively, as though shielding them from a world that had turned too sharp.

Halvar crouched over her bleeding arm, inspecting the half-healed wound.

"Could've been worse," he grunted. "Should've been worse. How in blazes did it close like that?"

Astrid traced the faint silver seam across her skin. "Embla did it."

Halvar raised an eyebrow. "With fire?"

"No," Astrid whispered. "With… something else."

Embla's eyes half-lidded.

I reminded your flesh how to be whole. Only a little. I cannot force it. Only guide.

Halvar let out a long breath. "Not sure if that's miraculous or terrifying."

Astrid leaned against Embla's warm flank, letting her eyes close for a moment.

Then Halvar spoke the question none of them wanted to face.

"What happens now?"

The Cost of Mercy

Astrid opened her eyes slowly.

"I don't know," she admitted. "Calven won't stop. Not after today."

"No," Halvar agreed. "You not killing him — that's a wound to his pride deeper than any blade. Worse, witnesses saw it. His own men saw it."

Astrid chewed her lip. "You think they'll talk?"

Halvar gave a humorless laugh. "Oh, they'll talk. They'll talk all the way back to their monastery. Every man will tell a different version — but all of them will include one thing."

He met her eyes.

"That their holy leader was brought to his knees in a ring of dragonfire."

Astrid's stomach twisted.

"He'll twist the story," she murmured.

"He has to," Halvar said. "If he doesn't, his entire order crumbles beneath him."

Embla's tail tightened around them.

He will call us monsters.

"Yes," Halvar said. "He'll say you bewitched the villagers. That Astrid used sorcery. That the storm answered to you."

"I didn't summon it," Astrid said sharply. "It was already there."

"But it helped you," he said. "And people don't forget what that looks like."

Astrid wrapped her arms around herself. "I didn't want to scare them."

"Maybe you should have," Halvar muttered under his breath.

Astrid looked at him sharply.

He sighed.

"You spared him," he said. "A good choice. A right choice. But it has consequences. You let him live, and now he'll return with double the men. Triple. With blessed spears. With priests who can light torches with a prayer."

Astrid stared into the snow.

"I know."

Embla's voice brushed both their minds, low and heavy.

I would have killed him. If you'd asked.

Astrid touched her snout gently. "I know."

You still can ask. Later.

Astrid blinked — surprised not by the offer, but the softness behind it.

"I don't want you to become a killer," she said.

Embla's eyes narrowed thoughtfully.

If he tries to take you, I already am.

Halvar shivered, though not from cold.

"Girl," he murmured, "your dragon loves you in the way storms love mountains. Beautiful. Terrifying. And impossible to stop."

Embla purred softly.

Astrid leaned into her again.

"I don't want storms and mountains," she whispered. "I want… peace."

Halvar placed a hand on her head.

"Then we fight for it," he said. "On our terms."

Across the Land: A Shift Begins

As they rested, the forest breathed around them — quiet, ancient, indifferent.

But outside that clearing…

The world was shifting.

Skarlund

Villagers moved through the ruined streets, whispering hushed words:

"A dragon spared him."
"She could have killed him."
"She didn't."
"The priest screamed."
"The sky itself fought her."

Some feared.
Some doubted.
Some wondered.

And wonder spreads like fire.

The Woods

The soldiers who survived fled, shaken. Some prayed. Some cursed. Some cried.

And rumors began:

"The dragon speaks."
"The girl commands storms."
"Calven failed."
"Calven was afraid."
"Calven burned us — not the beast."

Stories fracture.

Belief wavers.
Authority cracks.

The Monastery

Though they did not yet know it, messengers rode hard toward it, carrying tales that would ignite panic among the high priests.

Whispers would swirl:

Is the prophecy returning?
Did we miss something?
If Calven faltered… what does that mean?

The world was shifting — and for the first time in years, the monastery's hold on truth was not absolute.

The Night Watcher

Astrid eventually drifted into a restless sleep against Embla's side. Her dreams were filled with fire and storm and the ring of flame tightening around Calven's terrified face.

Embla did not sleep.

She watched the trees.

Listened to the wind.

Smelled the faintest traces of steel, smoke, and fear from miles away.

She nuzzled Astrid's hair gently.

My rider, my heart… rest. While I guard.

But in the darker part of her mind — the part the Heartforge had woken — a different fire burned.

A promise.

If he comes again. I will not spare him.

Not unless you ask me a second time.
And I do not think you will.

Morning's Warning

Astrid woke to a strange sound.

A rhythmic tapping.

She blinked, disoriented, then sat up sharply as she saw Halvar standing knee-deep in the stream, staring at something caught beneath the thin layer of ice.

"Papa?" she called, rising.

Halvar didn't answer.

Astrid walked toward him, brushing snow from her clothes.

"Is something wrong?"

He pointed at the ice.

Astrid knelt beside him.

It was a message.

Carved into a flat stone beneath the frozen surface.

**ASTRID HALVARSDOTTIR
THE WORLD IS WATCHING
CHOOSE WISELY**

The carving was precise, the letters marked by a hand that knew runes and power.

Astrid's breath hitched.

"The wizard," she whispered.

Halvar frowned. "Could be. Or someone else."

Astrid's blood chilled. "Someone else?"

Halvar nodded grimly. "Wizards aren't the only ones who carve warnings into stone."

Embla lifted her head sharply.

Look.

Astrid turned.

Footprints.

Dozens of them.

Not Calven's.
Not soldiers'.
Not villagers'.

A different pattern.

Bare feet.
Long strides.
Almost… clawed at the heel.

Astrid felt the skin of her neck prickle.

"Who else is out here?" she whispered.

Embla's pupils narrowed to slits.

Hunters, she said. **But not like Calven's. I smell… something old.**

Halvar's hand slid slowly to the hilt of his hunting knife.

Astrid swallowed hard.

"We need to move," she said. "Now."

The world had begun to shift around them.

But something else — something older than Calven, older than the monastery, older even than the prophecy —was beginning to move toward them.

A new danger.

A new player in the game.

And as Astrid mounted Embla again with Halvar close behind, she felt it like the first tremor before an avalanche:

The true war was only beginning.

The Footsteps in the Snow

The second Embla lifted off, Astrid felt it.

Eyes.

Watching.

Tracking.

Following.

The forest below blurred into streaks of pine and shadow as Embla soared low and fast, weaving between treetops to avoid open sky.

Halvar gripped the spines behind Astrid, leaning close. "Whatever left those prints… it was close. Too close."

Astrid nodded tightly. "I know."

But knowing wasn't enough.

Embla's wings cut through the cold air, breath steaming in controlled bursts. She scanned the forest below with sharp, predatory focus.

I smell them again, she murmured. **Not men. Not wolves. Not anything I know.**

Astrid shivered. "Do you think it's—"

Hunters, Embla said. **But not the monastery's.**

Halvar swore under his breath. "As if Calven wasn't enough."

Astrid swallowed hard.

"Papa… did dragons ever have other enemies?"

Halvar didn't speak for a moment.

Then, quietly: "Every great creature has something hunting it. Even kings."

Astrid didn't answer.

But a cold pit settled in her stomach.

A Clearing of Bones

Embla slowed suddenly, flaring her wings wide.

There.

She descended into a wide glade surrounded by ancient pines, their trunks dark and towering. Snow blanketed everything — except one stark patch where the white had been disturbed.

Bones.

Dozens of them.

Bleached white. Scattered. Broken.

"Saints," Halvar whispered.

Astrid slid off Embla's back, boots crunching in the snow. The air felt different here — colder, stiller, like sound didn't travel as far. She crouched beside a ribcage as long as she was tall.

"What animal is this?" she murmured.

Halvar knelt beside her, shaking his head.

"Not animal," he muttered. "Not one I've ever hunted. This… looks like something that walked upright."

Astrid recoiled.

Bones of a humanoid shape — but larger, thinner, elongated. And not all the same. A second skeleton lay nearby, smaller. A third was shattered completely.

Embla padded forward, head low.

She sniffed a femur, then jerked back, lips curling.

Wrong. Old. Hungry.

Astrid stood, brushing icy flakes from her gloves. "Hungry for what?"

For life, Embla murmured. **For fire. For… blood of magic.**

Astrid felt her heartbeat stutter.

"Are they… demons?" she whispered.

Halvar chuckled humorlessly. "If this is a demon, it died cold and alone like anything else."

Astrid wasn't soothed.

Embla's pupils narrowed, her wings twitching.

They hunted something. Not men. Not deer. Something… powerful.

Astrid stared at the bones.

"They're dead. Who killed them?"

Embla didn't answer.

Instead, she turned her head sharply toward the tree line.

Something moved.

The White Walker

Astrid spun.

A lone figure stood between two pines, tall and thin as a

sapling. Completely still. Completely silent.

Human silhouette.
Bare feet.
Clothes ragged.
Skin snow-pale.

Halvar moved behind Astrid, knife drawn.

"Don't move," he breathed.

The figure didn't advance.

Didn't breathe.

Didn't blink.

Astrid's pulse thundered in her ears.

"Hello?" she called, voice shaking. "Are you— do you need help?"

For a long moment, nothing happened.

Then the figure tilted its head.

The movement was slow. Too slow. Like a puppet being guided by strings.

Its hair hung in long, wet strands, unmoving in the breeze.

Astrid froze.

"Papa," she whispered, "what is that?"

Halvar tightened his grip on the knife. "Not a man."

The figure stepped forward.

Its feet made no sound on the snow.

Embla growled, wings half-spreading.

Back.

The figure stepped again.

Astrid could see its eyes now — milky white, unfocused, like someone seeing through a fog.

Halvar put an arm in front of her and stepped forward.

"That's close enough," he snapped.

The figure stopped.

Its lips parted slightly, revealing sharp, broken teeth.

Then — without warning —

It screamed.

A sound like metal tearing, like ice splitting on a lake, like every nightmare Astrid ever had collapsing into one moment.

Embla lunged forward, placing herself between the creature and Astrid, roaring back.

The scream stopped.

The creature cocked its head again.

Then—

It ran.

Not toward them.

Along the tree line. Faster than any human should be able to move. Its legs bent too far, its spine twisting unnaturally as it vanished into the darkness between the pines.

Astrid stumbled backward.

"What— what was that?" she gasped.

Halvar grabbed her shoulders. "We're leaving. Now. That thing wasn't hunting deer."

Embla's wings snapped open.

I smelled its hunger, she growled. **It wanted you.**

Astrid felt ice in her veins.

"Why me?"

Embla's gaze darkened.

**Because you shine.
And things that shine attract things that starve.**

The Wizard Speaks Again

As they lifted into the air, the clearing of bones shrank behind them. The trees blurred beneath Embla's wings.

Astrid's heart still hammered desperately.

"What was that thing?" she whispered. "It wasn't alive. Not properly."

Halvar nodded grimly. "The old stories mention things like that. Things from the long winters. Things that followed armies and starved villages."

"And hunted dragons?" Astrid said.

Halvar hesitated. "Some say they hunted anything with magic."

A cold wind cut across Embla's flight path.

Astrid felt a familiar presence slip into her mind — thin but urgent.

Child.

"The wizard," she gasped.

Embla faltered for a moment in flight, recognizing him.

You must listen, his voice whispered sharply. *The monastery is not the only danger. There are older forces in this world — forces that stirred when the egg you awakened cracked.*

Astrid swallowed hard. "The creature in the woods—"

—was a remnant, the wizard said. *A hunter born of famine, winter, and desperation centuries ago. They died when the last dragons died… or so we believed.*

Embla hissed through her thoughts.

Not dead.

No, the wizard agreed gravely. *Because a spark has re-entered the world. Fire has returned. And anything that once fed on fire is waking.*

Astrid's stomach twisted.

"What do we do?"

You flee, the wizard said. *You hide. You survive. And you strengthen the bond with the dragon, or the world will devour you both.*

Astrid clenched her fists.

"But Calven is burning villages—"

I know! the wizard snapped, unusually harsh. *But if you face both the monastery and the hungry things at once, you will die. And if you die, the world loses its only chance.*

Astrid froze.

"The only chance for what?"

The wizard hesitated — the longest pause he had ever given.

For balance.
A world with dragons. And humans. And something better than the ashes we once made.

Astrid stared ahead numbly.

"Where do we go?" she whispered.

North, the wizard said. *To the old stronghold of the dragon-riders. The ruins of Bryngard.*

Astrid gasped. "That's a myth."

So is a girl who hears the earth, the wizard replied. *And a dragon born under a mountain.*

Embla growled, wings adjusting as she banked northeast.

We go.

Halvar wrapped his arms around Astrid again, anchoring her physically, because everything else felt as though it were being pulled out from under them.

Hurry, the wizard whispered. *You are being tracked. By more than one enemy. And time is—*

His voice cut abruptly.

"Wizard?" Astrid called. "Wizard!"

Nothing.

Only wind.

Embla glanced back at her.

He is gone. Something silenced him.

Astrid's breath trembled.

"Something?" she repeated. "What something?"

Embla didn't answer.

Halvar did.

His voice was quiet.

"Something older than Calven."

And the forest below grew darker.

And the sky ahead thickened with gathering storm.

And Astrid felt, for the first time, the full weight of what she had become:

Not just a girl.

Not just a rider.

A spark in a world full of hungry shadows.

CHAPTER 22

THE CHOICE AND THE CHASE

The sky deepened to a dull iron gray as Embla carried them north, her wings laboring harder with each passing mile. The weight of three riders — even as light as Astrid was, even with Halvar's wiry frame — pressed on the young dragon's endurance. More than that, though, the weight of **what hunted them** dragged behind like a second shadow.

Astrid kept glancing back over her shoulder.

Not toward Skarlund.
Not toward Calven's armies.
But toward the treeline where the White Walker had vanished.

She could *feel* the place even now — an icy echo in her bones that had nothing to do with the winter air.

Embla felt her tension through the bond.

Do not look for it, the dragon murmured. **Look forward. There is danger ahead also.**

Halvar tightened his grip behind Astrid, nodding. "She's right. Whatever that thing was… it's not something you want to see twice."

Astrid swallowed. "It screamed like it was warning others. Calling them. Or calling something worse."

Halvar didn't answer, which was answer enough.

Embla angled her wings, catching a crosswind that lifted them above the forest canopy. Below, the trees stretched endlessly — dark pines dusted with snow, rising and falling over hills like a rumpled blanket. But even from this height, Astrid noticed something unsettling.

Patches of forest lay flattened.
As though something large had passed through.
Or many things.

Embla noticed too.

Those are new, she said. **The wind still tastes broken there. No regrowth. No healing.**

Astrid shivered. "Whatever left that clearing of bones… maybe it wasn't alone."

Halvar leaned closer to shout over the wind. "Girl, if there are more of those things, then north may be as dangerous as south."

"South is *certainly* dangerous," Astrid shot back, thinking of Calven's burned villages.

"True," he conceded. "But running blindly isn't the answer."

Astrid's breath fogged in the air. "I'm not running blindly. I'm following the wizard's last warning."

Halvar grunted. "And I trust him less than a hungry bear."

She stared ahead, eyes narrowed. "I trust him more than the monastery."

"Well," Halvar said dryly, "that's a low bar."

Astrid almost smiled — then Embla stiffened beneath them.

Movement, she warned. **Ahead. Small. Fast. Many.**

Astrid's heart lurched. "Calven's men?"

Embla inhaled deeply through her nose, the cold air whistling past her sharp teeth.

Not men.

A pause that felt like a fist tightening.
Wolves. And starving.

Halvar cursed under his breath. "Wonderful."

Embla folded her wings, gliding lower through the trees.

"Are they dangerous to you?" Astrid asked, gripping her neck ridge.

Not to me.
Embla's tone darkened.
But to you.

They descended toward the ground — and now Astrid heard them too.

Growls.
Snarls.
Branches snapping.
The frantic rhythm of a pack on the move.

But the wolves weren't coming *toward* Astrid.

They were running past her.

Fleeing.

Astrid blinked. "Embla… they're running *away* from something."

Embla landed in a shallow dip between hills, snow spraying up around them. She crouched low, wings half-open, sheltering Astrid and Halvar.

The wolves burst through the trees — a blur of gray fur and frothing jaws. Dozens of them. Some limping. Some with patches of fur ripped out. Eyes wide with fear.

Halvar's hand went to his knife. "Back, girl. Don't spook them."

But the wolves didn't look at them.

They didn't dare.

They sprinted past in a stampede of terror, whimpering, stumbling, fleeing so desperately they didn't even register Embla's massive presence.

Astrid's breath clouded in front of her face.

"What could scare wolves like that?"

Embla's answer came as a low growl rumbling through her chest.

Something that is not far behind them.

As if summoned, a new sound drifted through the forest.

Not footsteps.
Not growls.
Not the scream of the White Walker.

A rhythm.

Soft.
Measured.
Too controlled to be animal.

Astrid grabbed Embla's ridge. "Up. Now."

Embla leapt into the air —

But she didn't get far.

A shape moved in the trees.

Then another.

And another.

White figures.
Too thin.
Too tall.
Too fast.

Not one.
Not two.

A *pack* of White Walkers.

Their milky eyes glowed faintly as they turned upward, toward Astrid.

Halvar's grip tightened until his knuckles whitened. "Astrid…"

Embla beat her wings hard, gaining altitude —

But the White Walkers climbed.

They scrambled up the trees with spidery speed, claws digging into bark, ripping grooves into the trunks as they ascended.

Astrid's breath hitched. "They're chasing us."

Embla roared, sending shockwaves through the forest — but the creatures didn't flinch.

Up! Up! Embla cried. **They climb like spiders!**

But even as she climbed, the creatures followed, faster and faster.

One reached the top of a tree. The trunk bent under its weight — then snapped.

The creature launched itself into the air.

Astrid screamed.

Embla twisted mid-flight, dodging — the creature sailed past beneath them, crashing into the snow with a sickening thud.

It didn't scream.

It didn't cry.

It simply stood again.

And climbed the next tree.

Astrid's heart pounded. "What do they want? Why are they following us?"

Embla's wings beat harder, breath frost-thick.

They want your light.
Her voice trembled with the truth of it.
They hunger for magic. For warmth. For life. For blood that hears the earth.

Astrid's blood ran cold.

So it was her.

Not Embla.

Not Halvar.

They were hunting **her.**

Halvar swore violently. "They can smell her gift."

Astrid clutched Embla's scales. "Is there somewhere they *can't* follow?"

Embla hesitated.

Then —

Yes.

Her wings angled sharply northward.

Bryngard.

Astrid exhaled, shaking. "The wizard said to go there."

Then we go. Now. Before they catch us.

Halvar ducked lower as the wind whipped around them. "Girl, if these things reach us in the air—"

"They won't," Astrid said, voice trembling.

She tried to believe it.

But she could still see their pale shapes leaping through the trees…

Still hear the crack of wood under their claws…

Still feel their hunger in her bones.

Embla flew harder.

Faster.

Snow blasted beneath her like waves.

But the White Walkers did too.

Because the truth was now undeniable:

Calven wasn't the only one hunting Astrid.

Not the only one who believed she was dangerous.

Not the only one who wanted the bond between girl and dragon **broken**.

The White Walkers had survived centuries without dragons.

They would not let the world change again.

And if the wizard was telling the truth…

Astrid and Embla were the spark that would change everything.

A spark that predators would kill to extinguish.

The Pursuit Through the Pines

Embla burst above the treetops in a spray of snow and frozen pine needles. The cold wind slapped Astrid's cheeks raw, tearing at her hair, making her eyes water. But nothing — *nothing* — could shake loose the feeling of being hunted.

Halvar looked back over his shoulder. For a moment, Astrid thought the White Walkers had vanished.

Then she saw them.

The creatures were erupting from the forest canopy like grotesque white insects, hurling themselves between the tops of trees with terrifying speed. They were too thin to be human, their arms too long, their hands curled like talons.

And they were gaining.

Halvar's grip tightened. "They're climbing the whole bloody forest to get to you."

Astrid's lungs constricted.

Embla struggled upward, but the wind thickened, resisting her. She strained, wings beating with powerful strokes.

Astrid felt her exhaustion through the bond — a deep ache in Embla's wing joints, the weight in her chest, the fire within her struggling to sustain her speed.

"We need height," Astrid murmured. "We need open air."

Open air makes us easier to see. Embla grunted with effort. **But trees make them faster. Choose, Astrid.**

Astrid's heart spasmed.

Up, and risk being spotted by Calven's scouts or archers in the distance…

Or stay low, letting the White Walkers climb and leap until they could reach Embla's belly or wings.

She couldn't risk Embla being dragged from the sky.

"Up," Astrid said hoarsely. "Take us up."

Embla put every last ounce of strength into her wings.

The forest fell away beneath them — trees shrinking into scattered needles of green; hills flattening into long rolls of white.

It should have been beautiful.

It wasn't.

The White Walkers pursued relentlessly, climbing atop each other's backs, scaling trees in staggering bursts of speed.

One reached a high branch and *launched* itself upward — higher than before — a jagged shape spiraling through the air.

Astrid screamed, ducking as the creature's clawed hand swiped at Embla's tail.

Embla twisted violently, nearly throwing Astrid and Halvar off.

Astrid clung fiercely. "Just a little more—!"

Embla surged the last few dozen feet into open sky.

Wind blasted around them in clean, powerful streams.

Below, the creatures fell short — collapsing back into the forest with dull, heavy thuds. They writhed for a moment, then scrambled back up, but the canopy now blocked their ascent.

Embla rose another twenty feet, ensuring safety.

Only then did Astrid breathe again.

Halvar sagged in relief. "I'd rather fight a pack of wolves bare-handed than look at those things again."

Astrid rubbed her burning eyes. "Why are they here? Why now?"

Embla's thoughts were grim.

They are called to magic. To change. To storms. To you.

A thick silence weighed down on them.

Then a new sound cut through the wind.

Not a scream.
Not a howl.
Not a leap.

A **horn**.

Long.
Low.
Echoing over the distant hills.

Astrid's blood chilled instantly.

"Calven…" she breathed. "He's moved north."

Halvar cursed. "He must've sent scouts when we fled Skarlund. Or riders. They're sweeping the region."

Astrid stared northward.

Beyond the hills, smoke curled faintly into the sky — but not from burning towns. This smoke was darker. Controlled. Like the kind used to signal armies.

"We're trapped," Astrid whispered. "White Walkers behind us. Calven ahead."

Embla's wings flexed as she angled toward the northeast.

Not trapped. Guided. The wizard said Bryngard lies this way. We follow him.

But Astrid felt a knot in her stomach.

"What if the wizard wasn't warning us?" she whispered. "What if he was *steering* us somewhere? Into something?"

Halvar frowned. "Girl, we don't have time to argue with fate."

Astrid clenched her jaw.

He was right.

But a part of her — a growing part — didn't trust the wizard's influence.

Still, the choice was gone. North was the only direction not filled with predators or soldiers.

Unless…

"Wait," Astrid said suddenly. "Embla, land there."

She pointed to a narrow frozen river winding between two steep hills. Embla looked confused but obeyed, circling downward.

Halvar blinked. "Why are we stopping? Those creatures could—"

"We're not stopping," Astrid said. "We're choosing."

She dismounted before Embla fully settled in the snow. The cold bit instantly into her boots.

Halvar slid down beside her. "Astrid, what are you doing?"

Astrid turned to him.

"Two enemies are chasing us," she said. "One wants to kill us. One wants to 'save' the world by killing us more slowly."

Halvar stiffened.

Astrid continued.

"If we keep running blindly, they'll push us somewhere

we don't choose. Drive us like animals until we fall into their hands."

Embla lowered her head.
Her breath steamed along the ground.

So you choose here?

Astrid nodded.

"We need to decide right now — do we escape to Bryngard like the wizard said, or turn south and strike back at Calven before he gathers an army big enough to crush entire towns?"

Halvar blinked at her. "Astrid— we can't strike an army. Not yet."

"Then we die running," Astrid said.

For a moment, no one spoke.

The frozen river groaned beneath a shifting sheet of ice.

Embla watched Astrid intently.
Halvar's face was a storm of fear, pride, and dread.

And Astrid realized…

This was the moment the wizard meant.
This was the crossroads he couldn't show her.

She stared north — toward Bryngard, toward ancient ruins and forgotten power, toward a place the White Walkers feared.

Then south — toward Calven's spreading path of destruction, toward villages in danger, toward the people who needed saving *now*.

Embla nudged her shoulder gently.

Choose, Astrid.
I will follow.

Anywhere.

Astrid closed her eyes.

The fire of Embla's bond swirled through her.
The screams of Skarlund echoed in her memory.
The White Walkers' hunger prickled at the edge of her skin.
The wizard's warning pressed like a hand on her back.

And Astrid made her choice.

She opened her eyes.

The Decision That Changes Everything

Astrid stared into the vast white horizon, breathing hard, frost gathering on her eyelashes. Her heartbeat hammered in her chest, loud as war drums.

Bryngard to the north.
Calven's army to the south.
White Walkers behind.
The wizard's voice silent.
Embla's breath warm on her cheek.
Halvar watching her like he could feel the weight she carried.

For the first time in her life, *everyone* waited for her to decide the direction of the world.

Astrid drew a long, slow breath.

Then she whispered:

"We go north."

Embla exhaled sharply, a puff of warm smoke swirling around Astrid like relief.

Halvar nodded once, jaw clenched. "Bryngard it is."

Astrid turned toward the dragon. "If the wizard says it's

the only safe place left… then we trust him. For now."

Embla lowered herself, wings folding close.
Her eyes glowed with quiet pride.

I knew you would choose the sky over the sword, she
murmured.

Astrid touched her snout. "I didn't choose sky. I chose
survival. For all of us."

Halvar stepped forward. "Girl, if Bryngard is real — if
even half the old stories are true—"

"—then we'll find something there to help us," Astrid
finished. "Something to protect the people who can't run as
fast as we can."

Halvar's eyes softened.

She was no longer the child he'd kept hidden from
danger.
She was becoming the leader he feared she'd have to be.

Embla crouched lower.

Climb on. Before the pale ones return.

Astrid swung onto her back; Halvar followed. Embla
tensed her wings.

Then—

A sound froze them all.

A distant, echoing cry.

But not the White Walkers.
And not a wolf.
And not a human.

A sound like stone grinding against bone.
Like wind moving through a hollow skull.

Embla's wings trembled.

It follows us.

Astrid looked down the frozen river, into the trees.

Something white moved between the trunks.
Then another.
And another.

The White Walkers had found the river.

Halvar cursed. "Up! Up now!"

Embla launched into the air with a powerful leap—

But Astrid felt it instantly.

The wind shifted.

Hard.

As if something massive displaced the air behind them.

"Embla—?"

I know! the dragon cried. **Hold tight!**

She beat her wings, rising higher—

But the wind was wrong.
Twisting.
Pulling.
Dragging her sideways.

Astrid clutched her ridge. "What's happening?!"

Embla snarled.

The storm moves against me. Something stirs the sky.

Halvar leaned close. "That's no storm— girl, look!"

Astrid turned.

And her heart nearly stopped.

The White Walkers weren't chasing them anymore.

They were **kneeling**.

Every pale creature had dropped to one knee in the snow, heads bowed low, arms hanging loose at their sides.

Like worship.

Or fear.

Astrid's breath fogged. "Why are they—?"

Then she saw it.

A shape drifting between the trees.

Not walking.
Not running.
Not climbing.

Floating.

Wrapped in tatters of frost-burned cloth.
Limbs long and thin.
Face hidden beneath a hood of bone-white hair.
Bare feet not touching the snow.
A soft, unnatural glow radiating from beneath its cloak like cold moonlight.

Astrid trembled.

"Embla…" she whispered. "What is that?"

Embla's voice was a whisper of terror.

An ancient one.
A leader of the hungry dead.
A FROST WIGHT.

Halvar swore in a choked whisper. "Those things weren't just hunters… they were its pack."

The Frost Wight lifted its head.

And looked directly at Astrid.

Astrid felt the world tilt.
The air thinned.
Her breath vanished.
Her vision tightened into a small white tunnel.

Then—

A voice slipped into her mind.

Not like Embla's.
Not warm.
Not alive.

Cold.
Dead.
Hungering.

Child of fire.
A heart awake.
A pulse of earth.
Come.

Astrid screamed and clutched her skull, nearly falling.

Embla roared, wings snapping open as she fought the twisting wind.

OFF HER!
OUT OF HER MIND!

The Frost Wight extended one skeletal hand.

The White Walkers rose as one.

And the world exploded into motion.

The creatures burst forward, sprinting across the snow, their limbs tearing grooves into the ice. The Frost Wight glided behind them, untouched by the world, its presence bending the air around it.

Embla wrenched herself upward, wings straining violently.

Hold! she roared. **I cannot take us higher unless—**

Something slammed into them.

A White Walker had leapt from a rock ledge, catching Embla's hind leg mid-flight.

Embla shrieked, twisting, flinging the creature off — but three more leapt after it, claws scraping her scales.

Astrid screamed as one nearly grabbed her foot.

Halvar kicked it in the face, sending it spinning.

Embla fought the wind, her wings beating wildly.

Astrid, she gasped. **They want you—**

A blast of cold air hit Astrid like a hammer.

She toppled sideways—

Almost falling—

Embla twisted under her, catching her with one wing.

Hold me! Embla cried. **Don't let go—**

Astrid grabbed onto Embla's scale ridge again just as a second White Walker lunged for her leg—

And Halvar stabbed it through the throat, sending it tumbling.

"GO!" he shouted. "EMBLA, GO!"

Embla surged upward with a scream of raw power—

And this time she broke free.

The White Walkers fell away beneath them.
The Frost Wight reached upward—

But the wind snapped in Embla's favor, blasting her high, far, and fast.

Astrid gasped for breath, tears freezing on her cheeks.

Halvar clung to her.

Embla's wings shook with exhaustion.

But finally—

Finally—

They escaped the reach of the dead things.

The forest fell away.

The Frost Wight faded into the trees.

And the sky opened above them again.

Astrid collapsed forward against Embla's neck, trembling from head to toe.

Halvar's voice was hoarse. "Astrid… girl… you all right?"

Astrid tried to answer.

But the Frost Wight's voice still echoed in her skull.

Child of fire.
A heart awake.
Come.

Her voice cracked. "It spoke to me. Inside my mind."

Halvar stiffened. "Like the wizard?"

"No," Astrid whispered. "Nothing like the wizard."

Embla's voice shook through their bond.

Astrid… it knows you.
And it will follow.

Until we reach Bryngard.
Or until it feeds.

Astrid wiped her tears with a shaking hand.

"We have to get there," she whispered. "Whatever Bryngard is— whatever the wizard meant— it's the only place left that might stop that thing."

Halvar nodded slowly. "Then ride hard, girl."

Embla turned her wings northward.

And Astrid felt something settle into her chest.

Not fear.
Not panic.

Purpose.

The choice wasn't just made.

It was sealed.

North Into the Teeth of Winter

The sky grew darker as they pressed north, the air thinning into a sharp, metallic cold. Embla flew lower now, saving her strength, gliding along the curves of the land. Her wings trembled with each beat, but she pushed on doggedly.

Snow began to fall.

Not gently — but in quick, swirling flurries blown sideways by a rising wind. The storm ahead was building, a wall of gray that swallowed the horizon.

Halvar leaned forward, shouting over the howl. "Girl— are we flying into a blizzard?"

Astrid squinted through stinging snowflakes. "The wizard said Bryngard lies beyond the mountains. Maybe the storm… hides it?"

Halvar swore. "Or hides something that'll eat us."

Astrid ignored the dread creeping up her spine. The Frost Wight's voice still echoed faintly in her skull. She pressed her fingers to her temples, focusing on Embla's warmth.

Don't listen to it, Embla murmured. **Let my fire be louder.**

Astrid's chest ached with gratitude. "I'm trying."

Try harder. Embla huffed. **You humans let thoughts wander like lost goats. It makes you easy prey.**

Astrid might have laughed — if her fear hadn't been chewing holes in her ribs.

The wind grew stronger. Snow thickened. Embla angled her wings and descended into a ravine sheltered between two steep ridges. The sharp turn almost threw Halvar sideways.

"Warn me next time!" he shouted.

I warn you with the angle of my wings, Embla replied. **If you miss it, that is not my fault.**

"We're not dragons!" Halvar snapped back.

Whose fault is that? Embla muttered.

Astrid actually snorted — then froze.

At the ravine's bottom lay footprints.

Fresh.

Lots of them.

Astrid's stomach twisted. "Embla— land. Slowly."

Embla touched down cautiously, folding her wings tight. Snow piled around her claws.

Astrid slid down and crouched, brushing frost away from

the prints.

The tracks were human.
Boots.
Dozens of pairs.

Halvar crouched beside her, jaw tight. "Calven's scouts. We're close to their northern sweep."

"And they're heading the same direction we are," Astrid whispered.

Halvar looked grim. "If Calven or any of his priests reaches Bryngard first—"

"He won't," Astrid snapped.

Snow drifted over the tracks as she stood.

Embla sniffed the air.
Her pupils narrowed.

South. Riders.
Close.
And they smell… angry.

Astrid's pulse spiked. "It's Calven."

Halvar stiffened. "How many?"

Embla's nostrils flared. **More than before. And torches. Many torches.**

Astrid looked at the darkening storm ahead.

To the White Walkers behind.

To Calven moving in from the south.

And to the unknown north — Bryngard — a place of myth, power, and danger no one had survived in generations.

Her hands trembled.

But she stepped toward Embla.

"We keep going."

Halvar grabbed her arm. "Astrid— girl— if we fly into that blizzard and Embla tires—"

Astrid met his eyes. "If we stay here, Calven finds us. Or worse, the Frost Wight does."

Halvar went pale. "Don't say that thing's name."

Embla lifted her head, scanning the treeline.

I feel it.
A shiver rippled along her spine.
Far behind. But following. Always following.

Astrid swallowed. "It wants me. It won't stop."

Then we don't stop either. Embla crouched low. **Climb on. Quickly.**

Halvar didn't argue this time.

They mounted just as a distant horn cut through the trees — sharp, cold, unmistakable.

Astrid froze. "That's Calven's hunting horn."

"What direction?" Halvar barked.

Embla answered.

All directions.

Astrid's stomach dropped. "What?"

Embla's wings snapped wide.

Riders spread out. In a line. Sweeping north. They mean to trap us between their walls of men.

Astrid nearly swayed with dizziness. "He's hunting us like animals."

Halvar's face hardened. "Then show him why hunters go home with missing limbs."

Embla launched upward again, the ravine walls blurring beneath them.

The storm approached like a living thing — a shifting wall of swirling white that seemed to watch them.

And Astrid felt something else.

A pulse.

Like a heartbeat.

Far away.

North.

Slow, deep, ancient.

Embla felt it too.

Her thoughts slid into Astrid's mind, trembling with awe.

Do you hear that?

Astrid inhaled shakily.

"Yes."

Halvar blinked. "I don't hear anything but wind."

Astrid pointed toward the distant storm.

"It's not sound," she whispered. "It's… calling."

Embla's voice lowered.

Bryngard.

A shiver ran through both of them.

Halvar frowned. "So the ruins are real, then."

Astrid nodded slowly. "Yes. And something there wants

us."

Halvar's brow knitted tight. "Or wants the dragon."

Astrid didn't argue—because he wasn't wrong.

Something ancient lived in those ruins.
Something that still breathed magic.
Something the Frost Wight hungered for.
Something Calven feared.

Astrid tightened her grip on Embla's scales.

"We keep going," she said. "No matter what."

Embla beat her wings hard, rising into the curtain of snow ahead.

The storm swallowed them whole.

Inside the White

The world vanished.

Astrid's breath hitched. She couldn't see more than a few feet. The snow was so thick it felt like moving through a cloud. Embla's wings were shadows. Her scales were cold beneath Astrid's hands.

Halvar leaned close, shouting, "Can you see anything?!"

Astrid shook her head wildly. "Embla?"

The dragon answered through the bond, her voice thinner now:

I see shapes.
Stone.
Peaks.
Cliffs.
But the wind is wrong. Too strong. Too… guided.

Astrid's chest clenched. "Guided? By who?"

Embla's wings bucked as the air slammed sideways into them.

By something that doesn't want us here!

A gust hit them so hard Halvar nearly slid off. Astrid grabbed him.

"Hold on!"

He grunted. "Trying!"

Embla banked right, fighting the gale.

Astrid squinted through the storm—

And saw something.

Tall.
Dark.
Jagged.

A silhouette through the white.
A wall of stone rising like a broken tooth.

"Embla— look!"

Embla followed her gaze and screeched in triumph.

I see it! A tower! A ruin!

Halvar strained his eyes. "Bryngard?"

Before Astrid could answer—

A massive black shape burst out of the storm ahead.

Embla swerved hard—

And a spear of ice shot past, grazing her wing.

Astrid screamed.

Halvar cursed.

Embla roared—

As pale shapes emerged from the white.

Not White Walkers.

Worse.

Humans.

Wrapped in heavy furs.
Faces painted blue.
Eyes cold and empty.

A northern tribe — ancient, ruthless, and loyal to no king.

And they threw spears like lightning.

Halvar's face drained of color.

"We've flown into the Stormguard tribe's territory!"

Astrid gasped. "Who are they?!"

"Warriors!" Halvar shouted. "Killers! They protect the old ruins from outsiders!"

Embla growled.

They protect Bryngard.
They protect whatever sleeps there.

Astrid's voice cracked. "They're trying to force us back!"

Halvar's eyes widened as he saw movement in the swirling storm.

"NO— they're trying to drive us—"

Right when Embla turned—

A spear shattered against her shoulder.

She dropped several feet.

Astrid screamed—"EMBLA!"

Embla steadied herself, roaring in fury.

From the flurries of snow, dozens of Stormguard warriors appeared on rocky outcrops.

Silent.
Unmoving.
Waiting.

Spears drawn.

Embla circled desperately, dodging thrown weapons—

Until the tribe leader stepped forward.

A tall woman with braids of white-blond hair.
A cloak of wolf hides.
Eyes as gray and unyielding as the mountain.

She raised a spear—

Not to throw.

To point.

Straight at Astrid.

Embla hissed.

She sees you.
Not me.
You.

And Astrid felt the storm answer the woman's silent command.

A vortex of snow and wind tore toward them—

Not random.

Not natural.

A spell.

Astrid clutched Embla's ridge.

"We're not welcome here."

Halvar spat. "No one is."

Embla spread her wings.
The storm crashed around them.
The spear-army closed in.

Astrid clenched her jaw.

"Then we fight our way through."

Embla roared—

And dove straight into the heart of the storm.

The Stormguard and the Ruins of Bryngard

The blizzard thinned as Embla drove upward, her wings slicing through the final curtain of swirling snow. The moment they broke out of the storm's grip, the world changed sharply around them.

Below:
Spring waited — green valleys, thawed rivers glinting like silver threads, the faint blush of early wildflowers along the lower slopes.

Above:
Winter clung stubbornly to the high ridges — jagged cliffs streaked with ice, frozen waterfalls suspended like sharp teeth, snow swirling in patches where the wind carved hollows.

Astrid stared down at the spring valley. For a heartbeat, she longed for that warmth — the safety of green instead of white.

But fate dragged them higher.

Embla let out a rasping breath. **The air warms below. But the ruins lie above, where cold clings to stone.**

Halvar nodded grimly. "Old places hold onto winter. Hard to take it from them. Harder still to survive it."

Astrid tightened her grip. "Then we don't stop until we reach Bryngard."

But the mountains had other ideas.

As the storm thinned, the Stormguard tribe reappeared — not as silhouettes in the blizzard, but as warriors standing firm upon the icy ledges. Their heavy furs were rimed with frost, and their blue-painted faces looked carved from stone.

The northern spring had **not** touched them.
They lived in the cold, thrived in the cold, and became part of it.

The tribe leader — the tall, white-braided woman — stepped to the cliff edge. The wind snapped her wolf-hide cloak behind her.

This time she lifted her hand — not to cast wind or call the storm, but to **halt** her warriors.

Embla circled warily, keeping distance.

Astrid cried over the wind, "Why are they stopping?"

Halvar's voice was tight. "Maybe they see we're not attacking."

Embla snorted. **Or they wait for a sign.**

A horn blew from somewhere behind the leader — low, deep, and resonant. A ritual call.

The woman lifted her face toward the sky.

Then pointed again.

Not at Astrid.

Not at Embla.

Not at Halvar.

But toward a towering ridge behind them — its peak crowned not by snow, but by **shattered black stone**, as if the mountain had once been struck by lightning so fierce it split the world.

Astrid's breath caught.

"That's—"

"Bryngard," Halvar whispered.

The ruins loomed like broken fingers clawing at the sky.
Half-buried halls lay carved into the rock.
Massive archways rose from the ice.
Pillars lined a wide plateau — cracked, ancient, half-collapsed.

And at the center, on a platform dusted with snow, a massive stone circle stood upright like an enormous ring — engraved with runes Astrid didn't recognize.

The Stormguard leader dropped to one knee.

The entire tribe followed.

Astrid froze. "What are they doing?"

Halvar swallowed. "They're not trying to kill us. They're… presenting the path."

Embla blinked slowly.

**They guard the way.
But it is not us they bow to.
It is the place.**

Astrid stared at the kneeling warriors.

"They're letting us pass," she whispered. "But why?"

Halvar grimaced. "Because they think what waits in there will kill us for them."

Embla hissed.

Or because something in Bryngard wants us to enter.

A sudden, icy wind surged up the mountain. Not natural. Not spring. Not winter.

Worse.

Astrid's blood turned to ice. "It's here."

Halvar spun. "Where?!"

Embla snarled, baring her teeth.

Behind.
Below.
Moving up the slope.
FAST.

Astrid looked down the mountain's side — and saw shapes swarming up the lower ridges.

White Walkers.

Dozens of them.
Then hundreds.

They were climbing from the spring valleys into the winter peaks — but wherever they stepped, frost spread outward like veins of white lightning.

Spring withered at their touch.

Ice killed the thaw.

Snow returned where their hands struck the stone.

Astrid's heart pounded so hard she felt dizzy. "The Frost Wight is close."

Embla answered with a shiver that rippled down her spine.

It brings winter wherever it walks.

Halvar's voice trembled. "Girl… if it reaches Bryngard…"

Astrid knew.

If the Frost Wight reached the ancient dragon city —
If it touched whatever power the ruins held —
If it absorbed any magic left there —

It would become unstoppable.

Astrid looked again at the stone circle on the plateau — the heart of Bryngard. It pulsed faintly with a cold blue light.

Calling them.
Waiting.
Expecting.

She tightened her grip on Embla's scales.

"We fly straight to the ruins," Astrid said, voice firm. "Now."

Halvar grabbed her arm. "Astrid— whatever's in there —"

"I don't care!" she shouted, eyes burning. "If the Wight reaches it first, everything dies. Every village. Every family. Everyone."

Embla crouched low.

I go. Wherever you lead.

Astrid climbed on.

Halvar cursed and followed.

Below them, the Frost Wight's voice drifted up the mountainside — a cold whisper carried on hollow wind.

Child of fire…

Come to me...
Come...

Astrid clenched her teeth.

"Embla— fly."

Embla roared and launched upward.

The Stormguard tribe watched in total silence, kneeling as the dragon streaked toward the ancient circle carved into the mountain's heart.

The Frost Wight climbed ever closer.

Its pack swarmed beneath.

The storm twisted around the peak.

And Bryngard waited.

Ancient.
Silent.
Awakening.

Astrid's last thought before the ruins swallowed them:

This was the choice.
This was the chase.
Now comes the price.

CHAPTER 23

THE THRESHOLD OF BRYNGARD

Embla climbed the last stretch of cold mountain wind, her wings heaving as she pushed toward the plateau. Frost steamed from her nostrils with each breath, trailing behind her like pale banners. Astrid clung to her neck ridge, her fingers numb from gripping through the storm.

But nothing — not the cold, not the pain, not even the memory of the Frost Wight's voice — could pull her eyes from what loomed ahead.

Bryngard.

It rose from the mountainside like the ribs of a colossal beast long buried under snow. A shattered city of broken towers and collapsed bridges, its stone architecture older than anything Astrid had ever seen. Carved walkways spiraled along the cliff face. Enormous arches stretched between crags, some intact, others fallen into the abyss below.

And at the heart of it—

The **stone circle**.

A perfect ring of ancient black stone, wider than Embla's wingspan, etched with runes so deep they glowed through the frost. Snow swirled within its center, but did not touch the circle's surface.

Astrid felt its pull.

Not metaphorically.
Physically.
A low hum thrummed through her bones, echoing in her chest.

Halvar placed a hand on her shoulder, steadying her. "Girl… this place feels wrong."

Astrid shook her head slowly. "No. Not wrong. Old. Listening."

Embla beat her wings once more, climbing high enough for the wind to level out.

The storm above the peak raged — but the plateau itself was eerily still, as if Bryngard protected the land around it.

This place remembers dragons, Embla whispered. **I smell them. Old ones. Long dead. Long sleeping.**

Astrid pressed a hand to her chest. "I feel them too."

Embla descended toward the stone circle and landed with a heavy crunch of talons on frost-crusted stone. The plateau was wide enough to hold dozens of dragons at once — though none had been here in centuries.

Astrid slid off Embla's back and nearly collapsed. Embla steadied her with one wing.

Halvar landed behind them with more grace than expected, though he winced as his feet hit the cold stone. "By the gods… the air here feels strange."

"It feels like… memory," Astrid murmured.

She approached the circle.

The runes hummed beneath her feet — soft at first, then stronger when she stepped closer. She reached out a trembling hand toward the black stone.

"Careful," Halvar warned.

But Astrid barely heard him.

The surface felt warm.

Warm.

In the middle of endless winter ice.

Embla stepped forward beside her, lowering her head until her snout touched the stone.

The runes flared brighter.

The air thickened.

Astrid felt a pulse beneath her palm — not magic. Not heat.

A **heartbeat**.

The stone pulsed again.

The circle was alive.

Or waking.

Embla's pupils thinned to slits.

Astrid… something stirs beneath.
Not a creature.
A memory.
A door.

Astrid swallowed. "A door to where?"

Embla lifted her head slowly.

To the part of the world dragons were forced to forget.

Astrid's chest tightened.

"What does that mean?"

Halvar stepped closer, scanning the ruins nervously. "It means the wizard sent us straight into the jaws of something older than any monastery. Something that didn't want to be found."

Astrid opened her mouth to answer—

But the mountain answered first.

A distant roar of wind cut through the air. Not natural. Not wild.
A cold shriek carried on hollow lungs.

Astrid froze.

Halvar's face drained of color.

Embla's wings snapped open in fury.

It followed us.
The Frost Wight is climbing toward the plateau.

Astrid spun toward the mountain edge.

Below, the storm churned — not blowing upward anymore, but **pulling inward**, drawn to a point like a vortex forming around a dark center.

Shapes moved in the blizzard. Pale shapes.

The White Walkers had returned.

All of them.

Halvar stepped in front of Astrid. "Girl — move back. You're too close to the ledge."

But Astrid didn't move. She couldn't. Her breath caught as the storm peeled aside like a curtain.

And the Frost Wight emerged.

Its tattered cloak dragged frost behind it. Snow melted at its feet only to freeze again in patterns like spiderwebs. Its white-blind eyes locked onto Astrid with haunting precision.

Embla growled deep in her chest.

Stay back, pale one.
You touch her, you die.

The Wight tilted its head, floating effortlessly a few inches above the stone, its limbs dangling like broken branches.

Then it spoke.

Not aloud.

Inside their minds.

Child of fire.
Come.
The circle opens for the marked.
You belong within.

Astrid staggered backward, clutching her skull as the voice bored into her mind like ice dripping into bone.

Halvar caught her. "Stay with me, girl. Fight it!"

Embla snarled and advanced.

Do not speak to her.
Do not look at her.
Do not THINK of her.

The Frost Wight ignored the dragon completely. Its gaze was fixed on Astrid.

You carry the spark.
You hear the earth.
You open the stone.

Astrid gasped, eyes widening.

"It wants me," she whispered. "The circle reacts to me…"

Halvar gritted his teeth. "Then we smash the circle."

"No!" Astrid cried.

Embla froze and swung her head toward her.

Halvar stared in disbelief. "What do you mean 'no'?!"

Astrid touched the stone again — and the runes flared.

"I think the circle protects something. Or someone. Maybe even Embla. Maybe dragons used this place for training, or refuge, or—"

The Frost Wight's voice overrode hers.

It opens the way to the Chamber of Echoes.
Where the first riders met their dragons.
Where fire was born.

Astrid trembled. The words vibrated through her spine.

Halvar swore. "Girl — you're not going in there. We don't know what—"

But the stone circle pulsed again — louder.

Embla tensed. **Astrid… it calls to you. But we do not know if it calls to help… or to feed.**

Then—

A rumble shook the mountain.

The ground split near the far side of the plateau, and White Walkers began pouring over the edge — dozens of them scaling like spiders.

Astrid's heartbeat stuttered.

Halvar drew his knife. "We're surrounded."

The Frost Wight glided closer.

Come, it whispered.
Come to the circle.
Come to your fate.

Then it raised one skeletal hand—

And every White Walker froze in place.

Waiting.

The silence that followed was suffocating.

Embla bent low over Astrid, wings shielding her.

Tell me what to do, she whispered.
Fight?
Flee?
Break the stone?
Dive into it?
Say the word.

Astrid stared at the glowing runes.

At the Frost Wight.

At the horde closing in.

And she knew:

If they stayed on the plateau, they would be overrun.
If they fled, Embla would be exhausted before they reached
lower ground.
If they fought, Halvar would die.
If they hesitated—

Everyone would die.

The circle was the only unknown.

But it was the only door that the Wight wanted open.

And that terrified her most of all.

Astrid's breath shook.

"Embla…"

Embla lowered her head.

Yes, Astrid?

Astrid placed both hands on the stone.

"We're going into the circle."

Halvar shouted, "Astrid—NO!"

The runes flared blinding blue-white—

A shockwave burst outward from the circle—

And the mountain dissolved into light.

Light swallowed the mountain.

For a heartbeat, Astrid couldn't feel her body. There was no wind, no cold, no stone beneath her boots—only a weightless, soundless in-between, as if she'd stepped off the edge of the world and never hit the ground.

Then everything slammed back.

She hit her knees on smooth stone.

Air rushed into her lungs—warm, dry, tinged with something she couldn't quite name. Not smoke. Not snow.

Ash. Old and quiet, like the memory of long-dead fires.

"Astrid!" Halvar's voice, rough and close, echoed strangely.

"I'm here," she gasped.

Her own voice bounced back at her, repeating in faint layers—here… here… here…

She pushed herself up, palms scraping against stone.

It wasn't the plateau.

They were in a vast circular chamber so wide the opposite walls faded into shadow. The ceiling arched high overhead, disappearing into darkness. The floor beneath her hands was carved with overlapping spirals—runes etched deep and perfect into the rock.

They glowed faintly with the same soft blue light as the stone circle outside.

"Where… are we?" she whispered.

Embla's shadow fell over her. The dragon took a hesitant step forward, claws clicking softly.

Below, Embla murmured. **Deep. Beneath the city. Beneath the mountain.**

Halvar turned in a slow circle, knife still in his hand. "Feels like a tomb," he muttered. "Or a trap."

Astrid swallowed.

"No," she said quietly. "Listen."

They fell silent.

The chamber wasn't silent back.

It was filled with whispers.

Not words—not at first. Just the impression of breath, of motion, of something just beyond hearing. Then, slowly, threads of sound pulled into shape.

Laughter.
A roar.
The rhythm of wings.
A chant in a language Astrid didn't know.

She closed her eyes.

The echoes wrapped around her like fog.

Chamber of Echoes, she realized. **Not just a name. It's… what it is.**

Embla lifted her head, eyes going distant.

I hear them, she whispered. **Dragons. Many. Old. Bright.**

Astrid reached out with her gift, pushing her awareness down—into the stone, into the air, into the humming lines beneath her knees.

The world responded.

Images flickered at the edges of her mind—so fast she almost missed them.

A dragon the size of a house, scales like molten copper, soaring over Bryngard when it was whole—towers unbroken, banners streaming.

A rider standing in this very chamber, hand pressed to the stone, eyes blazing with reflected fire.

A circle of dragons and humans together, heads bowed around a central flame.

Then—

Swords.
Blood.
Smoke choking the sky.
Dragons falling from the air like burning stars.

Astrid jerked back, heart pounding.

"What did you see?" Halvar demanded, catching her elbow.

She tried to speak, but the images were still lodged behind her eyes.

"Riders," she managed. "Dragons. This was their place. Where they met. Where they trained. Where they… ended."

Embla lowered herself slightly, scales shivering.

I feel their fear, she whispered. **At the end. Not fear of men. Fear of… losing themselves. Becoming rage. Becoming weapon.**

Halvar's gaze flickered between them. "So this is where it started and where it broke. Grand. Exactly where I always wanted my little girl to visit."

Astrid managed a weak smile.

Something tugged at her attention.

At the far side of the chamber, shapes stood against the wall—tall, thin, and still. For a moment, panic flared— White Walkers?—

But these didn't move.

They were statues.

Twelve of them, spaced evenly in a circle around the room—six dragons, six humans. The dragons' stone wings were spread, their eyes carved with uncanny precision. The humans wore different armor, different clothing, faces from different eras, but every one of them bore the same mark on their forehead:

A circle divided by a jagged line.

Astrid's fingers tingled.

She reached up slowly, touching her own brow.

Nothing there.

Yet.

Embla padded closer to one of the dragon statues, nostrils flaring.

These are not just stone, she murmured. **They remember.**

Astrid frowned. "Remember what?"

Before Embla could answer, the runes on the floor flared brighter.

"Back," Halvar said sharply. "Astrid—"

Too late.

Light rose from the spirals beneath Astrid's feet, curling around her ankles like mist. It climbed her legs, her chest, her throat—a gentle, insistent pressure.

Embla lunged, trying to nudge her away.

Her muzzle hit something solid and invisible.

She snarled, shoving harder, but a transparent barrier held her back. Sparks skittered where her scales touched the air.

Astrid!

"I'm all right!" Astrid said, though her heart was racing. "I think. I—"

The floor dropped.

Not physically. It felt like falling without moving—like sinking through layers of time.

The chamber blurred.

Halvar shouted her name.

Embla roared.

Then they were gone.

Not from the room—but from *now*.

The Chamber had decided to show her what it remembered.

The one thing Astrid had never fully understood about her gift was this:

She didn't *really* hear the earth.

She heard what the earth remembered.

And Bryngard remembered everything.

She stood in the same chamber—but it wasn't old. It wasn't cracked. The runes burned bright and steady underfoot. Torches flickered in sconces along the walls. The statues were not statues.

They were people.

And dragons.

Living.

Breathing.

Watching.

Astrid gasped.

No one reacted to her. They moved as if she wasn't there. A woman with dark hair knelt by a young dragon, tying a strip of cloth around a fresh wound. A man in heavy furs laughed with a copper-scaled drake, their amusement echoing off the stone.

And at the center of the chamber stood a circle of twelve:

Six riders.
Six dragons.

A ritual.

Astrid's heart pounded.

A tall rider stepped forward—a man with hair like pale straw and eyes as hard as ice. The mark on his forehead glowed faintly—the circle with the jagged line.

He placed his hand on the stone.

"We gather," he said, his voice resonant. "For balance."

The word struck Astrid like a bell.

"Not for conquest," another rider said—a woman with a crooked nose and kind eyes. "Not for dominion."

"For balance," the dragons echoed, their voices overlapping in a layered chorus.

The copper dragon Astrid had glimpsed in the earlier flash spoke next.

"If we fly alone, we burn the sky," he said. "If you march alone, you break the earth. Together, we walk the line between."

Astrid's throat tightened.

That was what this had been.

Not dragons above humans.
Not humans above dragons.

A pact.

A partnership.

And somewhere, somehow, it had shattered.

The pale-haired rider looked up, directly toward where Astrid stood—even though he couldn't see her.

"The day will come," he said slowly, "when fear outweighs memory."

His gaze passed *through* her.

"When the ones who come after us remember the fire, but not the purpose."

The chamber flickered.

Suddenly it was filled with smoke.

Astrid coughed, eyes watering. The echoes around her twisted into screams. The riders were older now. Some were missing. The dragons were restless, wings flaring.

"We cannot hold them back forever!" someone shouted. "The kings want more. The priests want more. Every village asks for our fire!"

"We were never meant to be their weapons," a dragon roared.

"What were we meant to be?" a young rider cried.

"Bridges," a dragon whispered. "Between your world and what lies beneath."

The vision shifted again.

The chamber was almost empty.

The copper dragon lay bleeding on the floor, sides heaving. The pale-haired rider knelt beside him—older now, lines etched deeply into his face.

"They have turned us into monsters," the rider whispered. "Or we have let them."

The dragon's eyes fluttered open.

"Then give the world what it thinks it wants," he rasped. "No more bridges. No more balance."

The rider swallowed. "What are you saying?"

"End it," the dragon said. "All of it. Lock it away. Our flame. Your bond. Their memory."

The room trembled.

The runes pulsed.

Outside, dragonfire roared and people screamed.

The rider looked toward the ceiling, jaw shaking.

"What if someone needs us, someday?" he whispered.

The dragon's gaze drifted toward Astrid.

Though she knew he couldn't see her, the weight of his eyes still pinned her.

"Then let the earth decide," he said. "If the world is ever worthy of our fire again… it will grow another bridge."

His chest rose one last time.

Fell.

Stilled.

The rider pressed his hand to the stone.

"Then let this be my betrayal," he whispered. "And my act of faith."

Light flared, blinding.

Astrid cried out—

—and the vision shattered.

She was back in the chamber.

On her knees.

Hands pressed flat to the stone, fingers splayed.

Her skin burned where it touched the runes.

Embla's face loomed just beyond the invisible barrier, eyes wide, smoke coiling from her nostrils.

Astrid! Her thoughts crashed through like a wave. **You went still! You didn't breathe! I tried to break through—**

"I'm all right," Astrid croaked. "I think."

Halvar crouched just beyond the barrier, knuckles white on his knife. "You were… gone," he said roughly. "Your eyes were open but not seeing. You scared ten years off me, girl."

Astrid swallowed hard.

"It showed me," she whispered. "What this place was. What the riders were. What they did at the end."

Embla's pupils narrowed.

Tell me.

Astrid forced herself to sit up straighter, though her muscles trembled.

"They weren't tyrants," she said. "At least not at the start. They… they kept balance. They used dragonfire to stop wars, to heal the land after storms, to bridge gaps between kingdoms."

Halvar snorted faintly. "Didn't work out too well in the end."

"No," Astrid agreed. "Because people started treating dragons like tools. Like weapons for hire. And some riders… gave in. They burned on command. They broke armies. They forgot why they started."

Embla's tail flicked anxiously.

And at the end?

Astrid closed her eyes for a moment.

"At the end," she said softly, "one of them shut it all down. He locked away the bond. The fire. The *possibility* of it. He let dragons and humans tear each other apart rather than let the world keep twisting their connection."

Halvar stared at her. "You mean he killed them all?"

"Yes," Astrid whispered. "By letting the fear win. By letting the kings and priests push too far. By not stopping it sooner."

She lifted her head.

"But he also… left a door."

Embla's gaze sharpened.

The circle.

Astrid nodded.

"He told the earth—if it ever thinks the world deserves dragons again… it will grow a new bridge."

Embla's eyes softened.

You.

Astrid's throat worked.

"I don't know," she whispered. "Maybe. Or maybe any girl like me would've done. I'm just… the one who listened."

Halvar shook his head slowly. "I knew you were special, but this…" He huffed out a breath. "Somehow, 'bridge between worlds' didn't cross my mind."

A faint, dry voice echoed through the chamber.

Nor mine, at first.

Astrid's heart jolted.

"The wizard?" she called.

A familiar figure stepped out from behind one of the dragon statues, coalescing from drifting motes of light.

Cloak.
Staff.
Eyes like stormlit ice.

But he wasn't solid.

He shimmered slightly, as if seen through heat.

Embla bared her teeth.

I smelled you, she growled. **Dust and lightning.**

The wizard inclined his head. "My apologies for the abrupt silence earlier. The Frost Wight is… adept at drowning certain kinds of magic."

Astrid scrambled to her feet—only to find the invisible barrier still held.

She slammed her palms against it. "Why did you send us here without telling us what it was?"

"Because you would not have come," he said simply.

Halvar exploded. "You could have told us this was the tomb of dragon history and the place where the last bond was broken!"

The wizard's gaze flicked to him.

"And would you have brought her?" he asked quietly. "Or would your fear have dragged her south instead, straight into Calven's noose?"

Halvar's retort died on his tongue.

Astrid stared at the wizard.

"You knew what I was," she said. "From the beginning."

He smiled faintly.

"I knew what you *could* be. There's a difference."

Embla's wings twitched.

The dead thing climbs, she reminded him. **The Wight. It comes.**

The wizard's expression sobered.

"Yes," he said. "And we have little time."

He stepped closer to the barrier, studying Astrid.

"This chamber does not choose lightly," he said. "It only opens fully for those it deems… possible."

"Possible what?" Astrid whispered.

His eyes softened.

"Possible bridges," he said. "The question, Astrid Halvarsdottir, is what you will connect. And what you will refuse to let through."

The stone beneath her hands pulsed again.

Warmth seeped into her palms, up her arms, into her chest.

Embla inhaled sharply.

I feel it, she murmured. **Like the Heartforge, but… sideways. Not just for me. For you. For us. Together.**

The wizard nodded.

"This is not a forge for dragons alone," he said. "This is where riders were bound. Where they learned to hear as their dragons do. Where they shared more than thoughts."

Astrid's mouth went dry.

"What do you mean?"

The chamber darkened.

Runes flared.

The wizard's voice seemed to come from everywhere at once.

"You have three choices, Astrid."

She stiffened. "I hate when you say that."

He almost smiled.

"Choice the first," he said. "Turn away. Refuse the chamber. Walk out of here as you are—a girl with a dragon, hunted but unbound. You will live shorter. You will burn quicker. But your choices will be your own."

Embla snarled softly.

I do not like this 'turn away.'

"Choice the second," the wizard continued. "Take what power the chamber offers without accepting its limits. You and Embla will burn bright. Very bright. And very briefly. You will tear down Calven, the Frost Wight, and half the world with you."

Halvar paled. "Absolutely not."

"And the third?" Astrid whispered.

The wizard's gaze sharpened.

"Accept the bond as it was meant to be," he said. "Balanced. Shared. You will gain strength—but you will also be held by its rules. You will not be able to use dragonfire without cost. You will not be able to choose only for yourself. Every act will ripple through Embla. Every decision will change you both."

Embla tilted her head.

We are already changing each other, she said quietly.

"Not like this," the wizard said. "This is… permanent. Deeper than thought. Deeper than life. It may even reach beyond death."

Halvar sucked in a breath. "And if she chooses this—will it kill her?"

The wizard's gaze flickered.

"It will kill the girl she was," he said. "And the dragon Embla was. What comes after will be… something new."

Astrid's heart pounded.

Outside, the mountain shook faintly. A distant roar carried through the stone—white and hungry and old.

The Frost Wight was close.

Astrid looked at Embla.

At Halvar.

At the wizard.

At the glowing runes beneath her hands.

Fear swelled in her chest, thick and suffocating.

"I don't want to burn the world," she whispered. "I don't want to be anyone's weapon. Not the monastery's. Not the Wight's. Not yours."

The wizard inclined his head. "Then don't."

She laughed shakily. "It's not that simple."

"No," he agreed. "It's not. That's why it matters."

Embla leaned closer to the barrier until their foreheads almost touched.

Astrid felt her warmth, smelled the faint scent of lightning and smoke and frost.

I choose you, Embla said softly. **Whatever you choose.**

Astrid's eyes burned.

"If I turn away," she whispered, "we might die."

Embla's thoughts were a low, steady hum.

If you accept halfway power, we *will* die.

Astrid swallowed.

"And if I choose the bond?"

Embla hesitated.

Then:

Then we will be what we were meant to be.
Not just fear.
Not just fire.
Not just a girl hiding a dragon under the bracken.
Something… more.

Halvar pressed a hand against the invisible wall.

"You don't have to decide for the whole world," he said roughly. "Just decide what lets you look in the mirror without flinching."

Astrid's fingers tightened on the stone.

The runes flared in response.

Outside, the Frost Wight's voice whispered through the rock.

Child of fire.
Heart of earth.
Choose…

Astrid closed her eyes.

She saw Torndal.
Skarlund.
The ring of fire around Calven.
The boy who'd given her the fish-carved token with hopeful eyes.

She felt Embla's first awkward steps.
Their first flight.

Their first shared thought.

And beneath it all, the echo of the pale-haired rider's words:

If the world is ever worthy of our fire again... it will grow another bridge.

"I don't know if the world is worthy," Astrid whispered.

Her voice trembled.

"But I know *she* is."

She opened her eyes.

"I choose the bond," she said.

The chamber exhaled.

Light roared up from the runes, flooding her veins with heat and cold all at once. Her thoughts shattered like glass and reformed, not alone now but threaded through with Embla's presence—every heartbeat echoed, every breath mirrored.

Astrid screamed.

So did Embla.

The barrier exploded in a shower of blue sparks.

Halvar was thrown backward.

The wizard raised a hand, shielding his eyes.

For a moment, dragon and girl were outlines of light— one scaled, one small—overlapping, breathing in sync.

Then the glow dimmed.

Astrid collapsed.

Embla staggered, legs trembling.

Halvar dragged himself upright, vision swimming.

"Astrid…?"

She pushed herself to her knees, gasping.

Her eyes opened.

They glowed faintly—amber, like Embla's, with tiny sparks flickering in the depths.

Embla blinked slowly.

Astrid?

Astrid heard the thought inside her skull—clearer than ever. Not like a voice beside hers.

Like a voice braided *through* hers.

She smiled weakly.

"I'm here."

Embla shuddered.

I felt you fall and stand at the same time. It was… terrifying. I hated it. I loved it. I do not understand it.

Astrid laughed, half-sobbing. "That makes two of us."

The wizard watched them, expression unreadable.

"It is done," he said quietly. "Bryngard has accepted you."

Outside, a sound like the world cracking rolled through the chamber.

The Frost Wight had reached the plateau.

The wizard's gaze snapped toward the ceiling.

"Our time is up," he said. "The Wight cannot enter this chamber easily—but it will try. And when the hungry dead tear at the doors of an old power, nothing good follows."

Embla straightened, weariness warring with a new kind of steadiness.

We go back up, she said. **We face it.**

Astrid rose beside her.

Her knees shook.

But beneath the fear, something else burned:

Balance.

Bridges.

A promise made in a dead dragon's last breath.

She looked at Halvar.

He nodded once, eyes shining with something fierce and proud.

"At least now," he said, "you'll scare them half to death before they kill us."

Astrid grinned weakly. "That's the spirit."

The wizard lifted his staff.

"The circle will return you to the plateau," he said. "After that—what you do is not mine to say."

Astrid stepped toward the center of the runes with Embla at her side.

They stood together.

Heart pounding.
Fire waking.
Fear and hope tangled in equal measure.

The Chamber of Echoes hummed one last time, etching their choice into its long memory.

Then light rose again.

The world tilted.

The stone circle's threshold reached for them.

And as they vanished from the chamber and rushed back toward the waiting mountain, toward the Frost Wight and the White Walkers and whatever Calven would become…

Astrid had a single, blazing thought:

We are not their weapon.
We are not their monster.
We are the bridge.

Whatever that meant.

The mountain—and the world—were about to find out.

CHAPTER 24

THE BREATH OF THE FROST WIGHT

Back Into the Winter of Death

Light spat them out of the stone circle like a breath held too long.

Astrid hit the ground hard, knees slamming into the frost-lined stone of the plateau. Embla skidded beside her, claws scraping sparks. Halvar staggered out after them, dropping into a crouch, knife already drawn.

The world snapped back instantly.

The cold.
The wind.
The storm twisting above their heads.
And—

The Frost Wight.

It was closer than before.

Much closer.

It hovered twenty paces away, cloak slithering like living ice around skeletal limbs. The White Walkers surrounded the plateau in a ring of pale hunger, crawling over broken stone like insects swarming prey.

But none of them moved.

None of them breathed.

They waited.

For the Wight.

For Astrid.

Embla lowered herself protectively over Astrid, wings

half-spread, a low growl rolling like thunder from her chest.

Stay behind me, she warned. **Your fire is new. Mine is old. I take the first strike.**

Astrid pushed herself up, breath shuddering.
Her head spun.
Her chest burned.
The runes' warmth still glowed faintly under her skin, echoing in her heartbeat.

"I can't hide behind you anymore," she whispered. "Not after what we just chose."

Embla shot her a sharp look.

We chose together. That does not mean you walk in front of a storm for fun.

Astrid almost smiled despite the terror.

Halvar stepped beside them, jaw clenched so tightly his teeth might crack.

"All right," he growled. "What's the plan for killing a ghost king?"

They didn't get to answer.

The Frost Wight glided forward.

The air around it bent, folding like cold glass. Frost spread across the stone beneath it in branching veins. Its tattered cloak snapped in the windless air.

Embla snarled, taking a step toward it.

And the Wight **lifted its hand**.

The White Walkers fell to their knees instantly, like puppets with strings cut.

Astrid's breath caught.

The Wight spoke—not aloud, but inside their minds, cold and consuming.

Child of fire.
Marked of stone.
You open the chamber.
You take what was locked away.
You belong to me now.

Astrid's pulse exploded.

"NO," she said aloud, her voice cracking. "I belong to no one. Not you. Not the monastery. Not even the chamber."

The ground trembled.

Embla stepped forward, flame building behind her teeth.

Speak again, ice-thing, she growled, **and I will melt your bones.**

The Frost Wight tilted its head, studying the dragon.

Then it spoke again.

You are wrong, hatchling of fire.
She belongs to you.
As you belong to her.
One flame. One death.

Embla stiffened.

It knows, she whispered. **It sees the bond.**

Astrid felt her own heart stutter—because through the bond, she felt Embla's heartbeat echoing hers. Not just in sync.

Entwined.

Halvar stepped between them and the Wight, knife ready though hopelessly inadequate.

"You don't get her," he snarled. "You don't get either of

them."

The Wight did not even look at him.

It raised its other hand—slowly, deliberately.

The temperature dropped instantly.
Astrid's breath crystallized in her throat.
Her eyelashes froze together.

And then she felt it—

Clawing at the bond.

Give me the flame, the Wight whispered. *Give me the bridge. The world must freeze. The fire must end.*

Astrid gasped, staggering backward. Embla roared and shoved her with a wing, trying to protect her from the psychic assault—but the Wight wasn't attacking her body.

It was attacking the bond.

Astrid clutched her head.

"Embla—!"

I feel it— Embla hissed, shaking violently. **It touches the place where we connect. It wants to UNMAKE it—!**

Halvar moved to strike the Wight—

But before he even took a step—

A White Walker moved.

Fast.

It lunged the moment he turned, claws sweeping toward Halvar's throat.

"Astrid!" he shouted.

She didn't think.

She reacted.

She slammed her hand forward—

And **the rune-light in her veins erupted like lightning.**

A shockwave burst from her palm, invisible but forceful as a hammer. The White Walker flew backward, crashing into a stone pillar with a sickening crack.

It didn't get up.

Halvar blinked at her in disbelief. "Girl… what did you just—"

"I don't know," she said, trembling. "I just—did it."

Embla's eyes widened.

You used my fire.

Astrid froze.

"What?"

Not flame. Embla stepped closer, voice trembling. **But the thread of it. The echo. You took it. You pulled it through the bond without burning me. Astrid, that's—**

The Wight screamed.

The scream was silent, but the air warped. Every White Walker collapsed flat on the stone, hands over their ears though they had none.

The Frost Wight's blind eyes blazed with icy light.

Her fire is MINE.

Astrid stumbled back.

Embla whipped around her, wings tightly circling her like a shield.

Stay behind me now. We test your power another time.

Astrid grabbed Embla's front leg, breath ragged. "No. We do this together."

"We die together if you stand still long enough," Halvar muttered.

The Wight extended both skeletal arms.

The snow around them rose into a swirling vortex—
The wind shrieked—
White Walkers crawled toward the plateau edge—
The mountain's frost thickened under their feet—

Astrid felt the pressure in her chest spike, as if hands were crushing her heart.

Embla roared—

And pushed her flame upward.

Astrid felt it through the bond—pressure, heat, a bright, dangerous pulse.

Not enough, Embla whispered. **Not like this. We are too new —**

Astrid's fingers dug into Embla's scales.

"Take mine."

Embla stiffened.

Astrid—NO—

"I said take it!"

She pushed.

Heat surged from her chest into the bond, a hot rush like liquid sunlight.

Embla reared back, stunned.

Her pupils thinned to slits.

Her throat glowed bright gold.

The Frost Wight froze.

Astrid whispered—

"Burn him."

Embla opened her jaws—

And **breathed fire.**

Not blue.
Not gold.
Not the baby flame she'd used months ago.

A torrent of brilliant white-gold flame burst from her mouth, so bright it whitened the world.

The Frost Wight shrieked—
Its cloak erupted into fire—
Its bones glowed—
Cracks spread across its form—
The White Walkers convulsed on the stone—

For a heartbeat, Astrid thought it was enough.

That they'd won.

But the Wight did not fall apart.

It pulled the fire into itself.

A sucking pressure collapsed the air around it.

Astrid stumbled backward. "Embla—stop!"

But Embla couldn't.
The fire poured out of her like a flood.
She screamed, trying to cut it off, but the bond held it open.

Astrid—It's taking—It's TAKING me—

Astrid's vision blurred.

Halvar ran, trying to push Astrid away—but the heat threw him back.

The Frost Wight lifted its head—

Flame dancing inside its ribs.

Child of fire, it whispered, voice cracking with new power. *Your flame is mine now.*

Then it stepped forward.

Unafraid.

Unburned.

And stronger than before.

Astrid's heart stopped.

She had given it power.

Her fire—

Embla's fire—

The Wight had taken it.

She fell to her knees.

"Embla—what have I—?"

Embla collapsed beside her, smoke streaming from her jaws, chest heaving.

It drains me… she whispered. **Astrid… run…**

The Frost Wight glided closer, shadow falling over them.

Halvar stood between them again—knife shaking but raised.

"You want her," he rasped. "You go through me."

The Wight lifted a skeletal hand.

Snow began to swirl around Halvar's feet.

Astrid screamed—

Embla tried to rise—

And at that exact moment—

A voice rang out from behind the Wight.

Deep.
Human.
Familiar.

"ENOUGH."

The Frost Wight froze.

Halvar's eyes widened.

Astrid gasped.

Because the speaker—

Stepped out from the storm with a torch in one hand, sword in the other.

His black cloak whipped in the wind.

His eyes burned with righteous fury.

His voice carried cold fire.

Brother Calven had arrived.

And he had seen everything.

Calven's Claim

The torchlight made Calven look taller than he was, the flames snapping wildly in the storm winds that refused to touch him. Snow swirled around him in spirals, as if afraid to land on his cloak.

He walked toward them with slow, deliberate steps, blade

drawn, eyes locked on Astrid as though nothing else existed on the plateau.

"Child," he said, voice low and brimming with triumph, "you've done the unthinkable."

Embla groaned and shifted, trying to stand.

Calven didn't flinch at the sight of her — at the dragon fire smoldering beneath Embla's scales, the smoke curling from her nostrils.

He didn't fear her.
He *welcomed* her.

"Proof," he whispered, breath trembling in the frigid air. "A living dragon. A bound rider. The prophecy made flesh."

Astrid forced herself upright, legs shaking. "Stay away from her."

Calven almost smiled. "Oh, Astrid… I'm not here to harm the dragon."

His eyes glittered.

"I'm here to claim her."

Embla snarled, but her flame only flickered — weakened, pulled at from within by the Wight's theft.

Halvar planted himself between Calven and Astrid again. "You're not taking anyone from here alive."

"Alive?" Calven chuckled darkly. "Halvar, you misunderstand. I don't need to take them *alive*. I need only take them."

The Frost Wight turned slowly toward Calven, the glow of stolen fire flickering in its ribs. Snow drained from the air around it, sucked inward as if the cold itself fed on flame.

Calven saw it.

He froze.

A thin tremor crossed his face — not fear, but anticipation.

"You," Calven whispered to the Wight. "You are the corruption. You are the rot the priests warned us of."

The Wight's blind eyes fixed on him.

Calven lifted his sword, torchlight glittering off its edge. "And I have waited a lifetime to face something like you."

Astrid stared.

He meant it.
He wanted this.
He'd been dreaming of this moment — the moment a "holy warrior" finally met a monster worthy of his zeal.

The Frost Wight lifted its hand toward him.

Fire-taker, it whispered. *You do not belong to the flame.*

Calven's smile widened. "No," he breathed. "I belong to the Light."

He lunged.

Halvar swore under his breath. "Idiot—!"

Calven swung his sword in a wide arc, blade slicing through the air.

And to Astrid's horror—

The Wight flinched back.

It jerked as the sword passed near its ribs, the runes carved into the steel bursting with pale gold light.

"A blessed blade," Halvar whispered. "He brought a sanctified sword."

Calven advanced, cloak whipping behind him.

"You feed on her fire," he snarled, "but you cannot take *mine*."

He slashed again.

This time the blade hit, cutting through the Wight's cloak and biting into frozen bone.

The Wight screeched silently — the shriek rattling Astrid's teeth.

A crack spread across the Wight's side.

Halvar blinked. "He can hurt it. Calven can actually—"

The Wight lashed out with a burst of cold that slammed Calven off his feet. He hit the ground but rolled back up, sword raised again.

Calven laughed.

"Glorious," he breathed. "At last, a foe of worth."

Astrid wanted to scream at him. *This isn't a crusade!* But the words wouldn't come.

She was too busy trying to breathe again — because the Wight's cold still gripped the bond. Embla trembled violently, struggling to stay conscious.

Astrid pressed her forehead to Embla's side.

"I'm here," she whispered. "I'm here, breathe with me—"

Embla's voice flickered through the bond, thin as thread.

It takes our fire, Astrid.
We cannot win like this.

Astrid shook as she looked up.

Calven and the Wight clashed again — Calven's glowing blade sparking each time it struck icy bone. The Wight countered with flashes of freezing energy that cracked stone beneath his boots.

But even with his holy blade, Calven was faltering.

He was only human.

The Wight was not.

Astrid tightened her grip on Embla's scales.

"We need to pull back," she whispered. "We need to take our fire back from it."

Embla whimpered, smoke dripping from her mouth. Astrid felt the agony of it — the draining heat, the hollow ache in the chest, the desperate instinct to curl around her rider and shield her.

How? Embla asked weakly. **It took the fire we shared. We gave it willingly. A dragon's flame cannot be forced back.**

Astrid's breath caught.

But wasn't that exactly what the chamber had shown her?

The runes pulsed under her skin like a second heartbeat.

Balanced.
Shared.
Bridged.

"Maybe a dragon's fire can't be forced back," Astrid said. "But our fire isn't just dragon anymore."

Embla's eyes widened.

Astrid—no—

"I have to try."

You do not know what it will do!

"Neither do you!"

Another silent shriek raked across the plateau as the Wight knocked Calven backward, slamming him into a pillar. He hit the stone, gasped, and dropped to one knee.

The Wight turned toward Astrid.

Its cloak rose around it like wings made of ice.

Your flame tastes pure, it whispered. *Give it. All of it. And I will freeze the world into silence.*

Astrid grabbed Embla's horns and pressed her forehead to the dragon's.

Embla trembled.

"Astrid…" Halvar warned, voice cracking. "Girl, whatever you're thinking—don't."

"I have to," she whispered.

Then, through the bond—

She **pulled.**

Not flame.
Not heat.
Not Embla herself.

She pulled the thread between them.

The echo.
The resonance.
The *connection.*

A bright shock tore through her chest.

Embla roared — not in pain, but in sudden breathless surprise.

Astrid—what are you—

The Frost Wight staggered.

Its ribs dimmed.

Its cloak sagged.

The stolen fire flickered—

Astrid had pulled back the spark the Wight had taken.

It was working.

Calven spat blood and pushed himself to his feet. "What did she just—"

But Astrid didn't hear him.

Because the bond flared so brightly it nearly blinded her.

Embla's flame rekindled.

Weakly.

But real.

And Astrid felt—

Power.

Not like the wild blast that had knocked the White Walker away.
Not like Embla's blazing fire.

Something quieter.
Sharper.
Smoother.

A line of heat unfurled through her hands, like a glowing thread drawn taut.

Embla gasped.

Astrid—
You're wielding the bond—

Astrid raised her hand.

Energy sparked between her fingers.

The Wight's blind eyes widened.

This time, **it stepped back.**

Astrid's voice shook, but she lifted her chin.

"You can't take our fire," she whispered. "You can't take *me*. Not anymore."

The Wight shrieked, its cloak snapping like torn wings.

Calven staggered forward, sword raised. "Astrid—hold it there!"

Embla spread her wings, rising shakily.

Halvar grabbed Astrid's arm. "Girl—focus! Whatever you're doing, do it again!"

Astrid closed her eyes.

Reached into the bond.

Pulled.

Fire crackled across her skin.

Embla inhaled.

Calven charged.

The Frost Wight raised both hands—

And the plateau erupted as all four forces collided.

The Fourfold Clash

For one suspended second, the plateau held its breath.

Astrid pulling fire through the bond.
Embla spreading her wings, flame rekindling in her throat.
Calven charging with his blessed blade.
The Frost Wight rising, cold swirling around its skeletal

form.

Then—

Everything hit at once.

Embla roared, flames bursting from her jaws—white-gold, richer and deeper than before. Astrid felt the heat roar through her own chest like a second heartbeat.

Calven leapt, blade glowing with holy runes, striking downward.

The Frost Wight thrust both skeletal hands forward, releasing a torrent of freezing storm.

When the four powers collided—

The world screamed.

A shockwave blasted outward from the point of impact, throwing snow, stone fragments, and White Walkers high into the air. The entire plateau shook as cracks split through the frost-lined surface like spiderwebs.

Embla's flame split around Calven's blade.
Calven's blade carved a glowing arc through the Wight's storm.
Astrid's fire-thread lanced through the air like lightning.
And the Wight's cold swallowed everything it touched.

The collision burst into a swirling vortex of light and ice that crackled with raw power.

Astrid staggered backward, her ears ringing, breath torn from her lungs.

Embla fought the wind, claws carving trenches in the stone.

Halvar flattened himself to the ground, gripping the stone

edge to keep from being flung off.

Calven shoved forward, teeth bared, blade glowing brighter as he drove it toward the Wight's chest.

"You will FALL," he growled.

The Wight caught the blade between its skeletal hands.

The steel hissed as frost crawled along it.

Then the Wight spoke in a voice colder than winter itself:

Holy light is a child's toy.
Your faith is thin as breath.
You do not frighten me.

Calven snarled. "Then let me remind you—faith burns."

He pushed.

The runes on the blade burst into golden fire.

The Wight shrieked as the blade's light burned its fingers, cracking bone like glass in flame.

But even as it reeled, its other hand lashed outward—striking Calven's chest with crushing force.

Calven flew backward, hitting the ground so hard the air left his lungs in a violent gasp.

Embla seized her chance.

Flame erupted from her once more—

But only for a heartbeat.

Her knees buckled.

Smoke curled from her nostrils weakly.

Astrid felt the collapse in her gut—felt Embla's exhaustion through the bond.

"No—no, stay with me!" Astrid cried, pressing her hands to the dragon's scales. "Take whatever you need—take it!"

Embla's head shook violently.

No. You will burn from inside. The bond is not full enough yet—I take too much and you die.

"I don't care!" Astrid choked. "You need it more—"

ASTRID.

Embla's mind-voice slammed through her thoughts, fierce and trembling.

If you burn, I burn. If you fall, I fall. We do NOT throw each other to death. You said the bond had balance—now trust it.

Astrid sobbed but nodded.

Embla's flame dimmed—but stabilized.

For now.

The Frost Wight rose again, cloak flaring like wings of void-black frost. The cracks from Calven's strike glowed faintly in its ribs—but its fury outshone any wound.

Its hollow voice swept across the plateau:

Fire.
Light.
Faith.
Flesh.
You are all noise.
All passing.
All rot.

It raised both arms.

And the temperature *plunged.*

The air froze mid-breath.

Snow crystallized mid-fall.
The sky itself dimmed as if frost tried to smother the sun.

Astrid gasped—her lungs seizing.

The cold wasn't cold anymore.

It was **wrong.**

A dead cold.
A soul-killing cold.
A cold that erased.

Embla staggered, wings drooping.

Astrid—this is not wind—this is its HEART—

Calven dragged himself to his feet, trembling. "It's… trying to freeze the bond itself…"

Halvar's eyes widened. "It wants to kill the dragon through HER!"

Astrid fell to her knees, clutching her chest as the frost forced its way along the connection—cold needles stabbing into her heart.

Embla roared and collapsed beside her.

Calven shouted something she couldn't understand.

The Frost Wight glided closer.

Give me the flame, it whispered. *Give me the bridge. Let the world freeze in peace.*

Astrid screamed—

And in that scream—

Something answered.

Not the Wight.

Not Embla.

Something **below** the plateau.

Something **in Bryngard.**

The runes along the stone ring behind them ignited—
Glowing blue.
Then white.
Then gold.

Astrid felt warmth swelling beneath her, rising through the stone, racing toward the center of the plateau like a heartbeat in the mountain.

Embla's head lifted weakly.

Something wakes— she gasped.

Calven turned in shock. "By the Light—what is that—?"

A sound boomed beneath them.

A low, deep, ancient roar.

Not of a creature.

Of stone.

Of memory.

Of something that was never meant to sleep.

The Wight turned sharply, cloak snapping like broken wings.

For the first time—

It recoiled.

Astrid forced herself to her feet.

A faint glow pulsed under her skin—matching the runes.
Her breath warmed.
The frost in her chest cracked.

"What… is… that?" she whispered.

Embla's pupils narrowed to slits.

The chamber echoes us.
It answers us.
It defies the Wight.

Calven stepped back, eyes wide as the ground trembled.

"Something is rising," he breathed.

Halvar snarled, "We don't have time for riddles—WHAT is rising?"

Astrid swallowed, voice shaking.

"A guardian," she whispered. "The last rider said the earth would decide who was worthy. The chamber… thinks we are."

The plateau split down the center.

A massive stone shape rose from the rupture—

A colossal carving shaped like a dragon's head, eyes glowing with white-hot runes. Its jaw cracked open as ancient gears ground beneath the mountain.

The Frost Wight screamed.

The dragon statue roared.

Embla's wings flared despite her exhaustion.

Astrid—
It's calling you.

The statue's eyes locked onto Astrid—
Blinding white—
Filled with ancient judgment.

Calven shielded his face, sword trembling in his grip.

Halvar pressed back against Embla, awe-struck and pale.

The Frost Wight raised its arms in fury.

Astrid stepped forward—

And the stone dragon's eyes pulsed once.

A single beam of white-gold light shot from the statue—

Not at the Wight.

Not at Embla.

At **Astrid.**

The light struck her chest—

And the world exploded with a sound like a dragon taking its first breath.

The Awakening of the Fire-Thread

The beam of white-gold light struck Astrid square in the chest.

Her breath vanished.
Her knees buckled.
Her vision went white around the edges as if she were staring into the heart of the sun.

She tried to scream—but the sound never left her throat.

The light wasn't burning her.

It was **rewriting** her.

Runes spiraled across her skin like living fire, flickering in and out, too fast for the eye to follow. Her heart thundered in her chest—then synchronized with Embla's. For a fraction of a second, their hearts beat as one.

Embla staggered forward, pupils blown wide in fear and awe.

Astrid—
ASTRID—!

Astrid felt the dragon's terror.
Felt her soul tightening around the bond.
Felt a roaring pressure behind her ribs, threatening to crack her open from the inside.

Her body arched, lifting from the ground, hair floating as if underwater.

And in that suspended moment—

She heard voices.

Not living ones.

Echoes.

Hundreds of them.

Riders
Dragons
Flame
Stone
War
Grief
A covenant
Breaking
Healing
Ending
Beginning

They all flooded her mind in a single pulse.

Then—

A deeper voice cut through the chaos.

Ancient.
Massive.

Carved from the mountain's bones.

Little spark…
the world has grown thin in your absence.

Astrid choked.

"Wh-what—who—?"

The chamber knows your name.
Bryngard remembers your fire.
And the bridge awakens.

The light seared brighter—

And the stone dragon statue **roared.**

A blast of force rippled out from Astrid, forming a protective ring around her—shoving Embla back, pushing Halvar to the ground, sending Calven stumbling.

Even the Frost Wight slid backward, cloak whipping around its hollow frame as it hissed in fury.

Astrid's feet lifted off the stone.

Her eyes opened—

Glowing bright gold, swirling like flame trapped under glass.

Embla gasped through the bond.

Astrid…
you look…
you look like a RIDER.

But not like the old riders.

Something **new.**

A hybrid of dragon and human flame.
A bridge reshaped by the chamber itself.
Not a girl wielding a dragon.

A girl **forged** together with one.

Astrid felt fire coil through her veins—not burning her, not consuming her, but moving with purpose.

Her palm glowed.
Her spine hummed.
Her breath steamed with sparks.

She lowered her feet slowly to the stone, light flickering around her like embers caught in wind.

The Frost Wight recoiled farther.

The bridge lives again, it whispered in horror.
This was forbidden.
This was ended.
This must be ended again.

Calven stared at Astrid like he was witnessing a miracle —or a nightmare.

"Astrid…" he whispered, voice trembling. "What are you?"

She didn't know.

She only knew what she *felt.*

She felt Embla's heartbeat inside her own chest.

She felt the pulse of ancient power beneath the mountain.

She felt the Frost Wight's hunger scraping at her mind like claws on glass.

She felt Calven's fanatic hope and fear twisted together.

She felt Halvar's terror for her—and fierce, overwhelming pride.

And she felt the bond.

Not as a thread.

As a **pathway.**

A two-way river of fire.

She could push it.
She could pull it.
She could shape it.

She lifted her hand.

A line of fire flickered between her fingers—weak, small, but controlled.

The Frost Wight hissed.

You are not the flame.
You are the shell around it.
You will crack.

It lunged.

Calven acted first.

With a shout, he hurled himself in front of Astrid, blade raised to block the Wight's strike.

"LIGHT DEFEND ME!" he roared.

The Wight backhanded him with a blast of cold so powerful it tore the blade from his hand and flung him thirty paces across the plateau.

He hit the stone hard—

Slid—

And did not rise.

"Calven!!!" Astrid yelled.

Halvar ran toward him, slipping on the ice.

But Astrid couldn't move.

She felt the Wight's attention turn back to her.

Its hollow voice slithered through the air.

Your flame tastes of the chamber.
Ancient.
Pure.
I will take it.
I will devour the bridge.

Astrid's heart pounded—furious, bright.

Embla dragged herself forward despite her exhaustion, wings trembling.

If you touch her, the dragon snarled, **I will tear your bones apart with my teeth.**

The Wight floated closer.

Frost spread across the stone, reaching for Astrid's boots.

Astrid clenched her fists.

The rune-light flared.

The frost cracked.

Embla's eyes widened through the bond.

Astrid—
something is changing—
inside you—

Astrid felt it.

Something moving.
Stirring.
Like a second heartbeat.
Not hers.
Not Embla's.

Something from the chamber.

Something awakened by the stone dragon.

An ancient instinct stirred behind her ribs—
not human,
not dragon,
but the echo of riders long gone.

She lifted her hands.

The rune-fire coiled around her fingers.

Not like a flame.
Not like Embla's breath.

Like **shaped fire.**

A blade made of heat and light.

She didn't know how she formed it.

She only knew she needed it.

The Frost Wight recoiled.

Impossible.

Astrid's voice trembled—but held.

"You want my fire?" she whispered. "Come take it."

The Wight shrieked and lunged—

And Astrid swung the fire-blade.

The impact erupted into a blast of white light and freezing
storm that shattered stone beneath them.

The Wight stumbled back—a deep crack running
diagonally across its ribs where the fire-blade struck.

Halvar shouted in disbelief.

Embla stared, stunned.

**You SHAPED fire—
you SHAPED it—
Astrid—humans cannot—**

Astrid panted, sweat freezing on her brow.

"I didn't," she gasped. "*We* did."

The Frost Wight screamed again, enraged.

The bridge must be broken—
must be broken—
must be—

Its voice cut off sharply.

Because Calven—bloody, staggering, barely conscious—had risen behind it, gripping his fallen blessed blade with shaking hands.

His voice was hoarse—but filled with venom.

"You do not get to judge the living."

He drove the blade into the Frost Wight's back.

The Wight arched in agony, icicles bursting from its cloak like shards of glass.

Calven leaned close, face contorted with fury.

"You want the flame?" he rasped. "BURN ON IT."

He twisted the blade.

The Frost Wight convulsed—
Screeching—
Cracking—
Its stolen fire spilling out in flickering bursts.

Calven roared in triumph—

Then the Wight spun with impossible speed and struck him through the chest.

Calven gasped—
Blood blooming across the snow—

Sword falling from his hand—
Eyes wide in shock and fury.

"NO—!!" Astrid screamed.

Embla roared and surged forward—

But the Wight seized Calven by the throat, lifting him into the air like a broken doll.

Faith is fragile, the Wight whispered.
Fire is forever.
And hers—
is mine.

It turned toward Astrid—

Dragging Calven like a shield.

Halvar shouted in horror. "ASTRID—DON'T—!"

Astrid froze, fire-blade flickering.

The Wight held Calven between them.

A living barrier.

A cruel checkmate.

Astrid's breath hitched.

Her hands shook.

Embla's growl trembled with fury and helplessness.

Astrid—
we cannot strike—
he will die—

The Wight's hollow voice slithered through the wind.

Choose, bridge.
Your flame…
or his life.

Astrid's heart shattered.

And the mountain held its breath.

The Choice That Breaks the World

Calven dangled from the Frost Wight's skeletal hand, boots scraping against the frozen stone, blood dripping onto the plateau in dark splashes. His sword lay far behind him, the runes fading.

He coughed a thread of crimson, but he didn't look at the Wight.

He looked straight at Astrid.

His eyes—usually full of cold faith and hardened judgment—held something she had never seen before.

Fear, yes.
But also… understanding.
Recognition.
An echo of something painfully human.

"Astrid…" he rasped.

The Wight tightened its grip.

Astrid stepped forward.

"Let him go," she pleaded, fire-blade flickering in her hand. "He's not yours."

He is nothing, the Wight answered. *A vessel of noise. A breath of warmth to be extinguished. His life weighs less than your flame.*

Astrid's chest constricted. "If you kill him—"

Then I clear the path to you.

Embla crawled closer, using the last dregs of her strength to keep her body between Astrid and danger. She spread her wings weakly, trembling.

Astrid—if you surrender the flame, it dies inside both of us. We die. The world burns or freezes. Don't—

"But he'll—"

He is a man, Embla whispered gently. **You are the bond.**

Calven struggled weakly, eyes burning with something fierce and strangely calm.

"Astrid," he rasped, "you listen to me. Do NOT give your flame to that thing."

"Calven—"

"Look at me!" he barked, blood flying from his lips. "I have hunted monsters all my life. I know EXACTLY what this is."

The Wight turned its head toward him, as if offended that prey dared speak.

Calven wheezed a laugh. "You want her fire because you're afraid of what she is becoming."

The Wight's cloak curled in irritation.

She is nothing. A spark. A seed. A child who confuses light with strength.

Calven spat more blood, smiling through it.

"No. She is the first true rider in an age… and you fear her."

A shudder ran through the Wight—an unmistakable ripple of fury.

Astrid realized Calven was right.

The Wight *feared* the bond.

Feared Astrid.
Feared what she might become.
Feared the return of balance.

Halvar shouted across the plateau, voice cracking with desperation:

"Astrid! Don't you MOVE! You hear me? You don't give up a single ember! I'd rather bury him myself!"

"HALVAR," she cried, "he'll die—"

Halvar stepped forward, jaw locked. "Then he dies fighting the right side for once."

Calven let out a broken laugh. "I'd prefer not dying at all, thanks."

The Wight lifted him higher.

Choose, bridge.

The fire-blade in Astrid's hand trembled.

Her chest burned.

Her eyes stung.

She could feel Embla's heartbeat pounding faintly inside her bones—steadying her, grounding her, begging her to hold the flame.

Astrid… if you give it, you give ME.

Astrid's breath fractured.

Calven's voice sharpened, slicing through her fear.

"Astrid—LISTEN."

She forced her gaze back to him.

His voice wasn't cruel.
Or commanding.
Or righteous.

It was honest.

"You owe me NOTHING," he rasped. "Not your life. Not your flame. Not your heart."

His eyes softened.

"You only owe the world the chance to survive whatever comes next."

The Wight hissed and tightened its grip—

Cracks spreading along Calven's ribs.

Astrid broke.

"STOP!" she screamed. "STOP! PLEASE!"

Her fire-blade flickered violently, almost extinguishing.

The Wight drifted closer, whispering through the storm:

Give it to me… and he will be spared.

Calven forced a smile—bloody, aching.

"Don't… believe it…"

Astrid's knees buckled.

She couldn't breathe.

She couldn't think.

Embla's voice trembled.

Astrid… if you give in, it wins. Forever.

The Wight leaned close, breath colder than death.

Choose.

Astrid closed her eyes—

And made her choice.

She lifted her hand.

The fire-blade dissolved.

Embla screamed.
Halvar shouted in horror.
The Wight surged forward to claim the flame—

But Calven moved first.

With the last strength left in his body—

He grabbed the Frost Wight's wrist.

Not to break free.

To **pull himself closer.**

He looked directly into Astrid's eyes.

And mouthed—

RUN.

Then he used the last breath of his life to speak a single
word:

"Ignis."

The holy runes carved into his armor ignited—
a burst of pale gold light exploding outward.

The Wight shrieked—
its cloak tearing—
its ribs cracking—
fire spilling out in violent arcs.

Calven's body burned in golden flame—
not consuming him,
purifying him.

A self-sacrifice spell.
A forbidden one.
Reserved only for the highest priests.

Astrid screamed his name.

The Wight staggered back—
for the first time truly wounded—
fire eating at its form from the inside.

Calven collapsed to his knees—
face soft, peaceful—
eyes closing.

"Astrid…" he whispered through the flame.

"You were never the monster."

Then he fell.

The Wight—
howling—
reeled back—

And Embla rose.

Her fire—
rekindled by Calven's sacrifice—
exploded through the bond, flooding Astrid's chest.

Astrid felt the fire in her veins blaze like a living thing.

Embla opened her jaws—

AND BREATHED.

This time, the flame was not white-gold.

Not baby-blue.

It was **runefire.**

Ancient.
Pure.
The flame of Bryngard.

It struck the Frost Wight full in the chest.

The creature screamed—

not in hunger,
not in rage—

In *fear.*

The runefire burned through its stolen flame—
melting ice
cracking bone
shredding shadow.

Halvar shielded his face from the blast.

Astrid staggered forward, fire glowing beneath her skin,
eyes blazing.

The Frost Wight collapsed to one knee.

It stared at Astrid with hollow fury.

Bridge, it rasped.
This is not over.

And with one last shrieking flare—

It shattered into ice and ash.

Silence fell.

Embla collapsed.

Astrid dropped beside her, shaking.

Halvar stumbled toward them, breath heaving.

The Stormguard, who had watched from the cliffs, knelt
as one—
bowing to the glow that lingered around Astrid
and to the dragon who had breathed the flame of legends.

But Astrid couldn't look at them.

She crawled forward—

toward Calven.

He lay still.
Eyes closed.
A faint smile on his lips.

A man who had lived his whole life hunting monsters—

and died saving two.

Astrid touched his forehead gently.

"I'm sorry," she whispered. "I didn't want this."

The wind stirred his hair.

Embla rested her head beside Astrid, eyes soft with grief.

He chose, she murmured.
Even humans can be brave.
Even broken ones.

Astrid wiped her tears with shaking hands.

Halvar placed a hand on her shoulder, trembling.

"You did right, girl," he said hoarsely. "Even when there was no right choice left."

Astrid didn't reply.

She stared at Calven's still face
and whispered the hardest truth she had ever spoken:

"I don't think the world is ready for me."

Embla curled around her protectively.

Then we will make it ready.

Astrid closed her eyes, leaning into her dragon's warmth as the storm slowly died around them.

The Frost Wight was gone.
Calven was gone.
And the bond—

the ancient bond—
burned brighter than ever.

But far below the mountain, in the thawing valleys…

Other things were stirring.

Word would spread.
Fear would grow.
The monastery would come.
The kings would hear.

And Astrid was no longer a girl.

She was the bridge.

And the world would either rise to meet her—

Or burn around her.

CHAPTER 25

THE DRAGON-BORN DAWN

The Ashes of a Warrior

For a long time, no one moved.

The storm had died.
The wind had quieted.
The mountain had gone still.

Only the faint crackle of lingering runefire echoed across the plateau where the Frost Wight had fallen.

Astrid knelt beside Calven's body, her fingers trembling as she brushed away the frost forming on his hair. Embla curled around her in a half-protective, half-exhausted coil, smoke drifting from her nostrils with each ragged breath.

Halvar stood several paces away, shoulders slumped, staring at Calven with a complex mixture of sorrow and bitterness.

The Stormguard tribe remained on the cliffside—silent, bowed, unmoving.

Astrid finally lifted her head.

"Embla?" she whispered.

The dragon stirred slightly.

Still here, Embla murmured, her voice faint but steady. **Still breathing. You?**

Astrid pressed a hand to her chest. Her heart felt… different. Heavier. Brighter. Hotter. Like something had been lit inside her and would never go out again.

"I don't know," she whispered. "But I'm standing."

Embla huffed a small, tired plume of smoke.

Then that is enough. For now.

Astrid nodded and forced herself to look down at Calven.

His face was peaceful—strangely peaceful.
Gone was the zealot's fire, the righteous fury, the cold certainty.

In its place was a quiet resolve.

A man who had spent his life hunting monsters…
and died saving the very thing he had been taught to hate.

Astrid's throat tightened.

"I didn't understand him," she whispered. "Not ever. But he didn't deserve… this."

Halvar walked closer, boots crunching on shattered ice.

"No," he said quietly. "He didn't."

He crouched down beside Astrid, rubbing the back of his neck. "I hated him most days. But today…" He exhaled. "Today, he chose right."

Astrid swallowed. "He said I wasn't the monster."

Halvar squeezed her shoulder gently. "And he finally believed it."

Astrid bowed her head.

Embla shifted, lowering her snout to Calven's chest.

I smell no fear in him now, she murmured softly. **That is rare, Astrid. Fear follows humans long after breath leaves them. But he… let go.**

Astrid closed her eyes. "He deserves to be buried somewhere warm."

Halvar nodded. "Aye. Somewhere spring reaches."

Astrid rose shakily to her feet. The plateau spun for a moment—her newly awakened bond humming in her veins like a second pulse.

Embla nudged her gently.

The chamber changed you.
I can feel it.
You walk differently.
You breathe differently.
You burn differently.

Astrid managed a tired smile. "So do you."

Embla blinked slowly. **Do I?**

"Your flames," Astrid whispered. "They weren't just fire. They were… something older."

Embla lowered her gaze, flexing her claws.

The chamber remembers what dragons were.
A pause.
And it shared some of that memory with us.

Astrid felt the truth of it ripple through the bond.

Not strength.
Not power.
Memory.

Ancient riders.
Ancient fire.
Ancient purpose.

And they were only touching the edges of it.

Halvar stood and turned to the Stormguard. "What now?" he called. "Will you stand against us or let us go?"

The Stormguard leader—the white-haired woman with wolf pelts and steel eyes—stepped forward.

She moved with slow, deliberate reverence, her boots crunching frost as she approached Astrid and Embla. Her warriors followed in a disciplined line, forming a semicircle around the trio.

Astrid tensed.

Embla growled softly, wings shifting.

Halvar's hand went to his knife.

But the leader only knelt.

Then, with a sweeping motion, she struck her fist against her chest in a powerful salute—one that echoed against the mountainside like a drum.

Her warriors mirrored the gesture as one.

Astrid stared, breath caught in her throat.

The leader rose, stepped close, and extended her hand—not in attack.

In **recognition**.

Her voice was deep, steady, and respectful.

"You are the Fire-Bound," she said. "The first of the age reborn. The mountain has seen you. The stone has accepted you. And we—Stormguard—bow to that bond."

Embla shifted, startled.
Halvar blinked.
Astrid's heart thudded.

"I… I didn't ask for that," Astrid whispered.

"You did not need to," the woman replied. "The pulse of Bryngard answered for you."

The leader's gaze softened—barely.

"Your battle woke more than stone."

Astrid swallowed. "What do you mean?"

The woman stepped aside, gesturing toward the far end of the plateau.

Astrid turned—

And felt the breath freeze in her chest.

Because emerging from the storm's last drifting remnants…

Was a pair of young Stormguard children.

A girl and a boy.

Maybe ten.
Maybe younger.

They carried between them a bundle wrapped in thick furs.

And the bundle was **glowing**.

Embla lifted her head sharply.

Astrid.
That is not human fire.

The Stormguard leader spoke softly.

"Our ancestors left us the charge: if the chamber ever woke again, the next sign would come shortly after."

Astrid's hands trembled. "A sign?"

The leader nodded once.

"The sign… of another egg."

Astrid gasped.

Halvar inhaled sharply.

Embla choked on a breath and whispered through the bond—
a trembling mix of awe, longing, and fear:

Another…
another like me?

The children approached and knelt before Astrid.

They held out the fur-wrapped bundle with reverent hands.

The glow brightened.

A pulse.
A heartbeat.
A warmth that spread into the air like dawn breaking.

The girl whispered, voice almost shaking with wonder:

"Fire-Bound…
a new hatchling stirs."

Astrid's stomach dropped.

A dragon egg.

Alive.

And they were placing it in her hands.

She froze.

Embla's breath hitched.

Halvar whispered, "Astrid… this is bigger than you. Bigger than all of us."

The Stormguard leader bowed her head.

"Bryngard has returned," she said. "And with it, the age of dragons."

Astrid stood numb, staring at the glowing egg.

Her life—already turned upside down—twisted again, more violently than ever.

Her bond had awakened.
The Wight had fallen.
Calven had sacrificed himself.
And now, in her arms…

A new dragon waited to be born.

Her eyes burned.

Her breath shook.

"Embla…" she whispered.

Embla pressed her head into Astrid's shoulder.

I am here.
A soft rumble.
Always.

Astrid held the egg close as warmth seeped into her chest.

She whispered the words she didn't know she needed:

"I won't let anything harm you."

To Embla.
To the egg.
To herself.
To the world.

The Stormguard bowed again.

Halvar stared in weary, stunned silence.

And Astrid knew:

The world wasn't ready for her.

But it would have to be.

Because now…

It wasn't just *her* the world had to fear.

It was what she was going to protect.

The Weight of a Second Heart

The plateau had fallen quiet again.
Too quiet.

Astrid held the warm, glowing egg carefully against her chest, its pulse steady and alive beneath her hands. Embla pressed close beside her, wings tucked tight, eyes fixed on the egg with an intensity that made Astrid's heart twist.

Embla had never seen another of her kind.
Never felt one.
Never smelled one.

A hatchling… Embla whispered, breath hitching. **It smells like… hope.**

The word caught in Astrid's throat.

Hope.
Embla, who had grown up hunted and alone, was speaking of hope.

Astrid's voice cracked. "Do you want me to… give it to you?"

Embla flinched back slightly, shaking her head.

No.
Then softer:
Not yet. I do not know what I am with another. With you, I know myself. With another dragon… I do not know if I would be gentle.

Astrid touched Embla's snout gently. "You were gentle with me."

Embla blinked, a soft rumble in her throat.

You were small.
A pause.
This one is smaller. That frightens me.

Astrid's heart squeezed.

Before she could respond, the Stormguard leader stepped nearer, her wolf-pelt mantle brushing the frost. Her gaze lingered on the egg, then lifted to Astrid.

"You must understand the meaning of this gift," she said. "It is not merely an egg. It is a promise. And a demand."

Astrid swallowed. "A demand?"

"Yes. A dragon-child is not born into silence."
Her voice lowered.
"Where dragons rise, kings tremble."

Halvar muttered under his breath, "Aye, they will. And the monastery most of all."

The egg pulsed warmly in Astrid's arms.

The Stormguard leader continued, "Long ago, when dragons vanished, the world fractured. The monastery rose to power because nothing could challenge them."

Her eyes narrowed.

"Now something can."

Astrid's stomach twisted.

Embla stepped between Astrid and the leader, not aggressively—protectively.

She will not be your weapon, Embla growled softly.

The leader held up her hands. "Nor would we ever try. The Stormguard bow to fire, not command it."

Astrid didn't miss the flicker of respect in the woman's

eyes.

But Halvar did not trust it.

He crossed his arms. "What will you do now?"

The leader's gaze drifted toward the horizon, where the storm clouds were thinning to reveal the first streaks of dawn.

"We will prepare," she said. "Word will spread fast. Too fast. You have slain a Wight. Awakened the chamber. Stirred the runes. And now this…"
She nodded toward the egg.
"…this will shake the world."

Astrid's breath hitched. "I don't want to shake the world."

The leader's expression softened—but only slightly.

"Child. The world was already shaking. You merely revealed the fault line."

Embla nudged Astrid gently.

She is… not wrong.
A pause.
And the monastery already knows too much.

Astrid looked toward the edge of the plateau. Calven's body lay still, draped gently with Embla's wing. Halvar had covered him with a cloak.

Astrid's throat tightened. "We can't leave him here."

Halvar nodded. "No. We'll bring him home. Whatever he was… he deserves that."

The leader bowed her head. "Your fallen foe died with honor. We will honor that."

Astrid hesitated. "Why? You didn't even know him."

"We know sacrifice," the woman replied. "He gave his life to shield the Fire-Bound. That is enough."

Astrid's eyes stung.

The Stormguard were harsh, strange, frightening—but there was no deception in them. Their reverence was real.

Halvar stepped beside Astrid, voice low. "Girl… we need to move. The monastery won't stay blind for long."

As if summoned by his words, a faint horn echoed in the distance.

Low.
Mournful.
Unmistakably *monastery-made*.

Astrid froze.

Embla's wings snapped half-open, instinct blazing through her exhaustion.

Astrid—someone approaches.

Halvar swore. "Already? They're too fast—"

"No," Astrid whispered. "They're not here. They're calling from far down the ridge."

Embla sniffed the air.

Her pupils thinned to slits.

I smell blood. Human. Many humans.

The Stormguard warriors stiffened.

The leader's hand went to her spear. "Our scouts reported monastery riders near the southern pass. They were hunting. We thought it was for wolves."

"It wasn't," Halvar said grimly. "It was for Calven."

Astrid's heart dropped.

She clutched the egg tighter.

"They're coming for him," she whispered. "To find out why he didn't return."

Embla's voice trembled with fury.

And they will bring fire-nets. And chains. And blessed blades. They always bring blades.

The Stormguard leader nodded. "Then you cannot linger here."

Another horn sounded—closer this time.

Halvar grabbed Astrid's arm. "We need to go. Now."

Embla crouched low, trying to gather strength for flight.

Astrid felt her pain through the bond.

"No," Astrid whispered. "You can't fly yet. You're too weak."

Embla snarled.
Then I will RUN.

The leader stepped forward. "Take the eastern descent. It is steep but fast. My people will slow the monastery."

Astrid's breath caught. "You'd fight them?"

"For the Fire-Bound?" the leader said. "For what your bond woke? For the hope of dragons?"
She struck her chest with her fist.
"Yes. We would die for that."

Embla exhaled sharply.

I like her.

Astrid almost laughed through the fear.

The egg pulsed warmly in her arms.

Halvar took a step toward the path, scanning the horizon. "Come on, girl. Before they crest the ridge."

Astrid looked once more at the silent body of Calven.

She whispered, "I'll carry you home."

Then she turned toward the eastern path, Embla at her side, Halvar leading the way—

And behind them, the Stormguard formed a shield wall as the monastery horns drew closer.

The world was waking.
The world was coming.

And Astrid—holding the egg close, her bond burning bright—felt the truth settle like fire in her bones:

This was no longer the story of a girl and her dragon.

This was the beginning of an age.

The Horns of the Monastery

The eastern descent was narrow, almost vertical in places, carved by old avalanches and the natural collapse of ridgelines. Frost-slick stone crumbled underfoot.

Halvar moved first, testing each foothold.

Embla followed close behind, her wings partly spread to catch them if they slipped. She breathed heavily, every step draining what little strength she had left.

Astrid walked beside her, one arm around the dragon's neck, the other cradling the egg as if it were made of sunlight.

Every few minutes, a faint horn sounded somewhere far behind them—closer each time.

The monastery was coming.

Embla kept sniffing the air, her ears twitching.

They smell like Calven, she murmured darkly. **But colder. Harder. They smell like iron and incense and anger.**

Astrid swallowed. "Anger at what happened to him?"

Embla shook her head, eyes narrowing.

No. Anger that they were not the ones to end him.

Halvar muttered, "That's the monastery for you. Mercy is a foreign language to zealots."

A sharp wind gusted through the ravine, carrying with it the faint clang of armored boots.

Astrid tensed. "They're close."

Embla's wings fluttered in warning.

Hide your fire, Astrid. Your chest glows.

Astrid lifted a hand.

She hadn't noticed—the runes that had burned so brightly earlier were still faintly glowing beneath her skin, pulsing like warm embers.

She pulled her cloak tighter.

Halvar looked back at her, eyes widening slightly. "Girl… you're going to cause a panic just by breathing."

"I'm trying," she whispered. "I can't turn it off."

Because it isn't off, Embla murmured. **It's… becoming.**

Before Astrid could ask what she meant, a sudden BOOM echoed down from the plateau above—

Followed by desperate shouts.

Halvar grabbed Astrid's arm and pulled her beneath a rocky overhang. Embla crouched beside them, wings folded tight, eyes burning.

Through the gap in the stone, they saw **smoke rising**.

Not fire-smoke.

Incense-smoke.

And then—

Boots.

Dozens.
Dozens of boots.

And between them…

Robes.

Long, white, and marked with gold sigils.

The monastery had arrived.

Astrid's breath caught. "How did they get here so fast?"

Halvar's jaw clenched. "Calven had a mission seal. Grants passage, lifts travel bans, orders shelter. With that emblem, they can cross any guarded path in a day."

Embla growled softly.

They come like wolves.

The trio remained perfectly still as dozens of monastery soldiers poured onto the plateau above, forming a semicircle around Calven's fallen body.

Their armor glinted in the broken light—steel chased with runes designed to burn dragon-hide.

Then a tall figure stepped into view.

A man in black and gold robes.
Head shaved.
Eyes colder than the Frost Wight's breath.

A staff capped with a white flame-sigil glowed in his hand.

Astrid's stomach twisted painfully.

"The High Priest," Halvar whispered. "The Raven of the Cloister. Gods help us."

Embla stiffened.
I know him. Not by scent… but by hatred. Astrid—he is death.

The High Priest knelt beside Calven's body.

He said nothing at first.

He reached out with gentle hands—hands too gentle—closing Calven's eyes. He smoothed the torn robe, brushed away the frost.

Then he rose.

His voice rang across the plateau like a blade sliding from a sheath.

"Prepare him for the fires."

A soldier bowed. "He died in battle, High One. Honorably."

The High Priest did not turn.
Did not blink.
Did not breathe.

"He died because a dragon still lives."

Astrid's heart hammered.

The High Priest lifted Calven's sword—the blessed blade—and held it up to the light.

"When one flame falls," he said, "the others must rise."

Then he turned slowly, surveying the plateau.

His gaze fell on the cracks of battle.
On the place where the Frost Wight had stood.
On the scorch marks that glowed faintly with Bryngard's ancient flame.

He froze.

The air around him seemed to still.

"The chamber has awakened," he said quietly. "The bridge has returned."

A soldier stepped forward. "High One… if the dragon-child is still alive—"

"She is," the High Priest said coldly. "I smell her fire on the wind."

Astrid felt Embla tremble beside her.

Halvar whispered hoarsely, "Girl we gotta go—NOW—"

But the High Priest wasn't finished.

He raised Calven's blade high.

And his voice thundered across the mountain.

"Hear me, faithful!
The one who killed our brother walks still.
She bears dragonfire in her veins.
She has awakened the ancient bond.
She is no child—
she is the beginning of an age that must never rise!"

The soldiers slammed their weapons against their shields.

The High Priest's eyes burned like coals.

"We will find her.
We will burn her.
We will break the bridge again.
And this time…
it will never reform."

Astrid squeezed the egg so tightly she almost dropped it.

Embla's tail lashed in panic.

He means to kill you first, Embla whispered, voice trembling. **Not me. YOU.**

Astrid's blood ran cold.

Because she felt the truth in it—

The High Priest wasn't hunting a dragon.

He was hunting **the rider.**

Halvar motioned violently. "Move. Move now before he sets the mountain on fire!"

They crawled deeper beneath the ravine outcropping as monastery soldiers fanned across the plateau, torches lighting, incense burning, weapons drawn.

The High Priest lifted Calven's body gently as if lifting a fallen brother.

"We march at dawn," he said. "And the first place we burn…"

His eyes drifted toward the fjord valley below.

"…is Havngard."

Astrid choked.

Halvar froze.

Embla's wings shuddered open in terror and fury.

ASTRID—THEY GO AFTER YOUR HOME—

Astrid pressed her fist to her mouth to smother a sob.

Her village.
Her father's home.
Her childhood.
The people who raised her.

The monastery was going to turn it to ash.

Because of her.

Halvar grabbed Astrid's face gently but firmly.

"Girl," he whispered, voice shaking with urgency, "you have to stand up now. You have to move. You have to get ahead of them. Havngard needs you."

Astrid clutched the egg tighter.

Her heart felt like it might break.

Embla pressed her wing over Astrid's shoulders.

You are not alone. We fly together. We run together. We fight together.

Astrid nodded slowly—tearfully.

The world blurred for a moment.

Then focus snapped back like a flame catching air.

"Then we go," she whispered.

She wiped her face.
Tightened her grip on the egg.
Placed her other hand on Embla's warm side.

"They won't burn my home."

Embla exhaled smoke, bright with determination.

And they won't take you.

Halvar nodded once. "Down the ravine. Through the pines. If we're lucky, we can reach the fjord first."

Astrid took one last look toward the plateau where Calven lay under monastery torches.

"I'm sorry," she whispered. "I'll make this right."

Then she turned—

And the trio began their perilous descent toward home.

Behind them, the monastery prepared for war.

Where Fire Falters

The eastern ravine narrowed as they descended, jagged stone walls rising high on both sides, funnelling wind into a sharp, cutting howl. Snow drifted in thin sheets from the upper cliffs, shimmering like falling ash.

Embla stumbled.

Not tripped.
Not paused.
Stumbled.

Astrid gripped her side immediately. "Whoa—steady— steady—"

Embla's legs trembled. Her claws scraped desperately for purchase on the ice-slick path.

Halvar spun back to help. "She's near collapse—"

No— Embla growled weakly, **I can move—I can—**

But she couldn't.

Her front legs buckled, and she sank to her chest with a heavy thud, wings drooping to the ground like torn banners.

Astrid dropped beside her, heart seizing. "Embla!"

The dragon's breath came shallow, ragged. Smoke puffed in small, erratic bursts.

Too much… she whispered. **Too soon. The Wight drained me. The runefire… drained more. I'm—empty.**

Astrid's throat tightened painfully. "You saved us. You gave everything—"

I had to.
A soft rumble.
You needed me.

Halvar crouched beside them, eyes flicking nervously up toward the ridge above.

"If she stops here, we're dead," he whispered. "The monastery's close. The horns echo louder each minute."

Another horn sounded—this one sharp, signaling movement rather than mourning.

They were coming down the mountain.

Astrid looked at the path ahead—too narrow to run, too steep to carry Embla, too exposed to hide.

Then at the path behind—monastery priests and soldiers hunting in formation.

Her pulse raced.

"Halvar… we have to shelter her."

He nodded grimly. "I know. Look for caves, hollows, anything."

Astrid scanned the ravine, frantic—

And saw it.

A narrow crack in the cliffside, partly collapsed, half-hidden beneath heavy icicles.

"Here!" she whispered, running toward it.

Halvar tested it with his boot. "Small… but big enough for Astrid. Probably not for Embla."

Astrid glared at him. "We make it big enough."

Embla tried to rise again, but her wings shook violently.

Astrid… leave me. You can run. They want *you*. Not me.

Astrid's heart snapped.

"Never."

She placed her hands on Embla's scales.

"You hear me? Never."

Embla closed her eyes, pained and grateful all at once.

Halvar wedged his shoulder against the arched rock and began shoving loose rubble free.

"Help me break this open!"

Astrid shifted the egg into the crook of her arm and started prying away frozen slabs of shale. Every few seconds she flinched, expecting the monastery to crest the path above.

They worked like frantic miners clawing their way toward air.

Within minutes, Halvar cracked open enough stone for Embla to squeeze through—barely.

"Go," he urged. "Get her inside!"

Astrid tugged gently at Embla's horn. "Come on—lean this way—yes—good—careful—"

It hurt to watch.

Embla winced, forcing herself through the gap, scraping her wings and flank painfully against stone. She growled low, a rumble of both frustration and shame.

Astrid crawled in after her.

Halvar followed last, pulling loose snow across the entrance to disguise it.

Inside, the cave was dim—almost pitch black save for the faint glow of the egg in Astrid's arms.

Embla collapsed fully now, her wings folding awkwardly, her sides rising and falling too fast.

Astrid pressed her forehead to the dragon's neck.

"Hey," she whispered. "You're okay. You're safe now."

Embla's mental voice flickered like candlelight in a storm.

I am so tired, Astrid…

"I know," she murmured. "You rest now. I'll keep watch."

As she spoke, the egg pulsed—warm light washing over the cave walls.

Halvar frowned. "Is it… responding to her?"

Astrid lifted the egg slightly.

It glowed brighter near Embla's chest.

Embla cracked open a weary eye.

It hears me…

Astrid held her breath.

Embla's voice trembled.

It knows I'm hurt.

The egg pulsed again—stronger—stronger—

The heartbeat inside quickened.

The glow bled into the air, warm enough that frost melted from the rocks.

Halvar stepped back reflexively. "That's… new."

Astrid looked at Embla, alarmed. "Is it hurting you?"

Embla shook her head faintly.

No.
It feels… like comfort.
Like a clutchmate reaching out.
Like warmth I haven't felt since hatching.

Astrid's chest tightened with emotion.

She gently placed the egg beside Embla's chest.

The dragon's breath steadied.

Slowly.

Beautifully.

Astrid touched Embla's jaw. "You're not alone anymore."

Embla exhaled, smoke curling softly.

Nor are you.

They both fell quiet—

Until faint voices echoed faintly through the stone above them.

Angry voices.

Ordained voices.

Monastery voices.

Halvar crawled toward the cave entrance, listening.

After a tense few seconds, he turned back.

Face pale.

Voice low.

"Astrid… they found Calven."

Astrid's heart slammed into her ribs.

Embla lifted her head weakly, growling.

"What are they doing?" Astrid whispered.

Halvar swallowed. "Grieving. Blaming. Praying."

A pause.

"They're swearing oaths. And Astrid…"

His next words were barely a whisper.

"They're swearing to burn Havngard to the ground."

Astrid closed her eyes, tears burning.

Her village.
Her childhood.
Her home.

Embla pressed her nose into Astrid's chest.

We will protect it. You and I. No matter the cost.

Astrid nodded shakily.

But Halvar's final words chilled her more than the mountain wind.

"They say Calven's spirit will not rest until the dragon-child is slain."

Astrid leaned back against Embla, clutching the egg tightly, voice trembling:

"I don't think his spirit feels that way at all."

Embla hummed gently.

Nor do I.

Astrid inhaled deeply through her nose, steadying herself.

Then whispered the truth she'd been avoiding:

"We can't outrun them anymore."

Embla's tail curled around her protectively.

Then we fight.

Astrid nodded.

Her eyes burned gold in the dark.

And the egg glowed brighter.

The Path That Burns Ahead

Hours passed in the dim shelter of the cliffside cave.

Astrid kept her hand on Embla's flank, feeling the dragon's shallow breaths slowly deepen into steadier rhythm. The egg lay pressed to Embla's chest, pulsing in gentle, warm waves. The soft light washed over them, painting flickering patterns across the stone like a heartbeat shared between three souls instead of two.

Outside, the mountain breathed darkness. The monastery's voices rose and fell—sometimes distant, sometimes horribly close—like the tides of a storm that refused to break.

Halvar kept watch near the entrance, barely moving

except to brush frost from the stone or shift his weight quietly.

Finally, Embla spoke through the bond.

Astrid… you need to sleep.

Astrid shook her head stubbornly. "Not until you're better."

Embla nudged her gently, smoke curling from tired nostrils.

You forget who is the dragon and who is the girl. I am built to endure pain. You are built to break. Rest.

"Not while they're out there hunting us."

Halvar spoke from the entrance, voice low, but firm. "Embla's right. You've done more in one day than most warriors do in a lifetime. If you burn yourself out, no one survives."

Astrid hugged her knees, gripping her cloak tightly. "If we rest too long, Havngard burns."

Halvar hesitated. Then he lowered his head.

"They'll burn it whether you're exhausted or not. Best meet that fire standing, not crawling."

Those words hit her harder than any blow.

She turned her face toward him, voice trembling.

"We're not strong enough, Halvar. I'm not strong enough."

Halvar crawled deeper into the cave, took her face gently but firmly between his calloused hands.

"You listen to me, girl. You killed a Wight. You awakened Bryngard. You carry the first dragon egg the world has seen in two hundred years. And you've got a dragon who'd rip the moon from the sky to keep you breathing."

He leaned closer.

"You're strong enough for anything."

Astrid blinked back tears.

Embla's tail curled around her affectionately.

We do this together. Always.

Before Astrid could reply—

A sharp sound echoed through the ravine.

Not a horn.
Not a prayer.
Not a footstep.

A **crack.**

Then a **snap.**

Then an unnatural **screech**, distant but shrill.

Astrid's blood ran cold.

Halvar stiffened. "That… wasn't human."

Embla lifted her head sharply, nostrils flaring.

Something hunts. Not monastery. Not Stormguard. Something older. Something hungry.

Astrid swallowed hard. "What kind of something?"

Embla's wings twitched anxiously.

The kind Bryngard kept asleep.

The egg pulsed—once—

As if reacting to danger.

Halvar drew his knife, jaw tight. "Whatever it is, it's

down the path ahead of us. We can't stay here without being trapped."

Astrid clutched the egg protectively. "Then we can't go forward…"

Embla turned her head toward the cave entrance.

Her eyes blazed—weak, but determined.

Then we go *through* whatever waits.
Because we will not let the monastery burn your home.
And we will not die in a hole in the mountain.

Astrid rose slowly, the egg glowing against her chest, her braid brushing her shoulders as she straightened.

She walked toward the entrance and crouched beside Halvar.

Below the mountain, far down the ravine, a strange rustling sound echoed—soft, rhythmic, *wrong*.

Astrid licked her lips nervously. "We go into that?"

Halvar exhaled. "Seems we must."

Astrid touched Embla's jaw.

"Can you walk?"

Embla pushed herself shakily to her feet, wings dragging slightly against the stone.

I can walk. I cannot run. But I can fight.

Astrid nodded, steadying herself as the three of them—girl, dragon, father—moved toward the mouth of the cave.

Behind them, monastery horns blared.
Ahead of them, something ancient stirred.
Inside Astrid's arms, the egg glowed brighter, its heartbeat quickening.

Embla pressed her snout against Astrid's back.

Whatever waits… we face it together.

Astrid nodded once, fiercely.

"Then let's go."

She stepped out of the cave—
into the dawn's cold light—
into danger—
into destiny.

And the mountain exhaled, carrying her name down the ravine:

Astrid.
The Fire-Bound.
The bridge reborn.

CHAPTER 26

THE BURDEN OF FIRE

Footsteps in the Ravine

The dawn light was thin and cold, stretched between jagged cliffs like a knife-edge of pale gold. Astrid stepped out of the cave, boots sinking into wind-packed snow, the egg glowing faintly in her arms.

The ravine below slanted downward into a maze of icy switchbacks, spiked crags, and sharp overhangs that hid the world beyond. A place where sound traveled strangely. A place where dangers crawled in silence.

Halvar emerged behind her, checking the path with a hunter's eye.

Embla followed last.

Her wings drooped.
Her breath steamed weakly.
But her resolve simmered like a bed of coals.

She rested her tail across Astrid's feet.

I smell it again, she whispered. **The thing that waits. The thing that is not man.**

Astrid swallowed. "Where?"

Embla's pupils thinned.

Everywhere. And nowhere.
It moves like broken wind.

Halvar scanned the ravine carefully. "Old mountains keep old secrets. Things that aren't meant to leave their depths."

Another sound echoed—soft, skittering, hollow.

Like bone on stone.

Like something dragging itself through the dark.

Astrid tightened her hold on the egg instinctively. The hatchling inside pulsed in quick bursts, like its little heart recognized the same danger Embla sensed.

"Do we go left?" Astrid asked quietly.

Halvar nodded. "It's the fastest path to the fjord. If we're lucky—"

A distant horn cut him off.

Clear.
Sharp.
Closer than before.

Embla hissed. **Priests. Again. Spreading like frost.**

Halvar swore under his breath. "They're flanking the ridge. Cutting off escape routes."

Another horn answered from the opposite side of the ravine.

Astrid's breath caught. "They're surrounding the mountain."

"No," Halvar said grimly. "They're surrounding *us*."

Embla pushed her snout against Astrid's arm, voice trembling with anger.

We should fly.

"You can't," Astrid whispered. "Not yet. You'll fall."

Better to fall fighting than crawl into their hands!

Astrid reached for her muzzle and pressed gently.

"Not if I lose you."

Embla froze. Her anger dimmed into raw fear, then

softened into aching devotion.

You will not lose me.
Not while I breathe.

Astrid leaned her head against Embla's.

"Then walk with me."

Halvar motioned urgently. "We need to move now. That creature ahead of us might be the lesser danger."

Another skittering sound echoed down the ravine — faster this time, as though whatever stalked them had begun to run.

Astrid's skin prickled.

"What is that thing?"

Halvar's face went pale.

"A caveborn," he whispered. "Old legends. A mountain scavenger that feeds on… bodies left out in the frost."

Embla's wings flared weakly in alarm.

I know that smell. Death that breathes.
We go around.
Quickly.

Astrid glanced at the narrowing path. "Around… where?"

Halvar pointed upward. "There. Those switchbacks lead along the cliff face. Dangerous, but better than diving straight into a caveborn's jaws."

Embla sniffed the air again, scales rippling.

Not one caveborn.
Two.

Astrid's pulse spiked. "We're being… hunted?"

Yes. They smell your fire. And your blood.
Embla's voice darkened.
They think you are a wounded deer.

Astrid clutched the egg closer and stepped onto the narrow ledge. Wind clawed at her hair, pulling braids loose.

Halvar followed. Embla squeezed in last, wings brushing against the cliff.

Below them, the ravine floor suddenly shifted—

And a pale, elongated shape darted into view.

It was thin as a starving wolf, with long limbs and a split jaw dripping with cold saliva. Its spine jutted like broken knives. Its skin was stretched tight, translucent in places, showing bones beneath.

Its eyes—
Empty.
Hollow.
Milk-white.

The caveborn lifted its head.

Sniffed once.

Then hissed.

Astrid choked on a breath.

Another hiss answered from the shadows farther down the path.

Halvar's voice dropped to a strained whisper. "Keep moving. Slow and steady. Don't slip. Don't run. We outrun them up the ledge, not down the ravine."

Embla snarled at the creature below.

Come closer, corpse-thing.

I bite harder than I look.

The caveborn shrieked and began to climb the rock wall.

Fast.

Astrid's stomach plummeted. "Halvar—!"

"I see it—GO!"

They scrambled upward. The path was too narrow—every step threatened to send them tumbling hundreds of feet into jagged stone. The egg thudded rapidly against Astrid's ribs.

Embla forced herself up behind them, dragging her wings, growling through pain.

The caveborn scuttled closer, claws embedding in the stone like hooked nails.

Astrid felt her breath shortening, fear rising, but the runes under her skin pulsed faintly—warm, grounding, steady.

She clutched the egg tighter.

"Almost there—come on—just a few more—"

The caveborn leapt.

Embla swung her tail—

And the tail-smack smashed into the creature mid-air, sending it crashing into the ravine wall with a sickening crack.

But another one was already climbing fast, its limbs jerking at unnatural angles.

Embla staggered.
Astrid screamed.
Halvar reached for his knife—

But before the creature could strike—

A sudden, low, deep roar echoed through the mountain.

Not dragon.
Not human.
Not caveborn.

Something deeper.
Older.
Massive.

The sound vibrated through the stone beneath their feet, rattling loose snow and pebbles, making Astrid's bones tremble.

Embla went rigid.

**Astrid… that was not a caveborn.
Something else wakes.
Something huge.**

Astrid swallowed, frozen.

"What—what do we do?"

Halvar stared into the depths below, face pale.

"We pray it's not hungry."

The caveborns screamed—
and fled, scrambling into cracks and shadows as if running from a predator far worse than themselves.

The mountain fell silent again.

Then the horn of the monastery blasted above—

Close.
Very close.

Astrid looked up, breath burning.

Priests were coming down the ridge.
Creatures were rising from the deep.
Embla was too weak to fly.
The egg was close to hatching.

And Havngard would burn if she did nothing.

She tightened her grip on the egg and whispered:

"I won't let anything take you.
Not priests.
Not monsters.
Not fate."

Embla pressed her muzzle against Astrid's shoulder.

**Then keep climbing, little spark.
The fire ahead is ours to face.**

Astrid nodded—

And they continued upward into the narrowing ledge, with danger behind, danger ahead, and destiny closing around them like a tightening fist.

Smoke on the Wind

The ledge narrowed to no more than the width of Astrid's body. One misstep would send her plummeting into jagged rocks hundreds of feet below.

Halvar pressed himself flat to the cliff wall, moving sideways with careful, deliberate steps. Astrid followed, cradling the egg against her ribs. Embla trailed last, claws scraping the stone as she forced her trembling body to maneuver through a space never meant for dragons.

Every inch of this slope screamed danger.

But the danger behind them screamed louder.

The next monastery horn blasted.

Louder.

Closer.

Astrid froze when she heard voices echoing down the ravine:

"TRACK THE SMOKE! DRAGONS LEAVE SMOKE!"

Embla stiffened.

A thin coil of smoke rose from her nostrils — involuntary, a side-effect of exhaustion and pain.

Astrid... Embla whispered, shame and terror twisting through the bond.
I cannot stop it. My body burns from inside. The runefire will not lie quiet.

Astrid touched her muzzle gently. "That's not your fault. Not ever."

But the monastery was using it.

Voices echoed again:

"There! On the ledge! The trail is fresh!"

Halvar swore quietly. "They spotted the drift. We've got minutes."

"And the creature below?" Astrid whispered.

Halvar didn't answer.
He didn't have to.

The mountain trembled again — a low, deep groan that felt older than language. Snow sifted from the cliffs. A few loose stones cracked free and tumbled to the depths.

Embla shuddered.

That thing... knows we're here.
It stalks the smell of fire. And blood. And hatchlings.

Astrid's grip tightened around the egg.

The hatchling pressed back — a distinct twitch against her palm.

Her breath caught.

"Halvar… it moved."

Halvar's eyes widened. "By the gods… it's close to waking."

Astrid looked at Embla, overwhelmed. "What do we do?"

Embla nudged her gently.

We keep it alive.
We keep *you* alive.
We keep moving.

Astrid nodded and forced herself along the path.

Suddenly — a **shout** from above.

"There! On the cliff! I SEE THEM!!"

Astrid's heart lurched.

Armored silhouettes appeared on the upper ledge, barely visible through the snow flurries — cloaked priests and soldiers leaning over the drop.

A torch glowed in one of their hands.

"Bring me the ropes!" a priest commanded. "We descend NOW!"

Halvar muttered, "Damn zealots…"

Astrid's chest burned. "All they see is a monster."

Embla snarled low.
Then let them see one.

The first ropes dropped.

Astrid's pulse exploded.

"Halvar, they're coming right at us!"

Halvar pushed ahead. "There's a narrow outcropping up there — go, go!"

But the path was steep. Treacherous. Embla stumbled more than once, her claws slipping dangerously near the cliff's edge.

Astrid heard the scrape of metal — the sound of boots sliding down ropes.

Priests were descending like spiders.

One of them dropped faster than the others, landing on a narrow ledge only thirty paces above.

A zealot in gleaming white armor.

He saw Astrid — his eyes widened — and he screamed:

"THE BRIDGE! THE BRIDGE IS BELOW!
BRING THE BLADE!"

Astrid's legs nearly went out from under her.

Halvar pulled his knife. "Astrid — GET BEHIND ME!"

Embla roared, wings flaring despite her pain.

But the narrow ledge made fighting impossible. The priest lifted a throwing spear — a dragon-slayer's spear — designed to pierce scales.

He cocked his arm—

Embla couldn't dodge.
Halvar couldn't reach him.
Astrid's fire wasn't fast enough.

Time slowed.

Then—

Astrid felt the bond surge.

Heat swelled in her chest, rushing into her arm, coiling through her fingers.

The runes under her skin flared bright gold.

She lifted her hand without thinking—

And **shaped the fire.**

A thin blade of shimmering flame ignited along her palm.

The priest hesitated, stunned—

And Astrid SLASHED.

The fire-blade snapped outward in a sharp arc, cutting a glowing line through the air.

The priest's spear shattered in his hand.

He screamed as fragments of burning wood and melting iron rained over him.

Astrid staggered, gasping — the fire-blade flickering wildly.

Halvar stared at her, stunned. "Girl… you can do that on command? At will?"

"I don't know!" she cried. "I'm not choosing it — it's choosing me!"

Embla's voice trembled with awe.

No rider has shaped fire like that in centuries. Not since the first flames.

The priest above them fumbled backward, desperately scrambling away from the edge. His fear echoed down the ravine.

"She SHAPES it!
The prophecy is TRUE!
THE BRIDGE IS REAL!"

Astrid's stomach turned.

"I didn't want prophecy," she whispered.

Embla leaned against her.

**You didn't want me, either.
And yet here we are.**

Astrid almost smiled through the panic.

Then a new sound shattered the moment —

A deep, vibrating rumble.
Not from above.
Not from priests.
Not from the caveborns.

From **inside the mountain**.

Astrid felt it in her feet — a slow, deliberate shifting of stone.

Halvar paled. "That's not a tremor. That's something moving."

The egg in Astrid's arms pulsed frantically.

Embla's wings flared, fear slicing through the bond.

**Astrid—
RUN.
NOW.**

And the mountain split open behind them.

The Thing That Crawled from Stone

The ravine wall behind them **cracked**.

Not a small crack — not a falling stone — but a violent, jarring

tearing of earth, as if something inside the mountain had finally woken and wanted *out*.

Astrid spun, clutching the egg tighter.

Embla's wings shuddered open, her body arching protectively around Astrid even as her legs shook.

Halvar grabbed Astrid's arm, pulling her toward the narrow switchback. "Move, girl—MOVE!"

But the cliff face split wider.

Stone rained down.
Frost exploded outward.
An inhuman screech clawed the air.

And then—

It emerged.

A hulking, pale shape levered itself from the cracked stone, dragging a segmented body out of a crevice far too small to contain it. Its limbs were long and jointed wrong, bending backward, then sideways, then snapping into place with sickening precision.

Its hide was stone-gray and frost-pale, covered in bony plates that clicked and shifted. Its head—

Astrid gasped, stumbling back.

It had no eyes.

Just a skull-like face with a gaping maw lined with rows of teeth like jagged ice.

It breathed air with a choking, rasping sound…

…and the air **froze** where its breath touched.

Embla hissed, smoke rising from her nostrils.

A Frost-Chitin.

Her voice trembled.
A flesh-eater born of winter and earth.
A mountain hunter.
Older than priests. Older than riders.

Halvar swore violently. "A caveborn was bad enough. But *this*—!"

The creature twisted its head toward them, sniffing the air.

Searching.

Astrid's heart hammered.

"It's blind," she whispered. "Like the Wight's servants."

Embla nodded slowly.

Blind… but hungry. And it hears vibration. Breath. Fire. Life.

Halvar whispered sharply: "Astrid, don't move. Don't breathe loud. Don't—"

The egg **pulsed.**

Just once.

But loud enough.

The Frost-Chitin's head snapped toward them instantly.

Its maw yawned wide—
a gurgling cry echoing like a glacier cracking—
then it lunged.

"RUN!" Halvar roared.

They bolted up the narrow ledge.

The monster's claws crushed stone behind them, cracking footholds, sending chunks of rock exploding outward.

Astrid almost slipped as she leapt over a broken section

of the path.

Embla grabbed her cloak with her teeth, yanking her upright.

GO, ASTRID!
Embla's mental voice was frantic.
I can distract it—

"No!" Astrid cried. "You barely have strength to walk!"

I have strength to DIE.

"Not an option!"

But the creature lunged again.

Halvar shoved Astrid forward. "Up there — that wider ledge!"

They scrambled, slipping and clawing their way to a slightly broader outcropping overlooking the ravine.

Embla turned, planting herself between Astrid and the monster, wings extended as far as her pain allowed.

The Frost-Chitin climbed the cliff with horrifying speed. It pulled itself onto the ledge.
It opened its maw—

Embla roared, flame sputtering weakly.

But she had nothing left.

The creature stalked closer, mandibles clicking.

Then—

Something unexpected happened.

The egg in Astrid's arms started **glowing**, brighter and brighter, heat radiating through her arms, through her chest, through the air around them.

The Frost-Chitin froze.

Then SCREECHED, backing away, claws scrabbling on the ledge.

Astrid gasped. "It—It's afraid?"

Embla blinked, shocked.

**It fears the hatchling inside.
It fears dragonfire unborn.**

Astrid couldn't process it — the egg pulsed again, and the Frost-Chitin screamed louder, its eyeless head twisting away.

"It's driving it back!" Halvar shouted.

But the effect was brief.

The monster recovered, its fear snapping into enraged hunger.

Then it charged.

Astrid screamed.

Embla lunged—

And collapsed.

Her front legs buckled.

Her wings folded weakly.

She fell to her knees, head slamming the stone.

Her roar was small—pain-filled.

"Astrid—run—" Halvar cried.

"No!" Astrid shouted, tears streaming. "I won't leave her!"

The Frost-Chitin loomed over Embla's fallen form, breath

freezing the air around her. Its claws lifted—

Aim clear.

Astrid stepped forward.

She didn't think.
Didn't choose.
Didn't hesitate.

Her chest burned with a sudden, violent heat—

And flame erupted from her palm in a wide arc of gold-blue fire.

The blast struck the creature square in the head.

It reeled backward, shrieking, its bony plates glowing red-hot.

Astrid screamed with it, the power ripping through her body like white lightning.

Embla felt it too—
their bond flared—
fire surged between them—

Astrid dropped to one knee, gasping.

The Frost-Chitin staggered, shaking its skull violently, bits of melted bone clattering.

Halvar yelled, "Astrid! You hurt it!"

She pushed herself up.

"No."

Her eyes glowed.

"I *warned* it."

The creature roared and lunged again.

Astrid raised her hand—

Fire coiled into her fingers—

The runes blazed—

But the ground trembled violently.

Astrid lost her balance.

Halvar grabbed her.

Embla tried to stand—

And the entire ledge *collapsed.*

The Frost-Chitin lunged forward—
Halvar grabbed Astrid—
Embla tried to shield them—
the egg pulsed like a sun bursting—

And the world broke beneath them.

The Fall Beneath the Mountain

The ledge gave way with a thunderous crack.

Stone shattered.
Snow exploded upward.
Air ripped from Astrid's lungs.

She reached instinctively for Embla—
Embla lunged for her—
Halvar grabbed Astrid's cloak—

But gravity seized them all.

They fell.

Astrid's scream tore from her throat as she cartwheeled through open air. The egg slammed against her ribs; she curled around it protectively, clutching it to her chest.

Cold knifed past her face.

The world spun in blurs of rock and snow.

Halvar fell somewhere to her left, tumbling end over end, desperately clawing at empty air.

And above them—

The Frost-Chitin dropped from the broken ledge, shrieking, its bony limbs slashing at nothing, limbs flailing, mandibles gaping.

Embla unfurled her wings—

A broken roar tearing from her throat—

And forced them open against the screaming wind.

But they were weak.
Too weak.
Her left wing lagged behind, spasming with pain.

ASTRID—!
Her mind-voice cracked with desperation.
I'M COMING—HOLD—

Embla slammed into the air between Astrid and the cliff, wings shaking violently as she fought to stabilize her fall.

Astrid reached out—

Their fingers brushed—
Just for an instant—
Meaning everything—

Then a massive claw struck Embla's wing.

The Frost-Chitin, falling alongside them, had lashed out wildly and raked its jagged limb across the soft membrane.

Embla screamed, spiraling.

"EMBLA!" Astrid shrieked, voice raw.

Embla fell sideways, tumbling helplessly, blood trailing in the air like red ribbons against white snow.

The Frost-Chitin struck her again mid-tumble—
chitin smashing scale—
sending her careening into the ravine wall where she ricocheted downward.

Halvar hit a slanted outcropping, rolled, hit another, and finally slammed into a snowbank with a horrible thud.

Astrid saw none of it clearly.

Because she was falling too fast.

The ground rushed toward her—
Wind tearing the breath from her chest—
The egg pulsing frantically beneath her cloak—

Astrid curled tighter around it, whispering:

"Please—please—please—"

A shadow fell over her.

Embla.

Bruised. Bleeding. Wings shaking so violently she couldn't hold them straight.

But she **tried anyway.**

She dove under Astrid—
using her body as a shield—
still spiraling—still unable to fly—

I have you!
Embla cried through the bond.
I HAVE YOU—!

The Frost-Chitin plummeted after them, screeching, its limbs flailing like broken spears.

Astrid clung to Embla's neck, trying to soften the fall.

Embla wrapped a wing around Astrid—

HOLD TIGHT—

They crashed.

Hard.

Embla hit a slanted slope of packed snow and ice, sliding with violent speed. Her claws tore into the surface to slow them, leaving long raking furrows.

Astrid's head slammed into Embla's shoulder; she kept the egg pinned between her arms as their bodies scraped and bounced.

Halvar rolled again, coughing, struggling to rise.

The Frost-Chitin struck the same slope with a bone-shattering impact, smashing a crater into the snow, then rolled violently after them—
shriek still echoing—
mandibles clicking in fury.

Embla finally dug all four claws into the ice and skidded to a jarring stop near a cluster of boulders.

Astrid was flung from her back—
and landed in Halvar's arms as he caught her mid-fall, grunting in pain.

He sagged to his knees, clutching her tightly.

"You alive?" he gasped.

Astrid coughed, snow falling from her hair. "I—think so —"

The egg pulsed strongly in her arms.

Embla collapsed nearby, chest heaving, blood dripping

where the creature had torn her wing.

Astrid scrambled over the snow. "Embla!"

Embla lifted her head weakly, voice trembling.

I hurt…
but I breathe.
You live.
That is enough.

Astrid pressed her forehead against Embla's muzzle, tears spilling hot.

Halvar staggered closer, wincing, one arm wrapped around his ribs. "We need to get up. That thing will—"

A deafening screech cut him off.

The Frost-Chitin rose slowly from the crater it had made, dragging its segmented body upright. Bone plates cracked and reformed with sickening clicks. It turned its skull toward them—

And **charged**, claws slashing through snow like knives.

Halvar grabbed his knife—
Astrid lifted a shaking hand—
Embla tried to stand—

But everything froze.

Not by magic.

By sound.

A new horn — deeper, heavier, ancient — echoed across the mountain.

Not monastery.

Not Stormguard.

Something else.

Embla's head snapped toward the sound.

Astrid—
that is a hunting horn.
A BIG one.

The Frost-Chitin halted mid-charge, mandibles twitching.

And from above the ridge—

Shadows moved.

Not priests.
Not monks.

Massive silhouettes.
Huge.
Armored.
Carrying weapons the size of trees.

Halvar swore under his breath. "By the gods… those aren't monastery men."

Astrid squinted—

Trying to make out the figures.

The wind shifted—

Snow peeled back—

And enormous men in black-iron furs stepped into view, each carrying a weapon carved from blackened bone.

Embla sucked in a breath, stunned.

Astrid…
those are the Frostborn.
The mountain giants.
A tribe older than the Stormguard.
Hunters of monsters.

Halvar whispered, "If that's true… we're either saved—"

"—or dead," Astrid finished.

The Frostborn leader stepped forward, a mountain of a man with ice-white braids and a cloak made of stitched caveborn skins.

He pointed his massive bone-hammer toward the Frost-Chitin.

"TAKE IT."

The Frost-Chitin screeched—

And the Frostborn CHARGED.

Fire Between Giants

The Frostborn warriors thundered down the slope like an avalanche. Their bone-hammers and frost-forged axes caught the pale dawn light and flashed like shards of winter lightning.

The Frost-Chitin shrieked and lunged to meet them.

The two forces collided with a sound like the mountain cracking open.

The creature slammed one giant aside with terrifying force — the warrior hit a boulder so hard the stone split in two. Another Frostborn jammed a massive spear into the monster's side, but the Frost-Chitin twisted unnaturally, snapping its own rib to slide free.

Astrid watched in horror as the creature skittered up a rock face, its bony spine rippling.
It was fast.
It was strong.
It was relentless.

"Halvar—down!" Astrid cried.

A boulder rolled violently toward them — Halvar grabbed her and pulled her aside just as the stone smashed where she had stood.

Embla dragged herself forward, wings dragging in the snow, eyes burning with protective rage.

Stay behind me, she growled, voice shaking. **I will defend you. Even broken.**

Astrid grabbed her muzzle, tears in her eyes. "If you stand again, you'll die."

Embla bared her teeth weakly. **Then I die in front of you, not behind.**

Before Astrid could answer, a Frostborn giant was hurled across the clearing, crashing into a pine with a spine-splintering crack.

The Frost-Chitin turned toward Astrid, mandibles clicking.

It could smell her again.
Her fire.
Her blood.
Her egg.

It screeched and sprinted toward them.

Embla braced herself—

—and nearly fell trying to stand.

Halvar pushed her aside, raising his knife even though it was hopeless.

"Astrid, RUN!"

"I'm not leaving you!"

The monster lunged—

And Astrid's fire surged.

Her chest ignited —
runes flaring beneath her skin —
a violent, molten pulse ripping through her arm.

She lifted her hand—

And the air around her **glowed**.

Not a blade this time.

Not a whip.

Something new.

Something instinctive.

Something born of fear and love and ancient fire.

A **barrier** of shimmering gold erupted outward like a shield forged from living flame.

The Frost-Chitin struck it head-on.

And was thrown backward.

Hard.

It tumbled across the snow, shrieking in shock as its limbs twisted beneath it.

Astrid nearly collapsed from the force, falling to her knees, breath ragged.

Halvar stared at her like he'd never seen her before.

"Girl… you didn't strike it. You *blocked* it."

Embla's mind-voice was hushed with awe.

You shaped defensive fire…
That is a rider's art.
An ancient rider.

The Frostborn who still stood turned toward Astrid, stunned that a child had thrown the creature back. Their leader — the massive man in the caveborn cloak — froze, eyes widening.

He raised his bone-hammer.

But not at the creature.

At *Astrid.*

"STOP. HOLD."
His voice thundered like an avalanche.

Every Frostborn warrior halted instantly.

Even the Frost-Chitin froze, disoriented by the sudden stillness.

All eyes turned toward Astrid.

The leader stepped forward slowly, the earth trembling beneath each stride. He towered over her — nearly twice Halvar's height, with a chest broad as a boulder and arms corded with frost-scarred muscle.

He looked at Embla.
At Astrid.
At the glowing egg.

And then into Astrid's eyes.

The fire there reflected in his ice-white pupils.

He inhaled sharply.

"The flame…" he whispered.
"Alive… in human flesh…"

Astrid's stomach twisted. "I—I'm not here to fight you. We're just trying to get home."

The Frostborn leader knelt — the earth shuddering under

his weight.

He bowed his head.

A giant bowing to a girl.

"The Fire-Bound walks the mountain," he said. "And we — the Frostborn — do not raise weapons against the bond."

Astrid blinked. "You… you know about the bond?"

He nodded slowly.

"We were here when the last rider fell.
We buried the last dragon egg.
We waited for the mountain to speak again."

His gaze rose to the egg glowing in her arms.

"And now it screams."

Astrid clutched the egg closer, overwhelmed.

Halvar stood protectively beside her while Embla pressed her snout against Astrid's shoulder.

The Frost-Chitin shrieked weakly, trying to crawl away.

The Frostborn leader stood tall again, lifted his hammer

—

And smashed the creature's skull with a single brutal blow.

Bone shards flew across the snow.
The monster convulsed.
Then went still.

The leader turned back to Astrid.

"You carry fire," he said, "and fire carries you."
He pointed toward the mountain pass.
"We will escort you down the slopes. Your enemies are

many. But none may harm you while Frostborn breathe."

Astrid blinked hard, tears gathering.

"I… I don't know how to thank you."

He shook his head.

"It is not thanks we seek."

He stared at the egg — a reverent, frightened look.

"It is the returning dawn."

Astrid felt Embla's breath warm her back.
Felt Halvar steady himself at her side.
Felt the egg pulse with life against her chest.

The Frostborn stood in a solemn circle around them, giant shadows cast long across the snow.

Astrid whispered:

"Then let's go home."

CHAPTER 27

THE MONASTERY MOVES

The High Priest's Verdict

The bells of the Southern Monastery rang at dawn — not for prayer, not for ceremony, but for death.

Five slow tolls.
Each one echoing across the marble courtyards, across the high spires, and down the long stone steps where acolytes froze mid-task.

Five tolls meant only one thing.

A priest of rank had fallen.

A high-ranked one.

Brother Calven.

In the Hall of Proclamation — a cavernous chamber lit by walls of flickering candles — the High Priest waited, hands folded before him, expression carved from solemn stone.

His name was **Malrek of the Veil**, an old man wrapped in gold-threaded vestments, his eyes a sharp, cold blue that had once stared down a dragon with nothing but a ceremonial blade.

The last dragon.

He watched the doors open as the surviving priests stumbled in — burned, bruised, bloodied. Some limped. Some were carried. All were trembling with grief and terror.

They knelt as one.

The eldest survivor spoke.

"High Priest… our leader… Brother Calven… was slain on the northern cliffs."

Malrek lowered his head, masking the flicker of shock.

"Tell me how."

The priest swallowed hard.

"A girl, my lord."

Malrek lifted his gaze. "A *girl?*"

"A girl riding a dragon."

Gasps rippled through the hall.

Malrek's expression did not change, though a muscle in his cheek twitched.

"And the beast?" he asked. "Its color?"

"Blue-gold, my lord. Smoke from its nostrils. Flame from its throat."

Malrek's fingers tightened.

"And the rider?"

The priest's voice cracked.

"She wielded fire with her hands. Shaped it. Like the stories of old. The *Bridge* of prophecy."

A hush drowned the hall.

Even the candles seemed to shudder.

Malrek stepped forward, robes whispering across the stone.

"For two centuries," he said quietly, "we have kept the world safe from fireborn monsters. For two centuries we have hunted their shadows. For two centuries we have waited for the prophecy to fail."

He turned his gaze to the scorched armor of the kneeling priests.

"And now a child carries it on her skin."

The acolytes bowed lower.

"The girl's name?" Malrek asked.

"We… do not know for certain. She fled north long ago. But the villagers—"

He hesitated.

"—the villagers whispered a name before we left."

Malrek's voice dropped to a whisper.
A dangerous whisper.

"What name?"

"Astrid Halvarsdottir."

Malrek closed his eyes.

"Halvar's daughter."

The survivors glanced at each other. "You… you know her, my lord?"

Malrek inhaled deeply — a long, icy breath.

"Her father once walked our halls. He trained with our hunters. He witnessed the purge of the last brood… and fled from his duty."

He turned to the balcony overlooking the southern coast.

"Of course it would begin with his bloodline."

The room fell utterly silent.

Then Malrek lifted his staff — a long black rod crowned with a metal ring held together by old dragonbone bindings.

"Bring the banners."

Priests scrambled to obey, unrolling immense blue-and-gold tapestries embroidered with a dragon's skull cleaved by a sword — the symbol of the Order of Ablation.

Malrek slammed the butt of his staff against the stone.

"We march at once."

The chamber vibrated.

Acolytes whispered in terror.

"High Priest," one of the wounded priests dared to ask, "where do we march first?"

Malrek turned, eyes blazing.

"Havngard."

The hall stirred with unease.

"But my lord — that is a fisherman's village. Small. Remote. Barely protected."

"All the better," Malrek said. "Small things burn cleanest."

A flicker of grief crossed one survivor's face. "Their people are innocent."

Malrek's gaze sharpened.

"Innocent?" His voice was cold steel.
"They hid a dragon egg.
They protected a rider.
They defied their God."

He began descending the steps.

"Burn the boats. Burn the fields. Burn every home if needed.
Smoke out the girl.
Smoke out the dragon.

Smoke out the egg."

He paused at the doors.

"And when you find Astrid Halvarsdottir…"
His grip tightened on the staff.
"Bring her to me alive.
The Bridge must kneel before it is broken."

Astrid had no idea.

Havngard had less time than anyone knew.

And Malrek — the man who ended the age of dragons — was coming to finish what he began.

The Black Procession

Morning mist drifted across the monastery courtyard as High Priest Malrek stepped into the open air. The rising sun glinted off the polished white spires behind him, turning them from serene sanctuaries into towering spears of gold.

Acolytes bowed low.
Priests fell to their knees.
The air carried the crisp coolness of early spring — soft wind, damp stone, and the faint scent of thawed earth.

Malrek moved forward, his gold-threaded robes brushing the flagstones.

"Raise the armory," he commanded.

The great iron gates beneath the courtyard groaned open, releasing a gust of stale, untouched air from the deep vaults. Dust drifted upward as ancient weapon racks were drawn into the morning light.

Spears tipped with serpentsteel, forged in dragonfire.
Bows strung with twisted wyrm sinew.
Blades quenched in the blood of the last brood.

Even in the warming spring morning, the relics seemed to darken the air around them.

Priests whispered fearfully.

"These were used in the Purge…"
"Are we truly retrieving them again?"
"Against a child?"

Malrek placed a hand on a long black spear etched with runes.

"Against a prophecy," he said quietly.

A priest approached, bowing deeply.

"My lord… shall we deploy the Veilbound?"

The courtyard fell silent.

The Veilbound — monks who spoke no words, who lived and killed by absolute obedience.

Malrek nodded once.

"Wake them."

Moments later, figures emerged from the shadows beneath the sanctuary — tall forms draped in gray mourning cloth, faces hidden behind smooth, featureless white masks. They moved without sound, like drifting spirits.

Every acolyte backed away in dread.

The lead Veilbound knelt before Malrek.
The others mirrored the motion instantly.

Malrek leaned close, his voice low and cold.

"A dragon rises in the north. A rider rises with it.
The girl must be taken alive.
Her bond must be severed.

The beast must die.”

The Veilbound inclined their masked heads, then rose.

Malrek strode toward the sea gate overlooking the spring coastline.

“Ready the ships.”

The Mustering of the Fleet

Down at the harbor, the monastery's longships rocked gently in the rising morning tide. Spring wind filled the white sails, and the sea shimmered with sunlight, restless but unfrozen.

Soldiers loaded crates of burning oil.
Priests stacked censers, relic-stones, and dragon-slayer spears.
Hunters buckled on armor shaped like stylized dragon skulls.

A captain hurried to Malrek and bowed.

“My lord, the waters are calm. With today's wind, we can reach Havngard by nightfall.”

Malrek's gaze never left the horizon.

“Then we sail immediately.”

Behind him, the Veilbound boarded silently, their gray robes fluttering like mourning banners in the spring breeze.

Drums began to pound.
Sails unfurled.
The fleet lurched forward into the **spring-chilled sea**.

Malrek watched from the cliffs above, his expression unreadable.

“Let the world tremble,” he whispered.

"For the Bridge must break… before the world burns."

The Northern Warning

Far away, beyond the fjord, Havngard stirred.

Villagers noticed the sky darkening strangely over the southern horizon.

A farmer paused, shading his eyes.
"Looks like a storm."

A fisherwoman frowned.
"Tides aren't right for a storm."

A child pointed.

"Look! Sails!"

Dozens of white shapes crested the horizon.
Then hundreds.

The sea looked as though winter itself was marching north.

The bells of Havngard began to ring.

Old Jorunn limped into the **thaw-soaked street**, shouting:

"HAVNGARD! LIGHT YOUR BEACONS!
THE MONASTERY COMES!"

The Veilbound's Oath

Back on the monastery pier, the Veilbound boarded the first ship, moving like ghosts.

One of them paused beside Malrek before stepping aboard.

Malrek leaned close, his voice low and dark.

"Find the girl.
Find the dragon.

Bring me the prophecy's beating heart."

The masked figure bowed—
And stepped onto the ship.

The fleet surged north across the cold morning water.

Malrek watched from the cliffs above, wind tugging at his gold-threaded robes.

"Let the world tremble," he murmured.
"For the Bridge must break… before the world burns."

Havngard's Last Quiet Morning

The bells kept ringing.

Their haunting clangor rolled over the fjord, echoed off the thawing cliffs, and trembled through every cottage in Havngard. Seabirds scattered into the air, startled by the sudden chaos.

Halvar's cottage sat near the water on a small rise overlooking the village square. He stepped out onto his porch, hand shielding his eyes against the spring sunlight, and saw what everyone else saw:

White sails.
Dozens at first.
Then more.
Then too many.

A long line of ships cut through the fjord's mouth like a drifting wall of bone and silk.

The monastery.

Halvar's stomach sank.

It was too soon.
Too many.

Too organized.

Brother Calven had returned to them.

And Astrid… Astrid—

He closed his eyes, gripping the railing so tightly his knuckles turned white.

"Father," called a boy from the road, breathless, "the council is meeting in the longhouse! They're calling every able hand!"

Halvar nodded, his voice thick. "Tell them I'm coming."

But he didn't move immediately.

Not yet.

He stared out across the fjord, watching the monastery ships cut through the water in grim silence.

Spring sun glittered on the waves.
Wind tugged at the village banners.
Fishermen pulled children indoors.

A feeling settled over Havngard — a feeling like the moment before a storm breaks. Not of wind or rain, but something far worse.

Fear.

Not for themselves.
For Astrid.

Halvar turned at the sound of hurried footsteps.

Old Jorunn, leaning on her cane, approached him with frantic determination.

"Halvar," she rasped, "is it true? Did your girl… did she truly—"

"She is not what they say," he snapped, more harshly than intended.

Jorunn didn't back away. "But the monastery thinks she is."

Halvar swallowed hard, voice breaking.

"They're wrong."

"Then where is she?"

Halvar looked down.

He had no answer.

Only hope.
And dread.
And a desperate wish that she was far away — too far for the monastery's reach.

A horn sounded from the docks — a short, sharp blast.

The first monastery ship was turning toward Havngard's pier.

Jorunn gripped Halvar's arm.

"They're not here to talk, Halvar."

"I know."

"You have to warn her."

"I've tried."

Jorunn shook her head. "Try harder."

Halvar turned toward the longhouse, jaw tight. "If I could reach her, I would."

Jorunn watched the approaching ships with eyes full of old sorrow.

"Then pray she hears you," she whispered.

The Village Gathers

Inside the longhouse, smoke rose from the firepit as Havngard's leaders gathered in frightened circles.

Erik the Harbormaster stood at the center, slamming his fist against a table.

"They come with warships! Look at their numbers! The monks have brought hunters and steel—this isn't a visit!"

Freyja, the blacksmith's wife, stepped forward. "We can't fight the monastery. No one can."

"We can hide the children," someone murmured.

"We can hide the boats."

"They'll burn us out!"

"Why now? What have we done?!"

Whispers swelled and spiraled into panic.

Halvar stepped inside. Silence hit instantly.

Everyone turned.

Everyone knew.

He didn't bother pretending.

"It's Astrid," he said quietly. The words tasted like iron. "They come for her."

A murmur rippled through the crowd.

"But why?"
"She was always a strange one…"
"Is she dangerous?"
"She's Halvar's girl—she was born good…"

Halvar raised his hands for silence.

"My daughter is not a threat to any of you. She never has been. If the monks come asking questions, you tell them nothing. Do you hear me? Nothing."

Erik frowned. "Halvar… they won't accept silence."

"They can accept it or they can kill me," Halvar snapped.

A hush fell.

He wasn't angry at them.
He was angry at himself.
For not protecting her better.
For letting her run.
For everything.

Freyja stepped forward gently. "Halvar… what would you have us do?"

Halvar looked around the room — tired faces, frightened mothers, hardened sailors — people who just wanted to survive.

"The monastery will search every home," he said. "Ask every question. Tear apart anything they like."
He lowered his voice. "But Astrid is not here. We all know that. So keep it that way."

"And if they accuse us?" Erik asked.

Halvar's voice hardened.

"Then they accuse all of us.
As one village."

That struck something deep.
A unity forged by generations.

Jorunn nodded, firm and steady. "Havngard stands for its

own."

Murmurs of agreement spread.

But beneath it all… fear lingered.

Because even united, Havngard was **small**.
And the monastery fleet was **huge**.

Halvar stepped toward the door.

"Prepare for them," he said.
"I'll handle the first wave."

"Halvar—where are you going?"

He paused.

"I'm going down to the docks," he said. "If the monks
want someone to blame—"

He swallowed.

"They'll find me first."

The First Ship Approaches

Halvar reached the pier as the monastery ship glided
closer — sails billowing, oars cutting cleanly through the
water.

Along the rails stood priests in white-and-gold armor.
Hunters with dragonbone spears.
Silent Veilbound masked in gray.

The ship's prow cast a long shadow across the water as it
slowed.

Halvar stood alone at the edge of the dock, jaw tight, fists
clenched.

A priest at the bow raised a dragon-slayer's spear.
His voice carried across the water, amplified by the stillness.

"WHERE IS THE GIRL?"

Halvar didn't flinch.

He didn't move.

He only whispered, so softly the wind nearly swallowed it:

"Astrid… wherever you are… run."

The Price of Silence

The monastery ship slid against the pier with a low, hollow groan of wood and iron. Monks leapt off first, boots thudding onto the old planks. Their white-and-gold armor gleamed in the spring sun — far too bright against the weather-worn village.

Then the **Veilbound** stepped off.

Gray-robed.
Mask-faced.
Silent as death.

A chill rippled across the watching villagers.

Halvar did not move.

A priest stepped forward — tall, young, armored in polished plates engraved with the Order's sigil. His voice was sharp and cold.

"You are Halvar of Havngard."

A statement. Not a question.

Halvar met his gaze. "I am."

The priest scanned the villagers behind him — mothers clutching children, old men gripping walking sticks, fishermen shifting nervously in the mud.

"Bring him," the priest commanded.

Two hunters moved to grab Halvar's arms.

Halvar didn't resist — not yet.

"What do you want with my village?" he asked, voice steady.

"Only answers," the priest replied. "Nothing more."

"But lies," Halvar said, "will not satisfy you. Will they?"

The priest's jaw tightened.

"No," he admitted. "They will not."

They dragged Halvar toward the longhouse. Villagers parted reluctantly, fury and fear mixing in their eyes.

Jorunn cried out, "He's done nothing wrong!"

The priest didn't even look at her. "Silence."

The hunters shoved Halvar inside the longhouse. The priest followed. Two Veilbound stepped in behind them like gray phantoms.

The doors closed.

Interrogation

Inside, the longhouse felt suddenly too small. Smoke from the firepit curled in the air, mixing with incense from the priests' censers.

Halvar was forced to his knees.

The young priest crouched in front of him.

"You knew what your daughter was," he said quietly.

Halvar glared. "She is my daughter. That's what she is."

"A dragon-rider," the priest hissed. "A Bridge of

prophecy. A threat to all mankind."

Halvar didn't blink.

"She's a fisher girl. Nothing more."

One of the Veilbound stepped closer. Halvar felt it instantly — a strange pressure, like cold hands pressing against his chest, his skull, his breath.

The masked figure tilted its head slowly.

Searching.

Listening.

Sniffing the air.

The priest watched.

"Well?" he asked.

The Veilbound remained still for a moment.

Then it raised one thin, pale finger…

…and pointed toward the **north**.

Toward the mountains.

Toward Astrid.

The priest's eyes gleamed.

"Ah."

Halvar's heart slammed into his ribs.

"No," he said. "You follow that direction, you'll only find cliffs. Frozen caves. Nothing—"

"Silence," the priest snapped.

Another Veilbound glided outside.

The young priest stood, brushing dust from his knees.

"She is alive," he said. "We knew it the moment the Wight died. And now this one confirms it."

He leaned close to Halvar, voice low.

"She is close… very close. And we will find her."

Halvar met his gaze unflinchingly.

"You'll have to kill me first."

The priest smiled.

"If I wished you dead, I wouldn't waste iron."

He stepped backward.

"Set the village under watch," he ordered a hunter at the door.

"We will return to the mountains within the hour. But first —"

His voice hardened.
"Burn the boats."

Halvar's head snapped up.

"No."

"Yes," the priest said coldly. "If we deny the villagers escape, they'll have no way to hide her should she return."

"Don't you do this," Halvar growled. "These men need those boats to feed their families."

The priest shrugged. "Better they starve than shelter a dragon."

Halvar surged to his feet—

And a Veilbound slammed him into the floor with a single, impossibly fast strike.

Pain flared up his spine.

He gasped for breath.

The priest didn't even look down.

"Burn them," he repeated.

The Pier Ignites

Outside, hunters marched toward the docks carrying oil jars. Villagers shouted, scrambling to form a barrier between the monastery men and their boats.

Erik the Harbormaster stood at the front. "This is our livelihood! You can't—"

A hunter shoved him aside and smashed a jar against the nearest boat.

Oil splattered across the hull.

"NO!" a fisherman screamed.

Another jar.
Another splash.

Then one of the priests stepped forward, holding a burning censer.

Jorunn shouted, "Stop! PLEASE! We'll cooperate! Just don't—"

The priest tipped the censer.

Fire spilled out.

The first boat caught instantly.

Flames crawled up the wooden hull like hungry fingers.

Villagers screamed.

More priests began lighting the others.

Smoke rose.

Embers flew.
Havngard's boats — the heart of its survival — became a line of burning pyres along the shore.

Halvar staggered out of the longhouse just in time to see the last of the boats igniting.

He fell to his knees.

His village was dying.
His people were being punished.
And the monastery would not stop.

Not until Astrid was found.

He whispered into the smoke-choked air:

"Astrid… they're coming.
Run, girl.
Run."

The Priest's Final Command

The young priest stepped up beside him.

"You see now?" he said softly. "Your silence helps no one."

Halvar clenched his fists.

"She's nowhere near here."

The priest smiled coldly.

"Oh, she will be."

He turned to his men.

"Prepare for ascent.
We hunt at once.
Take the Veilbound and twenty hunters. The others remain here."

The Veilbound drifted together like a flock of silent ravens.

Halvar's breath halted.

They were heading for the mountains.

They were heading for Astrid.

He whispered, voice breaking:

"Please… let my girl live."

The priest paused.

"She will live," he said calmly.

Halvar looked up, surprised.

Then the priest's eyes sharpened.

"Until the High Priest breaks her."

Smoke from the Bay

The Frostborn moved with surprising grace for men of their size, cutting a sure path down the mountain's northern slope. Their heavy boots crushed thawed earth and patches of lingering snow as they descended, the early-spring sun glinting off their bone-forged weapons.

Astrid followed closely behind their leader, gripping Embla's torn wing for support. The dragon's body swayed with weakness; every few steps her claws dragged.

"Easy… easy…" Astrid whispered.
"We'll reach the valley soon. We'll rest there."

Embla's voice trembled through the bond:

I'm… trying, Astrid.
But the world spins.
My blood feels cold.

Astrid tightened her grip on the egg with her free hand. The shell pulsed stronger than ever — rapid, like a heartbeat racing to escape.

Halvar limped behind them, one arm pressed to cracked ribs, breath strained.

A Frostborn warrior noticed his struggle and wordlessly took Halvar's other arm to steady him.

Astrid exchanged a grateful glance.

The warrior grunted, "Your father is strong for a small man."

Astrid almost managed a smile.

But her heart was too heavy.

Embla stumbled again, nearly collapsing.

Astrid sprang under her neck, straining to hold her weight. "No—no, don't fall—stay with me—"

Embla's jaw trembled.

Do you… hear the egg?
It calls louder.
It feels my pain.

Astrid's throat tightened.

"Yes," she whispered.
"It wants out."

A Frostborn giant knelt beside Embla and pressed a thick, steadying hand to her ribs.

"Dragon is bleeding too much," he rumbled. "Needs shelter. Needs heat. Needs rest."

"We don't have any of those," Astrid said softly.

The Frostborn leader, Sorrek Stonehide, turned toward her.

"You will soon."

He nodded toward a thin column of smoke rising from behind a ridge.

Astrid froze.

Smoke?

She blinked hard, thinking her eyes deceived her.

But no—

It rose sharp, black, and spreading.

"Is that… from Havngard?" Astrid whispered.

Halvar squinted, dread twisting his face. "No. No, please–"

Sorrek's deep voice cut him off.

"Yes. Your village."

Embla's head snapped up, eyes widening.

Fire…?
Monastery fire?

Astrid's heart slammed into her ribs.

"No. It can't be. They didn't reach it that fast—it's too soon—it's—"

But the wind shifted.

And carried the smell.

Not campfire.
Not hearth-smoke.

Burnt wood.

Burnt tar.
Burnt boats.

Astrid felt her knees weaken.

"They're burning the harbor," Halvar whispered, his voice breaking. "Gods… they're burning the boats…"

Astrid clutched the egg to her chest, trembling. Tears stung her eyes.

"No," she said.
"No. They're not doing this because of me."

Halvar looked at her, guilt and love warring in his face.

"Child… they are."

Astrid shook her head violently, voice rising.

"No! This isn't my fault! They can't—"

Embla pressed her muzzle against Astrid's shoulder.

They can and they are.
Because they fear us.
Because they hate us.
Because they will burn anything to reach you.

Astrid's breath came in sharp, ragged bursts.

The Frostborn stopped walking.

Sorrek lowered himself beside her so his huge form didn't tower over her fear.

"Fire-child," he rumbled, "your village is in danger. If you go now, you run toward an army."

Astrid's hands trembled around the egg.

"I have to," she whispered. "They're hurting people I love."

Sorrek nodded once, solemnly.

"Then you will not go alone."

Another Frostborn thumped his chest. "Nor I."

"And I," a third rumbled.

Embla lifted her head, eyes burning blue.

And me.
I stand with you.
Even if it kills me.

Astrid wiped her eyes, heart pounding with grief, fury, and rising heat.

"Then we go."

She turned toward the black smoke rising into the spring sky.

Her home was burning.
Her childhood was ending.
And the monastery was waiting.

Astrid pressed her forehead to Embla's.

"We fight now."

Embla exhaled warm breath across Astrid's face.

We fight together.

Halvar swallowed hard, voice shaking.

"Then gods help everyone in our way."

The Frostborn thundered behind them, weapons drawn.

And Astrid, clutching the glowing egg, began the march toward the smoke.

Toward war.

CHAPTER 28

THE RETURN TO HAVNGARD

Smoke Over the Fjord

The smell reached her first.

Not campfire smoke.
Not cooking hearths.
Not the familiar sea-wind of drying nets.

This was acrid.
Sharp.
Wrong.

Burned wood.
Burned tar.
Burned livelihood.

Astrid descended the last bend of the mountain path with the Frostborn at her back, Halvar limping beside her, and Embla staggering forward, wings dragging weakly in the thawing mud.

The fjord opened before them.

And Havngard…
Havngard was **hurt.**

Astrid's breath caught.

Black smoke curled from the docks where the fishing boats once lined the shore. Half of them were burned to the waterline — charred ribs jutting from the surf like the skeletons of sea beasts.

Villagers huddled in small, terrified groups along the beach. Children sobbed into their mothers' skirts. Men knelt in the mud with their hands on their heads while monastery hunters stalked the shore, scanning every face.

Astrid felt her chest tighten painfully.

"This… this can't be real," she whispered.

Halvar's voice was small and hollow.
"It's real, Astrid."

She stared down at the ruined pier.

Her memories were there — woven into every charred board and broken mast.
Her first fishing knot.
Her first dive into the cold fjord.
Her first lesson in the tides.

All of it burned because of **her.**

Embla sensed the spiral of grief and pressed her head into Astrid's side.

No, she murmured.
They chose the fire.
You did not bring it.
They did.

Astrid clutched Embla's muzzle.

"I'm so sorry," she whispered. She didn't know if she was speaking to Embla, to Halvar, or to the village below.

Sorrek Stonehide, the Frostborn leader, stepped to her side.

"We must move carefully," he warned. His voice was a low rumble. "Hunters watch the roads. Priests watch anything that moves."

Astrid swallowed hard. "If they see Embla, they'll attack."

Sorrek nodded. "And if they see you, Fire-Bound, they will call for their god."

His face darkened.

"And they will try to kill you."

Astrid stared down at the monastery hunters pacing the beach, their dragonbone spears gleaming in the spring sun.

"Then they'll try," she whispered.

The egg pulsed.

Harder.

Astrid felt the movement again — a ripple beneath the shell like a tightening coil. She held it against her chest, feeling its warmth surge through her body.

Halvar noticed.

His breath hitched.

"It's… moving again."

Astrid nodded. "Stronger. It's close."

Embla's wings trembled.

The hatchling can feel the danger.
Its blood calls to mine.
It knows the world it wakes into is not safe.

Astrid swallowed, fighting tears.

"We'll make it safe."

Sorrek gestured for them to move.

"Come. The low ridge will give us cover. We circle around, approach from shadow."

They followed him along the narrow trail skirting the cliff. Astrid moved quietly, every step trembling with dread.

As they reached the final slope, Astrid froze.

Voices carried up from the square below.

Familiar voices.

"We know nothing!" someone shouted. "Stop asking!"

"We have no loyalty to the girl!" another cried. "We only want to live!"

"No one is hiding her!"

Astrid felt her stomach twist.

Villagers.
Her people.
Terrified.
Cornered.

A priest strode into view, his white armor glinting.

"Then why did she flee?" he demanded. "Why did she not stay to face judgment?"

Astrid's pulse pounded in her ears.

Halvar clenched his jaw, fists shaking. "That's Calven's second-in-command. Marrek."

"Him," Sorrek muttered. "The one with the eyes like broken ice."

Below, the priest raised his voice:

"Bring forward Halvar's neighbors. They may speak sense."

Villagers cried out. A young girl screamed as a hunter seized her arm.

Astrid took a step forward, fury rising like heat under her skin—

Sorrek grabbed her shoulder.

"No."

Astrid shook him off. "They're hurting my people."

"They will hurt more if you rush in blind. Choose your strike."

Embla's eyes glowed faintly.

Astrid.
If you go now…
I will follow.
But I cannot protect you.
My wings are failing.

Astrid swallowed.
Her eyes burned.
Her heart hammered.

Below, a priest shoved old Jorunn to her knees.

Astrid's breath shattered.

"Let her go," she whispered. "She's done nothing."

Halvar grabbed her arm gently. "Astrid—don't—"

But she couldn't look away.

Jorunn lifted her head, voice shaking:

"We will not betray a girl who did no wrong."

The priest slapped her across the face.

Astrid gasped out loud.

Her anger ignited.

Literally.

Tiny sparks flickered across her fingertips. The egg pulsed harder, heat building beneath the shell.

Embla froze.

Astrid—
The hatchling feels your rage—
Control it—

"I can't," she whispered. "Not this time."

Below, the priest raised his hand.

"Take her inside the longhouse!"

A hunter grabbed Jorunn's arm—

—and Astrid moved.

Not thinking.
Not planning.
Pure instinct.

She stepped through the trees onto the open slope.

Sorrek cursed and reached for her—
but she was already gone.

Embla lurched after her, struggling to follow.

Halvar's voice cracked.

"Astrid—NO!"

Too late.

Her boots hit the slope.
Her braid snapped in the wind.
The egg glowed against her chest like a tiny sun.

She walked straight toward the burning docks.

Toward the monastery.

Toward danger.

Toward destiny.

Hunters turned.

Priests froze.

Someone shouted:

"THE GIRL!
THE BRIDGE!"

Every head snapped toward her.

But Astrid didn't flinch.

She stepped into Havngard's ashes—
and glared at the man hurting her village.

Her voice rang across the square:

"Let her go."

The Girl in the Ashes

The moment Astrid stepped into the open, the entire village square fell silent.

A child gasped.
A fisherman dropped his net.
Jorunn froze where she knelt in the mud, disbelief widening her eyes.

The monastery hunters reacted first.

"THERE!" one shouted, pointing his spear.
"THE BRIDGE! THE GIRL!"

Priests snapped their heads toward her. Some stumbled backward as if they'd seen a ghost. Others gripped their weapons tighter.

Astrid kept walking.

Slow.
Deliberate.
Unafraid.

Smoke drifted around her, curling through her braid and cloak. Ash clung to her boots. The egg against her chest glowed stronger with every step she took.

Embla stumbled into view behind her.

The dragon was barely standing — wings dragging, pearls of blood dripping onto the mud — but when she raised her head, the village gasped in awe and terror.

A dragon.
A real dragon.
In Havngard.

"Mother above…" someone whispered.

A hunter took a nervous step back. "It's wounded…"

Another snarled, "Then now is the time to kill it!"

Astrid's voice cracked through the air like a whip.

"Don't touch her."

The words hit harder than steel.

Marrek, the young priest in white-and-gold armor, spun toward her.

He was the same man who had ordered the boats burned. The same who slapped Jorunn.

He smiled now — a tiny, triumphant thing.

"Astrid Halvarsdottir," he said, spreading his arms. "At last."

Astrid stopped a few paces from him.

"Let her go," she said, chin lifting. "She has nothing to do with this."

He grabbed Jorunn's arm and yanked her upright, dagger

pressed to her collar.

"Oh? And what about you?" he asked. "Where were you when your village sheltered you? When your father lied for you? When innocent people trembled because of *your* burden?"

Astrid swallowed hard.

Guilt sliced through her.

But behind her, Embla growled low.

He is wrong, Astrid.
You owe guilt to no one.
Only truth.

Astrid steadied herself. "Let. Her. Go."

"What will you do if I don't?" Marrek asked. "Burn me?"

Astrid closed her hand slowly, feeling the heat coil beneath her skin like a waiting serpent.

"Try me."

A ripple of fear passed through several hunters.

But Marrek only smirked. "Then prove it. Shape your flame. Show us why Calven died screaming."

Astrid's breath caught.
Her heart pounded.

But before she could answer—

The egg moved.

A sharp *crack* split the air.

The sound was small, but it echoed through Astrid like thunder. She froze, eyes widening as she looked down.

A thin fracture line glowed across the shell's surface, bright and molten as sunrise.

Embla gasped aloud.

It begins…
Astrid — the hatchling comes—

Marrek's eyes flicked to the egg, widening in horror.

"What… what is that?" he demanded.

Astrid's fingers curled around it protectively.

"Hope."

Marrek's expression shattered into rage.

"Take her!" he shouted. "Take the egg! KILL THE DRAGON—"

But before his men could move—

Embla collapsed.

Her legs buckled, wings crumpling beneath her as she fell hard into the mud, gasping in pain.

"Astrid!" she cried through the bond, voice full of panic.
I cannot… stand! I cannot—

Marrek laughed sharply.

"Pathetic. A dying beast. A dying bond."

Hunters raised their spears.

Villagers screamed.

Astrid stepped over Embla, positioning herself between the dragon and the monastery.

Her eyes blazed.

"Touch her," she said.

Fire curled up her arm, blue-gold and whispering like a living ribbon.

"And I will burn your order to its bones."

A few hunters staggered back.

But Marrek didn't.

He sneered.

"You are one girl. One spark. And we—"

He lifted his hand.

The Veilbound stepped forward.

Silent.
Mask-faced.
Sure.

The entire square drew a collective breath.

Jorunn whispered, trembling:

"Astrid… run…"

Astrid shook her head.

"No."

She glanced at the cracked egg.

At Embla struggling to breathe.

At her father, who had just limped into the square, bloodied and horrified at the sight.

At the Frostborn emerging behind her like silent mountains, weapons drawn.

Then back at Marrek.

"I'm done running."

Flame blazed up her arm.

The egg cracked again — louder.

A brilliant fissure split the shell in two.

A newborn roar echoed faintly from within.

And the world seemed to hold its breath—

just as the first spear was thrown.

When the Egg Breaks

The spear glinted in the spring sunlight as it cut through the air.

Astrid saw it only as a flash of silver—
aimed straight at Embla's exposed side.

"NO!" she screamed.

She threw herself forward, arms outstretched—

—but she wasn't fast enough.

Sorrek was.

The Frostborn leader lunged from behind her, massive body moving with the speed of a striking bear. His bone-axe swung upward, catching the spear mid-flight—

CRACK!

The shaft splintered, the tip spinning harmlessly into a patch of mud.

The entire village gasped.

Marrek's eyes widened. "What—those men—who are—"

Before he could finish, Sorrek planted himself between Astrid and the monastery forces, chest rising and falling like a mountain about to erupt.

"You touch the girl," he growled,
"you face *Frostborn steel.*"

Three more giants thundered down the slope, roaring

their war-cries. The ground itself seemed to shake beneath their boots.

The hunters recoiled in shock.

"Frostborn!? Here!?"
"They're not supposed to leave the northern pass—!"
"Gods above, what is happening?!"

Astrid didn't hear them.

Her world had narrowed to Embla's collapsed form and the egg pulsing in her hands.

Another crack split the shell.

A glow burst through—
blue-white, piercing, electric.

Embla gasped through the bond:

Astrid—
she comes—
she comes NOW—

A faint, newborn cry echoed from inside. Not a roar, not yet—
just a trembling squeak, raw and alive.

Tears pricked Astrid's eyes.

But Marrek saw something else.

"THE EGG IS ACTIVE!" he shouted. "THE PROPHECY UNFOLDS—SEIZE THEM ALL!"

The hunters surged forward.

The Veilbound stepped silently into their path—

And then **all hell broke loose.**

The Clash

Sorrek's axe came down with a thunderous crash, slicing a hunter's spear in half and sending the man sprawling.

Another Frostborn swung a hammer like a battering ram, knocking two monks off their feet with a single blow.

Villagers scattered, screaming, diving for cover as the monastery forces clashed with the giants in the muddy square.

Embla tried to rise.

She couldn't.

Astrid… I must protect you…
Her voice shivered with pain and fury.
I must stand—

"Don't move!" Astrid cried, kneeling beside her. "You'll tear your wing open!"

Embla let out a broken whine.

Behind her, a Veilbound figure glided toward them—mask empty, silent, hands raising like a pair of pale blades.

Astrid spun, fire rushing up her arms.

"Stay back!"

She thrust her palms forward—

A blast of blue-gold flame erupted from her hands, wild and unfocused, scorching the ground at the Veilbound's feet. The masked figure jerked back, robes singed, and tilted its head in eerie, analytical silence.

The egg cracked again.

This time the shell split down the center.

A brilliant burst of heat washed over Astrid's face.

A tiny snout pushed through—
glowing like a star being born.

Astrid stared, breath trembling.

"Hello," she whispered.

A small, quivering sound answered her.

A hungry, determined sound.

A sound ready to live.

Marrek Strikes

Marrek saw the opening.

He saw Astrid kneeling.
The egg splitting.
Embla helpless.
Sorrek locked in battle.

And the hatred on his face turned almost holy in its
intensity.

"There will be no hatching today," he hissed.

He raised his serrated relic-blade—

—and sprinted toward Astrid.

Halvar cried out from the edge of the square:

"ASTRID, MOVE!"

Astrid turned—

But before Marrek's blade could fall—

Embla surged to life.

Not with her wings.
Not with her strength.

But with her **fire.**

With a desperate scream, Embla exhaled a narrow jet of flame—not strong, not wide, but enough to force Marrek back a step, enough to singe his armor, enough to save Astrid by a heartbeat.

He stumbled, enraged and shocked.

"You should be dead!" he snarled at the dragon.

Embla bared her teeth, blood dripping down her chin.

Try again.

Marrek lifted his blade, fury boiling.

Astrid rose to her feet, fire curling around her arms.

The egg pulsed brighter, cracks widening—

Three battles colliding:

Astrid vs. Marrek
Embla vs. death
The hatchling vs. the world it was entering

Astrid tightened her grip on the egg.

"Stay away from my family."

The Shattering

The shell split.

Completely.

Light burst outward in a searing flare, engulfing Astrid, Embla, Marrek, the square, the entire world—

A newborn cry split the air—

high, sharp, fierce.

The hatchling was coming.

And nothing would stop it now.

Light exploded.

Astrid staggered backward, blinded as a wave of heat burst from the cracking egg and swept across the square like a summer storm. Sparks spiraled through the air. Every hunter froze. Even the Veilbound stopped mid-stride, tilting their mask-faces toward the brilliance.

The egg split open with a ringing, crystalline sound—

CRACK—SHHHH—FWOOM.

Inside, curled tight like a glowing ember come to life, was the hatchling.

Small.
But not weak.

Her scales shimmered with the same blue-gold fire that danced through Embla's breath — only brighter, younger, purer. Tiny horns like molten silver rose from her brow, and her wings—thin, translucent, radiant—fluttered for the very first time.

She blinked up at Astrid, pupils widening.

And Astrid's heart broke open.

"Hello, little one," she whispered.

The newborn answered with a trembling cry—

keeehhh—!

The sound was both frightened and fierce.

Marrek shielded his face from the light. "No—NO! Seize it! SEIZE THE CREATURE!"

The Veilbound moved first.

They surged forward, gliding rather than running, arms cutting through the smoke like blades.

"Back!" Astrid shouted.

Fire erupted along her arms, an instinctive flare powerful enough to crack the stones beneath her feet. Heat rolled off her in waves. Embla's flames responded, flickering brighter despite her pain.

The newborn turned toward Embla with a soft chirring sound—

A sound of recognition.

A sound of kin.

Embla's voice broke through the bond, trembling:

Sister…
My sister…

Astrid's breath caught.

Then everything happened at once.

The Veilbound Strike

A Veilbound figure lunged, hands outstretched to seize the newborn—

Sorrek's hammer came down with a thunderous blow.

BOOOOM.

The masked monk flew back, crashing through a stack of fishing crates.

Another Veilbound appeared behind Astrid, arms reaching for her throat—

—and Halvar, limping and furious, shoved a burning spar of wood into its chest.

"GET AWAY FROM MY GIRL!"

The blow didn't kill it—the Veilbound didn't scream or flinch—but it stumbled long enough for Halvar to drag Astrid aside.

"Run!" he gasped. "Take her and run!"

Astrid grabbed his wrist. "Not without you—"

SHRRKKK!

A blade sliced past her cheek, narrowly missing. Marrek snarled, using a fallen spear to cut toward her with wild, desperate rage.

"You will NOT leave with that abomination!"

Embla roared weakly, heat fluttering in her throat.

Astri—d… go…

"No!" Astrid cried, spinning toward her. "I'm not leaving you—"

The newborn hatchling let out a sudden, piercing wail.

KREEEHHH—!!

A shockwave burst outward — not flame, not light, something deeper — a raw pulse of newborn dragon-magic that blasted the mud into spirals and sent hunters sprawling.

The Veilbound staggered.

Astrid felt the surge sweep through her, lighting her nerves in brilliant fire.

Marrek choked, clutching his head. "What—what is that—?!"

Embla gasped, her voice barely a whisper through the bond:

She has the old fire… the first fire…
Astrid—help her shape it—
Help her LIVE—

Astrid Chooses

Astrid knelt, gathering the trembling newborn into her arms. The hatchling was warm—too warm—her body shaking with the effort of being alive.

"Stay with me," Astrid whispered. "Please—stay—"

Marrek lunged.

"GIVE IT TO ME!" he roared.

Embla moved.

With a scream of agony, she forced herself upright, wings dragging, blood dripping, but she stood—between Astrid and the blade.

Marrek's strike hit Embla's scales and skittered off with a shower of sparks.

He stared at her, disbelieving. "You should be dead!"

Embla bared her teeth.

Not while she breathes.

Marrek raised his weapon to strike again—

Sorrek grabbed him from behind.

The priest screamed, kicking wildly, but the Frostborn's arms locked around him like iron.

"You harm the Fire-Bound," Sorrek growled, "you answer to ME."

And he hurled Marrek across the square.

The priest slammed into the longhouse wall with a

sickening crack and collapsed into the mud.

The square fell silent.

Only the crackle of embers and the newborn's soft whimpers broke the air.

Astrid looked down at the tiny dragon in her arms—scared, shaking, alive.

Her heart surged with fierce love.

"We have to go," she whispered.

Sorrek nodded. "More ships will come. More hunters. The High Priest himself, perhaps."

Halvar stepped forward, eyes shining with tears.

"I'll hold them as long as I can," he said. "I'll lead them off. You run."

Astrid shook her head violently. "No—I'm not losing you —"

"Astrid."
Halvar cupped her cheek, voice trembling.
"You were born to protect them."

Embla leaned against Astrid's side, voice resonating with fierce determination:

We all go.
Together.

Sorrek raised his hammer. "Then we leave. Now."

Behind them, warriors clashed again as reinforcements poured from the monastery ships.

The newborn cried weakly, nuzzling into Astrid's chest.

Astrid held her close, fire curling around her hands

protectively.

She lifted her eyes toward the burning sky.

"Embla… Sorrek… Father… run."

They fled the square as the monastery forces surged forward—

and behind them, Marrek stirred in the mud, one eye opening.

Hatred burning.

The hunt wasn't over.

It had just begun.

The Flight Through Ash

Astrid ran.

Embla limped beside her—bleeding, breath ragged, wings dragging like torn banners in the mud. The newborn hatchling clung to Astrid's chest, tiny talons gripping her cloak, trembling with every distant roar and clash of steel.

Sorrek and the Frostborn formed a shield around them, moving like a living fortress. Halvar stumbled along, breath short, clutching his ribs but refusing to fall behind.

Smoke thickened the air.

Shouts rose from behind.

The monastery had regrouped.

Drums pounded from the ships.
More hunters spilled onto the beach.
Priests barked orders from the pier.

Astrid looked back once—just long enough to see Marrek staggering to his feet, blood running down his temple, eyes burning with hate.

"ASTRID!" he screamed.
"YOU CAN'T RUN FOREVER!"

She tightened her hold on the newborn.

"Watch me."

Sorrek pointed toward a narrow alley between two old storehouses. "Through there! The forest lies beyond!"

They sprinted toward the gap—

—and villagers stepped out.

Astrid skidded to a halt.

Men and women blocked the alleyway, armed with fishhooks, oars, butcher knives—whatever they could grab. Their faces were streaked with ash and fear.

Astrid's stomach dropped.

"Please," she begged. "Move — we have to go."

Old Jorunn stepped forward.

And for a heartbeat, Astrid feared she would give them up.

But Jorunn simply wiped soot from her cheek and said:

"Let the girl pass."

The crowd parted instantly.

A young fisherman grabbed Astrid's arm as she passed. "We'll hold them off as long as we can."

A mother with a baby on her hip nodded fiercely. "Go. Save your dragon."

Astrid choked back tears.

"You all already have."

Sorrek ushered her forward. "No time. Move!"

They plunged into the alley—just as monastery hunters turned the corner behind them.

The Final Race

The alley opened into Havngard's northern meadow, its spring grasses trampled by the monastery's arrival. The forest loomed ahead—dark, green, alive.

But Embla staggered.

Her claws slipped in the mud. She collapsed again, gasping, trembling all over.

"Astrid…" she whispered.
I can't… I can't move my wings… everything feels cold…

The newborn hatchling cried, crawling up Astrid's chest, trying to reach its sister.

Astrid knelt, placing a trembling hand on Embla's snout.

"Stay with me," she whispered, voice cracking. "Please—stay with me—"

Halvar sank to his knees beside them. "Astrid… they're coming."

Shouts echoed from the alley.

The pounding of boots.

The clatter of relic-steel.

They had seconds.

Sorrek slammed the haft of his hammer into the ground. "I stay. I hold them."

Another Frostborn slammed his shield down. "And I."

"And I," said a third.

Embla lifted her head weakly, eyes filled with fear.

No… they will kill you…

Sorrek smiled — the first smile Astrid had ever seen him give.

"Let them try."

Astrid's throat closed.

"No," she whispered. "I'm not leaving you here—"

"You must," Sorrek said gently. "Your fate is not in Havngard anymore. Nor in these ashes. Go, Fire-Bound. Go where the mountains call."

The newborn suddenly jerked in her arms.

Ffff—FWOOF!

A tiny spark of blue-gold fire shot from its mouth.

Not strong.
Not hot.
But enough to ignite a patch of grass in a sudden flash.

Embla blinked in wonder.
Halvar gasped softly.

Astrid stared down at the hatchling — so small, so fragile, but already carrying a flame that felt ancient.

And she made her choice.

She slid her arms beneath Embla's chest. "Sorrek — help me lift her."

The Frostborn didn't hesitate. He scooped Embla's body into one massive arm, grunting at her weight.

Astrid gathered the newborn against her heart.

"Father," she said, turning to Halvar, "go with Sorrek's men. They'll get you away from the village."

Halvar shook his head. "Astrid, I—"

"Papa," she whispered, her voice breaking, "I need you alive."

Halvar's face shattered into grief.

He pulled her into a fierce, desperate embrace, careful of the hatchling.

"I love you, Astrid," he whispered into her hair. "You were always more than I deserved."

Astrid sobbed once, then pulled away.

"I'll come back for you."

"I know," Halvar said.

Sorrek jerked his head toward the forest. "Astrid — now."

She turned.

And she ran.

Embla cradled in Sorrek's arms.
The newborn pressed to her chest.
Halvar limping beside the giants.
Villagers screaming behind them.
Monastery hunters bursting into the meadow—

But Astrid didn't look back.

She fled into the shadow of the forest—

and the trees swallowed them whole.

Behind Them — The Last Stand Begins

As Astrid vanished into the woods, Sorrek's three

Frostborn turned as one to face the monastery's advancing wave.

The first hunters burst from the alley.

They paused when they saw the giants.

Sorrek raised his hammer.

"For Bryngard," he growled.
"For the fire that wakes."

The giants roared—

—and crashed into the monastery line.

The sounds of battle erupted behind Astrid, echoing through the trees like thunder.

She didn't stop running.

Not until Havngard was nothing but smoke behind her.

537

CHAPTER 29

THE FOREST OF ECHOES

The Weight of Three Flames

The forest swallowed them whole.

Tall pines rose like pillars around Astrid, their branches netting out the sky. Soft spring mist clung to the undergrowth, carrying the scent of moss, thawed earth, and distant sea-spray. For the first time since the docks, the world fell quiet.

Too quiet.

Astrid pushed deeper into the trees, her breath ragged, the newborn hatchling clutched to her chest. Embla leaned heavily against Sorrek's arm, her steps uneven, her breath thin and trembling.

Halvar gritted his teeth with every movement, but he stayed near Astrid, refusing to fall behind.

After several minutes, the Frostborn leader raised a hand.

"Here. We stop."

They reached a small clearing surrounded by fallen logs and thick spring ferns. Light filtered through the treetops in wavering stripes, painting the space in shifting gold and shadow.

Astrid knelt, carefully lowering the newborn onto a bed of moss.

The tiny dragon squeaked in protest, wobbling on unsteady legs, wings fluttering weakly.

Embla collapsed beside her with a shudder, eyes half-lidded, her chest rising and falling in uneven bursts.

Astrid's heart clenched.

"Embla… please hold on."

Embla's voice brushed against her mind, faint but loving:

**I'm here…
I won't leave you…
Not now…**

Astrid swallowed hard and reached for the newborn. But the hatchling had already crawled to Embla on trembling limbs.

It pressed its tiny head against Embla's cheek.

A soft glow passed between them.

Embla exhaled, a sound halfway between a groan and a purr.

She knows me, Embla whispered weakly.
She knows my flame.

The newborn's chirps grew louder, more determined.

Astrid felt warmth blooming in her chest — not her fire, but something gentler, pulsing in rhythm with the newborn's movements.

Not Embla's bond.
Not dragon-to-dragon.

Something new.

Something reaching for her.

She knelt slowly.

"Hey," she whispered. "It's all right. I'm here."

The tiny dragon turned toward her.

Its eyes — bright blue with flecks of gold — focused on

Astrid as if memorizing her face. Then it took one wobbling step forward.

Then another.

It bumped its head against her palm.

And a sound like a soft bell chime echoed through her mind.

Astri…
Not a word.
Not quite a thought.

A feeling.

Recognition.
Need.
Love.

Halvar inhaled sharply behind her. "Astrid… it knows you."

Sorrek nodded solemnly. "It claims you as kin."

The newborn climbed into Astrid's lap, curling up like a cat seeking warmth. When it touched her skin—

Flame shivered through her veins.

Her heartbeat synced with two others:

Embla's steady, strained fire.
The newborn's fragile spark.

Astrid gasped softly.

"What… was that?"

Sorrek answered quietly.

"The bond of three flames."

Embla lifted her head weakly.

Astrid…
Her voice trembled with awe.
She shares you.
She shares *me*.
We are… bound together.

Astrid felt it then — a thread of warmth tying all three of their hearts like braided fire.

One for Embla.
One for the newborn.
One running straight through her.

She trembled, whispering:

"This… this is real."

Sorrek knelt beside her.

"It is rare," he said.
"Older than the monastery. Older than the Purge.
A triad flame was said to shape the fate of ages."

Halvar swallowed hard. "So the monks fear this for a reason."

Sorrek nodded.

"They fear what they cannot kill."

The Newborn's First Flame

The hatchling chirped again, climbing clumsily up Astrid's chest. It nuzzled her chin, tiny wings flapping.

Then—

fwip—fsshh—

A faint puff of blue smoke escaped its nostrils.

Astrid blinked. "Did she just…?"

Embla's eyes brightened with pride.

Her first breath.
My sister will grow fast.
Faster with you near.

Astrid laughed softly — the first laugh since the village burned. She stroked the newborn's head gently.

"Hello, little fireheart."

The dragon chirped happily and curled up under her throat, resting there as if that had always been her place.

Halvar sat down heavily on a log, wiping soot from his face. His eyes were tired, but a small smile tugged at the corner of his mouth.

"She already loves you," he said quietly.

Astrid hugged the newborn close.

"I love her too."

The Forest Speaks

Then the wind shifted.

A single crow burst from the treetops, cawing in alarm.

Sorrek's head snapped up.

"Hunters."

Astrid felt it too — the tremor beneath her feet, faint but wrong.

Embla's nostrils flared weakly.

They follow us…
I smell the oil on their armor.
They're close.

The newborn chirped anxiously, pressing deeper into Astrid's arms.

Halvar stood, wincing. "We need to move."

Sorrek shook his head. "No. Embla cannot walk farther tonight."

Astrid felt panic rising.

"Then what do we do?"

Sorrek's expression hardened.

"We choose our ground.
And we prepare to defend it."

Embla lifted her head.

**I will not run again.
Not while I have fire in me.**

Astrid stroked the newborn's back. "We'll protect her together."

Sorrek rose to his full height, raising his hammer.

"The hunters enter the Forest of Echoes," he rumbled. "They do not know what waits."

Astrid stood.

Fire rippled faintly across her fingers.

"I do."

When the Woods Listen

The forest changed as the hunters approached.

The wind stilled.
The birds fell silent.
Even the spring insects retreated into the bark.

Astrid felt it first — a prickling at the back of her neck, like invisible eyes opening all around them. Embla stirred uneasily, nostrils flaring. The newborn hatchling tightened her tiny claws into Astrid's cloak, pressing trembling warmth against her chest.

Sorrek stood at the edge of the clearing, hammer raised, muscles coiled.

"They come," he said quietly.

Halvar limped beside him, gripping a broken oar he'd snatched during the flight. It was barely a weapon, but he held it like a vow.

The forest floor shuddered faintly — rhythmical, steady.

Bootsteps.

Armor.

Many.

Astrid knelt beside Embla, brushing her fingers over the dragon's cheek.

"How far can you breathe?" she whispered.

Embla's reply was thin but determined:

Not far.
Not much.
But enough to burn one.
Maybe two.
No more.

Astrid nodded, swallowing hard.

"Then I'll handle the rest."

The newborn chirped, small wings fluttering in fright.

Astrid hugged her close. "Hey… hey, it's okay. Stay with me."

The hatchling pressed a glowing muzzle against Astrid's throat—

And suddenly Astrid felt everything:

Embla's pain like a low throb.
Sorrek's steady battle-readiness.
Halvar's fear wrapped in fierce love.
The forest… listening.

The newborn's small flame pulsed once—

—and Astrid's heartbeat synced with it.

A ripple of fire flickered along her arms.

Sorrek turned. "Your flames grow stronger. Why?"

"I don't know," Astrid whispered.

But she did.

The bond of three flames was waking.

The Hunters Arrive

Branches snapped in the distance — deliberate, measured, disciplined.

Sorrek lifted a hand.
"Hold."

Astrid crouched beside Embla and the newborn, her pulse thundering in her ears. Embla pressed her muzzle to Astrid's knee, trembling with exhaustion.

They're here…
Embla's voice was barely a breath.

Astrid stroked her cheek. "Rest. I've got you."

Halvar gripped his makeshift weapon, jaw clenched tight. "We won't let them take you again, Astrid."

She touched his arm, steadying him. "Don't fight unless you have to."

The first hunter stepped out from between the trees — a tall man with burns on his cheek and a relic-steel spear gripped tight.

He froze when he saw the newborn in Astrid's arms.

Then Embla.

Then Sorrek.

"Gods above…" he whispered.

His voice cracked as he shouted:

"Here! HERE! They're here!"

Monastery hunters poured from the shadows — two dozen, then more, forming a half-circle around the clearing. Their armor gleamed dully under the canopy. Their spears dropped into ready position.

Then the forest fell silent.

Truly silent.

No birds.
No wind.
Even the leaves stilled.

From between the hunters, the **Veilbound** moved forward — pale masks drifting like floating skulls, robes whispering over roots.

The newborn whimpered, pressing itself into Astrid's chest.

A young priest stepped out behind them — not Marrek, someone new. His armor was polished, almost ceremonial, his eyes wide with awe and fear.

"That is it," he breathed. "The second flame. The prophecy's child."

Astrid rose — not slowly, not dramatically, just with a

calmness that felt older than she was.

"You don't touch her."

The priest studied her warily. "You are only a girl."

Halvar barked a sharp, humorless laugh. "You fools keep saying that."

Sorrek lifted his hammer. "This 'girl' outlived your dragon slayer."

A ripple of anger passed over the hunters.

The priest raised his hand for silence.

He pointed at the newborn.

"You will surrender the hatchling. And the wounded dragon. And the Bridge."
His gaze locked on Astrid.
"Alive, if possible. Dead, if necessary."

Astrid stepped forward — just one pace — and the flame curled instinctively around her fingers.

Not bright.
Not violent.
But alive.

"You touch them," she said softly,
"and I burn your Order to the ground."

A murmur swept the hunters — unease, doubt, fear.

The priest swallowed. "You're bluffing."

Then something happened that none of them expected.

A low shiver passed through the soil beneath Astrid's feet — a vibration, like a heartbeat pulsing through the roots.

The trees seemed to lean in.

The newborn chirped once, sharply—

—and Astrid felt something inside her shift.

The forest was listening.

Sorrek inhaled sharply. "The Echoes awaken…"

Embla struggled upright on trembling limbs, glaring at the hunters with a fury far larger than her weakened body.

A hunter stepped forward. "Priest, she's rousing the forest —"

"Hold," the priest snapped, voice cracking. "Stand your ground!"

Astrid lifted her hand.

Leaves rustled.
Roots tightened.
The air warmed.

It wasn't dramatic.
It wasn't a storm.

It was like the forest had begun breathing in time with her own heartbeat.

And every hunter felt it.

Finally, the priest's composure broke.

"Veilbound—SEIZE HER!"

The masked figures stepped forward—

—and the clearing erupted into motion.

The Forest Echoes Her Flame

The trees whispered.

Leaves trembled.

Roots shifted beneath the soil.

The hunters noticed it too.

"Why are the trees moving?"
"Is this some kind of magic?"
"Hold formation!"

The priest stepped forward, spear raised.

"Fire-Bound," he warned, "stand down or—"

Astrid opened her palm.

Blue-gold fire curled upward, dancing like a living serpent of flame.

"No."

The newborn echoed her — letting out a tiny spark that flickered like a match.

Embla's eyes glowed faintly.

Three flames.

Three heartbeats.

Braided as one.

The forest reacted instantly.

Branches creaked overhead as if leaning toward her. Moss lit faintly with golden sparks. Shadows twisted like they were shifting into place.

A hunter whispered in fear:

"She's waking the old magic—"

The priest snapped,

"Veilbound — take her!"

The white-masked figures stepped forward.

Silent.
Swift.
Inhuman.

Astrid felt a cold spike of terror — but the newborn pressed against her heart, giving her its tiny flame.

And she understood.

"Together," she whispered.

The newborn squeaked.

Embla's weak flame flickered.

Astrid's pulse steadied.

"Together," she said again, louder.

The nearest Veilbound lunged.

Astrid thrust her hand forward—

—and the forest answered.

BOOOOM—FWOOSH—

A wall of flame erupted from the ground, ripping upward like a storm of light, forcing the Veilbound back. Hunters cried out, shields raised, eyes reflecting blue fire.

The trees themselves seemed to glow — not burning, but channeling.

Halvar stared in awe. "Astrid… what have you become?"

She didn't know.

But she felt something ancient, powerful, coiling inside her.

Not just her flame.
Not just the newborn's.
Not just Embla's.

A **triad flame** awakening.

Astrid took a step forward, fire swirling around her arms.

"This is your only warning," she said.
"Leave. Now."

The priest glared at her, face twisted with rage.

"You cannot resist the Order."

Astrid's eyes burned.

"I'm not resisting."

Her voice was soft as wind—
and sharp as steel.

"I'm protecting my family."

The First Echo-Fight

The Veilbound lunged.

Three masked figures cut through the clearing like shadows come alive, moving too fast, too silently to be human. Their robes whispered across the forest floor. Their hands — pale, long-fingered, sharpened to unnatural points — reached for Astrid with mechanical precision.

Astrid didn't think.

She *felt*.

The newborn's heartbeat against her chest.
Embla's weak but determined flame.
The forest's pulse under her feet.

"Together," Astrid repeated — and thrust her hand forward.

FWOOM—SHHH-BOOOOM!

A burst of fire ripped up from the ground like an erupting

geyser. The flames didn't just come from Astrid — they came from the *roots themselves,* from the soil, from the old magic buried beneath centuries of pine and stone.

The Veilbound nearest her jerked backward as the blast engulfed it, robes igniting in blue-gold fire. It didn't scream — it simply flailed once, mask cracking under the heat, then collapsed into the moss with a heavy thump.

The hunters recoiled.

"By the gods—"
"She controls the forest!"
"This shouldn't be possible—!"

The young priest's face drained of color. "This power… it shouldn't exist—"

Sorrek roared and barreled forward, hammer swinging in a massive arc.

His strike collided with a second Veilbound mid-lunge —
THOOOM —
slamming it into a pine trunk hard enough to splinter bark. The masked monk rose again immediately, unnervingly fluid, mask now tilted at a broken angle.

Sorrek snarled. "You should've stayed dead."

Embla struggled.

She forced her great head upward, wings quivering, blood dripping from her torn membranes.

Astrid… let me stand… let me fight—

"No!" Astrid cried. "Your wing—"

But Embla pushed anyway, claws gouging the soil, body shaking with effort. The newborn hatchling felt Embla's agony and let out a tremulous cry — a cry that sparked something dangerous.

Its eyes glowed — bright and wild.

"Astri—!"

Halvar shouted as a Veilbound darted past Sorrek, moving straight for Astrid. Halvar swung his broken oar at its head — the blow knocked the mask sideways but barely slowed it.

"Astrid, look out!"

Astrid spun, flames curling along her arms—

But the newborn moved first.

The tiny dragon inhaled.

Its chest swelled.

Its wings flared.

And with a shrill, cracking screech—

FWOOOOOOSH!

A blazing cone of blue-gold flame erupted from its open jaws — small but *piercingly* intense. It hit the Veilbound square in the chest.

The masked figure staggered, convulsing as blue fire ate through its robes. The flames clung like living threads, burrowing through cloth and skin alike.

The Veilbound collapsed into the ferns.

Halvar stared in disbelief. "The little one… can breathe already…"

Astrid held the newborn close. "She protected us."

The hatchling chirped and tucked its head under Astrid's chin, trembling.

But the priest didn't back down.

"Enough," he snarled. "You are children playing with ancient power."
His voice cracked.
"You cannot control what you've woken."

Astrid's flames dimmed slightly. "Watch me."

The priest raised his relic-blade.

"Hunters — advance!"

Two dozen hunters surged forward in a coordinated rush.

Embla roared — a weak, pained roar, but enough to make the front line falter.

Sorrek swung his hammer, knocking three hunters aside. His warriors joined him, forming a wall of Frostborn steel.

But the hunters pushed harder.

Spears clattered. Shields slammed. Voices rose in fury and fear.

A Veilbound slipped behind the main line.

Astrid felt it before she saw it — a cold pressure behind her, a shadow out of rhythm with the forest's pulse.

She spun—

Too slow.

The Veilbound struck.

Its pale hand slashed toward the newborn — not Astrid — the newborn.

Astrid screamed:

"NO!"

She didn't cast flame this time.

She *unleashed power.*

It surged from her in a blinding explosion — blue-white fire spiraling outward in a circular shockwave, tearing through grass, moss, fallen leaves.

The forest itself reacted.

Roots ripped up from the earth, coiling like serpents around the Veilbound's limbs. Branches snapped down and pinned its torso. The ground cracked beneath Astrid's feet.

Hunters screamed and stumbled backward.

The young priest shielded his face from the blast. "She's a conduit—! She's channeling the ancient fire—!"

Astrid gasped as the power bled out of her, her legs buckling.

The newborn squeaked in alarm. Embla cried out through the bond.

Astrid—stop—
You'll burn yourself—

But it was too late.

The shockwave blasted across the clearing, and the hunters were thrown like rag dolls, crashing into tree trunks, skidding across moss, tumbling through ferns.

Silence followed.

Crackling brush.

Falling soot.

The faint trembling breath of the newborn.

Astrid collapsed to her knees, vision swimming.

Halvar rushed to her side. "Astrid—Astrid, are you hurt?"

She swallowed, trying to steady her breath. "I… I didn't mean to do that."

Sorrek stared at her with awe and fear. "The Echo-Fire answered you. Even Frostborn can't command such magic."

Embla pressed her muzzle against Astrid's shoulder, weak but steady.

You protected us.
You saved her.
That is what matters.

Astrid hugged the newborn close. "I won't let them take you. Any of you."

A groan rose from the far end of the clearing.

The priest.

He staggered upright, trembling, eyes wild with terror.

He pointed at Astrid with a shaking hand.

"The High Priest… will… erase you."

He ripped a strip of fabric from his cloak, dipped it into his own blood, and slammed it against a nearby tree trunk — leaving a crimson sigil smeared across the bark.

A hunter's mark.

A death warrant.

"This forest will burn," he hissed. "The Order will not stop."

Then he stumbled backward into the pines, retreating with the few hunters still conscious.

The message was clear:

They weren't giving up.

They were regrouping.

And the High Priest was coming.

Astrid stood slowly, newborn in her arms, Embla leaning into her, her flames flickering weak but alive.

"We need to move," she whispered.

Sorrek nodded with grim certainty.

"The second wave will come," he said. "Stronger. Prepared."

Halvar placed a hand on Astrid's shoulder.

"Then we must be ready first."

Embla lifted her head.

We run…
but next time…
we fight.

Astrid looked toward the deeper forest, where shadows thickened like a waiting path.

She tightened her hold on her dragons.

"Then let's go."

They slipped into the trees just as the forest swallowed the clearing behind them —
and the Echo-Fire's glow faded into the roots of the earth.

Into the Deep Paths

The forest grew stranger the deeper they went.

The air grew cooler, denser — not with cold, but with age.
Light filtered down through the pine canopy in thin shafts, dancing across moss-covered stones like wandering spirits.

The ground dipped and rose in smooth, unnatural curves, as though shaped not by roots, but by memory.

Sorrek led the way, steps steady but wary.
Halvar followed behind him, hand pressed to his ribs, breath tight.
Astrid walked in the middle, newborn in her arms, Embla leaning against her side like a wounded wolf refusing to fall.

Every few steps, Embla stumbled.

Every stumble stabbed Astrid's heart.

"Slow down," Astrid whispered. "We can rest soon."

Embla shuddered, voice faint.

**No…
keep moving…
the hunters won't wait…**

The newborn chirped anxiously and pressed its glowing snout against Embla's cheek.

A faint, shimmering thread of warmth passed between them.

Embla inhaled sharply.

**She… gives heat…
Not fire…
but strength…**

Astrid blinked. "She can do that?"

Sorrek turned, astonished. "The young one shares vitality? That is a gift no Frostborn song speaks of."

Halvar gave the newborn a shaky smile. "She's stronger than she looks."

Astrid stroked the baby dragon's head. "She's everything."

The newborn preened under her touch — wings fluttering in sleepy pride.

But Embla still limped, still trembled, still bled.

The forest seemed to sense it.

Branches lowered overhead like hands reaching for them.
Moss shivered beneath their feet.
A distant hum — like a melody trapped in the wind —
drifted through the trees.

Sorrek slowed.

"You feel that?" he murmured.

Astrid nodded. "It's… calling."

Halvar frowned. "What is?"

Sorrek raised a finger.

The wind fell still.

The forest breathed in.

And Astrid heard it.

A whisper.
Soft.
Ancient.
Curling around her name like a leaf drawn into flame.

Astri—id…

She froze.

Her fire flickered along her skin in response — not summoned, but awakened.

Embla lifted her head.

**The forest knows you…
It knows what you carry.**

The newborn chirped excitedly, eyes glowing brighter than before.

Sorrek studied the trees with a reverence Astrid had never seen in him.

"I have heard tales," he rumbled. "Old stories, from before my grandfather's bones were dust. They say the Forest of Echoes remembers every flame that has lived."

Halvar swallowed. "Every flame?"

"Every dragon," Sorrek said, voice low. "And every rider."

The whisper came again — faint, like breath against Astrid's ear.

Come.
Come deeper.
Bring the flame.

Astrid took an involuntary step forward.

The newborn tensed in her arms.

Embla's eyes widened with sudden fear.

Astrid… don't…

But Astrid felt the pull — a gentle, undeniable tug somewhere beneath her ribs. A flame that wasn't quite hers.

"The forest wants us to follow," she whispered.

Sorrek nodded grimly. "Yes. And we must."

Halvar stared. "Why?"

"Because," Sorrek said, "if the Echoes call the triad flame, then something old has woken. Something that may save Embla. Something that may doom us all."

They walked on.

The Deep Path

The ground sloped downward, winding into a hollow where sunlight barely reached. Luminous moss clung to the rocks, glowing faintly blue — the same shade as dragonfire.

The newborn chirped excitedly, kicking tiny legs.

Embla shivered.
Astrid held her closer.

The whisper grew louder.

**Come, Flame-Bound.
Come to the heart.**

Astrid's breath quickened.

She felt the forest seeing her — not her body, not her face, but her *fire*, the braided flame she carried with her dragons.

She whispered, half in fear, half in awe:

"Is the forest alive?"

Sorrek shook his head. "It does not live."

Then he glanced around, eyes narrowing.

"It remembers."

Halvar tightened his grip on his makeshift weapon. "Memories don't whisper."

Sorrek gave him a grim look. "These do."

Embla whimpered suddenly, collapsing fully against Astrid.

"Astrid—!" Halvar cried.

The newborn screeched and scrambled closer, pressing its side to Embla's torn wing.

Astrid knelt, tears burning her eyes.

"Embla… Embla stay with me—"

Embla's breath hitched.

I feel… cold.
Too cold…

Astrid felt a surge of panic.

"No, no, no—just hold on—"

The forest went silent.

Utterly silent.

Then—

A sound echoed through the hollow.

A deep, resonant hum.

The ground glowed faintly beneath them, tracing curling shapes — runes? vines? bones? — that pulsed once like a heartbeat.

Sorrek's eyes widened.

"This place… this is no ordinary hollow. This is—"

The whisper rose, clear as a distant voice:

The Sanctum of the First Flame.
Enter, Fire-Bound.
Enter, and remember what was lost.

Astrid looked down at Embla's trembling form.

Then at the newborn pressed desperately against her.

Then at the glowing hollow opening ahead — a cavern mouth carved from gnarled roots and stone, pulsing faintly with dragon-colored light.

She stood on shaking legs.

"Come on," she whispered to Embla and the newborn.

"We're going in."

The Sanctum of the First Flame

The hollow swallowed them whole.

Its entrance wasn't a cave exactly — not rock, not soil. It was something *grown*, a twisting lattice of ancient roots fused together with stone so old it had turned smooth as polished bone. Moss glowed faintly along every curve, casting dim blue-gold light that shimmered like living fire.

Astrid stepped inside.

The newborn tightened itself around her collarbone, trembling with anticipation.
Embla pressed close, leaning so heavily that Astrid braced her with both arms.
Halvar ducked beneath the low archway, grimacing at the tight distance between walls.

Sorrek entered last, his massive frame nearly scraping the roots overhead.
"This place was not built for giants," he muttered.

The air grew warmer as they descended.

Not from heat — from *memory*.

Astrid felt it as a hum beneath her feet, a pulse in the walls, a subtle rhythm that matched the beat of her triad bond.

The whisper returned, clearer now:

Astri—id...
bring the flame...
bring the heart...

She swallowed hard.

"Do you hear that?" she asked.

Halvar shook his head. "I only hear my own nerves rattling."

Sorrek frowned. "I hear echoes, but not words."

Embla lifted her head.

**The voice... knows you.
It knew me... before I was born.**

Astrid felt her skin prickle. "What does that mean?"

Before anyone could answer, the tunnel opened into a vast chamber.

The Chamber of First Flame

The ceiling soared high above them, lost in swirling mist and strands of glowing moss. The walls curved in perfect circles, layered like the inside of an ancient shell.

In the center stood a stone basin, cracked with age.

Inside it burned—

not fire,
not light,
but a **memory of fire.**

A swirling ember-lit shape, hovering just above the basin, shifting like smoke trapped in amber.

The newborn gasped and wriggled out of Astrid's arms.

It scrambled toward the basin.

Embla followed weakly, dragging her damaged wing.

"Astrid," Halvar warned, "is this safe?"

"I... think it is."

The newborn reached the basin and chirped softly. The ember responded — pulsing brighter.

Embla leaned close.

And the ember flared—

FWOOOOOM—

A wave of heat rolled through the chamber — not burning, not painful, but deep, radiant, alive.

Astrid staggered.

Images flashed behind her eyes.

Not visions.
Not memories.
Echoes.

Echoes of the First Dragons

She saw a great dragon unfurl its wings above a blazing forest.
A woman riding on its back, her eyes glowing with the same braided fire Astrid now held.
A circle of monks kneeling in terror, their relic-spears cracking under scorching heat.

She saw another rider — a man this time — falling beside his dying dragon as a Veilbound sank a relic-blade into its heart.

She saw the last brood fleeing north beyond snow and ice, pursued by white-masked shadows.

She saw the Purge begin.

She saw the Purge end.

And in all of it, she saw **three flames.**

Always three.

A dragon.
A hatchling.
A rider.

Braided by fate.

Braided by fire.

When the vision faded, Astrid gasped and dropped to her knees.

Halvar rushed to her. "Astrid! Astrid, look at me—are you hurt?"

She shook her head, breath unsteady. "I saw them. The old riders. The first bond. They fought the Order… and died for it."

Sorrek knelt beside her.

"It means your bond is older than their fear," he said. "Older than the monastery. Older than the world as we know it."

Embla reached the basin and lowered her head.

The ember swirled.
Shifted.
Reached for her.

A tendril of golden light touched her snout.

Embla gasped — her whole body arching as warmth flowed through her like water.

Her torn wing twitched.
Her breathing steadied.
Her eyes brightened.

Astrid…
Her voice trembled with wonder.
It heals me…

Astrid cried out in relief.

But then the ember dimmed suddenly — the healing flickered — and a tremor ran through the chamber.

The newborn screeched in alarm.

The roots overhead shivered.

Sorrek rose, hammer ready. "Something's wrong."

Astrid felt it — a cold spear of dread piercing her chest.

"No," she whispered. "Not here. Not now."

The air twisted.

The whisper that had guided them all this time returned

—

—but it was no longer soft.

It was **urgent.**

Astri—id…
they come…
RUN.

Halvar stiffened. "Who—"

Then they heard it.

Bootsteps.

Echoing down the tunnel behind them.

Dozens.

Armor clattering.
Spears scraping.
Voices chanting a low, rhythmic prayer.

Sorrek swore under his breath.

"The second wave. The monastery found the entrance."

Astrid grabbed Embla, helping her up. The newborn scrambled into her arms, crying out in fear.

The ember flickered rapidly — like a heartbeat entering panic.

Another tremor shook the chamber.

And the whisper cried out:

Flee, Flame-Bound!
Flee!
The Bridge must live—
before the world burns!

Astrid turned toward the exit.

"We run," she said.

Embla pressed close.

Halvar lifted his makeshift weapon.

Sorrek's jaw set like iron.

The hunters' shadows spilled into the tunnel behind them.

And the Chamber of First Flame shuddered with the weight of prophecy.

The Sanctum of the First Flame

The hollow swallowed them whole.

Its entrance wasn't a cave exactly — not rock, not soil. It was something *grown*, a twisting lattice of ancient roots fused together with stone so old it had turned smooth as polished bone. Moss glowed faintly along every curve, casting dim blue-gold light that shimmered like living fire.

Astrid stepped inside.

The newborn tightened itself around her collarbone, trembling with anticipation.

Embla pressed close, leaning so heavily that Astrid braced her with both arms.
Halvar ducked beneath the low archway, grimacing at the tight distance between walls.

Sorrek entered last, his massive frame nearly scraping the roots overhead.
"This place was not built for giants," he muttered.

The air grew warmer as they descended.

Not from heat — from *memory*.

Astrid felt it as a hum beneath her feet, a pulse in the walls, a subtle rhythm that matched the beat of her triad bond.

The whisper returned, clearer now:

Astri—id…
bring the flame…
bring the heart…

She swallowed hard.

"Do you hear that?" she asked.

Halvar shook his head. "I only hear my own nerves rattling."

Sorrek frowned. "I hear echoes, but not words."

Embla lifted her head.

The voice… knows you.
It knew me… before I was born.

Astrid felt her skin prickle. "What does that mean?"

Before anyone could answer, the tunnel opened into a vast chamber.

The Chamber of First Flame

The ceiling soared high above them, lost in swirling mist and strands of glowing moss. The walls curved in perfect circles, layered like the inside of an ancient shell.

In the center stood a stone basin, cracked with age.

Inside it burned—

not fire,
not light,
but a **memory of fire.**

A swirling ember-lit shape, hovering just above the basin, shifting like smoke trapped in amber.

The newborn gasped and wriggled out of Astrid's arms.

It scrambled toward the basin.

Embla followed weakly, dragging her damaged wing.

"Astrid," Halvar warned, "is this safe?"

"I… think it is."

The newborn reached the basin and chirped softly. The ember responded — pulsing brighter.

Embla leaned close.

And the ember flared—

FWOOOOOM—

A wave of heat rolled through the chamber — not burning, not painful, but deep, radiant, alive.

Astrid staggered.

Images flashed behind her eyes.

Not visions.
Not memories.
Echoes.

Echoes of the First Dragons

She saw a great dragon unfurl its wings above a blazing forest.
A woman riding on its back, her eyes glowing with the same braided fire Astrid now held.
A circle of monks kneeling in terror, their relic-spears cracking under scorching heat.

She saw another rider — a man this time — falling beside his dying dragon as a Veilbound sank a relic-blade into its heart.

She saw the last brood fleeing north beyond snow and ice, pursued by white-masked shadows.

She saw the Purge begin.

She saw the Purge end.

And in all of it, she saw **three flames.**

Always three.

A dragon.
A hatchling.
A rider.

Braided by fate.

Braided by fire.

When the vision faded, Astrid gasped and dropped to her knees.

Halvar rushed to her. "Astrid! Astrid, look at me—are you hurt?"

She shook her head, breath unsteady. "I saw them. The old riders. The first bond. They fought the Order… and died for it."

Sorrek knelt beside her.

"It means your bond is older than their fear," he said. "Older than the monastery. Older than the world as we know it."

Embla reached the basin and lowered her head.

The ember swirled.
Shifted.
Reached for her.

A tendril of golden light touched her snout.

Embla gasped — her whole body arching as warmth flowed through her like water.

Her torn wing twitched.
Her breathing steadied.
Her eyes brightened.

Astrid…
Her voice trembled with wonder.
It heals me…

Astrid cried out in relief.

But then the ember dimmed suddenly — the healing flickered — and a tremor ran through the chamber.

The newborn screeched in alarm.

The roots overhead shivered.

Sorrek rose, hammer ready. "Something's wrong."

Astrid felt it — a cold spear of dread piercing her chest.

"No," she whispered. "Not here. Not now."

The air twisted.

The whisper that had guided them all this time returned

—

—but it was no longer soft.

It was **urgent.**

Astri—id…
they come…
RUN.

Halvar stiffened. "Who—"

Then they heard it.

Bootsteps.

Echoing down the tunnel behind them.

Dozens.

Armor clattering.
Spears scraping.
Voices chanting a low, rhythmic prayer.

Sorrek swore under his breath.

"The second wave. The monastery found the entrance."

Astrid grabbed Embla, helping her up. The newborn scrambled into her arms, crying out in fear.

The ember flickered rapidly — like a heartbeat entering panic.

Another tremor shook the chamber.

And the whisper cried out:

Flee, Flame-Bound!
Flee!
The Bridge must live—
before the world burns!

Astrid turned toward the exit.

"We run," she said.

Embla pressed close.

Halvar lifted his makeshift weapon.

Sorrek's jaw set like iron.

The hunters' shadows spilled into the tunnel behind them.

And the Chamber of First Flame shuddered with the weight of prophecy.

CHAPTER 30

THE FIRE OF CHOICES

When the Sanctum Trembles

The roots above the sanctum quivered.

Dust drifted from the ceiling.
The ember inside the stone basin pulsed in frantic bursts —
no longer a calm memory of fire, but a warning flame.

Sorrek planted his feet, hammer raised.
"Positions! They'll breach in seconds!"

Halvar tightened his grip on his broken oar, jaw clenched
so hard a vein stood out along his temple.
"I'll defend the rear. You get Astrid moving."

Astrid didn't move.

She stood frozen, staring at the trembling roots overhead,
the newborn wailing softly in her arms, Embla leaning
heavily against her leg.

Embla's newly healed strength flickered — not gone, but
fragile. Her wing twitched painfully.

Astrid... we cannot fight them here...
Not with the small one...
Not with the echo watching...

Astrid swallowed hard.

"But if we run again..."

Halvar turned, gripping her shoulders.

"You run," he said softly. "You run because you must live.
Because they fear *you*. Because they'll burn this whole forest down
just to break your bond."

His eyes glistened.

"And I won't lose you."

Footsteps thundered through the tunnel — boots on stone, armor clattering, men shouting orders.

Sorrek roared, "BRACE!"

A hunter slammed through the tunnel mouth with a shield raised — only for Sorrek's hammer to crash into it, sending him flying back into the men behind him.

A second hunter slid beneath Sorrek's guard, relic-steel spear thrusting toward Astrid.

Halvar intercepted him, wooden oar clattering against steel. The blow sent Halvar staggering, but he didn't fall.

"GO!" he shouted, shoving the hunter away.

Astrid clutched the newborn and turned to Embla. "Can you fly?"

Embla shook her head, pain wracking her body.

**Not high… not far…
but I can move.
I can run.**

Sorrek grabbed Astrid's arm, pulling her toward a narrow exit at the far side of the chamber — a tunnel partially hidden behind a curtain of glowing moss.

"This way! The sanctum has deep paths — old Frostborn routes!"

Astrid hesitated.

Her gaze drifted back to the stone basin — to the ember swirling above it.

It pulsed again —
thump
thump

like a heart.

And in the space between flame and memory, Astrid saw a flash:

A cloaked man striking a dragon's neck.
A rider falling to her knees.
A newborn dragon crushed beneath the heel of a Veilbound.
Calven raising a relic-spear drenched in dragonblood.
Malrek chanting beside a burning monastery altar.

A future.
A past.
A warning.

The newborn shrieked — the sound snapping Astrid back to the present.

"Astrid!" Halvar cried. "DO NOT FREEZE!"

Another hunter charged —

Sorrek blocked the blow and crushed him into the wall.

Embla nudged Astrid urgently.

Astrid… choose…

The word burned through Astrid like fire.

She wasn't choosing to run.

She was choosing them.

"Come on!" she gasped. "We're going!"

She grabbed Embla's foreleg, helping her up. Embla stumbled but rose, wings dragging, teeth bared.

The newborn clung to Astrid's shoulder, shaking.

They turned toward the moss-covered exit—

But the sanctum itself reacted.

As Astrid approached the glowing moss, the vines pulled back.

Revealing a tunnel she hadn't seen before.

A tunnel carved not by men or dragons —
but by **magic.**

Sorrek's eyes widened. "The sanctum opens for you."

Before Astrid could respond, a hunter shouted:

"THEY'RE ESCAPING—!"

Another wave of monastery soldiers surged into the chamber.
Veilbound stepped through the smoke-like shadows behind them, masks gleaming in the emberlight.

Embla growled.
Sorrek lifted his hammer.
Halvar readied his broken oar.

Astrid tightened her grip on the newborn.

And as they stepped into the newly opened tunnel, the whisper returned — no longer faint.

It echoed like a voice carved from flame:

Run, Flame-Bound.
Run to the heart.
For only there…
can the bridge be forged.

Astrid didn't look back.

She plunged into the tunnel.

The forest roots sealed behind her—

Just as the hunters reached the threshold.

The sanctum shook with their fury.

The Heart of the Deep Paths

The tunnel swallowed them in total darkness.

For several breathless seconds, Astrid could hear nothing but her own heartbeat — her own, and the newborn's, and Embla's, all weaving together in that pulsing triad rhythm.

Then the roots overhead began to glow.

Soft blue at first.
Then gold.
Then a shifting mixture of both, like dragonfire bottled behind bark and sap.

Sorrek let out a low breath. "By the ancestors…"

Halvar leaned against the wall, panting from the last fight. "This place is… alive."

Astrid touched the nearest root — it pulsed under her fingers like a warm vein.

"No," she whispered.
"It's awake."

Embla limped beside her, each step trembling, but her eyes gleamed brighter with every pulse of the root-light.

This is old magic…
older than the purge…
older than the first dragons…

The newborn chirped softly and pressed its snout to the wall. The roots recoiled as if ticklish — and then glowed brighter.

Sorrek took a cautious step forward. "The small one… she's guiding it."

The newborn chirped again — louder this time — and the tunnel shifted.

Literally shifted.

Roots peeled back.
The ground curved to the left.
Openings sealed behind them.
New paths opened ahead.

Halvar stiffened. "It's moving the tunnels?"

Astrid nodded slowly. "It's protecting us."

No, Embla whispered.
It's guiding us deeper.
Toward something… waiting.

Halvar swallowed hard. "And is that something good or bad?"

Embla didn't answer.

Because none of them knew.

The Walls Remember

As they moved deeper, the shifting walls began to show shapes imprinted in the bark.

Not carvings.

Not paintings.

Memories.

Flickering silhouettes like shadows caught in amber.

Astrid paused, breath catching.

"Do you see that?"

Halvar squinted. "I see… silhouettes? Are they alive?"

"No," Sorrek murmured. "Echoes."

Embla nodded weakly.

**The forest remembers fire…
remembers every dragon that lived…**

The newborn squeaked in excitement and pressed its face against another glowing patch.

A burst of images flared:

— A massive dragon swooping low over snow.
— A rider with hair braided in gold, laughing.
— A monastery tower crumbling under fire.
— A child draped in dragonhide, being sworn into a sacred bond.

Astrid recoiled.

"Did you see that?!"

Sorrek nodded grimly. "Old times. Old war. Old bonds."

Halvar wiped sweat from his brow.

"Why show us this now?"

Astrid touched the wall gently.

Because you are the next.
Because the forest sees your fire.
Because you are the bridge.

The whisper wasn't spoken — it simply pressed into her thoughts like a truth she'd always known.

The newborn whimpered softly, wings drooping.

Astrid hugged her close. "I know, little fireheart. It's a lot."

The Growing Fear

Embla stumbled.

Her wing scraped the tunnel floor, leaving a streak of

blood across glowing moss.

Astrid winced. "Embla — stop. Rest."

Embla shook her head violently.

No…
we cannot stop here…
something follows…

Sorrek stiffened. "Hunters?"

Embla's eyes darkened.

No.
Not men.
Something older.
Something that hates fire.

Halvar's grip tightened on his oar.
"That doesn't sound like anything I've met."

Sorrek glanced back down the passage behind them.

"The forest is shifting to hide us… but whatever follows doesn't need eyes to find flame."

Astrid swallowed hard.

"How close is it?"

Embla closed her eyes, trembling.

Close enough to smell us…
not close enough to strike.
Not yet.

The newborn clutched Astrid's tunic, shivering.

And suddenly, Astrid felt it too—

A cold wrongness.
Like frost on a grave.
Like breath that didn't belong to anything living.

She whispered:

"What is that…?"

The forest answered.

A shadow of the old purge.
Left behind.
Hungry.
Unfinished.

Halvar exhaled sharply. "A shadow? What kind of shadow?"

Sorrek shoved him forward. "One that wants to kill us. Move."

They quickened their pace.

The roots ahead parted again, showing a descending path lined with stones carved in circular patterns.

Embla hissed.

We descend… to its heart…
Astrid… are you ready?

Astrid clutched both dragons close.

"No," she whispered.
"But I will be."

And they stepped into the spiral of glowing stone.

The Hollow That Remembers Blood

The spiral path narrowed as they descended.

The glowing roots faded.
The stone beneath their feet grew colder.
The newborn tucked itself beneath Astrid's chin, shivering hard enough to shake.

Embla's wings twitched restlessly, her head low, breath

coming in short huffs.

It's close…
Her voice wavered with fear and instinct.
I smell… old death.
Hungry death.

Sorrek's grip tightened on his hammer.

Halvar shifted closer to Astrid, placing himself slightly ahead of her, as if his broken oar could do anything against the thing following them.

Astrid whispered, "What *is* this shadow?"

The forest seemed to exhale.

A cold wind whipped down the tunnel — sharp as knives. It extinguished the moss-light ahead, plunging half the passage into pitch-black.

The newborn squeaked in terror.

Sorrek raised his hammer, voice low and grim. "Whatever it is… it's not alive."

Halvar swallowed. "Dead?"

Sorrek shook his head slowly.

"Worse."

The First Glimpse

The darkness behind them stirred.

Astrid turned slowly.

A shape slithered out of the shadows — massive, but half-formed, as if made of smoke and ash instead of flesh.

It had wings — or the memory of them — tattered and broken.
Eyes — or hollow sockets where fire had once burned.

Claws — or streaks of blackened mist shaped like talons.

It crawled along the walls like a dying nightmare.

Embla staggered backward.

No… no, that's… that's a flame-eater…

Halvar's face drained of color. "A what?"

Sorrek stepped protectively in front of the group. "A dragon's shadow. Made after death. Born of relic-blades and broken magic."

Astrid clutched the newborn tight.

Sorrek continued, voice grim:

"They appear after a dragon is slain by the Order. The monks steal the fire. The body dies. But the **rage** lives."

Halvar whispered hoarsely, "A ghost…"

"No," Sorrek growled. "A wound."

When It Sees Astrid

The shadow paused.

It raised its head.

It inhaled.

Astrid felt its attention like a claw scraping her ribs.

The newborn screamed, its tiny body sparking with terrified flame.
Embla lunged in front of Astrid, wings flared, but her bad wing dragged limply behind her.

Astrid — RUN! she screamed into Astrid's mind.

Astrid didn't move.

She couldn't.

The shadow lowered itself, stalking closer.
The tunnel walls warped around its presence — roots shriveling, moss turning black.

Halvar raised his oar.

"Stay behind me."

The shadow hissed — a sound like burning bones.

And Astrid felt something slam through her mind.

A vision.

A dragon screaming as a relic-blade pierced its skull.
A monk chanting as its fire was drained.
A newborn crushed under armored boots.
A mother's flame torn from her chest.

The shadow lunged.

Astrid gasped and stumbled back.

The newborn clung to her neck, crying in pain.

Embla roared and forced herself between Astrid and the creature, even though her legs shook violently.

Sorrek charged, hammer swinging.

THOOOM—

He struck the shadow dead-on.

The hammer passed through it—
—but the creature recoiled as if hurt.

Sorrek staggered back.

"It feels impact… but it isn't flesh."

Halvar moved to Astrid.
"Astrid, we cannot fight this thing. You must run."

Embla snarled.

She won't abandon me—

But Astrid stepped forward.

Embla froze.

Halvar froze.

Sorrek froze.

Astrid's voice trembled.

"…I'm not running."

The shadow slithered forward.

Astrid raised her hand.

Her flame flickered weakly — too small, too afraid.

The shadow inhaled that fear like a feast.

The Newborn's Instinct

The newborn suddenly wriggled free of Astrid's arms.

"No!" Astrid cried as the tiny dragon dropped to the ground.

The hatchling planted its claws in the dirt, arched its back, and hissed with a sound far too large for its body.

Its wings flared—
Its eyes blazed gold—
Its throat lit with blue fire—

FWOOOM—

A beam of flame shot from its tiny jaw.

The shadow shrieked, recoiling violently as the newborn's fire burned through its misty shape.

Embla gasped.

She can burn the dead...
she burns shadows...
she burns memory—

Astrid stared in shock.

"What... what are you?"

The newborn chirped fiercely, then hissed again, flames curling around its jaws.

The shadow hissed back, retreating a step—

But then it gathered itself and surged forward with a roar like tearing metal.

Sorrek bellowed, "ASTRID, MOVE!"

The newborn leapt between Astrid and the shadow—

Embla tackled the newborn aside, protecting her.

The shadow reared back—

And Astrid made her choice.

Astrid's Fire Unleashed

"No."

Her voice cracked into flame.

She stepped forward, fire swirling around her arms — uncontrolled, wild, desperate.

The shadow lunged.

Astrid thrust both hands out—

KRAAAAAA—BOOOOM!

A shockwave of blue-gold fire exploded from her chest, through her arms, into the tunnel ahead.

The entire Deep Path lit up like lightning ripping through

roots.

The shadow screamed —
A tearing, ragged, unnatural shriek —
Its form unraveling in streams of smoke and ash.

It clawed the air, trying to hold itself together—

But Astrid's fire burned through it, burning memory, burning death, burning everything.

In one final shriek, the shadow shattered—
and dissolved into swirling sparks that faded into the ground.

Silence crashed down.

Astrid collapsed to her knees, lungs burning, vision spinning.

Sorrek caught her before she hit the floor.

Halvar knelt beside her, shaking. "Astrid, Astrid—can you hear me?"

Astrid swallowed, voice faint.

"I didn't mean to do that. I just… reacted."

Embla limped to her, pressing her forehead against Astrid's.

You saved us…
Fire-Bound…
You saved us all.

The newborn climbed into Astrid's lap and nuzzled her chin.

Sorrek stared at her like he'd never seen her before.

Then he whispered:

"You killed a flame-eater.
No mortal can do that.
Not even Frostborn."

Halvar whispered:

"My girl… what are you becoming?"

Astrid trembled.

"I don't know."

The tunnel ahead glowed faintly.

The whisper returned — softer this time.

**Come, Flame-Bound.
Only one path remains.**

Astrid stood, leaning on Embla and Halvar.

"Then let's finish this."

Together, they stepped deeper into the forest's heart.

The Heartstone Bridge

The tunnel widened without warning.

One moment they trudged through twisting roots and shifting stone,
the next they emerged into a chamber so vast it seemed impossible it lived beneath the forest.

Astrid stopped breathing.

Sorrek let out a low, reverent curse.

Halvar's hand found his daughter's shoulder in trembling awe.

Embla collapsed.

The Heartstone Chamber

The cavern's walls curved upward into a perfect dome. Every surface — roots, stone, moss, even air — glowed softly with swirling blue-gold light.

At the center rose a colossal stone archway, half-buried in the earth.

It was carved from the same material as the basin they'd seen before…
but cracked, ancient, etched with runes older than any language Astrid knew.

A shimmering film of starlight hung across the arch like a doorway made of breath.

The newborn gasped, eyes widening, pupils narrowing to slits.

Embla tried to rise —

—and failed.

She crumpled fully onto her side, chest heaving, wing dragging limply.

"Astrid—!" Halvar dropped to his knees beside her.

Astrid fell beside Embla, hands shaking. "No, no… Embla, stay with me—"

Embla's eyes fluttered weakly.

**My fire…
it's burning wrong…
I feel…
cold again…**

"No," Astrid whispered fiercely. "The sanctum healed you. It should have held."

Sorrek approached slowly, brow furrowed.

"It *was* healing her. But the flame-eater… its shadow touched her. Took part of her fire."

Astrid stared at him.
"What does that mean?"

Sorrek knelt, laying a hand on the stone floor.

"The only way to restore her fully… is through the Heartstone Bridge."

He pointed to the archway.

Halvar's eyes widened. "That's real? I thought it was just Frostborn legend."

Sorrek's voice dropped reverent and terrified.

"It's where a rider and dragon become one flame. Where they share core fire, not surface fire. It is the old ritual — the one the monastery burned from the world."

Astrid's heart slammed against her ribs.

"You mean…"

Sorrek nodded.

"If she passes through that arch with you, Astrid… you will be bound for life.
Not just through emotion.
Not just through magic."

His gaze deepened.

"Through spirit."

Astrid swallowed.
Her hands shook.

"Will it save her?"

Sorrek hesitated.

"The old songs say yes."

"And the price?" Halvar demanded.

Sorrek exhaled.

"The rider must give part of their own flame. Permanently."

Astrid froze.

Halvar grabbed her shoulders, panic rising in his voice. "No. Astrid, listen to me. You don't know what that does. You don't know what it costs."

Astrid stared at Embla — her Embla — shivering, gasping, fading.

"I can't lose her."

Halvar shook her.

"You are sixteen! You don't give up your life at sixteen!"

Astrid's voice broke.

"I'm not giving it up. I'm sharing it."

Embla whimpered, pressing her snout weakly against Astrid's knee.

Astri—d…
let me go…
do not burn yourself for me…

"Never."

Halvar's Secret Breaks

Halvar grabbed Astrid's wrists.

"Listen to me. Your fire — your ability — it isn't normal. It isn't chance. It isn't some miracle."

Astrid blinked through tears. "What are you talking

about?"

Halvar clenched his jaw, shaking.

"I should have told you years ago… but I was afraid. I thought I could protect you by staying silent."

"Protect me from what?"

He closed his eyes.

"When I was a young man… before the Purge ended… I rode with a monk order."

Astrid's blood went cold.

"No."

Halvar nodded, tears sliding down his soot-stained face.

"Yes. I was part of the Order of the Bridge."

Astrid staggered back as if struck.

Sorrek's hammer nearly fell from his grip.

"You?" he breathed. "A Bridge-Keeper?"

Halvar bowed his head.

"I helped hunt dragons."

Astrid's legs buckled.

Her voice came out barely audible.

"You helped… kill them?"

Halvar choked on the words.

"I held the spears. I held the torches. I followed orders like a coward. Until one day — a dragon saved my life instead of burning me."

Embla's eyes narrowed weakly, watching him.

The newborn growled softly.

Halvar wiped his face, shaking violently.

"That dragon… blessed me with a spark of its fire instead of killing me. A parting gift. A curse. A warning. I carried that spark in my blood — and I passed it to you."

Astrid whispered:

"My fire… came from…"

"Yes." Halvar swallowed hard.
"You are a child of dragonfire."

The newborn chirped in awe.

Embla stared at her with something like realization — and sorrow.

**Astrid… you were meant for this…
even before I hatched.**

Astrid clenched her fists, tears falling freely.

"If my fire came from them… then I owe them everything."

Halvar grabbed her again.

"No. You owe them nothing! You owe *yourself* a life. Not sacrifice. Not destiny."

But Astrid looked at Embla.

And she knew the truth.

"I choose her."

The Newborn's Purpose

The newborn crawled forward on trembling legs, placing itself between Astrid and the archway.

Its eyes glowed gold.

Then it lifted its tiny head, looked directly into Astrid's heart, and projected thought for the first time:

**You cannot cross alone.
A rider's fire is not enough.
A sister flame must join.**

Embla stared at the newborn.

**You… would give your fire?
Your birth-fire?**

The newborn chirped firmly.

**We are three.
We are one.
We cross together.**

Sorrek whispered, stunned,

"The triad flame… it was never meant for battle. It was meant for the Bridge."

Halvar shook his head, horror on his face.

"Astrid. If you do this… you will never be normal again."

Astrid kissed Embla's snout.

"Good."

She stood — newborn at her neck, Embla leaning on her, Halvar gripping her arm, Sorrek watching with reverence and fear.

She faced the shimmering archway.

And whispered:

"We cross."

The arch pulsed.

The chamber trembled.

The whisper rose loud and clear:

Enter, Flame-Bound.
Enter the Heartstone Bridge.
Enter — and become more.

Astrid took her first step—

The Bridge of Three Flames

The shimmering arch pulsed like a heartbeat.

Astrid stood before it, Embla leaning against her, the newborn wrapped around her shoulders like a trembling scarf of warm gold.

Sorrek and Halvar stayed a few paces behind, as if afraid of stepping any closer to the ancient magic humming in the air.

The Heartstone Bridge whispered —
soft, thunderous, and alive:

Enter.
Three flames.
One bond.

Embla's breath rattled painfully.

Astri... I am afraid.

Astrid ran her hand gently along Embla's jaw.

"I'm afraid too."

The newborn nuzzled between them, chirping a determined little cry.

Sorrek's voice broke the silence.
"Astrid, once you step through—there is no turning back. The bond will fuse. Your flame will never be yours alone again."

Astrid looked at him, fire glinting in her eyes.

"It already isn't."

Halvar grabbed her elbow.

"Astrid, please. Listen to me—"

She turned slowly, tears shining.

"I *know* what you did. Who you used to be. But you're not that man now. You saved me. You saved Embla. You tried."

Her voice cracked.

"But I was born into this fire. And Embla didn't choose to be hurt. I'll choose for both of us."

Halvar swallowed hard.

"You're my daughter. I want you to live a long life."

Astrid touched his hand.

"I will."

She stepped toward the arch.

The newborn chirped anxiously but did not resist.

Embla forced herself upright, wings trembling, leaning heavily against Astrid.

Together, the three approached the shimmering film of starlight.

The instant Astrid reached toward it—
the runes on the arch blazed.

FWOOM—

Golden fire spiraled upward, enveloping the arch.

Sorrek gasped. "It recognizes you!"

Halvar stumbled backward. "Astrid—!"

Astrid stepped through.

The Bridge Between Worlds

The instant they crossed the threshold, the air changed.

It was no longer a cavern.

No longer roots or stone.

They stood in a space between worlds —
a bridge made of swirling fire, suspended in an endless void
of memories.

Embers drifted like stars.
Shadows of dragons soared overhead.
Whispers filled the air — voices that belonged to no living
tongue.

The newborn clung tighter to Astrid, trembling in awe.

Embla stood straighter, no longer bleeding, though still
weak — as if the Bridge itself was holding her up.

Astrid... where are we?
Embla's voice echoed strangely, doubled, braided with the
newborn's flickering thought.

Astrid swallowed.

"In the old magic."

A shape approached from the glowing horizon.

A dragon — massive, spectral, wings spanning the entire
void.
A rider sat on its back, cloaked in burning light.

The rider raised a hand.

Flame-Bound.
We have waited for you.

Astrid blinked. "You... you're one of the first riders."

The figure nodded.

I am.
And now you must take your place.

Another dragon appeared —
then another.
Then dozens.

Spectral wings spanning eternity.
Eyes like molten gold.
Riders glowing like living stars.

They formed a circle around Astrid, Embla, and the newborn.

The newborn squeaked in fear, pressing into Astrid's neck.

Embla leaned close, eyes shining.

Do not fear, little one…
they honor us.

The first rider spoke:

Three flames.
One heart.
Step forward, Astrid.
Bring your dragons.

Astrid's pulse thundered.

She stepped toward the center of the bridge.

Embla pressed to her right side.

The newborn crawled down into her arms.

The void glowed brighter.

The Merging

The first rider lifted both hands.

Begin.

Fire erupted around Astrid — but it didn't burn.

It wrapped her.

Held her.

Lifted her slightly off the bridge.

The newborn floated from her hands, spinning gently in the air like a drifting firefly.

Embla rose too, her wings hanging limp but glowing with inner fire.

The rider's voice resonated through them:

Share your flames.
Braid them.
Become more.

Embla gasped —
her fire leaping from her chest like a living ribbon of blue-gold flame.

It wrapped around Astrid.

Astrid gasped, clutching her chest as her own fire leapt outward, entwining with Embla's.

The newborn squealed — its flame glowing white-hot — and it joined them, forming a third shining strand.

Three flames.

One bond.

The fire spun faster, brighter—
a braided helix of burning light.

Astrid's heartbeat synced with both dragons —
one steady, one young and flickering.

She felt Embla's memories.
The newborn's instincts.
Their fear.
Their love.
Their fire.

It became hers.

Her flame surged outward—
fierce, wild, ancient—
and the entire bridge blazed with blue-gold light.

The riders bowed.

The dragons roared in approval.

Astrid felt her fire fuse permanently with theirs—
a pulse, a snap, a blazing ignition—

WHOOOSH—

And a shockwave tore across the void.

Astrid fell to her knees.

Embla collapsed beside her, wings trembling but no
longer bleeding.

The newborn crawled to her shoulder, glowing bright as a
star.

The first rider spoke softly:

The Bridge is forged.
Your flames are one.
Your destiny begins now.

Astrid whispered:

"What… what am I now?"

The rider's eyes glowed like suns.

You are the Storm-Bound.

You are the Bridge Reborn.
You are the one the Order fears.

The spectral vision faded—

And Astrid, Embla, and the newborn collapsed back into the Heartstone Chamber.

Sorrek and Halvar caught them before they hit the ground.

Embla breathed steadily.
The newborn burned warm and bright.
Astrid glowed faintly, runes shimmering along her veins like rivers of light.

Halvar stared at her in stunned silence.

Sorrek bowed his head, whispering:

"By the old fires… she has become a legend."

Astrid opened her eyes.

The chamber shook violently.

Above them, distant footsteps grew closer.

The monastery's elite had arrived.

Astrid rose to her feet slowly.

Her fire flickered behind her eyes.

Her dragons stood beside her.

"We're done running," she whispered.

CHAPTER 31

THE UNBROKEN FIRE

The tremor hit first.

A deep, rolling shudder rippled through the Heartstone Chamber, sending dust drifting from the dome above and making the runes along the arch flicker like startled eyes.

Astrid braced herself on Embla's shoulder.

Sorrek turned toward the tunnel they'd sealed before — the one the roots had closed when the sanctum guided them deeper.

Now, the roots were pulling apart.

Not willingly.

They screamed.

The sound wasn't air or voice — it was wood and magic being forced aside, torn open by something that didn't belong in the old places.

Halvar stepped in front of Astrid without thinking, broken oar in his hands, shoulders squared.

The newborn tightened around Astrid's neck, claws digging into her cloak.

Embla's newly strengthened wings flexed — slow, stiff, but not broken anymore. Her breath came steadier now, fire pulsing under her scales.

They come again…
Her voice was low, no longer only afraid.
But we are not who we were.

The roots split.

The tunnel yawned open.

And the monastery's finest stepped through.

The High Priest's Fist

These were not the tired hunters from Havngard's docks.

The first through the tunnel was a man in blackened armor trimmed with gold, his chestplate engraved with a sun pierced by three spears. His face was calm, composed, eyes dark as riverstone.

He carried no spear.

Only a long, thin sword with a pale, glassy blade.

Behind him came soldiers in heavier mail, their shields marked with the monastery's crest. Their relic-spears were longer, etched with fresh runes, drinking in the chamber's light like thirsting mouths.

And behind *them* moved the Veilbound.

These were not like the ones in Havngard.

Their masks were darker. Their robes trimmed in crimson. Their movements too smooth, like they were breathing in someone else's pattern.

The man in blacked armor took in the chamber with one long, slow glance.

His gaze settled on the arch, on Astrid, on Embla, on the newborn dragon glittering at her throat.

He smiled.

"Remarkable."

Sorrek stepped forward, hammer raised. "Name yourself, monk."

The man inclined his head just a touch.

"I am Inquisitor Tareth. Voice of High Priest Malrek. I speak for the Order." His eyes lingered on Astrid. "And I see we have arrived just in time."

Halvar's jaw clenched.

"You're late," he said. "The Bridge is already forged."

Tareth's gaze flicked to him with cool curiosity.

"So it is," he murmured. "I can feel it. The old bond — dragon, hatchling, rider. The High Priest will be… interested."

Embla growled, a low rumble that made the chamber's air vibrate.

We are not yours to interest, little man.

Tareth didn't flinch.

"Astonishing," he said softly. "Its mind touches yours so openly? No discipline at all. No wonder the Purge was needed."

Astrid stepped forward, fire flickering along her arms.

"You don't get to talk about needed."

Tareth studied her closely.

"Child," he said, almost gently, "you have no idea what you are carrying. The Bridge bond is too powerful for a human soul. Left unchecked, it will burn you out from the inside. We are here to take that burden from you."

Astrid stared.

Halvar's voice was a rasp.

"That's how you justify it? You murder dragons and call it mercy?"

Tareth didn't look away from Astrid.

"Murder," he repeated mildly, as if tasting the word. "Such a small word for balancing a world."

Sorrek spat on the floor.

"Enough talk."

He raised his hammer.

Hunters lowered their spears.

The Veilbound stepped forward in eerie unison.

The newborn whimpered.

Embla's wings lifted, casting Astrid in shadow.

Astrid took a breath that tasted like stone and fire and fear.

"We're not going with you," she said.

Tareth sighed, almost regretful.

"I thought you might say that."

He raised his hand.

"Bind them."

The First Strike

The elite hunters moved as one.

Spears lowered. Boots slammed against stone. Shields locked.

They advanced in a tight wedge formation, Veilbound gliding at the flanks like smoke given bones.

Sorrek roared and charged first.

His hammer came down with the force of an avalanche, smashing into the lead shield and splintering it in a single blow. The impact rippled through the entire formation, staggering the front rank.

Halvar darted in behind him, striking with his broken oar like it was a blade — jabbing a hunter's ankle, shoving another off balance, never quite in the place a spear thought he'd be.

The Veilbound flowed around the disruption, ignoring Sorrek and Halvar. Their pale mask-faces turned toward Embla and Astrid.

Toward the triad flame.

Astrid felt their focus like icy fingers on her spine.

The newborn hissed, tiny chest heaving.

Embla took a step forward, planting herself between Astrid and the approaching monks, her breath already heating.

Stay behind me, Astrid.

"No," Astrid whispered. Her flame tingled along her palms. "We do this together."

The nearest Veilbound lunged.

Astrid raised her hand—

—but the forest did not answer here. There were no roots to pull, no trees to rouse. Only stone and echo and old, sleeping fire.

Fine.

Then she would wake that.

She dug down into the braid of their bond — felt Embla's fierce, stubborn flame, the newborn's wild, bright spark, her own uncertain blaze.

Together, she thought.

The newborn chirped, agreeing.

Embla's fire surged.

Astrid flung her hand forward.

FWOOM—

A thick ribbon of blue-gold fire blasted from her palm, arcing low across the stone. The Veilbound twisted aside, faster than any human, but the flame still caught their robes.

They didn't scream.

They burned.

Silent, still, bodies turning to ash that crumbled without a sound.

The hunters recoiled.

"Inquisitor!" one shouted. "She's using chamber-fire!"

Tareth's eyes narrowed, hunger creeping into his voice.

"Good," he said. "We need to see her limit."

He drew his pale-bladed sword.

The blade hummed — not like metal. Like a relic-stone carved into the shape of a weapon.

Embla's growl turned to a snarl.

That thing smells wrong.
Like emptied fire.
Like dragons… stolen.

Astrid swallowed.

"That sword was made from—"

"Yes," Tareth said quietly, almost pleasantly. "From those who chose not to submit."

He stepped forward, unhurried, as the hunters regrouped.

"Again," he ordered. "Press them. Wear her down."

Embla Tries to Rise

The next wave hit harder.

Hunters fanned out, trying to encircle Astrid and the dragons. Spears thrust, probing for gaps. Shields raised against fire, glinting with the oily sheen of sanctified oil meant to resist dragonflame.

Embla inhaled.

Her chest expanded.

She exhaled a roaring torrent of blue fire.

The front line broke beneath it.

Shields glowed red, some melting. Men fell back, armor smoking. One dropped his spear and fell to his knees, retching, as the heat stole his breath.

Embla staggered.

The fire had not been full strength.

Astrid felt the strain through their bond — Embla's pain flaring along the link like a pulled muscle.

"Easy," Astrid whispered. "Don't push—"

They won't stop, Embla snarled.
If I hold back, they kill you.

She lunged, snapping at a hunter who got too close, her claws scraping the stone.

Three spears struck her side — not deep, not fatal, but enough to make her cry out.

Astrid screamed, feeling each stab as if the spears had hit her own ribs.

She staggered back, hand flying to her side — no wound,

no blood, but pain bloomed there all the same.

Halvar shouted, "Astrid, your bond—!"

Tareth watched with clinical interest.

"Yes," he said. "There it is. The cost of the old ways. Shared fire. Shared damage. Shared death."

He smiled slightly.

"Unsustainable."

He moved forward, step by deliberate step.

The Newborn's Terrifying Gift

The newborn had been silent — pressed against Astrid's throat, trembling, eyes fixed on the advancing men.

Now, as Embla roared in pain and Astrid doubled over, something snapped inside the little dragon.

It dropped from Astrid's shoulders, landing with a soft thud on the stone.

Its tiny claws flexed.

Its eyes narrowed.

It inhaled.

Astrid felt it—

Not just flame.

Something else.

Something sharp and strange and ancient.

"Little one—wait—" she gasped.

Too late.

The hatchling opened its mouth—

—but no fire came out.

Not at first.

The sound did.

A sharp, piercing cry that knifed through the chamber like a blade of pure sound:

KREEEEEEEEE—!

The air shuddered.

The runes in the stone flickered.

The hunters screamed, clutching their heads as the sound tore through them. One dropped his spear. Another fell to his knees. A third collapsed, eyes rolling back.

Even Sorrek grunted, staggered by the force of it.

The Veilbound jerked as if yanked by invisible strings, masks tilting, movements stuttering for the first time.

Tareth hissed, eyes narrowing, jaw clenched against the pain.

"A dragonshrieker," he spat. "From a hatchling? Impossible—"

The sound cut off.

And then the flame followed.

Not a cone, not a rope—
a *pulse.*

A tight, concentrated blast like a thrown spear of fire.

It streaked across the chamber and slammed into the ceiling above the hunters, where the stone was already cracked.

BOOOOM—

Rock shattered.

Chunks of stone crashed down, smashing into shields, sending men sprawling, blocking half their advance with new debris.

Dust billowed.

The newborn swayed, panting, tiny body shaking from the effort.

Astrid scooped her up immediately, heart pounding.

"You did so well," she whispered. "You brave little terror."

The hatchling nuzzled her weakly, eyes dimming.

Embla stared.

**She turned voice to weapon…
and aimed it where the chamber would fall.**

Sorrek coughed, eyes wide.

"I have never seen a dragon do that," he rasped.

Tareth pushed rubble off his arm, face twisted in something finally cracking his composure.

Rage.

"Enough," he snapped.

He pointed his pale blade at Astrid.

"No more testing. Kill the elder dragon. Take the hatchling and the girl alive."

Astrid's blood went cold.

The hunters regrouped around their Inquisitor.

Sorrek tightened his grip on his hammer.

Halvar stepped up beside Astrid, breath shaking but eyes steady.

Embla forced herself upright again, blood trailing down her scales, fire burning stubbornly bright behind her eyes.

Astrid felt them both through the bond.

Their pain.
Their fear.
Their refusal to break.

"This ends now," she whispered.

The Triad Flame Unleashed

Astrid closed her eyes.

For a heartbeat, she shut out the chamber, the hunters, the Inquisitor's steady steps.

She only felt:

Embla's fire — old, bruised, unbowed.
The newborn's spark — sharp, clever, defiant.
Her own heart — terrified… and ready.

Together, she thought again.

This time, the answer wasn't just a feeling.

It was words.

Together, Embla agreed.
Together, the newborn echoed, clumsy but sure.

She stepped forward.

Stone hummed beneath her bare feet.

The runes along her arms — the ones that had traced along her veins when she fell from the Bridge — ignited, shining through her skin like molten script.

Sorrek took a step back, eyes wide.

Halvar whispered, "Astrid…?"

Tareth watched closely, sword at the ready.

"What are you?" he breathed.

Astrid opened her eyes.

They burned.

Not just with light.

With *them*.

"You wanted to see my limit," she said.

She lifted both hands.

"Here it is."

The triad flame surged.

It rose from her chest, from her dragons, from the very stone beneath her — a braided whirlwind of blue and gold and white that wrapped around her body, around Embla, around the newborn.

The air roared.

The chamber shook.

The hunters flinched back in instinctive terror.

Tareth did not.

He raised his pale blade, relic-edge gleaming.

"Stand firm!" he shouted. "Relic-steel can cut any flame —"

Astrid moved.

She didn't throw fire this time.

She *became* it.

One step—
and she was at the front of the storm.

Another—
and the braided flame whipped outward, a spiraling wave that wasn't just heat and light, but *will.*

It crashed into the shield line.

Metal screamed.

Sanctified oil sizzled.

The relic-steel spears glowed, then cracked, runes bursting like shattered glass. Shields were ripped from hands. Men were thrown back as if struck by a physical force.

The Veilbound tried to pass through it — their bodies flickering like failing candles.

The triad flame burned hotter around them.

Masks cracked. Robes disintegrated. One by one, they collapsed into ash.

Embla roared, a full-bodied sound that made the chamber ring.

The newborn shrieked again, this time without weaponizing the sound — just adding her voice to the storm.

Astrid walked through the inferno, untouched.

Her hair snapped in the wind of her own power. Her eyes were steady.

Tareth swung his relic-blade down, cutting at the heart of the flame coming toward him.

The pale edge bit into it.

The flame hissed.

For a moment, it parted.

Astrid staggered, feeling the drag — like something was trying to shear her bond in half.

The newborn screamed, clutching at Astrid's throat.

Embla snarled and lurched forward, pouring her fire into the braid.

Astrid grit her teeth.

"NO."

She grabbed the flame with her will — with all three wills braided together — and forced it closed around the blade.

The relic-glass screamed like something living.

Cracks spiderwebbed across its surface.

Tareth's eyes went wide.

"This is not possible—"

The sword exploded.

Shards of pale relic flew outward, evaporating before they struck the stone.

Tareth dropped to one knee, stunned, his hand bleeding where the hilt had been.

For the first time, fear flickered in his eyes.

Astrid stood over him, flames swirling around her like a cloak.

"You don't get to decide what's possible anymore," she

said quietly.

Silence fell.

The remaining hunters stared — half their number on the ground, shields broken, spears cracked, Veilbound gone.

Sorrek leaned on his hammer, chest heaving, watching Astrid as if seeing the shape of a legend forming in front of him.

Halvar's shoulders shook.

"My girl," he whispered. "You *really are* the Bridge."

Tareth rose slowly, breathing hard.

He looked at Astrid — at the dragons — at the shattered relics.

Then he did something none of his men expected.

He stepped back.

"Retreat," he said.

A hunter stared at him, aghast. "Inquisitor—"

"Retreat," Tareth repeated, cold and sharp. "We are not equipped for this fight. The High Priest must see this with his own eyes."

He locked his gaze with Astrid's as the hunters began to fall back.

"This is not surrender, girl," he warned. "This is study. When next we meet, I will not come to test. I will come to take."

Astrid held his stare.

"You can try."

A faint smile twitched at the corner of his mouth.

"Oh, I will."

He turned and walked toward the tunnel they had torn open, boots crunching over relic shards and ash.

Hunters followed, some limping, some helping others, all carefully avoiding stepping too close to Astrid and the dragons.

The chamber was quiet again.

The triad flame dimmed, folding back into Astrid's chest, into Embla's core, into the newborn's trembling heart.

Astrid's knees buckled.

She would have fallen if Embla hadn't caught her with her snout and Sorrek with his hand at her back.

"Easy," Sorrek rumbled. "You gave them a story to fear for a hundred winters. That takes strength."

Halvar wrapped his arms around her, trembling.

"I thought I'd lose you," he whispered into her hair.

Astrid let herself lean into him for a moment, eyes closed, feeling the dragons' warm presence pressed close on both sides.

Then she lifted her head.

"Tareth's going to tell Malrek everything," she said. "About us. About this place. About what we can do."

Sorrek nodded grimly.

"Good," he said. "Let him."

Halvar frowned. "Good?"

Sorrek's gaze found Astrid's.

"The High Priest will bring everything he has, now. The

world will not stay quiet. This was the last small battle, Astrid."

He nodded toward the Heartstone Bridge behind them.

"From here on… it's war."

Astrid looked up at the glowing dome, at the arch that had changed her forever, at the tunnels seething with distant monastery anger.

She laid a hand on Embla's warm scales.
The newborn curled against her collarbone, breathing softly.

Inside her, three heartbeats pulsed in perfect time.

She exhaled slowly.

"Then we don't stay here," she said.

"We get out of the forest. We find somewhere they can't follow us so easily. Somewhere the fire remembers us… but the Order has forgotten."

Halvar hesitated. "Does a place like that even exist?"

Astrid thought of the visions she'd seen.

Of dragons fleeing north over endless sea.
Of a hidden island wreathed in storm.
Of fire glinting on cliffs untouched by human hands.

"Yes," she said quietly.

"I think it does."

CHAPTER 32

A WORLD THAT TREMBLES

After the Storm Within the Earth

The forest welcomed them as they emerged from the Heartstone tunnels.

Sunlight filtered through the spring canopy in trembling beams, fluttering like moth-wings over Astrid's shoulders. The air tasted clean again — no relic-smoke, no iron, no charred oil. Just earth and sap and pine.

Embla limped beside her, leaning heavily on the rock walls when she had to, but breathing easier with every step. The newborn rode tucked against Astrid's chest, eyes half-lidded with exhaustion, small body warm as a stone left in the sun.

Halvar followed close, one hand always near Astrid's back as if afraid she might fall.

Sorrek led, clearing branches, listening to the wind as though it carried messages only the Frostborn could hear.

When they reached a clearing beside a small stream, Sorrek stopped.

"We rest," he said. "Astrid burned more fire than Embla — even the trees felt it. She needs stillness."

Astrid opened her mouth to argue, then her legs gave out.

Embla swung her wing beneath her before she hit the ground, lowering her gently onto moss.

Halvar knelt beside her, brushing hair from her face. "You don't have to be strong every heartbeat, Astrid."

She breathed in and out slowly until the rushing sensation behind her eyes calmed.

"I… didn't know the flame could do that," she whispered.

Embla lowered her muzzle to Astrid's shoulder, scales warm and steady.

Neither did I.
We are learning… together.

The newborn chirped and nuzzled her chin, tiny sparks slipping from its nostrils like flecks of starlight.

Astrid smiled weakly. "And you. You little storm spark."

The hatchling curled deeper into her arms.

For one fragile moment, the world was quiet.

Havngard — A Village Trying to Breathe Again

By the time they reached the fjord's edge, the sun had dipped low and the sea shone gold.

Havngard lay scarred — boats burned, docks broken, smoke rising from a few charred rooftops — but not ruined. The villagers moved through the wreckage with grim determination, hauling nets, repairing beams, passing buckets of water hand to hand.

Jorunn the herbalist was shouting instructions at two young men half her size.
Children gathered driftwood and hammered stakes into the thawing earth.
Old men worked ropes with shaking hands.

No one waited for rescue.

They rebuilt.

When Astrid stepped into the village with Embla behind her, silence rippled across the crowd.

Halvar stepped forward, voice steady though his eyes shone.

"My daughter has returned," he said. "And she has brought us hope."

Jorunn was the first to step closer. "Halvar," she breathed, "look at her. She looks like fire blessed her."

Astrid flushed. "Mostly I'm just tired."

Embla snorted and nudged her.

She saved the land from the monks, Embla told them all — projecting the thought in a sweeping wave of warmth. **She saved me. She saved us.**

Several villagers gasped as the dragon's voice touched their minds.

Then — astonishingly — some smiled.

A man just back from the docks bowed his head to Embla. "If she stands with you, dragon, she stands with us."

The villagers murmured agreement.

Sorrek looked around approvingly. "Your people have courage, Astrid Halvarsdottir. Not all lands greet dragons with open hearts."

Astrid exhaled, relief washing through her.

But the relief did not last.

A boy no older than eight tugged at her sleeve, eyes wide as he pointed south.

"Miss Astrid… why are there sails gathering on the horizon?"

Astrid's stomach dropped.

She looked at Sorrek.

He nodded grimly.

"The monastery is mustering," he said. "Your fire frightened them — but it also woke them."

The War Begins to Move

That evening, as the villagers lit a communal bonfire to drive back the chill, Astrid stood on the cliff path overlooking the sea.

Embla rested behind her, curled protectively around the newborn. Sorrek leaned against a pine trunk, sharpening his hammer's edge. Halvar sat on a boulder, eyes on the horizon.

The sea was darkening.

Not storm-dark.

Army-dark.

Dozens of faint white shapes dotted the far edges of the water.

Malrek's fleet.

Growing.

Spreading.

Preparing.

Halvar's voice trembled. "If they reach us tomorrow…"

Astrid closed her eyes. Memories of Calven burning Havngard once had been enough. But Malrek's ships were larger, better armed, commanded by men who would not hesitate.

"We can't fight them here," she said quietly. "We would only draw the battle to the village."

Sorrek nodded. "Correct. You must flee before the fleet reaches land."

Halvar stiffened. "I'm not sending her away again."

Astrid touched his hand. "Papa… if I stay, the monks won't stop until Havngard is ash."

Halvar shut his eyes.

"You're my daughter."

"And I'm also the Bridge," she whispered. "Embla and the newborn need me. The land needs us. I have to lead them away… somewhere safe."

Sorrek crossed his arms. "There is no safe place on the mainland anymore. Malrek has spies everywhere, and the Order will spread its net wide."

Astrid breathed slowly.

That vision in the chamber…

Dragons fleeing across storm-torn sea.
A hidden island where fire still lived.
Wings beating over untouched cliffs.

"I think," she said softly, "somewhere exists."

Embla lifted her head, eyes glowing.

The Storm-Isle.
The one you saw.
The dragons of the old days whispered of it.
We believed it lost.
But you… saw it.

Halvar stared at her.

"You mean to say… you want to fly across the sea?"

Astrid nodded.

"We can get there before the fleet reaches Havngard. They're heavier, slower. Embla can carry me, and the newborn rides light. Sorrek can guide the winds."

Sorrek grinned. "Frostborn do not fear sea storms."

Halvar's voice cracked.

"I just got you back."

Astrid wrapped her arms around him, pressing her forehead to his.

"I'll come back," she promised. "But first… I need to understand the fire inside me. And the only ones who can teach me are the ones who survived the Purge."

Halvar exhaled shakily.

"You've grown," he whispered, voice breaking, "and I barely noticed until now."

Astrid kissed his cheek.

"I'll always be your girl," she murmured.

He pulled her close, holding her as if trying to memorize her shape.

Embla watched with soft eyes.

He is fireless, she whispered.
But his heart burns bright.

Astrid laughed softly through her tears. "He really does."

Halvar released her reluctantly, wiping his face.

"Get some rest," he said. "I'll gather food and water for the journey."

Sorrek nodded. "I will see to the wind-path. At dawn, we fly."

Astrid looked out over the sea — the fleet growing closer.

She could feel the triad flame pulsing in her chest, warm and alive.

Tomorrow she would take to the sky with both dragons.

Tomorrow she would begin the next part of her story.

Tomorrow the world would tremble again.

CHAPTER 33

EPILOGUE: THE FIRST STORM

The Vision Returns

Night settled over Havngard in shades of silver and blue. Stars shimmered above the fjord like scattered embers, reflecting in the dark water. Embla stood on the cliff's edge, wings unfurled despite the ache in her healing muscles. The newborn clung to Astrid's shoulders, chirping restlessly at the scent of salt wind.

Astrid closed her eyes.

The triad flame pulsed inside her — faint, steady, waiting.

She breathed once…

…and the world shifted.

Not violently.
Not painfully.
Just *opened.*

Like a door in her mind swinging onto memory not her own.

Wind tore at her face.

Salt stung her lips.

The sky above was dark with storm clouds — not the soft gray of a spring squall, but the black-green fury of a world-ending tempest.

Lightning forked across the heavens, illuminating shapes in the air.

Dragons.

Dozens.

Wings like blades of midnight iron.

Wings shimmering gold, blue, crimson.
Wings torn, bleeding, scorched.

Their roars shook the sky. Their bodies writhed in exhaustion and terror as they fled the burning coastline behind them.

Astrid saw it clearly:

Villages engulfed in flame.
Monastery towers glowing with fire stolen from dragon hearts.
Priests with relic-spears cutting down anything that moved.

A young rider, armor cracked, clung desperately to a great bronze dragon's neck. Blood streaked his face. His eyes were raw with grief. He turned his head—

And saw Astrid.

Not truly.

Not physically.

But the bond bridged time, memory, and fire.

He looked *into her*, as if recognizing something in the braid of her flame.

"A Bridge," he whispered into the storm.
"The last Bridge…"

Another rider screamed behind him as lightning struck her mount. She plummeted into the sea, swallowed by the dark.

The bronze dragon banked sharply, following the others. Ahead, the clouds thinned—
and beyond them lay an island.

High cliffs of black stone.
Forests glowing with strange bioluminescent fire.

Waterfalls lit from beneath by molten roots.
Spiraling plumes of mist rising into the sky like smoke signals to the forgotten gods.

The Storm-Isle.

Dragons dove toward it, wings faltering, bodies blazing with exhaustion. When they crossed its boundary, the storm behind them peeled away like torn cloth.

Safety.
Refuge.
A last homeland.

Astrid saw the bronze dragon land on a ridge overlooking the sea. The rider dismounted, dropping to his knees. Tears burned his face.

"Storm-Isle," he whispered.
"Keeper of the last fires… shelter us."

And then—

He looked up again.

Straight at her.

Through time.
Through memory.
Through flame.

"Find us," he said.
"Bridge of the next age…
Find us before the monks do."

Lightning struck again—

—and the vision shattered.

Astrid stumbled, catching herself on Embla's warm flank.

Embla steadied her with a wing.

The dragons survived, Embla whispered in awe. **Not legends. Not ghosts. They lived.**

The newborn chirped fiercely, tiny wings flaring.

Astrid wiped a tear from her cheek.

"They're waiting for us," she whispered. "And the monastery is coming."

The Final Dawn

Havngard woke early.

Villagers stood on the cliff path, tools in hand, faces pale under the gathering dawn as the monastery fleet grew larger on the horizon.

Halvar hugged Astrid tightly, pressing his forehead to hers.

"You come back to me," he whispered.

"I will," she promised, though her voice wavered.

She turned to Sorrek. "You're sure you can guide the winds that far?"

Sorrek smirked. "Frostborn do not get lost."

Embla crouched low, wings opening fully for the first time since the Heartstone healed her scars. Light glimmered along her scales like dawn striking ice.

The newborn scrambled onto Astrid's shoulders, chirping excitedly.

"Ready, little flame?" Astrid whispered.

Ready, the hatchling echoed, voice tiny but fierce.

Embla lifted her head, eyes blazing.

Then let us fly, Astrid.

Let us find the island where fire still breathes.

Astrid climbed onto her back.

Halvar stepped away slowly, wiping his eyes with the back of his hand.

Sorrek stepped behind them, raising his hammer toward the sky.

"The winds answer," he said solemnly. "The path north opens."

Embla leapt.

Her wings snapped open—
catching the updraft—
lifting all three into the glowing dawn.

The newborn spread its tiny wings, catching its first real wind.

Astrid held tight as the fjord fell away beneath them.

Havngard grew small.
The sea grew wide.
The fleet behind them shrank into distant shadows.

Ahead—
in the far north—
clouds churned in slow spirals over a distant shape.

An island.
A storm.
A promise.

Astrid leaned forward, eyes fierce.

"Then let the monks chase the storm."

Embla roared—
a triumphant cry that split the sky—

and together they flew toward the island of lost fire.